Forever the Highlands
The Highlands Series

Samantha Young

Forever the Highlands

A Highlands Series Novel

By Samantha Young
Copyright © 2024 Samantha Young

Without limiting the rights under copyright reserved above, no part of this publication may be reproduced, stored in or introduced into a retrieval system, or transmitted, in any form, or by any means (electronic, mechanical, photocopying, recording or otherwise) without prior written permission of the above author of this book.

This is a work of fiction. Names, characters, places, and incidents are either the product of the author's imagination or are used fictitiously. Any resemblance to actual events, locales, or persons, living or dead, is coincidental.

This work is registered with and protected by Copyright House.

Cover Design By Hang Le
Couple Photography by Wander Aguiar
Edited by Jennifer Sommersby Young
Proofread by Julie Deaton

ALSO BY SAMANTHA YOUNG

Contemporary Romance

Play On

As Dust Dances

Black Tangled Heart

Hold On: A Play On Novella

Into the Deep

Out of the Shallows

Hero

Villain: A Hero Novella

One Day: A Valentine Novella

Fight or Flight

Much Ado About You

A Cosmic Kind of love

The Love Plot

On Dublin Street Series

On Dublin Street

Down London Road

Before Jamaica Lane

Fall From India Place

Echoes of Scotland Street

Moonlight on Nightingale Way

Until Fountain Bridge (a novella)

Castle Hill (a novella)
Valentine (a novella)
One King's Way (a novella)
On Hart's Boardwalk (a novella)

Hart's Boardwalk Series:

The One Real Thing

Every Little Thing

Things We Never Said

The Truest Thing

The Adair Family Series:

Here With Me

There With You

Always You

Be With Me

Only You

The Highlands Series:

Beyond the Thistles

Among the Heather

Through the Glen

A Highland Christmas: A Novella

Skies Over Caledonia

Northern Twilight

Forever the Highlands

Young Adult contemporary titles by Samantha Young

The Impossible Vastness of Us

The Fragile Ordinary

Titles Co-written with Kristen Callihan
Outmatched

Titles Written Under S. Young
Fear of Fire and Shadow

War of the Covens Trilogy:
Hunted
Destined
Ascended

The Seven Kings of Jinn Series:
Seven Kings of Jinn
Of Wish and Fury
Queen of Shadow and Ash
The Law of Stars and Sultans

True Immortality Series:
War of Hearts
Kiss of Fate
Kiss of Eternity: A True Immortality Short Story
Bound by Forever

About the Author

Samantha is a *New York Times*, *USA Today*, and *Wall Street Journal* bestselling author and a Goodreads Choice Awards Nominee. Samantha has written over 60 books and is published in 31 countries. She writes emotional and angsty romance, often set where she resides—in her beloved home country Scotland. Samantha splits her time between her family, writing and chasing after two very mischievous cavapoos.

ABOUT THE AUTHOR

ACKNOWLEDGMENTS

This one was bittersweet. Saying goodbye to a world that made me fall deeper in love with writing and my own country was difficult, even though I knew it was time. I've loved these characters and fictional Ardnoch so much, it's hard to believe they're not real. Thank you all so much for loving them too and for wanting to live in this world for a while. It's been a grand adventure and I couldn't have done it without you.

I also must thank my amazing editor Jennifer Sommersby Young who is always tremendous and encouraging and wise and smart and kind. Thank you, my friend.

Thank you to Julie Deaton for proofreading *Forever the Highlands*, catching all the things, and for all your lovely, encouraging comments along the way.

And thank you to my bestie and PA extraordinaire Ashleen Walker for helping to lighten the load and supporting me more than ever these past few years. I really couldn't do this without you.

The life of a writer doesn't stop with the book. Our job expands beyond the written word to marketing, advertising, graphic design, social media management, and more. Help from those in the know goes a long way. A huge thank-you to Nina Grinstead, Kim, Kelley, Sarah, Josette, Meagan and all the team at Valentine PR for your encouragement, support, insight, and advice. You all are amazing!

A huge thank you to Sydney Thisdelle for doing all your techy ad magic to deliver my stories into the hands of new readers. You make my life infinitely easier and I'm so grateful!

Thank you to every single blogger, Instagrammer, and book lover who has helped spread the word about my books. You all are appreciated so much! On that note, a massive thank-you to the fantastic readers in my private Facebook group, Samantha Young's Clan McBookish. You're truly special. You're a safe space of love and support on the internet and I couldn't be more grateful for you.

A massive thank-you to Hang Le for creating another stunning cover in this series. You are a tremendous talent! And thank you to Wander Aguiar for the beautiful couple photography that brings Eilidh and Fyfe to life.

As always, thank you to my agent Lauren Abramo for making it possible for readers all over the world to find my words. You're phenomenal, and I'm so lucky to have you.

A massive thank you to my wonderful family and friends, who are always supportive and loving. I couldn't do this without you.

And finally, a tremendous thank you to my producer Katie Robinson at Lyric Audiobooks, and narrators Shane East, Stella Hunter, and Zara Hampton-Brown. You all created magic with this series in audiobook and there aren't enough words to express how grateful I am to you all for bringing Ardnoch to life so beautifully.

AUTHOR NOTE

For all my lovely readers who've struggled to pronounce
"Eilidh" over the course of eleven books and yet still asked for
her love story:
Her name is pronounced *Haley* without the *H*: "A-ley."
Fyfe is pronounced *wife* with an *F*.
Love you all.
Happy reading!
Sam x

PROLOGUE
FYFE

Eleven years ago

Ardnoch, Scotland

It wasn't unusual for me to wake up and find my mum passed out on the kitchen floor. Well ... it didn't happen all the time because she was hardly ever home, but when she was, it usually ended up with her passed out.

I took her in for a second. Face down, limbs sprawled, taking up all the space in our tiny kitchen. Her nose was pressed against the peeling linoleum and loud snores escaped her mouth as it opened and closed in sleep.

Years ago, Mum had been pretty. I'd seen photos. But for as long as I could remember, her skin was dry, wrinkled before her time, and a dull gray. Her hair had also thinned. Brown like mine, but greasy and limply draped across her sharp cheekbone. That's what more than your fair share of alcohol did. And drugs. Whatever she could get her hands on.

Her slight frame took up so much space in the kitchen because it was a tiny room and she was tall. Her thin top had risen, flashing her bra. Her skirt or jeans or whatever she'd been wearing was gone. She was in nothing but a pair of ratty knickers, and she only had on one of a pair of cheap heels.

Sometimes I felt so fucking weary and old, right down to my bones.

I lifted my glasses off my nose to rub the sleep out of my eyes. When I pushed the frames back into place, I glanced at the clock. If Mum didn't give me any trouble, I could get her sorted before I had to leave for school. I couldn't miss school. Not for her, not for anyone. I'd realized a long time ago that I was going to use my brains and education to get me the fuck out of Ardnoch. To get me away from ... this.

It was hard to call which way this would go. Sometimes Mum fought like a tiger when you tried to rouse her. In rare moments, she was quiet and pitiful.

Hoping for the latter, I moved into the room and got my arms underneath her. This year I'd started to shoot up in height, so with her slight weight, it was easy enough to haul her into my arms.

My heart started to race when she grumbled under her breath, but she merely reached for me in her sleep and slung her arms around my neck to hold on. I carried her to the bed she rarely slept in.

As I was pulling the covers over her, she spoke. "Thank you."

I looked up and found her red-rimmed eyes on me. I got everything from my mum. Hair and eye color, height, and though no one would believe it, my intelligence. Mum had gotten into St. Andrews University and was studying to be an engineer when she fell pregnant. She told me bitterly (and often) that it happened on a drunken night out with some random bloke whose name she couldn't even remember. Her mum had insisted she come home and have me, and that was the worst thing that ever happened to my mother.

My grandmother died when I was three and Mum inherited her house.

She'd been leaving me alone in it ever since, working several jobs at a time in between partying, and she paid some of the bills when she remembered to.

The soft expression on her face told me she was in a self-pitying mood. "It's all right," I muttered, pulling back.

She grabbed my wrist, stopping me. "You're a good boy."

Then why can't you stand to be around me?

"Get some sleep." I yanked my wrist from her weak grasp and walked toward the door.

She whimpered, "I'm sorry I'm such a shit mum."

I halted, head bowed. My chest burned as a swelling sensation moved into my throat, a familiar choking feeling.

"I stay away so I won't hurt you," she admitted on a quiet sob.

I glanced back at her.

Her eyes begged for forgiveness for all the times she'd left me with no food in the house. For the times I'd had to rely on Deirdra, my elderly neighbor, who fed and took care of me whenever she could. For all the times Mum had beaten me black and blue while she was drunk or high and ragin' at a life she could have changed, if she'd only tried hard enough.

The truth was, I knew that's why she stayed away. Because some part of her didn't want to hurt me. "I know." I gave her a small nod, unable to give her anything more, and walked into the bathroom across the hall to get washed.

I stared at my reflection in the mirror above the sink. The bathroom was clean because I cleaned it. Our small, terraced home had become the place my friends crashed and hung out since there was no adult supervision. For so long I'd lived in filth as a kid, but as I got older, I learned to keep the house clean. People didn't need to know how bad my situation was, and a clean house helped pull the wool over everyone's eyes.

And ultimately, I could take care of myself. I knew how to cook, how to tidy, how to do my own laundry, and now that I was making some money online from game testing and reviewing and play-to-earn games, I could afford to pay the bills Mum forgot about. Deirdra let me use her bank details so I could get paid. She took the money I earned out in cash for me.

"You're a good boy."

Then why didn't Mum want me? I thought for the millionth time as I stared at my unremarkable face.

Why wasn't I enough?

"Fuck," I muttered, squeezing my eyes closed.

I needed to get my shit together.

It was stupid to let those thoughts in.

Better to do what I did daily and act like most people's opinions didn't matter. It seemed to work for me. Girls seemed to like my "couldn't give a shit" attitude. I'd lost my virginity a year ago and my best pal, Lewis, who was definitely better looking than me, was still a virgin. He'd made the mistake of falling in love at sixteen. Callie, his girlfriend, was a nice lassie, but love held you back. Love had you building sex into something it wasn't so you were still a virgin when you were dating the hottest girl in Sutherland. Not giving a shit had you losing your virginity on your fifteenth birthday to an eighteen-year-old stunner from Inverness.

What can I say? She liked my confidence.

And I'm a fast learner.

Since then, there had been three more girls. Until Carianne. I didn't love Carianne. She didn't love me. But she was pretty and she liked sex, so it was convenient for us both. But honestly, she was kind of irritating me lately. She wasn't academic, which was fine, but she was constantly on my back when I wanted to study. Calling me a geek had turned from an endearment into an insult. And I'd been insulted enough over the years to last a lifetime.

Time to end things with Carianne.

It had been a crap day.

Carianne did not want to be dumped. She made a scene and I hated scenes because, again, it's all I'd had my whole life with Mum, so I told her she could tell everyone she dumped me. That sorted her out.

But I'd gotten a B in my history class, again, and it was pissing me off. My history teacher, Mr. Martin, had taken a dislike to me and was always lowballing me with grades. This time I'd had enough and had a word with my favorite history teacher, Ms. Heron, and asked her to look at all my papers for the year. She'd been shocked by the request and I knew it probably put her in an uncomfortable position, but ballsy Ms. Heron said she'd look over them and get back to me. She knew how important it was for my grades to be top-notch. I needed to get into university.

Lewis was going to come over to study, but I was in a crap mood, so I told him to hang out with Callie instead. He tried his best not to be a bad friend by not forgetting about me, but I knew he enjoyed any chance he could to hang out with his girlfriend. I let him off the hook and trudged home, hoping Mum would be gone when I got there.

When I stepped in the door, I stumbled to a stop.

The living room had been ransacked. Cushions torn off our old sofa, the drawers in the sideboard pulled out, contents everywhere.

"Mum?" I called out, dropping my heavy backpack.

Nothing.

A feeling came over me.

A knowing.

"Fuck!" I bit out, rushing toward my bedroom.

Sure enough, it was completely upended.

And the drawer where I kept a stash of my money in a sock was on the bed, the socks all unraveled.

The money was gone.

Heart racing, I pulled up the rug by my bed and pressed down on the floorboard. It popped up and I sagged in relief when I found the majority of my earnings still secure. I'd planted the sock money as a red herring because I knew one day she'd look for it.

Getting up, I stalked into her bedroom and halted again.

Her closet was open and every item in it was gone. As was the suitcase she'd kept in there. She'd never taken all her things before.

And I knew. Deep in my bones.

This time, she was gone for good.

I stumbled back and lowered myself to her unmade bed. My chest ached. A dull, throbbing pain near my sternum.

But there was relief too.

And that made me feel as bad as the pain.

I tossed my glasses onto the bed and buried my head in my hands, shoulders shaking as I cried quietly in the silence of her empty bedroom.

Tears were the last thing I ever let that woman take from me.

The knock at the door had me wiping my face and eyes and reaching for my glasses. It was possible it was Deirdra and that she'd heard Mum make the commotion when she tore up the place. Hurrying through the mess to the front door that led straight into the living room, I yanked it open.

FOREVER THE HIGHLANDS

And then froze.

Lewis's wee sister, Eilidh, stood on the other side.

She was two years younger than us at fourteen, but with her height and confidence, she could pass for our age.

"What are you doing here?"

Eilidh shrugged with dramatic exaggeration. Since she'd started taking acting classes down in Glasgow during the summer (she'd even been on a Scottish TV show), Eilidh's natural drama had gone up a level or two. "I haven't been able to find my copy of *It Happened One Summer* since we went camping before school started." She pushed past me before I could stop her. "And I wondered if—" She stopped talking abruptly as she gaped at the mess.

My pulse jumped. The last person I wanted to find out about this was Eilidh. Despite her having flirted with me since she was eleven years old, I'd found Lewis's sister cute rather than annoying. Even when I agreed to let her sleep in my tent on the aforementioned camping trip and she'd prattled on and on about silly stuff until I eventually fell asleep.

But Eilidh was all about the drama, and I did not need that kind of reaction to this situation.

She whirled on me, her long dark curls whipping with the movement. Her blue eyes were striking against her olive skin and right now they were huge. "Fyfe, did you get robbed? Should we call the police?" She waved her hands frantically at the mess.

Fuck.

I slammed the front door shut. I honestly didn't know whether to be more annoyed with her terrible excuse to come round to my house and flirt with me, or the fact that I now had to explain the truth to someone when I'd had no intention of sharing the news about my mother's abandonment with anyone.

"I didn't get robbed and you're not telling anyone about this."

Eilidh gaped. "What am I not telling them?"

Narrowing my eyes, I wagged a finger at her. "If I tell you, I mean it, Eilidh—it stays between us. I'll never forgive you if you tell."

To my surprise, her expression softened with sympathy. Her tone was sincere as she replied, "I promise, Fyfe. I won't tell anyone. What's going on?"

At first, I was so surprised by her maturity and measured reaction that it took me a second to respond. Then I couldn't meet her eyes. "Mum left. Permanently. But first she tossed the place, looking for my money."

Suddenly, Eilidh's arms were around me, her cheek pressed to my chest as she squeezed me tight. I stiffened in her embrace, my anger rushing forth. Fury at my mum, and at Eilidh for being here when I wanted to be alone. My first thought was that she was using this moment to get close to me, which pissed me off.

Then she whispered, "I won't tell. I promise."

My tears from earlier burned in my eyes and I buried my head in Eilidh's hair, wrapping my arms around her so tight. She smelled fruity and fresh. Clean. Warm. Like the home she was brought up in. I shook. Mum had barely been around for most of my life, so I didn't know why being left alone was hitting me so hard.

But I felt like there was this crack in my chest and if I didn't stop it, it would only grow until I fell completely apart.

Eilidh held on tighter, as if her arms could stop the trembling.

"I hate her," I confessed harshly.

She didn't offer platitudes. "I hate her too."

Somehow that made me feel better.

I didn't know how long we stood there, but I finally

remembered I was holding my best friend's wee sister like she was a life jacket. In a way, she was. All the Adairs were. Lewis and I had different friends at primary school and it wasn't until we were thrown together in a class at high school that we realized we had so much in common.

From that moment on, he'd adopted me into his family. I'd had many a dinner at his house and hung out there all the time. Eilidh was part of that. Her silly crush on me annoyed Lewis, but as much as she was still only my best friend's wee sister, Eilidh made me feel seen.

And today she'd surprised me.

I released her and she reluctantly let go.

With her standing so close, I searched her face, needing reassurance she wasn't going to tell anyone about this. As I did, I realized for the first time that Eilidh Adair was a teenage stunner.

Before ... I recognized she was pretty in a vague, distant way. But it was the first time it hit me she was *more* than pretty.

"I won't tell anyone," she promised again. Quiet. No drama. "This isn't mine to tell, Fyfe."

Grateful, I nodded. "Thanks."

"Right." She swung around and gestured to the room. "Let's get this place sorted."

"You don't have to do that."

"But I'm going to." Eilidh pulled her phone out of her back pocket, hit the screen a few times, and then pop music blared from it. She grinned. "Need some tunes to help us along."

I rolled my eyes, my lips twitching, but I let her have that.

Then we set about tidying up my house.

We broke for a snack and a drink and we chatted in my kitchen about an audition she had in Glasgow in a few weeks. She'd been accepted into a prestigious summer drama school down there and had gotten some real acting work out of it already. Her parents weren't happy about the audition, because the agreement was that she could only take on acting jobs during the summer. But Eilidh could charm most people into doing anything, so I wasn't surprised she'd talked them into letting her go.

We were finishing up fixing my room when I noticed the time. "Come on, I need to get you home."

"I can ride back myself."

"But you won't."

We rode our bikes out of Ardnoch to a wee tiny place on the outskirts called Caelmore. It was where Lewis and Eilidh's architect dad had designed homes for himself and his brothers and sister. Their five homes sat spread in a row overlooking the North Sea. I didn't know of many siblings who'd want to stay that close to each other in adulthood, and I thought it was pretty cool that Lewis and Eilidh got to grow up surrounded by aunts and uncles and younger cousins.

We stopped at the top of the long, narrow country road that led into their small family estate. Eilidh hopped off her bike, and I had to straddle mine to keep my balance as she threw herself at me.

When she pulled back, she kept her hands planted on my shoulders and stared unabashedly into my eyes. With all the maturity of a wise forty-year-old, she said, "You have to know that your mum's actions aren't about you."

Renewed anger flushed through me. "That's where you're wrong."

"I'm not. Your mum is a deeply selfish person, Fyfe. That's not on you. You're amazing."

Her soft eyes made me wary. I gently nudged her away. "Eils."

She released me with a sigh and a sad smile. "I know you think this is some stupid wee girl crush, and it's never bothered me that you think that. But it bothers me today. Because I need you to know that you're amazing and that's why I like you more than anyone else. You're brave and smart. You stand up for people." I assumed she referred to the time I chased off those boys who were bullying her when she was about eleven. Her hero worship of me had started after that. "And next to me, you're, like, the most ambitious person I know. One day you'll get out of here and you'll do amazing things because you're destined to."

I smiled indulgently. "Eils."

"I mean it. You're a special person."

I inwardly ached because ... I could see she really did mean it. "Eilidh."

She shrugged, giving me a cheeky grin. "I know I'm just Lewis's wee sister and my opinion doesn't mean much. But I wanted you to know that. Oh, and I won't tell anyone. Not Lewis. Not anyone. Promise." She pushed up on her tiptoes and kissed my cheek before I could stop her. Then she hopped back onto her bike and rode toward her family home.

THAT NIGHT AS I LAY IN BED FOR THE FIRST TIME truly alone, I held on to Eilidh's words. They kept the question of why my mum couldn't stand to stay around me at bay, when usually it would have tortured me into insomnia.

Instead, I wrapped myself in the phrase "You're a special person" like it was sleep medication, hearing Eilidh Adair say those words over and over until I finally drifted off.

ONE
EILIDH

Three years ago

"Just a few more weeks and then you don't have to deal with him ever again," my makeup artist Suze reminded me as we sat in the costume trailer between takes.

Since I'd set foot in British Columbia, Canada, and met Eddie Coltrane, he'd been a pompous arsehole. I was the Bonnie in the Bonnie and Clyde–style indie movie I'd signed on to as soon as the second season of *Young Adult* ended. *Young Adult* had been my big break. We'd started filming when I was nineteen and I'd moved down to London to do it. My big brother Lewis was at college in the city, so he kept an eye on me. The show was a dramedy about a group of eighteen-year-olds who'd left school and started—or floundered about starting—"adulthood." I played Mikayla, a foster child who grew up in London's East End, a talented artist, and a drug addict.

The show was funny, emotional, harrowing at times, and

even though none of us had known each other before, our cast gelled. And so the show took off in a way none of us could quite believe, becoming number one on the streaming platform. My Instagram followers went from a couple hundred to a hundred thousand in a few days. Now I had over a million followers.

To my agent Danny's delight, the offers came flooding in after that first season of *Young Adult* aired. Feeling like I needed to keep the momentum going, I'd filmed a movie last autumn before filming restarted for the show, and now I was on set of another movie the following summer. I'd flown home to see my family at Christmas. But that was it.

And I missed them.

The missing them had grown into something approaching unbearable.

Being on set with someone who made me feel as uncomfortable as Eddie Coltrane pissed me off because I could be home in Ardnoch with my family instead of acting opposite this douche canoe.

The Clyde to my Bonnie was played by my fellow *Young Adult* castmate, Jasper Richmond. Jasper was one of my on-screen romances on the show. He was bisexual in the show and in real life, and we had great chemistry. But off-screen, that chemistry felt more familial. There had never been anything romantic between us, despite media and fan speculation.

Eddie Coltrane, however, was an actor I'd not met until now. He was playing a "friend" who betrayed us. To be honest, Jasper and I were playing very similar roles to what we played on the show, but that's why the production company wanted us.

Suze, whom I met on *Young Adult*, had become my go-to makeup artist. I liked having her with me whenever possible. Someone familiar. My life sometimes felt like a nomad's, surrounded by new people on every production. That had sounded exciting, like a dream, when I was a teenager. The reality of it was very different. Very isolating and lonely. You spend all this time with a cast on a movie, every day with them, growing close with them, and then once the movie wraps, everyone goes their own way. These people who had become your family for a few months go back to being almost strangers.

I found it disconcerting and upsetting, and I didn't think I'd ever get used to the highs and lows of that part of the experience. Maybe that's why this time, I had walls up. But that wasn't my issue with Eddie.

Eddie had proven himself an arsehole from day one.

Suze was the only person to notice my reticence with Eddie. Usually, I could flirt with a lamppost. It was kind of my nature. I couldn't help it.

But the first day I stepped on set and Eddie made it clear he thought I was an untalented nepo baby, I'd distanced myself from our costar.

I'd confessed to Suze about how I'd flubbed a line and Eddie had whispered in my ear I should switch to modeling because I was too stupid to act. I'd been so shocked, I hadn't responded. Or told anyone but the makeup artist, who was well known as a trusted confidante.

If I told anyone else, they'd probably laugh it off and say it was merely Eddie's weird sense of humor. And I didn't want to delay finishing this movie. I was tired, I missed my family, and I wanted to get away from a set where one of the actors seemed to enjoy watching me fuck up. His negativity was stressing me out and getting in my head, and so I was flubbing more of my lines than usual. That pissed me off because I shouldn't be letting him get to me.

But it was just bad timing.

Two days ago, my management team had contacted me about creepy fan emails addressed to me. I had received weird fan mail in the past. Most of it they filed away in a folder they kept for reference (and evidence). This person was one of them, but they noted lately there had been an increase in the number of emails this person was sending. They'd decided to forward them to the police, but honestly, there wasn't anything the police could do unless creepy fan-mail person made a physical move toward me. So I was a little on edge about that, though I felt safe on set. We had plenty of security.

But mostly, I was spiraling about something else.

Because what I hadn't confessed to anyone was how much social media was chipping away at me mentally and emotionally.

"Do you think if I take a ten-minute nap, my makeup will smudge?" I asked Suze as I crumpled my sandwich wrapper and tossed it into the rubbish bin.

"You should be fine. Just come back here if you need it. You're on set in twenty minutes," she reminded me.

I nodded, pushed up out of the chair in front of the light-adorned mirror, and pressed a kiss to the top of Suze's head. "Thanks, doll."

I stepped out into the baking heat. Locals told me this kind of heat had not been normal to the area during summer. But climate change was showing its ugly face, and the once-moderate summer temperatures of Vancouver had been over-ruled by record-breaking temps.

I smiled at crew members I passed as I made my way to my trailer. At twenty-two years old, I felt at least twice that. Which was probably why daytime naps had become a regular thing for me. Anything to escape my own mind. Normally, while filming, I was fine. I was in the character and I enjoyed playing someone else.

But off set, a weary emptiness plagued me. And when that didn't plague me, the nasty comments on social media did. You know, most of them were great and lovely and I had the best fans. However, there were a goodly amount of shitty comments about how bad of an actor I was, how my cockney accent could use some work, how I was such a bitch for cheating on a fictional character, how I should kill myself, and I wasn't even that pretty, but also how they wanted to fuck my mouth.

My DMs were filled with unsolicited nudes, messages of love interspersed with messages from organizations trying to "save" me, viewers sending me articles on addiction and mental health as though I were really the character I played on the show. DMs berated me for my lifestyle. And my acting. Messages filled with hate and jealousy. I'd even been sent an article on how to commit suicide.

It was shocking. I was exhausted.

And that level of intensity on social media happened to me overnight. There was no buildup to it.

Suddenly, I was everywhere.

I couldn't go into my favorite coffee place around the corner from my London flat without people recognizing me. A lot of people called me Mikayla, as if I were the character from the show.

I could not be more opposite. Mikayla was abandoned, broken, an addict. She had a good heart, but she was so desperate to feel loved and special, she trampled over people's feelings. The last season had ended with her cheating on Jasper's character with a fellow artist she'd befriended. A guy who had made it his life's mission to get Mikayla sober. I knew the writers well enough to know that was not going to go smoothly in season three.

I'd need to gird myself for how the audience would react to the next round of chaos Mikayla incited. Problem was, I wasn't sure I could brace myself for any more of this.

Tired, so tired, and needing something to boost my energy, I stepped into my trailer with thoughts of a power nap.

The trailer was about twenty years old, in need of an update, but I didn't care. The bed in the back was comfy.

Then my phone buzzed in my pocket.

Sighing, I took it out and slumped onto the end of the bed. I had a Google Alert set for myself and members of my family.

I tapped on the notification and my stomach plummeted.

FANS OUTRAGED AT ACTOR EILIDH ADAIR

"What the fuck?" I muttered, my stomach turning, my cheeks hot as I scrolled through the article. "Oh my God." I tapped on a social media icon and started scrolling through the comments on my last post.

I'd shared a photo from our night out last week. The cast of the movie had been invited to attend a charity benefit hosted by a politician. It was a children's charity that provided water, food, and emergency response to children in many countries across the globe, including a country caught up in an international political crisis. I was a villain for giving my support to the charity because they were providing aid to innocent *children* from a country whose government was the problem.

The comments were disgusting.

I'd betrayed them. I was fucking stupid. Ignorant. They were done with me. They wished I'd rot in hell. They were canceling their subscription to the streaming service in protest to my affiliation. Calling for the streaming service to drop me. I was a talentless hack, anyway. My uncles had gotten my foot in the door. I didn't deserve my success.

On and on.

Hundreds upon hundreds of nasty comments.

Fingers shaking, I tapped on Jasper's profile. He hadn't shared a photo from the benefit, but he'd been there too and

Forever the Highlands

was in my photos. No one had commented on his Instagram, though.

My phone rang in my hand. It was my publicist. I stared at the screen in shock, so overwhelmed I wanted the world to bloody disappear. The ringing stopped and then started again. My agent. The room spun. I couldn't breathe. I ducked my head between my legs, sobbing between trying to catch my breath.

"Fuck, shit, fuck." Jasper was there, his hands on my face, his thumbs wiping away tears. "Danny just called. Everyone's talking about it on set. Are you okay?"

"I ... it was only a photo," I whispered numbly.

"I know, I know. Look, call Greta back." Jasper tapped my phone. "She'll help take care of this. It'll all blow over."

Numbly, I hit the Call button.

"Oh, thank God." Greta's familiar posh accent filled my ear. "Right, my darling. First thing you're going to do is delete that photo. We've already put together an apology statement for you to share. We've emailed it over. Take a look. If there's anything you want to tweak, let me know."

"Apology?" I croaked out. "Apology for what? I supported a charity that provides aid to children."

"I know, darling. The world's gone crazy. But best to just say you're sorry and they'll forget about it within a week."

"And if I don't?"

There was a moment of silence. "Danny's already had a conversation with the PR team on the show, and they feel this is what's best for everyone."

"Will they fire me if I don't apologize?" At that moment, I hoped she'd say yes.

Because I couldn't take this.

This hate and vitriol. Living online in a world where you had to choose sides, where you weren't allowed to see both sides of an argument, where nuance had died several years ago, and we were all treating each other like we were the worst dregs of society if we showed even an ounce of common sense during a discussion.

There were hundreds and hundreds of vile comments on my social media.

And not only from that post.

So many people thought I was worthless and stupid and had gotten this far ahead in the business out of nepotism.

Maybe I wasn't cut out to be an actor.

"They won't fire you, but they won't be happy if you don't do this."

Jasper squeezed my hand. His expression was pleading. "Just post the apology," he offered quietly, "and this will all blow over."

Until the next time I did something I thought was innocuous but the world took offense to.

Feeling totally disconnected from the moment, I deleted the post that had started the furor and shared the apology statement. I switched off the comments for that post and then turned off my phone just as Dad called. I couldn't talk to him. I knew he would be calling to check if I was okay, but he was the most principled man I knew, and he wouldn't have apologized for something he didn't believe he needed to apologize for.

I'd never felt like a bigger coward.

"Let's get you back into makeup." Jasper took my hand and led me out of the trailer.

Suze fussed over me as I took a seat before her.

As I stared past my reflection in the mirror to my friends who hovered over me worriedly, it was the first time in my short career that I thought "I hate this job, I hate being here, I wish I wasn't *this*, I wish no one knew me, I wish I was home."

Unfortunately for me, it wouldn't be the last time those wishes escaped my heart.

Two
FYFE

Two years ago

I drove down Castle Street, the main street through Ardnoch, an avenue of identical nineteenth-century terraced houses with dormer windows. Most of the homes had been converted into boutiques, cafés, and inns. In among them was Morag's, a small grocery store and deli, Flora's, the most popular café in the village, and Callie's Wee Cakery, Callie's mum's bakery.

The cobbled streets and old-fashioned lampposts, the creeping ivy and hanging flower baskets in bright bloom for the summer, made the village picture-perfect. Once upon a time, I'd never imagined returning here, no matter how quaint and idyllic it was.

Yet, two years ago, I found my way back. Maybe fate had a hand.

Or maybe Deirdra.

When my old neighbor passed away, I'd gone home to

Ardnoch for her funeral. I was pissed off at myself for not being better at staying in touch when she'd done so much for me. While I was drowning my sorrows in the Gloaming (a hotel, pub, and restaurant owned by Lewis's uncles), my best mate's dad, Thane, approached me, along with his brother Lachlan. Lachlan Adair owned and ran Ardnoch Castle and Estate, a private members-only club that catered to film and TV industry people.

Somehow, our conversation turned into a job proposition, and I found myself bringing my cybersecurity company home to Ardnoch. My team all worked from home, so it was easy enough for me to make the move. We now protected all of Lachlan's (and the rest of the Adairs') businesses from digital threats, as well as some of the club members, so being able to use the estate as a base to meet those clients made the most sense. Since I was proficient in all types of security, I also advised on the security system for the estate. Lachlan used a drone perimeter, but I'd boosted its digital defenses so it was nigh impossible to hack.

I'd gone from wondering how I'd feed myself as a teen to having more money than I knew what to do with. At uni, I'd created an online game in my spare time that grew so popular, I sold it for millions to a large gaming company. They also offered me a job. Fans of the game wanted more from me, but creating games was just something I was good at. Not something I particularly enjoyed.

When one of my favorite uni professors realized what a great fucking hacker I was, he decided to employ my talents for good. After I'd freelanced for him, he recruited me to join his cybersecurity company. After graduation, I decided to set up my own company because I liked being my own boss. Money. I had it now. Financial independence. Pride, I had that too. In my achievements and in my company. My job meant protecting people from digital threats, people I chose to work for. I refused to work for individuals or companies whose morals didn't align with mine. I could feel good about that.

I'd been home for two years, had bought a fancy architect-designed house, and traveled any chance I got. Once I was a forgotten kid from the Highlands and now I was a man who had seen a bit of the world, only to discover, he craved home after all.

But Ardnoch wasn't the same without Lewis and Callie.

Not once in those first years in Edinburgh did I contemplate returning to my hometown. Yet as the years passed, the bitter memories faded and were overtaken by the good ones. While I'd met friends at uni, none of them had Lewis and Callie's staying power. Those others were surface friends who you had a good time with. It made me realize Lewis and Callie were my home.

Yet they were broken apart. Callie was off in Paris at a pastry school and Lewis was in London.

Until now.

Driving straight through the village, I continued until I hit the small development of architect homes on the McCulloch farm. Locals Jared and Allegra McCulloch had developed the small neighborhood on their land and sold off the lots for a small fortune. My house had plenty of land around it and floor-to-ceiling windows that captured the views of rolling hills and surrounding woodlands.

I'd barely been in the house five minutes when I heard Lewis's Harley growl to a stop on my driveway.

After seven years apart, Lewis and Callie had reconnected in London with a drunken one-night stand. It was the push Lewis needed to get his finger out of his arse and go after the woman he loved. While I might not understand his obsession with only one woman, I believed my best mate was incapable of loving any but her. So I was rooting for them. Lewis had graduated and was now a fully fledged architect, and he'd accepted a job at his father's firm in Inverness so he could come back to Ardnoch to pursue Callie.

They'd split up as teens because Lewis hadn't wanted to stay in Ardnoch and Callie did. Lewis had realized over the years that all he'd wanted was to see the world. He'd been pining for his ex and his childhood home ever since.

I was damned happy my best mate had returned.

Lewis Adair was as tall as me. Back in Edinburgh, I usually felt like the biggest bloke in the room, but maybe there was something in the water in the Highlands. Lewis got his height from two of his uncles. His uncle by marriage was tall too, as was Callie's father. There were quite a few big guys you wouldn't want to mess with walking the streets of Ardnoch.

Unlike me, Lewis didn't stroll around in suits and Derby shoes. He kept his long hair in a man bun, his beard wasn't nearly as neat and trim as mine, and while I had no tattoos, Lewis had many. One of his arms was covered in a sleeve of meaningful tattoos I was pretty sure only I knew were mostly about Callie. He strolled into my house in jeans, biker boots, and a long-sleeve tee, looking very much like the biker who'd parked his Harley outside my front door.

It was great that he could drop by anytime we wanted now.

And I had to remind myself of that when Lewis stalked inside, preoccupied over Callie. I'd been about to share with my friend my plans to open the house up even more by removing the wall between the entrance and the rest of the living space, but he looked like he had something on his mind. That's when he explained Carianne's moronic plan to get him and Callie back together.

Carianne and I hadn't seen much of each other since my return, but now that Callie was home, I was sure we'd bump into each other. She was already doling out her usual nonsense because she'd suggested Lewis fake date her to make Callie jealous. And she suggested this after admitting she had feelings for Lewis and wanted to date him for real.

He'd barely finished relaying this to me when I told him it was the worst idea I'd ever heard. It would only push Callie further away, and I could tell by his expression, deep down, he knew that too.

Before he could respond, his phone rang and he answered a video call.

It was his wee sister.

Eilidh.

A pang of emotion I couldn't quite identify echoed inside, and I sat down next to Lewis to speak to her.

For the last few years, I'd watched from afar as Eilidh Adair became a famous actor. A bloody great one at that. I was a fan of her TV show *Young Adult*. Though I found it difficult to watch her portray such a harrowing character and I fast-forwarded through the sexier scenes she acted out. The last time I'd seen her was in London at a wrap party for the first season of the show. I was visiting Lewis and I tagged along. She'd been flirty as ever, but there was a disconnect. Like there was a wall between us and she was no longer the wee girl I once knew. Seeing her in national ad campaigns and movies, hearing the internet gossip about her love life, and her being so beautiful she didn't seem real ... it only heightened the distance.

Once we'd been close, but now we were worlds apart.

Right then, however, with no makeup on, Eilidh was more like the teenager I remembered.

"Fyfe Moray, I always knew you were a smoke show," she said upon seeing me.

It was a knee-jerk reaction to roll my eyes and get up off the couch. "And you haven't changed a bit." I sat on the opposite couch again, giving Lewis space with his sister. But I felt something like relief. Because the Eilidh I'd just seen was nothing like the unattainable goddess who'd broken away from her family. From Ardnoch. From us all.

Christ, it was possible that pang I felt was ... maybe I'd missed her a little.

"So, what's perfect timing?" I heard her ask her big brother.

Lewis frowned at his phone screen. "Are you okay?"

Why wouldn't she be? I sat up straight, waiting for her answer.

"I'm fantastic. For the first time in ages, I have a few weeks off before the next project."

"Is that the film you're shooting in Romania?"

"The very one. I've been lounging around my flat, doing bugger all for a few days. It's nice, but I'll get bored soon enough, I suppose."

I scowled as Lewis's concern ratcheted up. I knew Lewis and their whole family worried about Eilidh. She didn't check in with them nearly enough. And I realized I resented her a little for it. While Lewis fucked off to London, he never lost contact with any of us. I spoke to him nearly every day, and I knew he checked in with his family all the time. There was no doubt in my mind that distance wouldn't keep him from us. However, Eilidh had made her own family with show biz people. It was like she didn't need the Adairs anymore. As someone who'd found solace in them because my own family was shit, it pissed me off that Eilidh took hers for granted.

I was pulled from my musings as I realized Lewis was filling Eilidh in on Carianne's plans.

"After asking him out!" I called, getting up to sit back down beside Lewis. Needing someone else to agree that her plan was terrible, I continued, "He forgot to mention Carianne asked him out for real first."

"Not surprising." Eilidh shrugged. I noted the dark circles

under her eyes and wondered if she was working or partying too hard. Or both. "I always knew she fancied Lewis."

It would have been nice if I'd known that back then. "Aye, apparently even when she was dating me."

"I remember telling you she wasn't good enough for you," Eils said, and then turned to her brother. "And you're an idiot if you trust a woman who has admitted to secretly harboring feelings for her friend's boyfriend and boyfriend's friend for years. Let me tell you, Carianne is hoping that by pretending to date her, you'll fall in love with *her* instead, like some fucking stupid rom-com."

And there it was. I'd forgotten beneath Eilidh's devil-may-care attitude and flirting, she was perceptive as hell. It was what made her such a good actor. Understanding the human condition. "That sounds like Carianne," I agreed.

Lewis huffed. "Carianne's nice, no? I mean, she loves Callie."

"Maybe." Eilidh grimaced. "But she's also always been jealous of Callie. When we were kids, it didn't matter what Callie had, Carianne had to have it too."

"I remember that." I nodded. "When we were dating, if Callie got something, Carianne wouldn't shut up about it until she got it too. I just thought it was what girls did."

"No." Eilidh screwed her face up at me. "Way to generalize us."

My lips twitched with amusement. "It's called assessing female behavior on fact-based evidence."

"A report based on the behavior of one subject is ludicrously flawed and inaccurate."

A spark of enjoyment flickered through me. "It's based on all the girls I've dated."

"Then maybe you should be more discerning in your choice of sexual partners. And according to Lewis, those are many."

"Pot meet kettle, no?"

She narrowed her eyes. "I'm discerning."

"Really?" I thought of the guy I saw her hook up with at a wrap party a few years ago. "Do we really think so?"

Eilidh opened her mouth to retort, and I realized I was anticipating her response because I was disappointed when Lewis cut her off.

"You're both right," he admitted.

"We are?" Eilidh wrinkled her nose in a way that made her look all of fourteen. "About what again? Fyfe befuddled me with his mild misogynism."

"Uh!" I gaped at her, trying not to laugh. "How dare you?"

Eilidh grinned, and I felt a flush of pleasure at seeing her beautiful smile brighten her expression. "You're so easy to wind up."

I rolled my eyes because we both knew I was *letting* her wind me up. Then I turned to Lewis. "What are we right about?"

"That pretending to date Carianne to make Callie jealous is a bad idea. Not only is it childish, but I think it would push Callie further away."

"Agreed," Eilidh and I said in unison and then shot each other a scowl neither of us meant.

"So ..." Lewis sighed heavily. "Any ideas on what I should do next?"

"Well." Eilidh smirked. "I know this might not make you happy, Mr. Impatient, but I think you should try a different tactic. It'll take longer, but it's more likely to work."

"And what's that?"

"Ask her if you can try to be just friends."

"Just friends?"

"Just friends. Then you can spend time together without

all the pressure, and you can remind Callie that you're a loyal, good person she can trust."

There Eilidh went again, being all smart and wise and perceptive. I wondered how many people in her life missed how deep Eilidh's waters were because they were so blinded by the beauty and flirt and charm.

Lewis looked at me.

"She's right," I agreed.

"Did it hurt you to admit that?" Eilidh teased.

"Why? Because I'm mildly misogynistic?"

"Did I say mildly? I meant wildly."

Amusement curled the corners of my mouth. I couldn't remember the last time I'd had this much fun bantering with someone.

"Friends," Lewis interrupted us. "You both think I should propose friendship?"

"If you want to prove that your first thoughts are to Callie, then aye," Eilidh insisted. "She needs trust to build between you again."

A few minutes later, to my surprising disappointment, Eilidh hung up. Lewis left to consider his options over Callie, and I got back to work. However, that feeling lingered throughout the day. The disappointment. The gnawing sense that something was missing.

Then, as I was getting ready for bed that night, my phone buzzed.

I picked it up to find a text from an unknown number.

> Despite your mild misogynism, it was nice catching up today.

Grinning, I saved Eilidh as a contact and replied:

> If you call insulting me catching up. It felt more like a roast.

My phone binged and my smile stretched my face.

> I also called you a smoke show. Trust you to home in on the negative. Also I miss your glasses. Did you get laser eye surgery, Fyfe Moray?

Nope. Contacts. I'm wearing my glasses as we speak.

> Well, that's a relief. For a minute there, I thought my Fyfe had disappeared.

Her Fyfe.

That felt better than it should.

Shoving that thought away, I replied honestly.

> You're one to talk. Today is the first time I saw the real Eils.

> What does that mean?

> You were you and not the untouchable BAFTA Award-winning Eilidh Adair.

> Is that what I am?

Somehow I sensed the melancholy in her reply. I hadn't meant to upset her.

> It's been a while since we spoke. All I've known of you is what I see on TV or on ad campaigns.

> Well, I'm still me.

FOREVER THE HIGHLANDS

> I got that today. It was good to see.

I waited for a response, but a minute passed and nothing. Disappointed, I put my phone down and reached for my e-reader. I hoped I hadn't offended her.

Then a minute or so later, my phone binged again. I dropped my e-reader in my rush to pick up the mobile.

> If I tell you something, do you promise not to tell Lewis or anyone?

Disquiet filled me. I didn't like the idea of keeping anything from Lewis, especially pertaining to his sister. But once, almost ten years ago, Eilidh had kept a secret for me.

> You can tell me anything and I promise not to share it.

I waited impatiently for her response.

> I'm lonely

Fuck.

My thumbs hovered over the screen.

I hated the idea of Eilidh out in the world, alone and lonely.

I knew what loneliness felt like. Didn't wish it on my worst enemy.

> Come home, Eils.

She took a few seconds to reply again.

> I can't. I'm under contract to do this film in Romania.

Shit. My thumbs flew over the screen.

Then text me, call me, anytime. I'm here.

I don't want to bother you.

Eilidh, you're never bothering me. Promise me you'll keep in touch.

Okay. I promise.

THREE
FYFE

Two years ago

Suffice it to say I'd had my fill of drama, and that was only spectating from the sidelines. The past month I'd watched Lewis and Callie fight and clash, come to a tentative truce, only to discover they were pregnant from their one night together in London. Lewis was handling this news better than I would have. The thought of being responsible for a child filled me with abject terror. I never planned to have kids. But it didn't surprise me Lewis took it in stride, and though he might not admit it out loud, I think he was ecstatic he and Callie were now tied together for life.

Callie had even agreed to start dating him.

Their drama seemed to be over (other than the infant cooking in Cal's belly), and I was glad because the whole thing had been a whirlwind of secondhand emotions. Eilidh and I had kept in touch almost every day and had been sharing our commentary over the situation like we were on the TV show *Gogglebox*.

Now, however, I was hoping for calm.

When I opened my door that morning, I realized fate wasn't ready for me to have my calm.

Standing outside next to a small Nissan parked on my driveway was the woman I hadn't seen or heard from in nearly a decade.

"What are you doing here?" I bit out.

My mum blanched, shifting her weight nervously. The past nine years had been kind to her. Her skin looked healthier. And her hair fuller, shinier. She'd put on a bit of weight and was dressed in a fitted shirt tucked into jeans.

She looked ... sober.

"Hiya, son."

I flinched. "Don't call me that."

Mum nodded, biting her lip. "Can I ... can I come in?"

Blood whooshed in my ears. "I'm on my way to work."

"I won't be long. Please."

With an abrupt nod, I turned and strode into the open-plan living and kitchen area. A construction company Thane recommended was coming in a few weeks to take down the wall between the entrance and the rest of this floor so it was all open. It involved expensive beam work, but I thought it would be worth it to be able to walk into the house and see all the way to the floor-to-ceiling windows at the other side and out to the view.

My mind stuck on thoughts about the demo because it was easier to think about that than to think about the woman behind me.

I heard Mum close the door and follow me in. My mind raced with confusion, hurt, and questions. A hundred fucking questions.

Arms crossed over my chest, I leaned against the kitchen island. Tried to look unaffected by her sudden appearance.

"Wow, you've done well for yourself." Mum gestured to the house. "You've got a beautiful home, Fyfe."

I jerked my chin. "So what do you want? I'm not in the mood for a family reunion."

"I deserve that." She nodded shakily. "That and so much more."

"Are you back in Ardnoch?"

"No." She smoothed a hand over her hair and that's when I noticed the wedding ring. "I live in Glasgow."

My jaw clenched and it took me a second to choke out. "With a husband?"

Mum followed my gaze to her hand. She brought it up, looking at the ring with affection. "With my wife, actually."

Shock rooted me to the spot. Never, not once, had I ever seen my mother with another woman.

She gave me a sad smile. "I used alcohol and drugs to deny a lot of things about myself, Fyfe."

"Do you think I would have cared?"

"No, of course not. I ... it's a long story, but my father once caught me kissing a girl when I was fourteen. He always lifted his hands to me, but that night he beat me so badly, Mum finally kicked him out."

What the fuck?

I threw my hands up. "So you disappear for years, after years of saying fuck all to me about anything, and suddenly, in the space of a minute, you're here, you're gay, and you grew up with an abusive father?"

"Why do you think I was the way I was? Why do you think I did my mum's bidding and came home and had you? I owed her. She saved my life that night, and she got rid of the man she loved to protect me."

My chest felt tight. "I can't ... I can't believe this shit."

"Fyfe ... I was so afraid of turning into my father. That's why I left. To protect you."

After years of neglecting me? She thought abandoning her son was protecting me?

I narrowed my eyes, suspicious of her motives. "How long have you been sober?"

Mum swallowed hard. "Six years."

"Married?"

"Five."

All that time, she'd been better ... and she never thought to come find me? Until now.

"Why has it taken you this long to show your face?"

"I didn't think you'd want to see me."

"Then why the change of heart?"

"I ... uh ... I read about you. There was an article online about the work you've done for Ardnoch Estate. About how successful you've become. Cybersecurity. I always knew you'd do well."

"And you ... wanted to come congratulate me?"

She flinched at the sneer in my voice.

"I ... uh ... I wanted to know what happened to the cottage. My mum's house."

Cold shivered through me and then a splintering pain scored across my upper torso. I didn't know it was possible for this woman to hurt me any more than she had.

But here she was. Doing just that.

"You want the cottage."

She swallowed hard. "I ... my wife, Jay, has a daughter from her previous marriage. We want to give her a good life, and finances are a bit tight right now."

"Are you fucking kidding me?" I whispered hoarsely.

"Fyfe—"

"Since I was three years old, you left me in that house on my own."

FOREVER THE HIGHLANDS 37

Her eyes filled with tears, but I felt nothing but resentment and anger toward her.

"Deirdra next door fed me more times than not because you fucking forgot to. And from age twelve on, I paid the bills from the money I made online. Do you know the debt that was on that house for missed council tax payments? Do you know what that amounted to? And *I* paid that debt off. My solicitors attempted to find you and could not."

"I ... I changed my name."

"When? My solicitors couldn't find you."

"I—"

"Never mind. The house belongs to me. It's now a holiday rental and source of income. And there's nothing you can do about it. It's called a Benjamin order. When we couldn't locate you, your mother's estate went to me. Now you can fight me in court for your share, but you'll have a helluva time convincing a judge to give you back that house." I took spiteful satisfaction in the way she paled.

"Fyfe ..." She gestured around. "Look at all you have. What do you need the extra money for?"

"I don't. The cottage is a reminder of all the valuable lessons you've taught me about independence." I took a step toward her. "How dare you come here asking me for money for your new family after you neglected, abused, stole from, and abandoned me."

"I was a different person then!"

I stayed calm, even though the rage threatened to choke me alive. "Really? Because you still seem like the same self-centered narcissist I remember. Only you don't have the excuse of being drunk. Fuck off, Innes." My tone was calm as I used her first name. "And don't ever darken my doorstep again."

She lifted her chin, eyes flashing. "I'll take you to court."

"You do that," I called her bluff. She wouldn't want her

past dragged out through the courts for all to see. All her sins laid bare.

Innes's expression fell. "I didn't mean to hurt you by coming here."

"Maybe not. But you're intelligent. You knew it could happen. You cared more about getting what you wanted than you cared about my feelings. Nothing new there. I expect nothing less from you."

"Fyfe, please—"

"Get out of my house and get the fuck out of Ardnoch. I won't ask again."

She burst into tears and whirled, hurrying from me.

It took me more than a few minutes to calm the agony swirling inside. Then, like always, I distracted myself from the pain with action.

Pulling out my phone, I tapped on the app for my home security system. I found the feed from the driveway and zoomed in on the registration plate on Innes's Nissan. I screenshot it and sent it to Lore, an employee who did legal work for me. But Lore was also one of the best hackers in the country and did freelance less-than-legal work on the side.

I had no intention of tracking Innes down. But information was power, and I wanted to have tabs on her so I could make sure she stayed gone.

If she'd ever cared even a bit for me, she would have stayed gone forever. Today was more proof that she couldn't give a damn about me. Never had. Never would.

AGATA WAS FIVE TEN, ALL LEGS, LONG BLOND HAIR, and a charming Polish accent. Any other night, this woman would have my undivided attention. Especially because I was in desperate need of distraction after my mother's appearance

FOREVER THE HIGHLANDS 39

this morning. The truth was we both knew what tonight was. Agata lived in Inverness. We'd met on a hookup app.

Dinner was just a nod to civility, but we both knew the date would end in her bed.

That's what I thought I needed when I drove to Inverness to meet up with her.

Then as we walked into the restaurant, my phone binged. It was Eilidh.

> I leave for Romania tomorrow. Wish I was coming home instead.

Unsettled by the thought of leaving Eils hanging, I apologized to Agata and told her I needed to respond to my text.

> Where are you now?

We sat at the table and my phone sounded with Eilidh's reply.

> At my flat. Jasper asked me to party tonight, but I'm not in the mood.

I felt relief at that. I didn't want her out partying and hooking up with random arseholes.

Agata cleared her throat as my thumbs flew over my phone screen. "Sorry," I muttered to her, knowing I was being a rude bastard and somehow unable to help myself.

> You should put something on the telly. Distract yourself.

The waiter took our drinks order, and I'd just asked Agata what she did for a living when my phone vibrated on the table.

My date scowled at my phone and then at me as if daring me to look at it.

I winced. "Look, I'm sorry. I've got a friend who needs me right now. Let me check it."

Her lips parted in disbelief, but I was already picking up my phone.

> I don't suppose you're around for a chat?

· Fuck.

I glanced over at Agata who appeared ready to murder me if I didn't turn off my phone. I could ... I could tell Eilidh I was busy, switch it off, have some food, and get laid.

"I'm sorry." I stood, pulling out my wallet to lay some cash on the table. "Something has come up and I have to go. I'm sorry."

"Are you joking with me?" My date's eyes almost popped out of her head.

"Sorry. Really sorry." I hurried from the restaurant and texted Eilidh back.

> Give me two minutes.

FOUR
EILIDH

Give me two minutes.

I stared at my phone screen, almost counting those two minutes in my head.

The truth was it would scare Fyfe to know how much of a life raft he'd become these last few weeks. I didn't know why I found it so easy to be honest with him about my feelings. Perhaps because I knew he understood loneliness. I'd always sensed it in him as a kid, knew how abandoned and neglected he'd been, and so I'd gone overboard to make him feel special back then.

I wasn't abandoned or neglected.

But I was lost.

And feeling lost was extremely lonely.

It was no wonder I grabbed onto Fyfe as soon as he offered his support.

My London flat had seen many parties over the years. In fact, for a while, it was barely ever empty. I'd started renting the loft-like flat when I first moved here for *Young Adult*. I could have moved somewhere bigger, somewhere closer to the studio, and at one point I was going to. I'd wanted a place I could furnish and decorate myself, but my neighbors had told me Pete, our landlord, didn't allow that in his flats. However, when I told Pete I was moving and why, he offered me rent control for a decade. A decade! In London. It was unheard of. And he said he'd have guys come and remove everything so I could furnish it and redecorate how I wished. I couldn't turn down such a deal. Plus, he was a great landlord. Every year he did all the safety checks on the smoke alarms and the heating system, like a landlord was supposed to but rarely ever did. More reason to stay put.

Now, however, my flat seemed ... empty. An interior designer had made it look cool and chic. There was expensive modern art on the walls, unique pieces of furniture. It was a Tribeca loft but with a ton of color and art.

The midcentury chaise sofa was the comfiest piece of furniture in the place, and I was curled up on it with a glass of wine while sweat stuck the hair to the back of my neck. A fan blew in the corner, but it did little to stave off the London summer heat that had built up over the days inside the brick building. And AC wasn't a thing in most residential homes here. I vaguely wondered if AC was a thing in Romania. Gawd, I hoped so.

My suitcases were laid out in my bedroom, and I'd packed what I hoped were enough clothes for the three months of filming.

Three months.

A wave of homesickness crashed over me.

Not for this place. Not for this beautiful piece of art that would never feel like home.

But for Ardnoch.

For Lewis and Callie, Mum and Dad, and my wee sister Morwenna who was growing up while I missed it.

For Fyfe.

FOREVER THE HIGHLANDS

My phone buzzed and I snatched it up, accepting the call. I was hoping for a video chat because I missed Fyfe's face, but I understood when I heard the hum of traffic in the background.

"Are you driving?"

"Aye, just coming back from the city. How are you?" Fyfe's deep rumble of a voice was like ocean waves. The rhythm of it soothed me.

I sighed, feeling better for having him on the other end of the line. The last few days had been a shit show. "I had to hand over my social media accounts to my management team today."

"What happened?"

"I posted a photo this week of me hanging out with friends on my roof terrace here and ..." I squeezed my eyes closed, still seeing the comments in my mind's eye. "I can't take it anymore. I try to let the comments roll off my back, but I can't. Every time I think I have a handle on it, I realize I don't. I've decided to let someone else deal with it so I don't have to see it anymore."

"What kind of comments?" Fyfe's voice was sharp.

"Fyfe—"

"I can easily check, you know."

"Well, we reported some of them."

"Jesus. Eilidh, what are they saying?"

"*Young Adult* is back at number one on the streaming platform and there's this whole new audience finding us. They're not happy my character cheats ... I've been threatened with physical and sexual violence on my social media."

All I heard was the humming sound of his vehicle on the road.

"Fyfe?"

"I'm trying not to lose my mind. Give me a second."

His concern warmed me. "I'm okay."

"They're threatening you over a fictional fucking character, Eilidh. That's insane."

"I am aware. That's why I handed it over so I don't have to see it or deal with it."

"It was the right decision." I heard his heavy sigh. "Please tell me you're safe."

"Aye. I'm safe."

"Does your family know?"

"After we reported the comments, we switched them off. I haven't heard from my family, so I doubt it. Please don't tell them. They don't need to worry any more than they already do."

"Maybe if you started talking to them about all of this, you'd feel better. They know something is up with you, Eils."

I winced because it was true. There was an emotional wall between me and my family. I wasn't quite sure how it had sprung up between us or how I could pull it down. "I need to figure some things out first. Once I do, I'll be more open with them."

"Well, at least keep talking to me."

"Of course." I smiled, wishing he were here with me. "How has your day been? Why were you in the city?"

"Uh ... just ... you know."

My stomach dropped. "I didn't interrupt a date, did I?"

"Aye, and thankfully. I wasn't in the mood."

Ignoring the jealous churning in my gut, I forced out, "Why? Has something happened?"

Fyfe was quiet for a moment and then, "If I tell you, will you keep it between us?"

"You know I will." It seemed to be all we did these days. We were each other's confidants. Being the person Fyfe could talk to made me feel more special than any award or accolade ever could.

"Innes, my mother ... she showed up at my house this morning."

Hearing the seething anger in his voice, I braced myself. "What happened?"

"She changed her name, has been sober for six years, lives in the Lowlands, and is married to a woman who has a daughter from a previous marriage."

What the heck? "Fyfe ..."

"She wants the house. Her mum's house."

Fury lashed through me in an instant, my cheeks turning hot with it. "What?"

"Says they're having financial problems and she wants to give her stepdaughter a good life. Wanted the house so she could sell it for the money, I suppose."

"That bitch!" I shot up off my couch. All the hurt and pain she'd inflicted on Fyfe as a boy ... I'd seen him the day she'd abandoned him for good. Seen something shatter in him. And she came back for the house instead of him?

I wanted to kill her. Pacing the room, I shook with the rage I couldn't expel. "I'm going to hunt that cow down and eviscerate her. She thinks she has financial problems now? Wait until I get my hands on her. She'll have to swim out of the fucking shipwreck of her life when I'm done with her! Fuck!"

A few seconds after the last expletive left my mouth, I was shocked by the sound of Fyfe's laughter.

I froze mid pacing. "Fyfe?"

His amusement petered off. "Thank you."

Puzzled and still infuriated I snapped, "For what?"

"Making me laugh on a day I didn't think I could."

"Oh." That warm feeling cut through the anger.

"She's not getting the house, Eils. I told her to get out of Ardnoch."

I slumped back onto my sofa. "Good. But that doesn't take away from the damage she inflicted today."

"No," he replied quietly. "It doesn't."

Tears burned my eyes. I hated that she could make him feel so unworthy and unwanted. "She's a selfish fool, Fyfe. She doesn't deserve to be your mother. She doesn't deserve someone as special as you."

"Eilidh ..." His voice was hoarse around my name, his tone grateful, like I was salve on an open wound.

"She's not your family, anyway. We are. The Adairs. You're ours. We're yours." The urge to clarify that *I* was *his* the second he woke up to what could be between us was strong. But I held back.

I heard the smile in Fyfe's voice as he replied, "I'm a grown man. Been on my own since I was a boy. And yet ... I needed to hear that, Eils. Thank you."

"Anytime, honey." The endearment slipped out before I could stop it. "I'm always here for you."

Five
EILIDH

Eighteen months ago

Despite my well-known sassy attitude, I had never fought with a director or producer or writer before in my life. I was a professional hired to do a job, and while I'd had careful discussions about script and direction if I wasn't entirely happy with something, I'd never had an out-and-out barney with a director before.

The movie we were filming in Romania was a sci-fi romance. My costar was an up-and-coming actor, and I was grateful he was down-to-earth, easy to work with, and utterly devoted to his childhood sweetheart, so there was no weird sexual tension between us beyond the chemistry we brought to the screen.

That made being in Romania away from all my friends and family a wee bit easier. Especially because I was merely going through the motions of the movie. I'd realized over the last few that I'd begun rewriting parts of the scripts my manager sent me, and this movie was one of them. No one knew, but I'd started writing my own pilot script to pass the time when we weren't filming. It was based on my family, on the Adair family and my uncle Lachlan's members-only estate. I'd planned to write multiple episodes for a TV show.

I didn't know if it was any good.

If I was talented enough.

But it *felt* better than the drivel they had me doing and spouting on this bloody film.

The truth was I was already on edge being "alone" in a Romanian forest for three months. I was missing Callie's pregnancy and her and my brother falling back in love (or at least admitting they'd never actually fallen out of love). Lewis had bought a house, and I was the only one who hadn't seen it yet! Moreover, Lewis had told me Morwenna confessed she felt neglected by both of us. That made me feel like utter crap, so I was trying to connect more with my wee sister but she wasn't making it easy. I needed to be in her physical presence. And this stupid film contract was standing in my way.

Fyfe was my saving grace. Our daily texts and biweekly calls kept me sane.

When my father called to tell me Callie's cottage had been broken into, I cracked. I had to get home. I had to check in on my brother and Callie.

My director said no.

When I threatened to walk away from the film entirely if he didn't let me leave, he'd bellowed at me, so I'd yelled back, and Liz, the producer, had to step between us. She was calm, collected, and amazing. Somehow she managed to convince my arse of a director to do without me for the weekend. Look, I wasn't stupid. I knew delays equaled money. But sometimes people were more important than a budget.

We got straight on the phone to Uncle Lachlan and he

gave us permission to land a chartered plane on the private airfield on his estate.

I'd deal with the tension between me and the director when I returned. I was only in Scotland for two nights, and I was like a kid at Christmas as the plane landed, desperate to deboard.

Uncle Lachlan greeted me as soon as I bounded off the plane. After hugs and reassurances, he gave me the keys to one of the vehicles in his estate fleet and sent me on my way to the village. I'd called Mum and she'd told me I could find Lewis at the Gloaming. I needed to reassure myself he was all right. I knew he had to be sick with worry over Callie. It made sense to pop into the pub first since it was on the route home. When Mum mentioned he was meeting Fyfe, I experienced a mass fluttering of butterflies in my stomach.

I couldn't wait to see him. We'd been chatting every day for months either via text or call, but this would be the first time I'd seen Fyfe in person in a few years.

Pulling the SUV into an empty spot outside the Gloaming, I jumped out and locked it, anticipation fizzing through me. So many emotions. Plus exhaustion. I was a jittery mess as I hurried into the pub, not making eye contact with anyone in the hopes of getting to Lewis and Fyfe without interruption.

Striding into the restaurant, I sidestepped a waiter and caught sight of my big brother at a booth table with Fyfe.

They were in profile, and Fyfe ... Fyfe was beautiful.

I mean, I already knew that. But in real life, he was bigger than I remembered. He was now a tae kwon do instructor and the physicality of that showed in his body.

The expensive blue shirt he wore stretched across his broad shoulders and he'd turned the sleeves up to reveal thick, veiny forearms. He gestured with his large manly hands as he chatted with my brother.

Fyfe Moray had grown from a wiry, slightly nerdy but

unbelievably cute teenager into a *man*. His brown hair swept back off his forehead in thick waves. A short beard made him look older. Older than twenty-five. Closer to thirty.

It worked for him.

He was so handsome, he took my breath away, and that was only in profile.

My attention reluctantly moved to Lewis. If Fyfe looked like a sexy businessman with a casual edge, my big brother looked like a biker. Long hair in a man bun, his beard thicker than Fyfe's. Tattooed. Jeans that had seen better days. Biker boots. Chunky silver rings adorning his fingers. Impossibly, Lewis was taller and broader than Fyfe but not by much.

Homesickness swept over me.

I missed my brother.

As I approached the table, their conversation drifted to my ears, and I almost faltered when I realized I was the subject.

"Eilidh is getting cynical in her old age," Lewis replied to something Fyfe had said. "And since when do you talk to Eils?"

Fyfe's gaze dropped to his menu. "She reached out after that video call. We text now and then."

Now and then?

Try every bloody day.

Something about his blasé demeanor bothered me.

"All above board, aye?" The warning in Lewis's voice made my pulse leap as I drew closer to their table. They hadn't even noticed me.

"For fuck's sake, Lew, what kind of question is that? It's Eilidh. I wouldn't touch her if she was the last woman on earth."

Fyfe's words might as well have been bullets for the way they ripped through me.

I was at their table now, though. They were seconds from noticing me.

And I didn't want Fyfe to look up and see the truth.

That I was in love with him and he'd just devastated me.

Good thing I was a damn good actor.

I crossed my arms over my chest, making sure the internal wound he'd inflicted had no chance to bleed outwardly. "Good to know."

My brother's and Fyfe's heads whipped around in surprise. Fyfe blanched as he realized I'd overheard everything.

My smirk was firmly in place, but I couldn't quite keep the bite out of my tone as I continued, "And for the record, I'd rather have a love affair with my right hand than repopulate the world with you, Fyfe Moray."

Remorse flickered in his dark eyes and he parted his lips to speak, but Lewis beat him to it.

My brother slid out of the booth and yanked me into his arms.

I squeezed my eyes closed, gripping onto his strong back as I melted into him.

Home.

"What are you doing here?" Lewis huffed out in delight.

"Weekend off. Thought I'd fly home to make sure you and Callie are okay."

My brother gently eased out of my embrace. "You came all the way from Romania for a weekend?"

"I was worried, and my production team is great." No need to burden him with the truth. "They chartered a private flight for me in the early hours of the morning. Uncle Lachlan let us use the airfield on the estate. Are you okay?"

"Weirdly wonderful and fucked at the same time."

Seeing the happiness in his eyes (a joy I'd worried Lewis would never find again after he and Callie broke up), I chuckled, delighted for him. I adamantly avoided looking at Fyfe because I was afraid if I did, I'd lose hold on containing my hurt. "I'll bet. Mum knew I was coming and told me you'd be here, so I thought I'd stop in before I go home. I didn't mean to interrupt."

"Join us." Lewis gestured to the booth.

The thought of sharing a meal with Fyfe after what I'd overheard filled me with panic. "No, I should check in with Mum, Dad, and Mor."

"Are you sure?" Fyfe asked, and I could hear the plea in his tone, even though I didn't look at him. "You're more than welcome to stay."

My gaze flickered in his direction but deliberately glanced past his eyes. "Nah, I'm good." And I wasn't here for him, I reminded myself. What I thought was between us was not what was between us. I'd built up a fantasy in my head, and it was time for a reality check.

Anyway, I was home for my family, not a man. I moved up onto my tiptoes to press a kiss to Lewis's cheek. "I'll stop by tonight so I can see the new house in person and check on Callie. That okay?"

"Of course."

"See you then." I turned on my heel and strode out of the restaurant, aware that people had noticed me, and tourists had their phones out. Ignoring the sound of camera shutters as they took photos of me, I rushed from the pub and jumped back into the SUV.

"It's Eilidh. I wouldn't touch her if she was the last woman on earth."

Fyfe's words echoed in my head, over and over, like an earworm as I drove out of Ardnoch to Caelmore. To my family home.

What were the last few months between us, then?

To Lewis, he made it seem like our friendship was merely the odd text here and there.

Did that mean he was ashamed of it? Why would he hide it from my brother? I hadn't told Lewis, but that was because

I'd been avoiding meaningful conversations with my family until I figured out what it was that needed to change in my life.

But Fyfe ... obviously our daily conversations didn't mean to him what they meant to me. In fact, maybe I'd imagined the close friendship I thought had grown between us. I'd imagined that beneath the surface, it was *more* than friendship.

As soon as I pulled into the driveway of my childhood home, my mum came flying out the door. I rushed from the SUV and straight into her arms.

Tears clogged my throat when we embraced as if we hadn't seen each other in years.

"It's so good to have you home, sweetheart," she whispered, not hiding her tears. Mum never hid a single emotion.

I always knew, despite her not being my birth mother, that she loved me as if I were her own.

And I knew then, with sudden, jarring clarity, that I wanted to come home.

For good.

Even with Fyfe's ugly confession ringing in my ears.

I wanted to come home.

Only ... I didn't know how to make it happen without admitting I'd failed.

AN HOUR HAD PASSED. I'D FORCED A HUG ON MY WEE sister Morwenna who clearly resented my sudden desire to be more involved in her life. Dad was at work, so I knew I'd see him when he returned. Tired, I decided to take a nap. Morwenna was in what used to be my room, so I settled into my parents' smaller guest room, a room that used to be Mor's.

Callie and Lewis were crashing in the guest annex while damage to the cottage was being repaired after the break-in.

54 SAMANTHA YOUNG

Lewis had no furniture in his new place yet, so they couldn't stay there. I happily took the guest room in the main house. And not just because Callie and Lewis needed the privacy of the annex more than me. I'd never told anyone, but I hated the place. I'd hated it ever since Mum's ex-friend tied us up and left us in there when we were kids.

I was so young. I didn't remember much from that age, but I remembered every second of that terrifying night. It was before Regan was technically our mother. She was still our nanny at the time. What we didn't know, but I'd learned later as a teen, was that Mum was running from an old friend who was in love with her. She had no idea how obsessed he'd become until he showed up in Ardnoch and broke into the house.

Mum and Dad weren't home. Our aunt Eredine was babysitting. It's funny how so many of those early childhood years were a vague mashup of feeling rather than memory, but there were some moments I remembered as if they'd happened yesterday. The moment that strange man appeared and knocked out Aunt Ery, only to manhandle me and Lewis into the annex to tie us up, was vivid. I could still hear Lewis screaming my name as he tried to fight the man off. Could hear my brother's terror for me and his little boy rage that he couldn't protect me.

I could still smell that man's aftershave. To this day, anytime I caught a whiff of the familiar designer cologne, I felt nauseated. It sounds awful, but I was relieved he'd been killed. He'd attacked Mum and in defending herself, he went flying over a cliff into the North Sea.

That year was traumatic. But kids are resilient. We were resilient. And we got Mum out of it.

Still.

I hated that bloody annex.

I was settling onto the guest bed for a power nap when my phone vibrated on the nightstand.

Reaching out, I swiped the screen, and a burning pang lit across my breast.

> Are we okay?

Fyfe's text glared at me.

I didn't answer.

Instead, I put the phone down and grabbed the remote for the blackout blinds. As soon as the room plunged into darkness, I closed my eyes.

The tears leaked free.

Yet somehow, out of sheer exhaustion, I drifted to sleep.

When I woke, I had a missed call from Fyfe.

Sighing, I groggily texted back.

> Why wouldn't we be okay?

He replied immediately.

> What I said to Lew came off harsher than I meant.

Hurt pierced me.

But he had meant it.

> It's all good. You and I can take a roast.

> Aye, good. Glad you're back. Hopefully see you tomorrow at Lew's.

> Yup. Anyway, gonna go spend some time with the fam. Talk later.

> See you tomorrow.

I threw my phone down on the bed, abandoning it, so I could give my family the full attention they deserved. Everyone was downstairs and I realized I'd slept longer than I meant to. Dad swept me up into a bear-crushing hug that caused a painful lump of emotion to burn in my throat. It didn't help he cupped my face in his hands and searched it like he knew there was something terribly wrong. I grinned cockily for him, trying to dissuade the concern I saw in his eyes. Shrugging on my best acting skills, I hugged Callie next, joking about her as yet nonexistent pregnant belly, and gave my family the version of me they were used to.

The version that didn't have a care in the world.

They bought it.

Or at least they pretended to buy it.

Because any time someone tried to push me to be honest with them, I disappeared.

And I knew them so well. I knew they were scared I was going to disappear for good if they pushed too hard.

Hating myself for making the people I loved feel that way, I cloaked myself in the part I played, with the promise to figure out my bloody life. And soon. Before I missed any more of what was truly important.

Six
FYFE

Nine months ago

> Eils, I'm in London. I'd love to see you.

A mess of emotions churned inside as I stared down at my unanswered text. The London cabbie prattled on about the weather, the traffic, content to hear his own voice and not requiring any response from me.

I'd come to London two days ago for a meeting with a potential client who I'd only gotten word from this morning was now an actual client. The truth was, I should have returned home yesterday. But the text I'd sent Eilidh two days ago had gone unanswered, and I knew for a fact from Lewis that she was in the city.

Nine months.

That's how long it had been since she and I had a real conversation.

Ever since she overheard those stupid words come out of my mouth to Lewis.

She acted coolly toward me. No one else noticed the difference. But the daily text conversations and the weekly video calls abruptly ended. I'd attempted to get us back there, but despite her protestations that "we're fine," her short, uninterested responses to my texts proved otherwise.

I'd hurt her.

And Eilidh Adair was adept at throwing up mile-high walls.

But nine months of very little after having months of her —the real Eilidh—I was pissed off. I was hurt.

Truthfully, I felt fucking abandoned all over again.

Now this.

I shoved my phone into my pocket as the cab neared Eilidh's street.

Not answering me at all. Avoiding me.

I hadn't realized what a light Eilidh's presence in my life was until she took that light away. The whole reason I hadn't yet left London was because I wanted her friendship back the way I had it last year. I didn't want to explode nine months of built-up resentment all over her so I attempted to cool my temper as the cab stopped outside her building.

After paying the cabbie, I jumped out and was hit by the thick London heat. It was early June, but summer had reached London early. Record-breaking temperatures made me long for Ardnoch where, the weather app on my phone informed me, the temperatures were that of chilly spring.

Sweat beaded on my forehead as I pressed Eilidh's flat number on the buzzer. The last time I'd been here was years ago.

The intercom crackled. "Hello?" I heard her familiar voice for the first time in ages.

We hadn't seen each other in person in two months. The

FOREVER THE HIGHLANDS

last time she'd visited Ardnoch. Callie gave birth to her and Lewis's baby girl, Harley, in early February. Eilidh was filming the fourth season of *Young Adult* and had come home for the weekend to meet her niece. I could tell it broke her heart to leave again, but she was under contract. She'd only managed to get home to see Harley again a few months later. Now that filming had wrapped on her show, I wondered why she hadn't returned.

I hoped like fuck it wasn't because she was still avoiding me.

The thought felt a wee bit too self-centered to have merit.

"Eilidh, it's Fyfe. Can I come up?" I held my breath, hoping like hell I hadn't underestimated her ability to hold a grudge.

The front entrance door clicked open and relief flooded me as I pushed into it. I made sure it was closed behind me before I took the stairs two at a time until I reached her floor.

Eilidh stood in her doorway, looking adorably young and fresh-faced with no makeup on. As I approached, drinking her in, a burning sensation flared near my sternum. Her thick dark hair wasn't straightened but left in its natural curls and piled on top of her head. She wore a pair of tiny pink cotton shorts, revealing her long, toned legs. Her blue tank top clung to her like a second skin and as soon as I realized she wasn't wearing a bra, I kept my eyes fixed firmly on her face. Her olive skin was flushed from the heat and aglow with perspiration.

It was a problem.

How beautiful she was.

"Hey." She stepped back to let me in. "This heat is pretty insane, eh?"

Her loft-like apartment was muggy as fuck. Even with windows thrown open and three fans blowing, it was stifling. Considering the UK only had hot weather for a few weeks out of the year, homes were not outfitted with air conditioning.

Those few weeks out of the year were miserable as hell. And London, being in the south, almost always got hit with higher temps than Scotland.

Even in a T-shirt and cargo shorts, walking into Eilidh's flat was like walking into a wall of heat. It was worse in here than outside.

"Jesus." I grabbed the neck of my tee and shook it. "How are you not dying?"

"After a while, you kind of get used to it." She strode away, not looking at me. Her unbound breasts bounced with the movement, and I swallowed hard. "Want a drink?"

"What you got?" I followed her into the kitchen.

"A cold beer?"

"Sounds heavenly."

"So ..." Eilidh yanked open her fridge. "What brings you here?"

Suddenly remembering I was pissed off, I replied, "Didn't you get my text?"

"Oh. Aye. Sorry. I thought I'd replied."

"Liar," I blurted.

Turning, she held out the bottle of chilled beer with a raised eyebrow. I took it, taking a step into her personal space. For the first time in what felt like forever, she met my gaze directly. Hers searched mine before she slid past me, taking a deep pull from her own bottle.

"Why would I lie?"

Might as well get this shit out in the open and deal with it. "Because I hurt your feelings last year and you've never forgiven me."

Eilidh whipped around, eyes narrowed. "Not true."

"Bullshit. We went from talking every day to almost nothing."

She shrugged casually. Her words, however, were not casual. "Well, that's because your friendship had become the most important friendship in my life, and you acted like you were ashamed of it. Or worse, like it meant nothing to you."

My lips parted in unpleasant surprise. All this time I thought she was pissed off about what I'd said about her being the last woman on earth I'd ever want. A comment, I might add, I'd only said to alleviate any concerns Lewis might have about my intentions toward Eilidh. It didn't matter if I thought Eilidh Adair was the sexiest woman alive. She was my best friend's wee sister, and his friendship meant too much to me to jeopardize it for something that could never be serious. And not because Eilidh wasn't worthy of a man giving her that. But because I was incapable of giving *any* woman more than a good time in bed.

Nine months and I'd thought the wrong thing had pricked her feelings. Something silly and vain. But it wasn't that.

It was something important and now I understood the distance.

She was wounded by me hiding what we'd become to each other.

I *had* made it seem like she meant nothing to me.

Fuck.

"Sweetheart ..." The endearment slipped out. "I'm sorry. I didn't ... you know that's not what I believe, though, right? Your friendship means a helluva lot to me. Or I wouldn't be here right now."

"Then why?" She nibbled on her lower lip, the action betraying her.

I took a step closer. "I didn't want Lewis to get the wrong idea. He and Callie had so much going on." It turned out that the break-in at the cottage hadn't been random. After Lewis's house had gotten broken into, we thought Callie's criminal father might be behind what was clearly a threat to Callie.

But a few months later, Callie was attacked in her bakery,

and it turned out the whole thing had to do with her French ex-boyfriend. She'd just gotten caught up in his tragic story. Thankfully, she made it out fairly unscathed, and she and Lewis welcomed Harley into the world, and they were getting married in October. At the time, however, it was stressful not knowing what was going on or who was behind the break-ins. "I didn't want to give Lewis something else to worry about."

"Why would he worry about us being friends? Haven't we always been?"

"Talking every day kind of friends, though? He might think it was something it wasn't. You didn't tell him either," I pointed out.

We both took a long swallow of beer as Eilidh processed this. Then she said, "I wasn't telling him *anything* about my life. It wasn't a deliberate secret I was keeping."

"I didn't mean for it to seem like I was keeping you a secret."

She considered me and nodded with a heavy sigh. "Okay."

Relief started to slide through me. "So ... are we good? Like, actually good this time?"

Eilidh wiped her forehead and I became fully aware of the heat again, sweat trickling down my back beneath my T-shirt. "If we're friends again, then I don't want to hide that from people. Hiding it makes it seem like there's something to hide. Right?"

I nodded, willing to agree to anything to have her back in my life. "I will tell Lewis I came here and that you and I are good friends. I promise."

A sexy wee smirk curled the corner of her mouth, and she bridged the distance between us to clink her bottle against mine. "It's nice to have you back."

My gaze devoured her gorgeous face, her big, expressive blue eyes. "You too, sweetheart."

SEVEN
FYFE

"You're on holiday?" I repeated, because I wasn't quite sure I believed her. Eilidh had been working nonstop since she was a teenager.

She was sitting on the cool hardwood floor of her flat, her back to an armchair and her knees drawn toward her torso. Sweat glistened on her chest as she drank from her fourth beer. I was on my fifth. The alcohol was making our hot bodies already hotter and had loosened us both up. As I sprawled on her couch, beer bottle dangling from my fingers, it pleased me that it hadn't taken too much for those nine months of distance to melt away.

"My agent wasn't very happy about it. Says I could lose momentum since the show isn't as talked about anymore. But I'm exhausted. When a fellow actor offers you a pill to give you energy and you seriously consider taking it, that's when you know you've got a problem."

Anxiety flickered hotly through me at the thought of Eilidh going down that path. "Fuck, Eils, please tell me you're exaggerating?"

She shook her head grimly. "I didn't take it, of course. But the fact that I considered it scared the shit out of me. That was around the time Harley was born. I was about to sign on to a movie shooting this summer, but I know I'm burned out, so I said no. That went down like a lead balloon with my agent."

"Fuck your agent." I'd like to mash the bastard for overworking her. "You're really taking a break all summer until the next season of *Young Adult* starts filming?"

"I am."

I narrowed my eyes. "Were you planning on coming home?"

She gave me an exasperated look. "Of course. But Mor is coming to stay with me for a few weeks as soon as school's out. She wants to spend some time in London, and I want to get to know my wee sister again. I didn't see any point coming to Ardnoch now. I'll visit when I bring Mor back."

Looking around her flat, I hated that she was here alone in this place. It was more art gallery than home. Not that I could talk. My house had very few knickknacks in it or personal touches.

"What is it?"

"Merely wondering if it's a break you need or a change of career," I told her bluntly. Eilidh hadn't been happy for at least a few years now. She was only twenty-four and she couldn't go on like this.

"Well ... I have been writing." She didn't meet my eyes, and I couldn't tell if the flush on her cheeks was the heat, the beer, or her insecurity. Most likely all three.

I sat up, intrigued. "Writing?"

"Screenwriting." Finally she looked at me. "I've been writing a script. It's inspired by my family. By Ardnoch Estate. The club. The members. The weird shit that's happened to us." She grinned wryly, yet just as abruptly, her amusement fled. "I think it might be something, but I'm not sure and ... I don't know if my family would see it as a violation of their privacy."

Eils was writing a script?

Awed, impressed, I shook my head. "Sweetheart, their lives have been splashed across national news. Also you said *inspired*, right?"

"Right. Different names, fictional village and estate, etc."

"Then I don't think they'd see it as a violation. This is amazing. I can't wait to read it."

"Really?" Her eyes were adorably round with surprise. "It might be shit."

"I doubt it."

A pleased smile curled her lush mouth. "Fyfe ... I ... it feels right. Writing. It feels right in a way I'm not sure acting does. But at least with acting, I know I'm good at it."

"You are twenty-four years old and you've been acting since you were fourteen. I think you'd know by now if it's what you wanted to do with your life. If it's not, you're *only* twenty-four. You've still got time to figure it out."

"I miss home." She exhaled the confession. "I feel like a failure because I miss it so much."

"How is that failing?" I pushed up off the couch and crossed the room to sit down on the floor beside her. Wrapping my arm around her shoulders, I drew her against me. "Eils, when I was eighteen, I couldn't wait to get the hell out of Ardnoch and leave behind ... all of that shit with my mum. But being away from Lewis and Callie and ... you ... I realized I'd been so focused on the bad stuff that I didn't pay attention to what I'd found there. *You* all gave me a home, a family ... and that's why I ended up back in a place I never thought I would. It's not failing to *need* people."

She rested her head on my shoulder and I could smell her perfume beneath the slight musk of our sweat. "I'm glad you found your way home."

I kissed the top of her head. "You will too."

Eilidh clinked her empty bottle against my nearly empty. "Want another?"

"Why not? Got any food?"

"I could order takeout." She pushed to her feet and stumbled a little.

I instinctually reached out to steady her with my free hand, and it landed on her pert arse for a second before she straightened. Eilidh's giggle was almost but not quite enough to distract me from the flash of smooth, tan skin beneath her shorts.

"Maybe food is a good idea." She chuckled as she wandered into the kitchen. "Soak up some of the beer."

Twenty minutes later, the Thai food from the takeaway place down the street arrived, and it helped a little with the alcohol. However, two hours after that, we were drunk.

Not wasted, can't see straight drunk.

But tongues loose, feeling good and relaxed kind of drunk.

We'd been talking for hours. I don't think I'd ever been able to chat away with someone for so long with this much ease. We didn't have any awkward pauses or moments of grasping for conversation. The topics veered from trips down memory lane to shows we were enjoying lately, to work, to family, to places in the world we wanted to visit. And back to family again.

"Have you heard from your mum?" Eilidh asked. We were both on her leather sofa now, sitting close, our hands almost touching where they met on the back of the couch.

"Nope. Not since last year. Thank fuck."

"Good. Then I don't have to kill her."

I flashed her a buzzed grin. "You would too, wouldn't you?"

Our eyes locked and Eilidh's expression was intense. Heated. "I'd do anything for you."

All evening, I'd been doing my very best to ignore the way her tank clung to her breasts. There was a difficult moment when she stood in front of the fan to cool down for a bit and turned around, nipples visibly hard through the material. The thought of mouthing those nipples flashed across my mind before I put an abrupt halt to it.

Now, brain hazy with alcohol, skin hot and already coated in a layer of sweat, I lost control of my wandering eyes. There was very little material between me and her skin. Just a flimsy tank top and barely there shorts. I could peel them down her legs and have my mouth on her pussy in seconds.

The horniness that had been building slowly over the evening hit peak hunger.

Abruptly, Eilidh threw herself into my arms. I stiffened, blood rushing toward my dick as her soft curves pressed against me. She tucked her face into my neck, her arms wrapped around my shoulders. Fuck, she felt so good.

"What's happening?" I asked gruffly, my arms closing around her.

"I missed you." Her words were muffled but audible.

I tightened my embrace, breathing her in. My hand rested on the bare, damp skin between her tank and shorts. "Me too, sweetheart."

She didn't move. Instead she buried her nose deeper against my skin and inhaled.

My balls tightened. "Eils ..."

Her lips were at my ear now. "You smell good."

The husky words, her breasts flush against my chest, the feel of her skin under my hand ... I was too drunk to think straight. All I could think about was how amazing Eilidh felt in my arms and how much I'd give my left nut to bury my dick inside her. My hand moved of its own accord, sliding down inside her shorts and knickers to cup her round arse. I squeezed, pressing her closer, my erection pushing against her.

68 SAMANTHA YOUNG

Her breath hitched and then she pulled back to stare into my eyes.

Hers were hooded, smoky with want. She searched mine for a second and then leaned in to brush her lips against my mouth in a whisper of a kiss. I didn't move. There was this tiny wee voice in the back of my head yelling at me. But yelling what, I didn't know. Eilidh's mouth brushed over mine again. And again. The fourth time, her tongue gently licked along my bottom lip.

It was like a spark on kindling.

I groaned, crushing my mouth over hers. She tasted of beer and something sweet. And her tongue ... fuck, the woman could kiss. I licked at her, devouring her, sucking on her tongue until she whimpered, clawing at my shoulders. I groaned as she pressed deeper into my body. When we came up for air, my skin was on fire, sweat trickling down my spine, and I had no thought other than the animalistic need to be inside this woman.

My fingers dipped inside her shorts as the desperate need to feel her, claim her, battled and won. Possessiveness roared through me when I discovered she was already wet. She gasped as my thumb found her clit and my mind blanked. I became nothing but my *wanting*. It took me over. Nothing else mattered but Eilidh and sex.

Eight
EILIDH

One minute we were kissing on the couch, the next Fyfe picked me up and carried me into my bedroom. Seconds after that we were naked.

Fyfe lowered himself to my bed and pulled me onto his lap to straddle him. I dropped my gaze to his cock as it pushed insistently against my belly. He was impressive as he swelled under my attention. I was at once turned on and a little curious to how Fyfe planned to fit that monster inside me.

His arms tightened and I pressed my lips to his, our kiss charged and erotic. My fingers threaded through his hair as I pushed against his erection. Fyfe's fingertips glided down the curve of my waist, across my belly, and down between my legs. I moaned into his mouth as he pushed two fingers inside me, the moan turning to gasps as he pumped in and out. His lips trailed down my chin, my throat, my chest before they danced across my breast and closed around my nipple.

I threw my head back on a groan of pleasure as the pull of his mouth shot streaks of heat from my breasts to between my legs. So wet. I was so wet. The only time I'd been this turned on was with my vibrator in one hand and my imagination in the other.

I clasped Fyfe's head to me as he sucked and licked my nipples. My hips undulated against the thrust of his fingers inside me.

I was panting loudly now, his name falling in encouraging pleas for more as the tension inside me increased. It tightened and tightened and tightened until I tensed upon the precipice of release. Fyfe scraped his teeth against my nipple and quickened his fingers, and just like that I shattered around him.

My inner muscles clenched around his fingers as if trying to trap him inside. "Fyfe!"

The orgasm was long and spectacular, and I could barely catch my breath as it eventually faded. I trembled as I sagged against him, satisfaction weighting my limbs.

Fyfe lifted my head off his shoulder, taking my chin in his hand to bring my lips to his. He pressed a sweet kiss on them. "I think you're ready for more."

I nodded. "So ready."

He kissed me again, hungry and dirty, all tongue and mouth fucking. His confidence and innate eroticism were shocking in the best way. He broke the kiss to demand, "You're going to take every inch of me, baby."

I reached for his cock, curling my hand around its impressive width, my grip firm as I stroked and squeezed him until he flexed his hips into my touch, his expression slack with pleasure.

"Eilidh, fuck, Eilidh. Put me inside you. I want your sweet pussy wrapped around me."

I gasped with arousal at his filthy words and lifted myself up onto my knees, so excited I knew before I even guided him inside me, I was drenched enough to ease his way considerably. I slowly lowered myself back down.

FOREVER THE HIGHLANDS

71

"So wet." His grip on my hips was painful. "Fuck, you want this. You need this."

"I do. For so long," I panted, feeling overwhelmingly full.

I clutched Fyfe's broad, hard shoulders, watching the way his teeth gritted and his eyes darkened as his dick slid snugly inside me. He growled, tipping his head back as I lifted myself up slowly, torturously.

His eyes flashed open. "Ride me, Eilidh. Or I'll make you."

"Make me." I licked teasingly at his lips.

He grabbed my hips and brought me back down. I couldn't move, pinned over his cock, and it was so exciting, I was afraid I was about to come again. "Oh my god!"

Taking control of the rhythm, Fyfe fucked me from the bottom. I wrapped my arms around his neck, bringing us flush so my hard, swollen nipples rubbed against him as I rode him.

We gasped against each other's lips, our grips tightening as we soared toward climax.

"Come for me, Eilidh," Fyfe demanded. "Squeeze my cock, baby."

I nodded on a whimper as I neared climax. Fyfe slid his hand between my thighs, and his thumb pressed circles around my clit.

The sensation was too much. I stiffened, arching my back as the orgasm exploded through me.

"Fuck," Fyfe gritted out, a hoarse shout falling from his mouth, his fingers digging into my hips as he jerked up in one last hard thrust. I felt him swell even thicker inside me before he throbbed and his hot, wet release filled me. "Oh, fuck." His chest heaved against mine as I collapsed on him, my head burrowed in the crook of his neck.

Fyfe's cock continued to pulse as my inner muscles quivered around it.

When our breathing calmed, he warned, "We're not done."

With ease, he lifted me off his dick and gently lowered me to my feet. Then he stood, towering over me, his wet cock still semi-hard. "Now you can sit on my face so I can taste you like I've been fantasizing about tasting you for months."

My belly clenched at what he described. "Uh, yes, please."

He grinned at my enthusiasm, and I wondered about his newfound attitude. Fyfe seemed to have shed all of his hangups about us being together. I wanted to question it. But I wanted Fyfe-induced orgasms more.

A few seconds later, Fyfe was sprawled on the bed, growing harder by the minute as I crawled up his beautiful body. I'd never done this before. Of course, I'd had boyfriends put their mouths on me, but I'd never done it this way. It seemed so visceral and filthy, and I was here for how turned on I was merely thinking about it.

My legs shaking with anticipation, I smiled at his smug smirk as I raised my hips over his face.

Fyfe guided me over him.

I felt his tongue thrust into me, and my back bowed as I gripped the headboard and undulated into his hungry exploration. His fingers were bruising on my hips as my pants and cries for more filled the bedroom. His tongue was magical, licking and fucking and sucking until I was mindless with need.

I shattered, and Fyfe pulled me harder on his mouth, voraciously eating up every second of my orgasm. Then, I was on my back and he was over me, his hands squeezing my breasts, his face a mask of so much need and desire, he looked almost angry with it. His thumbs stroked my pebbled nipples. "You're the sexiest woman I've ever been with." His right hand disappeared between my legs as he held my gaze and slid two fingers into my slick heat. "Beautiful here too." His breathing escalated. "You feel fucking amazing." He groaned the last word as

Forever the Highlands

he prodded between my legs with his hard, hot length and thrust into me.

I cried out, my hands gripping his back, my fingernails biting into muscle as Fyfe fucked me. Our gasps and groans and the wet drive of his cock turned me on as much as the realization that Fyfe Moray was inside me—

BEEP! BEEP! BEEP BEEP! BEEP!

My eyes flew open.

Confusion flooded over me as I stared up at my bedroom ceiling.

What the ...?

I sat up, feeling the sweat slickening the back of my neck.

No Fyfe.

A harsh, almost painful throb pulsed between my legs as reality came crashing in.

I'd just had the most vivid sex dream I'd ever had in my life.

Nine
EILIDH

"You have got to be kidding me." I growled in sleepy frustration as I flopped back on the pillow.

Tears filled my eyes. Part sexual frustration, part memory.

Last night, Fyfe and I kissed. Not just a kiss. Like filthy, prelude to dirty sex kind of kissing. Much like the kind of kissing we'd done in my dream. He'd slipped his hand down my knickers, his thumb on my clit ... and then his fucking phone had beeped on the coffee table. He'd jerked away to look at it and my brother's name was on the screen.

He abruptly remembered I was Lewis's wee sister.

I'd tried to hide my hurt, but his rejection was so painful, it was bloody difficult.

It seemed like pouring salt on the wound for my mind to conjure the most vivid sex dream I'd ever had. I winced feeling how wet I was. Jesus, had I come in my sleep?

Reaching over into my side table, I took out my vibrator.

"Do not think about Fyfe," I whispered as I shoved my pajama shorts down.

After he'd left my flat last night, I'd vowed to keep the man at arm's length.

Closing my eyes, I took care of myself, but I couldn't stop my mind from wandering, from conjuring the dream. I came with his face in my mind, but I promised it would be the last time.

TEN
EILIDH

Eight months ago

The sight of my wee sister's beaming smile filled me with joy.

Morwenna's arrival couldn't have come at a better time.

Lewis had mentioned last year that Morwenna admitted to feeling neglected by us. Mor was technically our half sister and because our mum was so much younger than our father, there was a big age gap between me and Mor. She was turning fifteen in November.

While I had always been a loud, smart-mouthed child who liked attention and, quite frankly, had preened beneath it, Mor was quieter. More reserved. She was actually a lot like our father.

I was envious of how much Mor looked like Mum with her copper-red hair, chestnut-brown eyes, and dimples. She was tall and slender. Lewis and I didn't look like the Adairs or, of course, Mum. We both took after our birth mother, Francine. Dark hair, blue eyes. The only thing we'd inherited from our father was our olive skin.

Maybe that envy was a betrayal of Francine, but I didn't know the woman who'd birthed me. I was a baby when she died. Regan was my mum. And I had to admit to no small amount of envy when Mor was born because I worried that deep down, Mum could never love me with the same intensity that she loved a child she actually gave birth to.

It was something I'd never admitted out loud to anyone.

And maybe subconsciously, it had held me back from Mor. At first, I was excited to have a baby around and had looked after her almost as much as my parents. But as she grew into a toddler and I realized how much of my parents' time she required, I'd backed off. Lewis was the one who had given her his attention when we were teenagers. I was off acting, desperate to fulfil my dream of becoming a movie star.

Sometimes I didn't recognize the girl I used to be.

So selfish and self-involved. It hurt knowing that was who I used to be.

Lewis informing me that we'd upset Mor with our neglect ... I'd never felt like a bigger arsehole. It had taken patience to get past my sister's defenses, but finally she trusted me enough to spend time with me.

And the past few weeks had been a balm to the soul.

Despite her reserve, Mor was excited about London and I was excited that I got to do all the things I'd never done before. We took a bus tour together, visited the Tower of London, Buckingham Palace, went on the London Eye, Big Ben, Westminster Abbey. We even took a day tour of Stonehenge, Windsor Castle, and Bath. Then there were the West End shows we'd attended. I'd gotten us tickets to see two shows a week for the three weeks she was in London. We ate out most nights, then snuggled up on my couch to watch TV. When

Mor opened up, she was funny and sharp and sweet all at the same time.

It was the best three weeks I'd had in as long as I could remember.

On our final day, I'd gotten permission to take Mor to the studio where we filmed *Young Adult* to show her how it all worked behind the scenes. She drank in every second of it, eager to learn what it was I did with my days, and I kicked myself for not doing it sooner.

That night, with our suitcases packed and waiting at my door for us to return to Ardnoch the next day, I confessed to my wee sister that this was the best time I'd had in a long time.

She gaped at me, her brown eyes wide with uncertainty. "Uh-uh."

Her denial wilted my smile. "I mean it," I promised her. "Mor, I've had the best time ever. You'll never know how much these last few weeks have meant to me."

"Really?"

Mor was curled up with me on the couch and there wasn't much distance between us. The summer weather that hit London when Fyfe visited had continued for most of Mor's trip. But this past week, it had rained. A lot. We could hear it now, pinging off the floor-to-ceiling, black-framed loft windows. To cast off the damp chill, Mor had settled a throw over her knees. Her hands were under it so I couldn't reach for them. Instead, I patted her arm. "Really."

She bit her lower lip, eyes bright with unshed emotion. "It's meant a lot to me too. Kids ... kids at school would tease me about you. I didn't know how to react because I felt like I didn't know you."

I frowned, hating that my job had put her in the crosshairs of shitty teenagers, but even more that she felt like she didn't know her own sister. "I'm sorry."

"But I know you now." Her smile trembled. "I can tell

them to get lost and stop talking about you because I know now that they're misinformed."

I didn't even want to ask what gossip they were spreading. Probably just repeating the same garbage people posted online, only for a million people to share it as if it were the gospel truth.

My phone buzzed on the table, breaking the moment. Mor was closer to it. "I'll get it." She picked it up and raised an eyebrow before handing it over. "It's Fyfe. Again."

Ignoring the suspicion in my wee sister's voice, I took the phone from her. My heart lurched unpleasantly.

Talk to me. Please.

Mor had seen that.

I tapped on the text and saw that was it. That's all he'd said.

But above it was all the unanswered texts he'd sent over the past few weeks.

Basically all of them begged me to talk to him.

I couldn't.

Fyfe Moray was my dream guy. And he'd finally made it clear that while he might find me physically attractive, there wasn't anything about me that was special enough to warrant him falling for his best friend's wee sister. Lewis was who he cared about.

"You're in love with him, aren't you?"

My eyes flew up from my phone.

Mor's expression was soft. Sympathetic.

"What?" I gasped, feeling as if I'd had the breath knocked out of me.

"I remember." Mor shrugged. "You ... you never paid much attention to me, but I paid attention to you. Aye, I was just wee, but I remember you flirting with Fyfe. Lewis and everyone joke about it like it's a cute story because you're so flirty. But I always thought you meant it with Fyfe. And now" —she gestured to my phone—"it looks like something's happened. And maybe that something is the reason why every time we have a quiet moment together, you look sad. I thought it was maybe because you're miserable acting and you don't want anyone to know for some reason. But now I think it might be Fyfe. Or both."

A renewed sense of guilt hit me. I'd missed out on this. This perceptive, kind wee girl who saw me. Who clearly saw me ... when no one else seemed to. And I'd abandoned her.

"Mor." I blinked as a tear escaped.

Her eyes widened. "I didn't mean to upset you."

"No." I shook my head, sniffling. "It's ... just ... I've been such a shit sister to you. I'm sorry." I pulled her into a tight hug. "I'm going to do better."

Mor's arms came around me. "Eils, this has been the best summer I've ever had. We're good. I promise."

I pulled back but only to cup her pretty face in my hands. "I love you."

She smiled shyly and mumbled, "I love you too. Does that mean I'm right? About Fyfe? About your job?"

"I'm ... I'm not sure I'm ready to talk about it."

She lowered her gaze, perhaps upset.

I hurried to explain, "Everything just hurts a bit too much right now. But know that I'm grateful you *see* me."

Seeming to understand, she nodded.

"You look so much like Mum."

"Really?" A pleased flush hit her cheeks.

"So like her. I used to be so jealous you looked like her."

"No way."

"Yes way." I released her and settled back against the couch.

"But you're beautiful."

FOREVER THE HIGHLANDS

"Thank you, sweetie. I think it was more about a connection to Mum, you know. I never knew my birth mother so Mum's all I've ever known."

Mor looked away, her smile falling. "Do ... do you think about her? Your birth mum?"

Something about her tense demeanor worried me. "I ... I do."

"Did you ever ask Dad about her?"

"What do you mean? Like about who she was and stuff?"

She nodded, still not meeting my eyes.

"When I was younger, all the time. But when Mum came into our lives, I ... I didn't want her to feel like I didn't accept her as my mum, so I stopped asking about Francine."

Mor met my gaze again. "Aren't you curious about her?"

"I did a little digging when I was your age," I admitted, because I hadn't told anyone about it. Not even Lewis. "I found out what her parents did for a living. Her parents died not long after Francine died. She didn't have any siblings. There was very little information, to be honest. The rest I got from Dad when I was a kid. That Francine died of an aneurysm in her sleep. That they were university sweethearts. That they were in love. I guess that's all I need to know."

I felt sad about it. For her. That she'd missed so much. That I didn't get a chance to know this person who made up half of my DNA. To know if there were reasons I was the way I was or if it was all nature or all Adair. I felt horrified for Dad and how it must have been to wake up to find her gone. I knew that must have scarred him forever.

But I also knew that Francine wasn't the love of his life. Not that Dad had ever said so. He'd loved her, yes. He'd grieved her.

I knew firsthand that Dad was madly, desperately in love with Regan. I'd watched it happen as a child when she came into our lives as our aunt Robyn's sister and then as our nanny.

For years, I'd secretly longed to find someone who would look at me the way my dad looked at Mum.

I grew up in a house with so much love, and I guess that's all I needed to know.

"That's it?" Mor asked. Her voice shook a bit.

Suspicion flickered through me. "Mor ... do you know something?"

"I... I overheard something. And I thought maybe Lewis would have told you. Maybe he did and you don't want to mention it to me." Her expression was hopeful.

My stomach, however, was in knots. "Lewis hasn't told me anything about our birth mother."

Mor looked like she wanted the floor to open and swallow her. "I ... I think this is something you should know, but I don't want you to hate me for telling you."

I grabbed her hand and squeezed. "I could never hate you."

She nodded, biting her lip. After a few very long seconds, she spoke again. "I overheard Mum and Dad talking last year. Dad was telling Mum that he had a chat with Lewis about your birth mum. That he'd told Lewis the truth about Francine."

Blood whooshed in my ears. "What truth?"

"That ... that ... well ... there was some man who hurt you when you were a kid. Tried to take you."

Sean McClintock.

Even though I was young when it happened, it had been so traumatizing I'd never forget it. Or his name. The same year Mum's ex-friend tied us up in the annex, another man tried to kidnap me from school. Sean McClintock. Whenever I think back on that year, I'm amazed at my resilience as a child. Because that shit was fucked up.

FOREVER THE HIGHLANDS 83

And the man who'd come for me ... Dad told me I looked like Sean's daughter who'd died and he was a grieving widow and father who'd mistaken me for his lost child.

I'd tried to feel sympathy, but I'd watched him beat and punch at my mum while she protected me with her body, so it was difficult to feel anything but anger toward him.

"What about him?"

"He ... he had an affair with your birth mum. They were teachers together." Mor's face paled as I reared in shock. "He tried to take you after his wife and kid died because he thought you were actually his."

A crushing sensation on my chest made me gasp for breath. I wasn't an Adair? I wasn't Dad's?

"You aren't his!" Mor reached for me. "Eilidh, I heard Dad tell Lewis he got a DNA test. You're Dad's."

Relief tore through me so rapidly, the emotional roller coaster so swift and volatile, I burst into tears.

"Oh, Eils, I'm so sorry. I shouldn't have said anything."

"No," I sobbed. "Y-you sh-should h-have." But that wasn't true. The person who should have told me was my father. Or fucking Lewis! They'd kept this from me. My birth mother cheated on my dad with the man who attempted to kidnap me as a wee girl!

Through my tears, I saw Mor crying. I reached for her, pulling her into my arms. "It's okay. I'm okay."

"I'm s-sorry." She hiccupped.

Soothing a hand over her back, I pressed a kiss to her temple, my tears miraculously settling at the sight of my sister's. "Don't be. Don't be, sweetie. I'm okay. Please don't cry."

"I'm going to get in so much trouble for telling you. For eavesdropping."

"No, you won't. I'm not going to tell anyone." Resentment flickered through me. Toward my dad. My brother. I didn't understand why Dad would tell Lewis and not me. Lewis wasn't the one Sean had come after. Or the one Dad had to get a DNA test for. Why would they hide this? "It's our secret," I promised her. "I won't say a thing."

At least not until I understood why they hadn't trusted me with the truth.

ELEVEN
FYFE

Seven months ago

You know that feeling that hovers over you when something in your life isn't right?

Like dread.

That sensation had knotted in my gut from the moment I left Eilidh's flat in London two months ago. I knew I'd handled it badly, but I was taken aback by Eilidh's continued silence.

It wasn't like we'd slept together. It was a one-off kiss.

The memory of that night stuck with me. I remembered our conversation word for word.

"Ignore it," Eilidh had whispered, reaching in to kiss me again.

It was too late.

I'd turned my head to look at my phone on the coffee table.

Lewis's name was on the screen.

Fuck.

This was not just any woman pressed up against me. Whose clit pulsed beneath my thumb. This was Eilidh. To be protected at all costs Eilidh Adair. The sister of my best mate in the whole world.

She was off-limits in every way.

I yanked my hand out of her shorts. "What are we doing?" I gently set Eilidh away from me and stood up. "Shit, sweetheart, I'm sorry. I've had too much to drink."

Pain tautened Eilidh's features as she hopped off the couch and straightened her top.

I felt another pierce of panic. "We can't just sleep together because we're attracted to each other. It would mess things up. And Lewis would kill me."

"Is that all it is?" Her expression was sad, resigned. "Just physical attraction?"

Pretending not to understand, I gave her a small, reassuring smile. "You can't help the fact that you're gorgeous. But I can help where my hands wander."

"Right." She laughed hollowly. "Fyfe Moray, Sutherland's biggest player. I keep forgetting about that."

Guilt turned my cheeks hot. "I would never play you."

Eilidh ran a hand over her hair, not meeting my eyes. "Clearly."

"We're drunk."

"Right."

"Eilidh."

"Maybe you should return to your hotel."

I nodded, running a hand over my face, my beard scratching against my palm. "And us? Are we okay?"

"Sure."

My head jerked back at the lie. I knew her well enough to recognize her "whatever" tone. "Eilidh. Please. Let's just put this aside and go back to being friends."

"I said sure."

FOREVER THE HIGHLANDS   87

"For a great actress, you're a terrible liar." I took a step toward her, but she retreated. It was like a gut punch. "Eils. I don't want to go through another nine months without you ..." I gestured helplessly to the couch where the hottest kiss of my life had just taken place.

"I said we're fine. I'm just out of sorts. We'll talk later."

"You matter to me. Our friendship matters to me."

"Same." But her tone was coolly detached in a way that filled me with dread. I watched as she strode toward her front door. "Do you want me to call you a cab?"

"No ... I'll be fine." Reluctantly, I crossed the room. "We'll talk when we're both a bit more sober. All will be good between us again, sweetheart."

Eilidh flinched ever so slightly.

I couldn't help myself. I reached out and stroked my thumb over her cheekbone. "Talk soon." With another sigh, I walked out of the flat and winced at the sound of the door crashing shut behind me.

My head throbbed with every step I took away from her. So did a spot in my chest near my heart. I had to believe I could fix things with Eilidh. That this would never get back to Lewis. It was just a stupid kiss and some foreplay. A hot, never wanted to fuck anyone more kiss and foreplay ... but just that. *Everything would return to normal between me and Eilidh.*

It had to.

But it hadn't.

All the talking and confiding we'd done ... I thought Eilidh would understand me better than this. She had to know that I wouldn't jeopardize our friendship for anything. Least of all a drunken night of sex. And I wouldn't betray Lewis like that either.

Therefore, I didn't get it.

I didn't get why my reaction was so unforgivable.

Eilidh had brought Morwenna home a month ago. My

texts had gone unanswered. My calls too. She'd done a valiant job of avoiding me but couldn't whenever I was invited to Sunday family dinner. Lewis and Callie were busy being new parents and organizing their wedding, which was to take place in two months' time. But Lewis wasn't too busy to notice that Eilidh was even more distant than usual.

"And just with me," he'd told me gruffly one morning as he changed Harley's nappy. "She's all over Harley and Mor and even Callie. But when I touch her, she tenses. When I try to talk to her, she just gives me one-word answers. I don't know what the fuck I've done, but I don't have time for it." He gestured to his daughter. "I have other responsibilities. I don't need to add worrying about Eils to the list."

I'd frowned. "What? You have a kid and Eilidh is no longer a priority?"

Lewis had cut me a dark look. "It's not like that. I don't have time for childish behavior. If she's got a problem, she should talk to me."

I feared her problem was me. Was Eilidh taking her resentment of me out on Lewis?

Whatever her issue was, I was done being avoided.

I got my chance the night of her last Sunday dinner before she returned to London. Eilidh had been quiet, morose almost. I knew from the exchanged looks among her family that they'd noticed. But they also seemed to be growing impatient with Eilidh's distance and attitude. They no longer pressed her to tell them what was wrong and their frustration was written all over their faces.

After dinner, their uncle Lachlan and aunt Robyn and cousins left, leaving Thane, Regan, Mor, Lewis, Callie, Harley, Eilidh, and me. Everyone settled around the sitting room with after-dinner drinks, but Eilidh quietly slipped out of the sliding doors and shut them behind her.

FOREVER THE HIGHLANDS 89

Uncomfortable silence fell over the room. Thane stood as if to go after her, but I cut him off. "Let me talk to her."

"You?" Lewis asked, eyebrows raised.

"We're friends." At least we were.

"Friends?"

"I told you that." I had, but only in vague terms. "We talk."

"You talk?"

Callie shifted Harley to one arm and gently slapped Lewis's biceps. "Quit it."

He shot his fiancée a frown. "I'm not doing anything."

"You're in protective big brother mode with Fyfe, which is the most ridiculous thing I've ever heard."

Internally, I winced at Callie's defense of me. If only she knew I'd had my hand down Eilidh's shorts two months ago and that I might have done more if Lewis hadn't called.

Opening the heavy sliding glass door, I watched the lines of Eilidh's back tense as she leaned against the deck balustrade, staring out at the water. I made sure the door was shut behind me. Between the heavy-duty glass and the ocean waves beyond us, no one inside would hear our conversation. Salt air filled my nose and I inhaled it as I leaned my elbows on the balustrade next to her.

Exhaling, I said, "If you're mad at me, be mad at me. But don't take it out on your family."

Eilidh let out a bitter little laugh. I hated the sound. It wasn't her. "My problem with my family has nothing to do with my problem with you. Those are two separate things."

Problem with her family. "Christ, Eils, just tell us what's going on in that head of yours. It feels like you've been miserable for years and your family is worried about you. Can't you see that?"

The low late-summer sun cast a glow over her beautiful face as she turned toward me, eyes flashing angrily. "I am perfectly aware that there is shit I need to figure out. But up until a month ago, I didn't know understanding my family and how they see me was one of them."

"What are you talking about?"

Furious tears glimmered in her eyes as she looked away. "Nothing."

"This." I couldn't help but grab her arm, pulling her toward me. "Shutting people out. People who give a damn about you. It fucking hurts, Eilidh. And you just keep doing it."

Her lips parted as she glared up at me incredulously. Something happened behind her eyes, something I didn't quite understand. Then she wrenched her arm from my grasp. "You're right. You're absolutely right. Come." She gestured toward the house. "You're an honorary Adair. You should hear this."

Something in her tone lifted the hair on the back of my neck. "Eilidh, what—"

She was already yanking open the door and marching into the house.

"We need to talk." I heard her say loudly as I hurried in after her.

Eilidh stood before her family, hands on her hips, as they all stared up at her expectantly.

My palms grew clammy. Was she about to tell them what happened between us? No. She wouldn't do that to me.

She crossed her arms defensively and I saw the telltale tremble in her lips that she was holding back emotion.

This wasn't about me. About us. It couldn't be.

Lowering myself onto the arm of the sofa, I watched her, a renewed worry washing over me.

"A while ago, I decided to investigate my birth mother. Francine."

Everyone tensed.

FOREVER THE HIGHLANDS 91

"I wanted to know a little about her."

"Why didn't you just ask me?" Thane frowned.

"Because I wanted to know who she really was. Not the perfect woman you painted her as."

He flinched at her tone and Regan reached for his hand.

"Eilidh—" Lewis's admonishing tone induced a sharp "back off" glare from his sister.

"I found out about our grandparents, about Francine's schooling, even found her yearbook from high school. I also found her yearbook from working as a teacher. The school has all their yearbooks available to view online. Including the last year Francine taught. There was an individual photo of her and then there was a group teacher photo. And I couldn't believe it when I looked at that photograph because standing next to her with his arm around her was the man who tried to kidnap me when I was a child."

What the actual fuck?

Not where I thought this was going.

Eilidh's expression was baleful as she searched her father's face.

"Eilidh—"

"That kind of brought up some horrible stuff that I'd suppressed, and I found myself reaching out to that man. Sean McClintock. I drove to Inverness to see him two weeks ago. He was quite happy to see me so he could apologize in person. Apparently, prison and a therapist sorted out his head, and he has a lot of remorse for traumatizing me." Her casual tone discussing something so painful was like nails on a chalkboard. I gritted my teeth, forcing myself not to go to her.

Thane stood up, his pain turning to anger. "You went to see that man? Alone?"

"Don't," Eilidh seethed. "How dare you? Were you ever going to tell me Francine cheated on you with that man? That they had an affair?"

Holy fuck.

Her pain became all too clear.

Was ... was Eilidh not Thane's?

The very thought twisted my stomach, and I had to hold myself back from rushing to her, from wrapping my arms around her to protect her from a truth that would break her heart.

"You are not his." Thane stepped toward his daughter. "If that's what's in your head or what he put in your head. You're not his. I had a DNA test done when he tried to claim custody."

"I know," Eilidh whispered harshly, her tears slipping free. "I know because *he* told me. My question is, why didn't you?" She turned to her brother who stared up her, eyes bright with emotion. "Did you know?"

To my shock, Lewis nodded.

He knew and hadn't told her?

"Dad told me last year."

Eilidh wiped at her tears. "I already knew that. I just already knew that. You can be trusted with the truth, but apparently I'm too much of a loose cannon to be treated like an adult."

"That's not ... is this ... is that why you've been weird with me?" Lewis stood, reaching for her.

She stumbled back, holding up her palms toward both father and brother. "Why didn't you tell me? If I'm yours, why didn't you tell me? Why did I have to find out from someone else that this woman you painted as a perfect wife and mother was actually a selfish bitch who cheated on you?"

Thane winced. "It was more complicated than that."

"It was an affair. According to McClintock, it was an affair, and he wanted to stay with his wife and child. And you took Francine back, even though it was an *affair*."

"My reasons for taking back your mother were my own.

Forever the Highlands 93

You don't get to judge me for that, Eilidh Francine Adair," Thane told her sternly.

She flinched and I stood up off the couch, edging closer to her.

"You're right. I don't get to judge you for that. I do get to judge you for not telling me. Why did you tell Lewis and not me? *I'm* the one whose parentage was in question. I'm the one Sean came after. So why did Lewis get to complete that puzzle while I was left with the lies? What is it about me, Dad? Why wasn't I worthy of the truth?"

Thane's features strained with remorse. "Oh, sweetheart, it's not about being worthy of the truth. I was trying to protect you from the truth. Back then. And now I didn't see the point in sharing. I only told your brother because he asked me directly to my face what my relationship with Francine was like. And I wanted to be honest."

"Do you think I'm like her?" Eilidh asked, voice breaking. "Is that why you didn't tell me? You didn't want me to self-fulfil my genetics by becoming even more of a flaky, disloyal, selfish bitch?"

Thane held up a finger. "One, stop calling your mother a bitch. Two, don't refer to yourself that way either."

"I didn't call my mother a bitch," Eilidh snarled, gesturing to Regan who pressed her lips tightly together, suppressing a reaction. "That's my mother. Francine was just the woman who gave birth to me."

"Francine didn't leave you, Eilidh. She died. And she loved you. More than anything. And people are allowed to make mistakes."

"Even if they keep repeating them?" The tears fell fast and free now. "I think that's why you didn't tell me. I think you look at me and you see her. Why wouldn't you? I made everyone dance to my fucking tune as a kid. Wanting what I wanted without caring how it affected anybody else. Then I fucked off and left my family behind to become a movie star!" She sobbed on a hysterical laugh. "And I hate every second of this life I was so determined to have. And because I can't face what a selfish bitch I've been, it makes me even more of a bitch. I *hate* who I am. I hate myself! And now I know why. I'm my mother's daughter!" With another sob, Eilidh's knees seemed to give out.

A burning pain lodged in my sternum as I moved toward her.

Her father got there first. Thane fell to his knees and pulled his daughter into his arms, gripping her tight as she cried against his chest like a little girl.

Regan was in tears, as were Mor and Callie. Lewis got up and knelt by his sister and father, his hand on Eilidh's back as he and Thane exchanged deeply concerned looks.

No fucking wonder.

Eilidh had told me over and over again that she was miserable. That she was trying to figure things out. But I hadn't realized it was this bad.

I hadn't paid enough attention.

Pushed enough.

Because I was trying to keep her at a safe distance.

I'd failed her.

TWELVE
EILIDH

Five months ago

For the first time in years, I felt free.

In hindsight, it seemed obvious that what I'd needed all along was to just admit to the people I loved that I'd made a mistake. And that I hated the person I'd become. In hindsight, the latter especially wasn't easy to face, let alone confess.

I feared changing my life. Feared disappointing them. Feared no one would take me seriously ever again because I'd made such a colossal error with the path I'd forged so far. Mostly I think I was terrified that if I admitted I didn't like who I was, they would admit, at least to themselves, that they didn't like me very much either.

The very thought of that was so painful, I couldn't bear it.

I hadn't lied when I told my family about visiting Sean McClintock. I arranged to visit him because I needed to make sure what Mor had overheard was true. It meant confirming it and protecting her so they didn't find out she was the one who'd told me the truth.

I was sick to my stomach meeting Sean, but he seemed so normal. So nice, actually. I couldn't forgive him for what he'd done, coming after me or having an affair with my mother, but I was grateful he was willing to meet and be honest with me. Sean told me Francine had been afraid of losing her youth after she gave birth to me. That she didn't want to be an ordinary wife and mum. She'd wanted excitement. Not to be stuck in a tiny village in the Highlands. That last one had hit its mark because for so long, I'd thought the same. That staying in Ardnoch equated to living an unremarkable life. Francine's answer was to start an affair with a married man, even though it blew up both their lives.

Somehow discovering my birth mother had cheated on my dad who was so wonderful, and all because she was *bored,* hit me in a place I never expected. It royally fucked with my head. I saw all the things I hated about myself in *her* in that moment.

The breakdown in front of my family was the culmination of everything that had happened in the past few years.

The stress of my job, the way the public picked me apart, finding out about Francine, and Fyfe. He was the one person who knew everything I was going through ... and he didn't want me enough to want to risk the status quo. I'd never connected with someone the way I connected with Fyfe. It seemed to me then that if he didn't want me, there had to be something wrong with me. That everything I'd grown to hate about myself must be true.

That was the breaking point. I had work to do to stop focusing on all the things I didn't like about myself.

I had to change my life.

FOREVER THE HIGHLANDS

Now I had the support of my family to do that.

Mum, Dad, Lewis, and Mor were so concerned after that awful scene, they suggested I speak with someone. Honestly, I felt a ton better just unleashing everything that had been roiling inside me for years. But for them, I agreed to see a therapist.

I had a session a week while I worked on my final season of *Young Adult*.

And it *was* my final season.

I'd decided to retire from acting.

While I felt nothing but relief, and with the help of my family and therapy, a sense of excitement about the possibilities of my future, I lost a friendship that mattered to me.

Jasper.

When I refused to sign on for another season of the show, the writers decided it was time to reboot it with a younger cast. The show was, after all, titled *Young Adult*. Those remaining from the original lineup, including Jasper, were out of a job. And my friend blamed me.

That was crushing.

A person who had stood by me through this crazy business seemed to only find me useful as a friend if I was acting and offering him something in return other than friendship. That awful realization made me more grateful to my family, who had been in constant communication these past few months.

I'd never seen my dad so happy and relieved to see me as when he picked me up at the airport. The showrunner had given me permission to take a long weekend off filming. To be in my brother's wedding.

The drive from Inverness Airport was the first time Dad and I had been alone since my wee breakdown a few months ago.

"How's my Eilidh-Bug doing?" he asked as we hit the A9 toward home.

At the endearment, one he hadn't used since I was a young teen, a swell of emotion filled me. It took me a minute to speak before I reached out and squeezed his arm. "I'm better, Dad. So much better. I have to keep my socials for another eight months to help with the promo of the show's final season because they buried that in the contract, but once it's done, I'll delete my social media and I'm going to try to be just Eilidh again."

"And it's definitely what you want?"

"It is."

"How's ... how's the therapy going?" he asked tentatively.

"You know I didn't want to go." I offered him a dry smile because I'd gone for his and my family's sake. "But Diana, my therapist, is making me see that I've allowed all the shitty things that have been said about me online, in the media, to fester more than I consciously knew."

His fists tightened around the steering wheel, but Dad didn't respond. I knew that one of the reasons he hadn't wanted me to go into acting was because of the fame aspect and the deadly court of public opinion.

"We've been talking about how those things have given me a warped sense of self and how I conflated the opinions of strangers with the reality of who I was because I was secretly unhappy with my career choice. I'd turned that unhappiness into failure and catastrophized how big that failure is. She's making me see that most young people end up not enjoying what they choose as their first career. The difference is the one I chose involved fame, which is a strange beast for anyone to deal with. She's making me see that it doesn't mean I'm a failure if I'm not built to handle the scrutiny. It's so much worse for celebrities now because of social media. Someone will always find a reason to hate you or be outraged, and when it's on the level I had to deal with, it's basically mass harassment and bullying masquerading as opinions, and no one can admit that because they genuinely think they're entitled to say whatever the fuck they want about you. So, long story short, I can't do fame and social media, and that's okay."

Dad's expression was tender. "She sounds like a very wise woman."

I nodded, tears burning my eyes. I'd also been extremely emotional since I'd started therapy. It was great for my work on the show but frustrating in real life. Diana told me it was normal. I'd been suppressing my feelings for so long, they were just spilling out of me. "I'm sorry for what I said to you that day. About Francine."

"You don't need to apologize, Eilidh-Bug."

"I do, Dad. I blew that up into something it wasn't. I know if I'd come to you as Lewis did that you would have told me the truth."

"I would have." He cleared his throat. "Eilidh, Francine made a mistake. A big mistake. But she was going through something. Looking back, now that we know more, I often wonder if she had postpartum depression. Her moods, the affair, it was out of character."

This new information stunned me. "Do you really think so?"

"I don't know for sure. I do know that your birth mother was a good woman who made a bad decision. I wouldn't have given our marriage another chance if I hadn't truly believed that. And you were right, I look at you and I see Francine. Not for negative reasons. I see Francine because you have her coloring. You have her fire. But I also see your uncle Brodan and your uncle Arran when I look at you." He flashed me a grin. "And I see your mum, Regan, because she brought you up and she instilled you with her kindness. I know you are struggling to see what we see, Eilidh, but you *are* good and kind. As a little girl, you were the first to stand up to bullies, to make the quiet kids in your class your friend. You spot someone who needs a light shone on them, and you give that to them. You make people feel special. And maybe that's the reason you can't handle the negative scrutiny of social media. Because you're kind to everyone and the injustice of cruel behavior hurts you too much."

Tears streamed down my cheeks as Dad continued.

"For the past few years, your light has dimmed, and I've worried every day that the longer I left you to try to figure things out that I would lose you. That you would lose you." His voice was gruff with emotion. "So as hard as it was to watch you admit everything you were feeling, as hard as it was to hear how you saw yourself, I'm glad it happened. I'm glad it led to this moment so you can hear about who you really are and hopefully really *hear* it, Eilidh."

I swiped at my tears and my now running nose. "Thank you, Daddy," I whispered. "I love you."

"I love you more than you'll ever know, my sweet girl," he replied hoarsely.

———

EVERYONE WAS AT MUM AND DAD'S THE NIGHT before the wedding, so Dad waited patiently in the car for me to fix my makeup before we entered the house. I felt overwhelming love from my family as they all got up to welcome me home.

Uncle Lachlan's and Uncle Brodan's hugs were the tightest. "How's my Eilidh?" Uncle Lachlan asked, not letting me go as I pulled back because he was searching my face, as if he could find the truth for himself. Uncle Brodan stood pressed to his brother's side, his expression just as probing.

Uncle Lachlan was the first of us Adairs to hit Hollywood.

FOREVER THE HIGHLANDS

He kind of fell into acting and became an action movie star. That life wasn't for him, though, so he retired in his midthirties, took the money he'd earned and wisely invested, and created a proposal to turn our family's ancestral castle and estate into the successful members-only club it was now. He and my uncle Brodan also owned Ardnoch Whisky, one of the most popular whisky distilleries in Scotland. Along the way, he'd married my aunt Robyn, a badass ex-cop from Boston. She was his best friend and the once estranged daughter of Lachlan's bodyguard, Mac Galbraith. It was very complicated, but Lachlan and Robyn fell madly in love while Robyn was helping to catch the person who'd begun stalking Uncle Lachlan and terrorizing the estate.

Through Robyn, Regan arrived and, of course, Dad fell in love with her, despite the age gap. Thank goodness. Regan was the best mum anyone could ask for.

As for Uncle Brodan, he followed Uncle Lachlan into show business but had become a far more critically acclaimed actor. He'd stayed away from the family for years, and when I was little, I remembered him as the charming, funny uncle I only got to see on special occasions. While he did enjoy acting, he missed his siblings and Ardnoch. When the woman he'd loved and lost as a teen returned to Ardnoch to teach, Uncle Brodan could resist the pull of home no longer.

He and my aunt Monroe fell back in love so quickly, she was pregnant by the end of their first year together. Uncle Brodan, who was already burned out by this point, retired from acting and started managing the whisky distillery.

My dad had gone to them about my breakdown and my uncles reached out to talk to me. Along with Diana, they were extremely helpful in making me see it was okay to realize that acting wasn't my ideal career. Uncle Lachlan said if he'd had to deal with social media back when he was acting, he wouldn't have lasted in the movie industry as long as he did.

That was comforting to know.

Just because I'd always liked attention when I was little didn't mean I could handle the level that had been thrown at me over the course of the past few years. Plus, when I was a kid, that attention had been positive. As my fame increased, the breadth of the negative attention became a monster in the dark of my mind that I'd kept convincing myself I could fight.

I couldn't.

And there was no shame in knowing your limits. I understood that now.

My uncles had been in contact with me regularly, checking in, reminding me that I was doing the right thing, and I kicked myself for not going to them sooner.

"I'm all good," I promised them, beaming.

Whatever they saw in my smile made them relax.

"Aye." Uncle Lachlan cupped my face. "There's my Eilidh."

Embracing my family was easy.

Fyfe, not so much.

Seeing him there, looking handsome in the black suit pants and dark cashmere sweater that molded to his strong physique, my pulse fluttered. Though I'd responded to his texts lately, I hadn't encouraged a return to our old friendship. Fyfe had no idea how I felt about him, and I couldn't punish him for reacting the way he had to our kiss.

I'd decided to be kinder to him, but for the sake of my heart to keep him at a distance.

We hugged, but I released him quickly, not wanting to feel him against me.

Fyfe appeared relieved by the embrace. Concern hollowed his gaze, though, as he looked me over. "How are you?"

"I'm good." I turned from him, announcing to the room. "Where's the champagne?"

Uncle Arran immediately held out a glass to me.

I laughed, grinning. "Ever the bartender."

He gave me a mock bow. "At your service."

Raising my glass, I turned to my brother and Callie. "To Lewis! For finally pulling his finger out of his arse to claim the kindest, smartest, prettiest girl in Ardnoch before she realized she could do better."

Everyone burst into laughter, including the bride-to-be, while Lewis mock glared. I grinned at him and called over the titters, "No, no, in all seriousness ... I have the best big brother in the world." Tears blurred my gaze, and Lewis's expression turned tender. "No one else but Callie could ever hope to deserve you. I'm so happy you found your way back to each other. I love you both. To Lewis and Callie!"

"To Lewis and Callie!"

My brother crossed the room to pull me into his bear hug. "It's good to have you back," he whispered before planting a gruff kiss to the top of my head.

"You too."

"Love you, Eils."

"Love you, Lew."

A FEW HOURS LATER, SOME OF THE YOUNGER members of our family had dispersed to get sleep before the big day. I was sitting with Mor and Callie. Lewis had gone upstairs to put Harley down. My gorgeous wee niece was staying the night with us because my parents were babysitting.

We were going over last-minute options for our hair tomorrow. Callie had bought a bunch of different clasps, clips, and hair gems, and we were deciding what would work best. I was maid of honor and Mor was a bridesmaid.

Callie's wedding dress was very boho princess, so I was naysaying the sparkly diamante clips.

"Pearls and flowers," I said quietly, because we didn't want to give away anything regarding Callie's dress.

Mor fingered the diamante star, and I saw the disappointment on her face. Callie looked at me and we shared a silent conversation.

"You know." I picked up the star and placed it against Mor's beautiful red hair. "Maybe it would be nice for our bridesmaid to have a point of difference. This would look gorgeous at the top or bottom of a fishtail braid."

Mor pretended not to be hopeful. "Do you think?"

"Absolutely," Callie agreed. "I like it."

My wee sister tried to hide her smile and failed. "Okay."

A shadow fell over our small group and I looked up, my skin buzzing with awareness at the sight of Fyfe.

"Hey."

"Hi."

He nodded toward the deck outside. "You got a minute?"

The balcony was lit up in the evening dark. The last time we'd stood out there, it was still summer. But autumn had arrived and so had the shorter days. Not wanting to be disagreeable on the eve of my brother's wedding, I nodded and stood. Following Fyfe out, I braced against the rush of chilly air.

"Too cold?" Fyfe asked, leaning against the balcony.

I tried not to let my gaze devour his long, strong body as I approached. "A bit. What's up?"

"We just haven't had a chance to talk in what feels like ages."

Settling beside him but with enough distance so we weren't touching, I said, "I've been busy sorting out my life."

Fyfe heaved a shaky exhale. "Eilidh ... I ... I've been a shit friend."

My eyes flew to his.

His expression was anguished. "I should have pushed

harder, made you admit how you were feeling, asked more, talked you into coming home—"

I pressed a hand to his arm. "Stop." My goodness, this man could tear me up. Knowing he cared this much was torture because ... it made me hope for *more* from him. "Nothing or no one could have done that. I needed to hit that point by myself. And I did. I'm doing much better."

"I can see that." He reached out to touch my cheek and I forced myself not to react. "You seemed so much more like yourself in there."

"I'm getting back to that person. But hopefully to a better version of her." I slowly eased away so it didn't seem like a rejection. "How are you?"

"I'm not done asking about you. When do you come home?"

"What do you mean?"

"You said you're retiring. That you'll be announcing it soon, right? So when do you come home?"

"Oh." I'd battled with the idea of returning to Ardnoch and landed on splitting my time between here and London. "I'm not. I'm staying in London. While I figure things out. I'll spend a few months in Ardnoch over the summer, though."

"You should come home." He scowled. "You know that's where you need to be."

"I know I need to take all the changes that are happening in my life one step at a time," I replied calmly.

The muscle in his jaw twitched as he turned to glower out at the darkness beyond. We could hear the water crashing against the shore below and see glimmers of waves catching in the half-moon light.

"How are you?" I repeated.

"All right." He shot me a reluctant smile. "Been worrying about losing those damn wedding rings."

Fyfe was Lewis's best man.

106   SAMANTHA YOUNG

I laughed. "The pressure." Then, because I was a masochist, "Are you bringing a date to the wedding?"

He tensed for a millisecond, shot me a look out of the corner of his eye, and then returned to staring straight ahead. "No. I am ... I'm casually seeing someone, though."

The thought of him with someone other than me was so painful, I had to shut all emotion down.

"It's not serious." He turned to me now. "You know I don't do serious."

"Right." I smirked as I created a mental shield between myself and my jealousy.

"We started seeing each other last month. She's from the US. Here on a work visa until January. We're just passing the time together. There's not a huge selection in the Highlands, you know. So it's just ... fun. Can't invite her to the wedding. It would give her the wrong idea."

Please stop talking.

"Are you seeing anyone?"

"Aye."

Fyfe flinched like I'd hit him. "Who? When?"

"Oh, I'm not seeing someone romantically." I took perverse pleasure in his reaction. "I'm seeing a therapist. Her name is Diana."

His shoulders seemed to slump with relief. My eyes narrowed. Interesting.

"That's good. Is it helping?"

"Definitely." I relayed to him what I'd told Dad, falling so easily into that place of sharing with Fyfe because I couldn't seem to help myself.

He reached out and curved his hand over mine. "Eilidh ... it kills me that you ever felt those things about yourself. Do you not know that your friendship has meant so much to me and to others over the years?"

Friendship.

FOREVER THE HIGHLANDS

Bloody friendship.

I smiled tightly and pulled my hand away. "Thank you. I better get back inside. I'll see you tomorrow."

Fyfe searched my face for a second, then nodded. "Aye. See you tomorrow."

Thirteen
FYFE

The combined noise of the fiddle, accordion, guitar, bodhran drum, and flute filled the village hall as Lewis's family, friends, and neighbors danced with abandon. My best friend's face was lit with laughter and happiness as he spun his bride out and pulled her back against his body. Callie's head tipped back, her laughter ringing out above the music. She was beautiful in her wedding dress and all eyes were on the blissed-out couple.

Well, not all eyes.

Mine kept pulling toward the maid of honor.

I sipped at my whisky, watching as Eilidh showed Morwenna the steps to the ceilidh music. Not everyone was proper ceilidh dancing (including the bride and groom), but some were. Eilidh looked beautiful and relaxed, and Mor lit up under her big sister's attention. I'd noted a marked difference in their relationship, how close they seemed now, and I was glad for Eils.

What I wasn't glad for was this continued distance between us.

Forever the Highlands

So much distance, even though she assured me we were fine after our kiss. That moment between us seemed like a fuzzy dream and not reality.

Because I'd never get to touch her like that again.

And apparently, I was never getting her back the way I had her.

That now-familiar burn scored across my chest.

I wanted to leave.

As much as I was over the moon for Lewis and had stood proudly at his side as he and Callie got married across the street in Ardnoch Church earlier today, I wanted to get away from this *thing* that was slowly turning into agony.

Everyone's eyes had been on Callie as she'd walked down the aisle toward Lewis. I'd had to force my gaze to her because Eilidh had walked down the aisle before her in her maid of honor gown, and I could barely hear anything over the sudden rush of blood in my ears.

She'd worn a pale green silk dress with thin straps, and the top part of it seemed almost corseted, pushing her breasts up. It skimmed her figure, tight at the waist and hips but then flowing loosely around her ankles. I thought bridesmaids weren't supposed to be sexy so they didn't pull attention from the bride. But that color against Eilidh's dark hair and olive skin was striking.

It was like seeing one of her red-carpet moments in real life. Untouchable Eilidh Adair suddenly at my fingertips.

I watched now as she hopped easily on her high heels, her arm around Mor's shoulders. Mor giggled as she attempted to copy her big sister. Eilidh seemed the happiest I'd seen her in a long time, and the immensity of my relief was a balm to my agitation. Smiling over my glass of whisky, I noted the tendrils of dark curls falling loose from Eilidh's updo.

I imagined all that hair spilled across my pillow, her lying breathless on her back beneath me, her dress bunched up to the waist, and her breasts shaking with the fierceness of my thrusts into her.

Fuck.

I should leave. Go to my American. She knew the score. What we were. And what we were was extremely far from complicated. Which was what I needed.

It was getting too hot in this fucking kilt anyway. I wore the Sutherland tartan, which was what the Adair family wore. A dark green with red, black, and white accents. All the Adair men wore a black evening kilt jacket with regulation doublet and vest. White shirt beneath. Black bow tie. Sporran. Socks. Dress shoes. The whole works. Lewis stood out in his biker boots instead.

A kilt was hot, though. Time to divest of the jacket at least.

"You, Fyfe Moray, should be dancing." Lewis's mum appeared at my side. She took the glass out of my hand, rested it on a nearby table, and then tugged me out onto the dance floor. We ended up next to Eilidh and Mor, and my heart lurched when Eilidh beamed up at me. Now Regan was attempting to show me the ceilidh moves, but I didn't care because Eilidh joined in, her hands touching me, her perfume filling my senses as her laughter filled that empty place inside me.

NOT LONG LATER, SO AWARE OF HER EVERY MOVE, I saw Eilidh duck out of the village hall by herself. Unable to resist, I followed her. The chilly October air pierced through my shirt and I welcomed it. Though I'd shrugged off the kilt jacket a while ago, I was still fucking roasting in this getup.

FOREVER THE HIGHLANDS 111

The cool air blowing up my bare legs was welcome too. After a few seconds of searching, I found Eilidh down the narrow lane between the hall and the building next door. Barely a shaft of moonlight lit her as she braced against the side of the village hall, her chin tilted as if she was looking at the slice of sky she could see above her.

"Hey."

She jerked, pushing off the wall at my approach. "What are you doing here?"

"Just checking in with you." I stopped, searching her expression, blurred by the darkness though it was.

"I'm fine. Just hot." She chuckled, and a strand of hair that had fallen loose cascaded over her shoulder.

Instinctually, I reached out to tuck it behind her ear, and Eilidh sucked in a breath.

Her awareness sent a jolt of sensation to my dick. Maybe I'd had too many whiskies, after all.

She stepped away, pressing against the building. "I just needed a breath of air. I'll see you back in there."

I smirked at her attempt at dismissal. "I'm not leaving you out here alone."

"It's Ardnoch, Fyfe."

"Aye. But once upon a time, this place was considered the crime capital of the Highlands."

Eilidh chuckled. "It's been quiet for a long time."

"Has it? Because I thought Carianne had to run down a bloke to save Callie from being shot in the face last year." I referred to the mess Callie's French ex had sucked her into and how my high school ex had surprised us all by extracting her from that situation.

Carianne was at the wedding reception earlier but left with some bloke. Last month she'd moved to Inverness with her new partner, and I doubted we'd see much of her going forward. Callie mentioned Carianne had thrown herself into her relationship with this single dad and wasn't interested in anything or anyone else now. We'd exchanged a few words. I was grateful for her and how she'd saved Callie, but that was the extent of any feeling between us.

"Fair enough." Eilidh snorted. "But before then, it was quiet for a good while."

I settled next to her against the wall. "You happy, Eils?"

"Happier than I have been in ages. I'm so glad Lewis and Callie found their way back to each other."

I nudged her. "You know Lewis told me that you're the reason they did. Apparently, you invited them to the same party in London and it was deliberate."

"You have to remember that I was still friends with Callie. I could tell, despite her gorgeous French boyfriend, that she was changed by losing Lewis. That she hadn't gotten over it. And Lewis ..." Eilidh pushed off the wall, turning to face me. "My God, how many times did you catch him creeping on Callie's socials?"

I chuckled. "Aye, more times than was healthy."

"Right. And they wouldn't tell anybody what happened between them and I thought if it was so awful, neither of them would still be hung up on the other. So I took the risk and shoved them together." I could see her cheeky grin in the dark. "I didn't think they'd sleep together and get pregnant."

I gave a bark of laughter. "Then you don't remember how horny for each other they were as teenagers."

She wrinkled her nose adorably. "Do not say the word *horny* when talking about my brother."

Unable to stop myself, I reached out to stroke a thumb over her smooth cheek. There was that rushing sound in my ears again and a foggy need blocking out my rationale. "It's so fucking good to see you like this."

"Fyfe—"

FOREVER THE HIGHLANDS 113

I crashed my mouth over hers, swallowing her words, my hand sliding around the nape of her neck to hold her where I wanted her. She tasted of champagne and something that was all Eilidh. Her whimper made my blood flush even hotter as I turned and pressed her up against the building, pushing my body into hers.

Her tongue licked at mine, her arms around my back, fingers curling into my shirt as she moaned and arched her hips against me. I pulled at the silk of her dress, trying to get under it. To feel her wet heat, to sink inside her.

Aye.

Fuck. Aye. I needed that. I wanted it so badly, my heart felt like it was about to explode.

"Eilidh!" The young female voice cut through the haze in my head. "Eilidh!"

Then Eilidh was pushing at my chest.

I forced myself to release her, stumbling back. She stared up at me in shock, lips swollen from my kisses. "That's Mor," she whispered.

Shit.

Oh my fucking ... what the hell was I doing?

"Eilidh ..." Her name came out thick and hoarse as I shoved a hand through my hair and stumbled back. "I'm sorry, sweetheart. I've had too much to drink. That won't happen again."

Hurt tightened her features. "Really? You're pulling the 'I'm drunk' card again."

"Eils—"

"No. You know what? Fuck you, Fyfe Moray." She pushed off the wall, her heels clicking on the cobbles as she hurried away.

Panic suffused me. "Eilidh!"

I moved to go after her but then saw Mor appear at the end of the lane. Halting, I watched as Eilidh reached her, put

114   SAMANTHA YOUNG

an arm around her sister, and pulled her away before she could see me.

"Fuck!" I collapsed against the wall, scrubbing a hand down my face.

In that messed-up moment, something became very clear.

For Eilidh's sake, I needed to stay the hell away from her.

Fourteen
EILIDH

Present day

Last week the cast and crew of *Young Adult* held a wrap party at a London hotel. I hadn't wanted to attend because I didn't feel welcome by the cast, but the showrunner insisted I celebrate my part in making the show successful.

It was a mistake. Not all the cast were arseholes to me. In fact, most of them weren't. They understood that I wasn't just giving up the show. I was giving up my career, and if I was doing that, then this is what I needed. I was grateful to them.

I was devastated that Jasper wasn't one of them. That my friend who had experienced the craziness of obscurity to instant fame right along with me was acting like a spoiled, entitled, petulant stranger.

He wouldn't look at me at the party, wouldn't talk to or acknowledge me. It had been like this on set, but luckily the antagonism had translated well to the screen.

The night before last, I'd returned to my flat to find the door already open and Jasper lounging drunkenly on my sofa.

"What are you doing here?" I'd asked, wary of that nasty look in his eyes.

He'd stood up, wobbling unsteadily as he threw keys at me. I ducked just before they hit my face. "What the fuck?" I cried angrily.

"Just returning your keysh," he slurred. "Don't need them no more."

"Fine. Get out."

"I protected you!" Jasper yelled, tears filling his eyes. "Anytime you needed me, I protected you and thish is how you repays me?" He swayed, somehow managing to glare and blink rapidly at the same time. "I have nothing without thish show. Wesht End. Thatsh all the offers I'm getting. Fucking Wesht End."

"Then you should take the offers," I replied. "Those are good offers. And the other jobs will come in. It just takes time. But I won't apologize again for choosing to leave. If you were any friend, you'd understand that."

"I undershtand shit." He spat at me as he stumbled past. "I undershtand that the pershon I need to get through all thish shit is abandoning me."

"Jasper, I will never abandon you. I'm always here."

"Fuck that. You're already gone." He slammed out of my flat before I could stop him.

Diana and I spoke about Jasper's reaction. She'd made me see the narcissism in his response. Deciding I didn't need anyone making me feel bad about myself when I'd been working so hard for the past nine months to love myself again, I hadn't gone after him. Maybe it was selfish. But I comforted myself with the knowledge that Jasper was acting even more selfishly.

FOREVER THE HIGHLANDS

It was March. I had no jobs lined up. Last month, I'd announced my retirement on social media. Or at least my team had. I didn't look at the comments. My team would take care of my socials until *Young Adult* aired and then I could delete myself from all those platforms. The thought filled me with overwhelming relief. Yes, there was this deep-seated fear that I'd never reach the same success in life again (the pressure of having reached the pinnacle of success in my early twenties was not lost on me), but I felt mostly relief. I knew I wouldn't automatically become some anonymous person. Yet over time, I had hope that most people would forget me. That I could walk down the street without being recognized or stalked by paparazzi.

Grabbing my laptop, I settled at the dining table and opened my screenplay. I'd finished writing two episodes of the TV show inspired by Ardnoch Estate. I could send it to my agent, but I still didn't feel confident enough in it. Uncle Brodan had dabbled in screenwriting—I could share it with him. But there was someone else I'd thought about sending it to.

Theo Cavendish.

He was Mum's friend Sarah's husband. Sarah was a famous crime fiction writer who had worked at the estate as a housekeeper all the while making millions off her independently published crime series. She eventually left Ardnoch to start living her life as a writer out in the open. Theo was a well-known and respected screenwriter and producer and an estate member. He and Sarah had fallen in love while adapting her series for screen. They were not the most obvious pairing. Sarah had always been a shy, quiet woman, and Theo was this intimidating, scorchingly hot aristocratic playboy. Yet I'd never seen a man more in love.

He was still intimidating, though.

But he was honest and I respected him.

If he thought my screenplay was good, then it would buoy my confidence.

I could email him, but it might be better to talk to him face-to-face. Which I could do now, since I was home.

But I needed time.

I needed patience with myself. Just some time to ... merely *be*. And yes, I knew I was privileged to take that time. Most people had to keep working through life and its struggles. Most people also hadn't experienced the amount of international pressure I'd dealt with.

I needed time to enjoy writing, enjoy my family, without all that other stuff clouding my mind. Ultimately, I'd decided to give up London. Ardnoch was where I wanted to be, so I didn't sign another rental agreement on my flat. My landlord Peter practically begged me to stay and offered me a longer term of rent control. I'd thanked him but packed up all my belongings. Most of it was in storage while I moved back into my childhood home.

The sea breeze fluttered over me as I rested my arms against the balcony railing on the deck of my parents' house. Being home was all about fresh starts. With everyone. Mum and Dad had redecorated the annex knowing I was coming home, and I was bravely facing my fears of the space. Last night was my first night in the detached guest suite, and it took me a while to fall asleep. But I was determined to persevere. The guest annex allowed me to be near my family while still providing some privacy. Of course, I could get my own place now that I was home, but I wasn't ready to do that either.

They'd even set up a desk for me so I could write. Once I told them what my aspirations were, they threw themselves into supporting me. Not only was there a desk but there were notepads and a cork pin board above the desk with pins and empty note cards all ready for my thoughts and ideas.

An ache moved through me as I stared out at the North

Sea. Years. I'd kept myself from them for years. No wonder I'd been miserable. I'd separated myself from the people who made me whole.

Yet despite our reunion, there was still an emptiness in me.

It had a name.

Fyfe Moray.

His warm dark eyes filled my mind and I flushed, remembering the last time we were together. I'd avoided my brother's best friend for six months. Ever since he kissed me at Lewis and Callie's wedding and then blamed it on alcohol again. Fyfe had tried calling. For weeks and weeks. About six weeks in, he gave up. He sent me a text promising he'd leave me alone and reiterating how sorry he was.

Ignoring Fyfe wasn't part of my new approach to life. No, avoiding him was temporary. I needed to deal with all this other stuff first and fully intended to have a serious discussion with him upon my return home.

I knew Fyfe was terrified of commitment.

I also knew we were drawn together. That there was a connection between us neither could deny. And I was done denying it. I was going to admit my feelings to Fyfe. Either he'd reciprocate and together we'd deal with how that affected Lewis ... or he'd reject me. The latter would hurt like a motherfucker. But I'd have my answer and I could move on.

I was done with being dishonest with myself and others.

Butterflies erupted in my belly as I pushed away from the balcony and turned to open the sliding doors to the living room. Stepping inside, I shut it behind me and locked up. Mor was at school, Mum was at the childcare center she ran, and Dad was at his office in Inverness.

The house was empty, but their warmth still lingered. Mor had asked me a question about the William Shakespeare project she was doing for English, and I'd helped her with it over breakfast. She'd hugged me before she left for school and it had felt wonderful. Mum had fluttered around us all, multi-tasking like a boss, taking care of us even as she readied herself for work. Between helping Mor, I'd watched her and Dad in the kitchen. She stopped what she was doing to tie his tie for him and then he'd handed her a coffee as she offered him a plate of scrambled eggs on toast. Afterward, he'd taken both their plates to wash them and urged her out of the kitchen to finish getting ready for the day.

Before Dad left for work, because he thought Mor and I were preoccupied, he'd kissed Mum thoroughly. When she was flushed and smiling, dimples appearing, he dropped a tender kiss on the tip of her nose and just stared at her for a few seconds. Like she was a miracle.

After all these years.

I'd returned my focus to Mor because I was afraid I might burst into tears. Ones of happiness for my parents. Maybe ones of sadness and longing for myself.

I think because ... I knew what the outcome of my quest would be today.

And I still intended to do it.

FYFE WAS NOT AT HOME.

I tried calling him, but it rang out so I called Lewis instead.

"He's at my place," my brother told me. "There's some new security system he wants to install. We told him the one we have is good enough, but ever since those guys broke in without him knowing, he's paranoid."

Lewis referred to the Frenchmen who had been looking for a piece of vital evidence Callie's police officer ex-boyfriend had hidden in a gift. They'd ransacked my brother and sister-in-law's beautiful home. It didn't surprise me Fyfe still held guilt about the fact that he'd been charged with installing their

FOREVER THE HIGHLANDS 121

security, but he hadn't gotten it up and running when the break-in occurred.

"Is he still there?"

"Aye, he just got there."

"Is he alone?"

"Callie and Harley are at the bakery. Why?"

"I just need to talk to him about something. Thanks." I hung up before he could pester me for more details.

Thankfully, the drive to Lewis and Callie's wasn't that far from Fyfe's. My dad had designed my brother's home for a wealthy client who ran into financial difficulties and had to sell the spectacular house for a steal.

It was situated on a small piece of private land, nestled in woodland, between Ardnoch and Golspie. The modern midcentury home was designed so that the living space was upstairs and the bedrooms downstairs. On the first floor there were two walls made entirely of glass. With woodland at the back of the home, the living space emulated the experience of being in a treehouse. The stairs brought you up into the kitchen, and beyond that was a living and dining area.

Off the dining area, Dad had designed an oversized square window box you could sit in. There were windows on all three sides and it literally felt like you were hanging in the trees. Below you could see the twinkle of water from the man-made moat around the house. Water was taken from a downhill stream on the back of the property through underground pipes and pumped into the moat, where propeller turbines attached to a hydropower system created hydroelectricity to power the home. There was also a bank of solar panels out front where there were no trees to block the sunlight.

On the ground floor were four bedrooms. The primary suite had a floor-to-ceiling window that abutted the moat so while lying in bed, it was like being on a boat. Similar to the primary suite, Harley's nursery had a floor-to-ceiling window so you could see the moat that surrounded the house. Lewis, Walker, and my family had decorated the nursery for Callie before Harley arrived and it looked like a fairy glen.

The house was a dream and a beautiful representation of my father's imagination and talent. I was a little envious my brother owned it, but I was also happy for him, Callie, and my niece. They got to raise Harley in a magical place, in a house filled with love.

Sure enough, a vehicle was parked outside my brother's dreamy home. A Volvo SUV I didn't recognize. It had to be Fyfe's. Those butterflies returned in force as I got out of my borrowed Range Rover, my legs shaky. If I was staying in Ardnoch, I'd need a car. The infrastructure for driving electric was rubbish up here, but Dad and Regan had hybrid cars and had installed their own electric charging point at home. Maybe I could do the same. The random thought of car buying was a good distraction as nerves unlike anything I'd experienced shivered through me.

During auditions, there had always been butterflies, but the good kind. I was one of those lucky people who didn't get stage fright and enjoyed an audition.

This was not that.

I clenched and unclenched my trembling fingers before pushing open the front door. "Hello!" I called as I stepped into the house.

"Who's there?" Fyfe's deep voice called from upstairs. The first floor was pretty much a mezzanine level so you could hear everything happening up there from the ground floor hall.

"It's me," I said as I began walking upstairs. "Eilidh."

Footsteps hurried toward me and then Fyfe was in view as I climbed.

He wore his glasses today and a rush of nostalgia moved over me as I stepped off the stairs and into the open-plan living space.

Fyfe gaped like he hadn't seen me in years. "Eilidh," he breathed my name.

He held an iPad that he lowered to his side as he continued to stare.

Not quite sure what to do with my body, I strode into the living space so I could stare out at the treetops. "How are you?"

"I ... Aye, I'm fine. It's ... I tried ... I tried calling."

I turned to face him again.

Fyfe set the iPad down on the kitchen island and crossed his arms over his chest defensively. The movement caused the Henley he wore to stretch around his powerful biceps. His strong features were neutral, his expression not giving much away. But his eyes gleamed with questions behind the dark frames.

He looked hot with his glasses on. "You should wear your glasses more often."

Fyfe raised an eyebrow. "Oh?"

I nodded. "I always liked your glasses." A noise downstairs made me freeze. "Is there someone else here?"

Fyfe glanced over his shoulder. "There's no one here. I left a window open in one of the bedrooms while I was mapping it for the new system. It probably blew the door shut. Remind me to close it before I leave."

"Oh." I guess my nerves were making me jumpy.

"So. Is that why you're here? To tell me I should wear my glasses more often?"

Nausea roiled in my stomach again and I took a deep breath. "No. I came to tell you something."

His arms dropped to his sides. "Okay?"

Where to start? Where to start? I didn't know what to do with my arms. I was an actor. Whenever I had a monologue, I knew exactly what to do with my body. But I had no idea how to keep my legs from buckling as I laid bare my heart to this man.

I strode toward him but stopped at the end of the island so I could lean against it for support. "I'm sorry for not answering your calls or texts. I never intended to ignore you forever. I just needed to deal with tying up my old life first."

Fyfe scowled. "You couldn't tell me that? Eilidh, I've been miserable for six months thinking I'd fucked things up between us for good. All the while lying to Lewis. I told him we were good friends and then all of a sudden we're not talking. I lied and told him we were still in contact."

There was a part of me, a selfish part, that was annoyed we were talking about Lewis. "Can we just focus on us and leave my brother out of this for a second?"

Fyfe pressed his lips together. I didn't know what his expression meant. Disapproval. Compliance. Who knew?

I continued, "I am sorry. But maybe once I tell you what's in my heart and mind, you'll understand why I just needed some time."

"Six months is a hell of a lot of time, just saying."

"Fyfe."

He sighed. "I'm sorry. Continue."

"First ... are you and the American still together?" I'd dreaded knowing, so I hadn't asked Callie or Lewis about it.

Fyfe frowned. "No. Of course not. We stopped seeing each other last October."

Oh.

After the wedding?

Why?

Because of our kiss?

Hope fluttered through me. I sucked in a shaky breath. "Since we were kids, you, everyone, has waved off my feelings for you like they were nothing. 'Oh, it's just Eilidh being a flirt.'" I smiled sadly and watched Fyfe tense, gaze alert. "But I wasn't just being a flirt." My stomach whooshed. *Here goes nothing*. Or everything, in fact. "I have loved you, Fyfe Moray, in some capacity since I was a wee girl. And the reason it hurt so much for you to kiss me and then immediately regret it is because I'm in love with you."

I released another shaky exhale as his eyes widened. "I loved you as a kid and then I fell in love with you again when we became friends as adults. Every day I woke up feeling more alive than I had in a long time because I knew I'd get to talk to you. And when that went away, when I pushed you away after overhearing you tell Lewis our friendship was nothing ... it was so unbearable being without you, I couldn't even acknowledge it. You kissing me at my place and then again at his wedding and blaming both moments on alcohol ... I reacted the way I did because I'm in love with you and it hurts to think that maybe all that's between us ... well, that for you ... is it only physical attraction for you?"

There.

I'd said it.

I shook against the counter as he wrenched his gaze from mine and stalked across the room. Fyfe dragged a hand through his hair, his fingers clenching in the thick strands. It was the pose of a man in anguish.

I braced myself.

FIFTEEN
FYFE

Panic.

It rioted through me as Eilidh's confession filled the space between us.

No.

No, no, no.

I didn't believe her.

And I couldn't believe her.

And I was fucking pissed off that she'd do this to us!

Couldn't she see who I was? How I'd already failed her?

I ignored her question and spun around from pacing Lewis's living room. "No."

Eilidh stared at me wide-eyed, so goddamn beautiful and untouchable. "No?"

The hope in her expression made me furious. At her. At myself. Anger was a tight fist around my throat. "No as in ... I ... I can't love you like that."

Startled, she reared back like I'd hit her. "You can't?"

"I care about you. I do. But I ... no. You and I will never be *that*. All I can ever give you is friendship."

Tears burned in her eyes and it killed me to see them. To

FOREVER THE HIGHLANDS 127

know I'd put them there. "I ... I can't be friends with you, Fyfe. I'm sorry."

Renewed panic had me striding toward her. "Eilidh, please. Don't do this to us. I need you."

She gaped at me in disbelief. "I just told you I'm in love with you, and you just told me you don't love me back ... and you want me to put aside how that makes me feel because *you* need our friendship?"

Fuck.

"Eilidh." I reached for her.

"Don't touch me."

"Eilidh, please."

Footsteps thundered up the stairs behind us and I whirled around just as Lewis appeared at the top of them. His features were hard as granite. "You heard her."

"Lew—"

He cut me off with a shake of his head, his gaze bouncing to Eilidh before hardening as it swung back to me. "Did you sleep with my sister?"

"No!" both Eilidh and I cried.

Lewis's shoulders slumped ever so slightly. "But something happened."

"Aye." I nodded grimly. "I kissed her. Twice."

"Even though you don't love her?"

I'll never know what stupid fucking gremlin possessed me in the next moment as I huffed, "Not all of us need to be in love with a woman to want to shag her, Lewis. That's just you, mate."

At Eilidh's in-drawn breath, I squeezed my eyes closed in anguish.

"Fuck." I reached for her. "Eilidh, I didn't—"

My words were cut off by Lewis who was suddenly in my face, his fist clenched in the front of my shirt as he shoved me away from Eilidh.

I stumbled back, fear rioting through me at the rage on my friend's expression. "I'm sorry. I didn't mean it like that." I looked at Eilidh but she'd turned away, her chin trembling as if she was attempting to hold back tears.

It felt like my guts were being ripped open. "Sweetheart, I'm so sorry."

"Don't talk to her. Just get out, Fyfe." Lewis drew his sister behind him as if she needed protection.

From me.

I felt like I might be sick.

"I never meant to hurt you, Eilidh."

"But you did." Lewis glowered at me. "And this is why I never wanted you two to get close. Because I know how fucked up you are about women."

I flinched. "I never intended to hurt her. Lewis, I'd protect Eilidh with my life and you know it."

"It doesn't feel that way right now." He shook his head in disappointment. "I'm sorry ... I just ... I need you to leave." I could hear the weary despondency in his voice as he warned, "Don't make me ask you again."

On that note, I left before I lost my dignity and begged them both to understand. I loved Eilidh.

I just wasn't capable of loving her the way she loved me.

She deserved more than I could give.

Sixteen
EILIDH

Typing out the end of the scene, I hit the last key on the keyboard with satisfaction and then saved the document.

My script was coming along.

I'd thrown myself into it the last few weeks, supported by my family who treated my writing time like it was precious. I'd taken to writing early in the mornings and when I went next door for a coffee, Mum already had one waiting. No one interrupted me in that time and whoever greeted me when I came out of my writing cave asked me excitedly, "How did it go?"

I loved my family.

When I wasn't writing, I spent most days with them and our large group of friends. Ardnoch was a small place, but our social circle was not.

Unfortunately, that meant gossip traveled fast.

Although no one knew why, everyone seemed to know there was discord between Fyfe and Lewis. My parents had asked about it, but I'd told Lewis not to tell them. I suspected he was relieved he didn't have to. He loved Fyfe and I'd told him he didn't need to choose between us. But he seemed to be taking Fyfe's rejection of me almost as badly as I was. My nosy brother had known something was going on between us and he'd decided to drop in on us. He told me he never meant to, but when he'd heard me confessing my love, he'd "accidentally" eavesdropped.

As devastated but unsurprised as I was by Fyfe's inability to love me, I couldn't have it coming between him and Lewis. The problem with loving someone was that you wanted them to be happy even if they couldn't be happy with you. Lewis was Fyfe's family. I couldn't be the reason that was taken from him. I was biding my time before I urged Lewis to mend fences with his best friend.

I said as much to Callie as I accompanied her and Harley to the doctor's office. My beautiful wee niece was already fifteen months. She was a heavy, warm weight in my arms as she snuggled against my chest, coughing now and then, as we walked into the small general practitioners' building. Harley had a cold that wasn't shifting, so Callie was done being anxious about it and wanted to see a doctor.

"I agree." Callie held the door open to the reception area. "But you have to give Lewis time."

"Three weeks is plenty of time. It's not like Fyfe and I slept together behind his back. I told a man I loved him and he rejected me. He shouldn't be punished for that," I said with a calmness I didn't feel.

Callie shot me a look that said she could see right through me. "He hurt you, and Lewis and I take people hurting you very seriously."

I lowered my voice. "Fyfe can't help his feelings."

Callie stopped us, smoothing a hand over her daughter's back as she whispered harshly, "He can help denying his feelings to protect himself."

"What does that mean?"

She pressed her lips together in contemplation.

Forever the Highlands

"Callie ... you can't possibly want Fyfe to lose the only family he has over this?"

Her expression fell. "Of course not. And he won't. Lewis just needs time."

With a sigh, I nodded, and we walked over to the receptionist to announce ourselves.

After Callie checked in, we took a seat at the back of the quiet reception area and Harley started wriggling in my arms. She made a few whimpering noises before announcing loudly, "Bah mum mum!"

"She wants her mummy."

My sister-in-law took her daughter and rubbed her cheek against hers. "I'm here, my darling," she soothed. "I know, my baby girl, but Mummy is going to make the doctor make you all better again. Yes, yes, my sweet girl."

I experienced a pang of longing watching Harley smile at her mother's affection and cuddles. Even as poorly as she felt, she was happy to be in her mum's arms. It wasn't like I wanted kids right this second, but after watching how well Callie and Lewis had adapted to parenthood, I thought it might be nice to have kids in my late twenties. While I still had energy like they did. Mum hadn't been too bad when she had Mor because she was still pretty young, but Dad was in his forties and I remember the new-baby tiredness hitting him hard.

Problem was, I'd have to meet Mr. Right soon if I planned to start having children in the next few years. Despite everything, Fyfe's face still popped into my head at the thought. It hurt. Now I knew for a fact he wasn't my Mr. Right. I had to keep looking.

"Have you heard from your friend Jasper?" Callie asked as Harley snuggled her face against her mother's neck and closed her eyes.

I brushed my knuckles over her soft but slightly reddened

baby cheek before I answered, "No. I tried texting and calling, but I think he's blocked me."

"I'm sorry, Eilidh."

"There's a part of me that's so mad at him for treating me this way ... but another part of me that just wants to give up trying with him. I'm tired of chasing after people who don't want me."

Callie searched my face, considering. "I think in *his* case, perhaps it's time to let go. In the case of certain other people ... I never told Lewis this, but I saw the way Fyfe looked at you at our wedding and I knew."

My pulse leapt. "Knew what?"

"It's not just an attraction for him, Eilidh. He watched you that night and it ... well, it reminded me of the way I catch Lewis looking at me."

This time that flicker of hope terrified me. "Callie, don't."

Whatever she heard in my voice caused regret to flash over her pretty face. "I'm sorry. I didn't mean to muddle the waters with my observation."

"It's fine." I was a wee bit breathless as I tried to coach my heart to ignore what she'd said.

"Harley Adair?"

We both glanced up to find an attractive man with dark blond hair and a warm expression standing in the middle of the reception. He dressed similarly to Fyfe and wore an expensive shirt and suit trousers, the shirt sleeves rolled up to his elbows showcasing strong forearms.

Who the heck was he?

Callie stood up. "That's us."

I followed, grabbing Callie's large bag filled with baby stuff.

"Dr. Cameron Phillips." The doctor held out a hand to Callie, his gaze flickering to me.

"Nice to meet you, Dr. Phillips. This is my daughter

FOREVER THE HIGHLANDS   133

Harley. Oh, and this is my sister-in-law, Eilidh. Is it okay if she accompanies us in?"

"Of course. Nice to meet you." Up close I could see his eyes were a light hazel. Very nice.

I gave him a flirty smile without thinking about it. "You too."

His eyebrows rose ever so slightly, and I saw a small smile curl his lips before he turned, gesturing for us to follow.

"You must be the new doctor all my customers have been talking about," Callie observed. This was news to me.

"Customers?" The doctor held open the door to the back of the clinic and we filed past him. He smelled good.

"I run Callie's Wee Cakery with my mum."

"Oh, the bakery. I've heard amazing things. I just haven't had a chance to pop in yet." Dr. Phillips turned to Harley. "Now, how can I help this little beauty?"

I watched as the doctor examined my niece, talking softly to her in a soothing, calm voice. He was great with her and she even offered him a small, tearful smile by the end.

"Oh, you're a heartbreaker, aren't you?" Dr. Phillips looked up at Callie with a sympathetic smile. "Seeing her like this must be hard. But it is just a cold that's taking a wee bit longer to shift than we'd all like. She's very congested. I'm going to give you a prescription for saline nasal drops and a nasal aspirator. Harley will definitely not appreciate the experience, but it should help clear the congestion right up."

"Okay, thank you, Doctor." Callie cuddled her daughter into her chest as the doctor filled out the prescription.

"So, what made you move to Ardnoch?" I asked nosily.

He looked over at me. "Needed a change of pace. I was working in a very busy clinic in Leith in Edinburgh and I just wanted a little quiet. This surgery has more doctors than some of the city clinics, which means I can take my time with patients rather than rushing them out of the door like they're

134 SAMANTHA YOUNG

an inconvenience." Dr. Phillips handed Callie the prescription. "Bring little Harley back if you don't see a difference in a week or if she's getting worse."

"Thank you, Doctor."

"Aye, thank you, Doctor." I grinned at him and I swear I saw a little flush on his cheeks before Callie led us out.

As soon as we were outside, my sister-in-law frowned at me. "What was that?"

"What was what?"

"You were flirting with my doctor."

"Was I?" I shrugged as I opened the door to Callie's SUV and placed her bag inside. "He was good-looking and being all sweet to my niece. It flipped my flirt switch."

Callie chuckled but shook her head. "Well, just keep in mind that three weeks ago, you told a man you were in love with him. The last thing you need is another guy messing with your head."

"I know. It's just harmless flirting," I promised. It was nice for a minute not to think about Fyfe and the crushing emotions that accompanied thoughts of him.

"Eilidh, right?"

I looked up from the rosé selection in William's Wine Cellar and stared into the handsome face of Dr. Cameron Phillips.

It had been two days since Harley's appointment, and I was searching for a couple of bottles of wine to go with the Italian dinner I was making for my family this evening. Mum and Dad were always working so hard, so I'd roped Mor into helping me. Lewis and Callie were bringing Harley over too.

"Hi." I blinked, surprised to see the doctor so soon. I

didn't know why. Ardnoch was a tiny place and it was inevitable we'd run into each other. "Yes. Eilidh."

"Cameron." He gestured to himself.

I smiled. "I remember."

"Special evening planned?" Cameron gestured to the wine.

"For my parents. I'm staying in their guest annex for a while and thought I'd make dinner to say thank you."

"Oh, you don't live in Ardnoch permanently?"

I stiffened. Did he not know who I was? A slight thrill coursed through me at the thought. "Now I do. But I've just returned home after a few years away working."

He leaned in, looking genuinely interested. "What do you do for work?"

He didn't.

He didn't know who I was.

A flutter of excitement caused my lips to curl at the corners. "Acting."

Cameron winced. "That's a hard game. But I guess being near a place like the Ardnoch Estate is inspiring. So ... it just didn't work out?"

Oh my goodness, this was hilarious and amazing all at once. And I technically wasn't lying when I replied, "No, it wasn't for me. I've come home to rediscover myself. Does that sound terribly self-indulgent?"

"Not at all. I think it's great that you have family support so you can do that. When I told my friends and family I was leaving Edinburgh for the middle of nowhere in the Scottish Highlands, they all thought I was having a midlife crisis."

"You're not old enough for a midlife crisis."

"That's what I said." He grinned, pleased. He had a very nice smile. I even felt a flicker of attraction.

"So ... did you come here alone?" Not exactly subtle.

Cameron rubbed a hand across the nape of his neck as if

slightly embarrassed. "All alone. My fiancée and I broke up, which was another reason for the move."

"Oh, I'm sorry."

"It's fine. Better to know before the wedding that she was screwing around with the best mate she promised over and over again was just her best mate and nothing else." He blanched. "Shit, that's an awkward amount of oversharing. I'm sorry."

I found him refreshingly endearing. "I'm sorry that happened. But you're right. You're better off in the long run."

"Speaking from experience?"

I thought of Fyfe and it hurt like always. "In a way."

"So ... You came home alone?" Cameron asked, his gaze drifting to the wine.

A little flutter in my belly surprised and pleased me. "I did."

His eyes flew to mine. "Oh. That's ... good."

I grinned. "Is it?"

He laughed softly. "I am clearly out of practice when it comes to talking to beautiful women."

"That was pretty good." I shoved him teasingly and he chuckled again, flashing me a shy but interested look.

"Would you ... would you maybe like to go out for dinner this weekend? I hear the food at the Gloaming is good."

"It is. My uncle owns it."

"Oh really? Of course." A light bulb seemed to go off in his eyes. "If you're Harley's auntie and she's an Adair—"

"That makes me an Adair. You've heard of us?"

"Hard not to."

He just hadn't heard of Eilidh Adair, BAFTA Award–winning actor. I hid my mischievous grin and replied, "I'd love to have dinner with you."

Cameron didn't hide his pleasure. "Great. Shall we

exchange numbers?" He pulled his phone from his back pocket.

I had a slight moment of hesitation giving out my number, a knee-jerk reaction to my longing to maintain my privacy. We swapped numbers, though, and Cameron reached out to grab a bottle of rosé. "My new neighbor cut my lawn this week. And though I didn't ask him to do that, I feel like I owe him a bottle of rosé and I feel this way because he very pointedly told me the exact label of rosé wine he likes to drink upon sharing that he cut my lawn."

I burst out laughing. "Welcome to small-town life."

Cameron's smile was sexier, more heated. "I think I'm going to like it."

SEVENTEEN
FYFE

It could have been hours I'd lain in bed just staring at my ceiling. I didn't know. My sleep had been broken and shit for the past few weeks. My appetite wasn't much better, and my energy was fucked because of it. I joint-led a tae kwon do class in Thurso every week, and it had taken everything within me to make myself attend. Lewis and Callie still attended, but it was awkward. Callie tried to make conversation but apparently, Lewis still wasn't ready.

For the first time since he'd returned to Ardnoch, I hadn't seen Lewis in almost a month. The longest we went without seeing each other was a few days. I'd visit the family multiple times a week. Harley, in my mind, was my niece. I wondered if she missed me. If she was even aware of my absence.

Did this mean Harley would grow up not knowing who I was? I would no longer be Uncle Fyfe?

The thought hurt like fuck, so I threw it away.

I'd lost both my best friends because I couldn't love Eilidh the way she needed. As shitty as that made me feel, I also was angry that I was being punished for something I couldn't help.

But I could help that I'd kissed her. Twice.

FOREVER THE HIGHLANDS 139

I'd led her on.

If I were them, I'd hate me for that.

She deserved an apology. So did Lewis.

I was well aware if I waited too long, I could lose them forever.

There was a part of me, though, that thought maybe that's what I deserved.

Eilidh bared her soul to me, gave me something precious —something I knew for a fact I did not deserve—and I'd rejected her and said something fucking stupid when I did.

That beautiful girl ... how could I have done that to her?

I sat up in bed before my alarm went off.

The truth was, I wasn't sure I was ready to face Eilidh *ever* because my apology would be to soothe my own guilt as much as it would be to offer her my regrets. Plus, she was right. It was selfish of me to plead with her to be my friend after she'd told me she was in love with me.

Yet Lewis ... I had to believe he and I could get over this. If I left things between us any longer, we might not.

Before I could back out, I reached over for my phone and hit Lewis's number.

I was about to hang up on the sixth ring when the line clicked open.

"You better be dying," he bit out hoarsely, sounding half-asleep.

Wincing, I glanced at the clock on my phone. In my sudden decision to do this, I didn't think of the time. "Thought you'd be up with Harley," I replied quietly.

"I have been up with Harley. I'd just fallen back asleep when an arsehole called."

"Lewis." I heard Callie's whispered admonishment in the background.

I winced at Lewis's words and Callie's kindness.

"Well, are you going to speak or just call me before the crack of dawn to irritate the fuck out of me?"

"Can we meet, Lew? Please."

He was silent so long, I squeezed my eyes closed against the emotion boiling within.

"Meet me at Isla's Point in thirty minutes." He hung up before I could say anything else.

I felt a flicker of hope. Lewis's place was not far from mine, and Isla's Point was a hidden spot on the coast, right between my house and Lewis and Callie's, where you could access the beach. Most tourists missed it, but locals knew of it.

Thirty minutes later, I'd showered and dressed and stood on the beach at Isla's Point. My car was parked behind the dunes.

I waited with my hands in my jacket pockets, staring out at the calm North Sea. It was a chilly but beautiful spring morning, the rising sun spilling across the water in ripples of sparkling light.

A gentle but cold breeze ruffled through my hair as I watched the seemingly never-ending horizon. There was no one else out here on the small cove. It was a tiny portion of sandy beach compared to Ardnoch Beach. Another reason it didn't attract many visitors.

I didn't hear his footsteps in the sand. Lewis just appeared at my side. His long hair was tied up in a messy bun, his beard needed trimming, and he looked knackered. Yet the fury I'd seen on his face the last time we shared space was gone.

The words, the apology, it stuck inside me for so long, Lewis sighed and flicked me a look. "This is Callie's day off from the bakery, which means I could be in bed with my wife right now, so if you're going to speak, speak."

"I'm so sorry, Lewis." The words were out, but my voice was like gravel, like I'd had to force them out.

FOREVER THE HIGHLANDS

141

We turned to face each other now. Lewis's gaze was searching. "Did you apologize to Eilidh?"

It hurt too fucking much to think about her, let alone speak to her. I shook my head. "What can I say to her that will help? Nothing. I asked her to be my friend after she told me she loved me. Selfish bastard that I am."

"You really don't love her?"

My hands clenched into fists at my sides. "I can't love anyone."

"Can't or won't?"

"What?" We locked eyes.

Lewis appeared half pissed off, half sympathetic. "Can't or won't love her?"

"Lewis ..."

"I was there." A muscle flexed in his jaw, blue eyes flashing angrily. "I saw you look after yourself because your mum was never there and when she was home, she was usually drunk, and even though you denied it, she was hitting you, wasn't she?"

A different shame crawled over and I nodded reluctantly.

Lewis let out a shuddering breath. "Then she just abandoned you."

"Lew—"

"You've moved from woman to woman, never letting them close. Never trusting them enough to. But you let Eilidh in. Didn't you?"

I dragged a hand through my hair, shifting restlessly because I was desperately trying not to fucking cry in front of my best mate. It took me a second to get around the lump in my throat. "I *can't* love her. Eilidh ... is meant for more than me. For more than this place."

"Then why did she come home?"

"Because she's feeling a bit lost and this is a safe place while she figures things out. She's just ... lost and clinging to here. To me. She'll realize soon enough she doesn't love me."

Lewis's expression hardened. "You patronizing fucker."

I flinched, my chin jerking back.

"Eilidh is a grown woman who has worked extremely hard to be honest with herself about what she wants and where she wants to be. She's chosen to come home. And she chose you as the man she loves. Now you can decide you don't want to be with her, but you do not fucking get to tell her she doesn't love you or love being home in Ardnoch. I had someone I loved make a choice for me, and I lost her for seven years. Don't you dare think you know better than Eilidh." He took a step toward me. "If you want some harsh home truths, Fyfe ... you're so intelligent, you think you know best in every situation. But when it comes to emotions ... you're an immature prick."

I raised an eyebrow. "Immature prick? I've been independent since I was seven years old."

"Aye, and you've been compartmentalizing your emotions ever since as an act of self-protection."

"What, are you a therapist now?"

"I'm your best friend. And I'm telling you that Eilidh is much more emotionally mature than you, pal."

Dropping my defensiveness, I recognized there was a lot of truth in what he said. "Which is why she deserves better."

Lewis laughed.

I scowled. "What?"

"Fuck, Fyfe ... every man in my life has better than he deserves in the woman who shares his bed."

"Not you. You're good to Callie."

"Now. But for seven years, I let her go when I should have fought for her. We all regret something."

"I ..." I turned to look out at the water, the truth bubbling inside me. "It's just bloody typical that the person I want most is the one most likely to leave. I couldn't have latched on to some ordinary woman who likes quiet, small-town life?" I winced. "Fuck, that makes me sound like an arsehole."

Lewis patted me on the shoulder. "Look, it's hard for me to see Eils as anything but my wee sister, but I recognize she's a talented celebrity and she's cute."

"Cute." I grimaced. "Eils isn't *cute*. She's ... she walks into a room and she knocks the fucking breath from your body, she's that beautiful."

Lewis smirked. "Is that so?"

I squeezed the bridge of my nose at his smug know-it-all expression. "That's the point. I'm just Fyfe Moray. Some big shot from the estate could come sweeping in and turn her head and whisk her away to live on some exotic island and that would make sense. But I'd be left behind."

"If that was going to happen, it would have happened. Eilidh's had more than enough opportunities for the celebrity life and celebrity relationships. She doesn't want it. She wants you. She wants *real*. My wee sister decided a long time ago you were the one for her."

I forced myself to meet my best friend's gaze, my voice filled with apology. "I can't give her that."

He sighed wearily. "I know you actually believe that."

"So ... what now?"

Lewis's features hardened ever so slightly. "You stay away from Eilidh."

Pain ricocheted through me. "Lew—"

"If you are stubbornly refusing to be with her ... then she needs space to get over you, okay. I mean it. You stay away from Eilidh, and you and I will be fine."

Even as it hurt to do it, I nodded in agreement.

I HAD JUST ENOUGH TIME TO MAKE BREAKFAST (something I actually could eat now that some things had been resolved between me and Lewis) and dress properly for work.

I gathered from the lack of fathers and uncles banging on my door that neither Lewis nor Eilidh had told anyone what had happened between us. Therefore, I could head into my meeting at Ardnoch Estate today without worrying one of the elder Adairs was waiting to bash my face in.

As I drove up my driveway, an object sitting outside my front door drew my attention. The hair on my nape rose the closer I got. The security system app on my phone hadn't gone off to alert me to someone being at the house ... Fuck. I'd left my phone in the car while I was talking to Lewis.

Was that ...

Was that ... no ... it couldn't be.

Braking hard, I shut off the engine and lunged from the vehicle, hurrying toward the front door.

Yes, it was.

A baby in a pink cardigan with a hood, bundled inside a blanket inside a car seat looked up at me and promptly burst into shrieking tears.

"What the ..." I gaped, looking up.

There was no one there.

Just my car in the drive.

I brought my phone up and tapped on my security system. There were the alerts I missed. Opening them, I saw that approximately twenty minutes ago, an old Vauxhall drove up and a brunette got out of the driver's seat. I zoomed in again and let out another curse.

I knew that brunette.

Pamela. We'd had a casual fling for about six weeks. Almost two years ago. It was during the time Eilidh disappeared from my life after she overheard me telling Lewis our friendship didn't mean anything.

My gaze moved from the video feed to the baby as Pamela took the car seat out of the back of the Vauxhall and left it at the door. She didn't even glance back. Merely hurried into the vehicle and sped off.

She'd left a baby outside on a cold spring morning.

"Fuck." I picked up the carrier. "Hey, cutie," I shushed the crying baby as I pulled out my house keys and opened the door to bring her inside. "It's all right, wee yin. We'll get this figured out."

A note tucked inside the baby's blanket caught my eye as I carried her into the living space and set her on my dining table.

"Let's have a look, eh, and see what this madness is all about." My soft words seemed to quiet her, and she watched me curiously as I opened the note. "Eh, what does your mummy have to say?" Seeing my voice had calmed her, I read the note out loud, "Fyfe, she's yours—" My heart jolted. "Her name is Millie. I tried to take care of her by myself, but I can't. She's better off with you. You can give her a comfortable, safe life. Sorry for doing it this way. Take good care of her— Pamela." The note tumbled from my hand as I looked at the baby girl whose face crumpled as if she sensed my emotions. She opened her tiny mouth and extremely loud noises squealed out of it. Millie sobbed like she was dying.

Oh fuck.

That's when I smelled it.

"Have you pooped?" I leaned in and wrinkled my nose. "That is either a dangerous fart or you have cacked in your breeks, wee yin. And I bet you're hungry too. Bugger. Fuck. Shit." Panic coursed through me. "I should not be swearing in front of a baby."

My immediate thought was I was fucked.

My second thought was to call Eilidh.

Third to call Lewis.

Fourth to call Callie.

A million thoughts flew through my head. Was Millie mine? I'd worn protection and Pamela had sworn she was on the pill. Not 100 percent effective but still. DNA test. I'd need to do a DNA test. Should I contact the police? I needed to get my team on tracking down Pamela.

First and foremost, however, I had to put my abject terror to one side because there was a wee girl in my house most likely hungry and she definitely needed her nappy changed.

"Right. Nappies. Supplies. Food." I grabbed her car seat and snatched up my keys. "We can do this, Millie. You and I, we've got this." My breathing was a bit shallow as we hurried from the house. "I know we've just met, but together we can do this."

Her crying slowed to a whimper as I googled how to buckle the car seat into my vehicle.

"There. We're intelligent human beings." I tapped her nose and she sniffled, her fists curling angrily. "Aye, I understand, wee babe. I've been sitting in shite of my own making for four weeks and it's uncomfortable as fuck. Let's get you out of your shitty breeks and into a clean nappy." I brushed her cute chubby wee cheek with my knuckles and hurried into the driver's seat.

As I pulled away from the house, I waited for my phone to connect to the car and then I called Walker Ironside, head of security at Ardnoch Estate, and told him an emergency had come up and I couldn't make our meeting. I hung up before he could ask questions and drove to the supermarket in Thurso.

Trying to shop in a hurry while carrying a baby in a car seat was not ideal, but I prioritized the nappy change first, grabbed the supplies, and headed into the baby changing room in the supermarket.

Luckily for me, Lewis had forced me to change Harley's nappy a few times in case I ever needed to do it when he or

FOREVER THE HIGHLANDS 147

Callie wasn't there. I tried not to gag as I discarded the dirty nappy in the facilities and cleaned Millie's red wee bum. Now that I was changing her, she'd grown docile and quiet, gazing up at me with dark blue eyes filled with childish curiosity. "That was a lot of shite, Millie," I told her quietly. "For such a tiny wee thing, you can shoot the poop."

She giggled, like she understood me.

That's when it hit me.

This wee human being might actually belong to me.

Holy fuck.

"Right, let's not think too hard on that or I might have a panic attack and you need me in good working order, don't you?"

Millie made a gurgling sound, as if in agreement.

"Aye, that's what I thought." New nappy on, I pulled her floral leggings back up and shirked her wee top over her rounded belly. Soft wisps of dark hair, and lots of it, curled on her head beneath a white beanie hat and she had pale skin. She was a beautiful wee thing and had her mother's coloring. I winced remembering how I'd been depressed at Eilidh's distance and I'd met Pamela on a hookup app. She'd just graduated and taken on a job as a solicitor in Inverness. She wasn't interested in a relationship, but the sex was good so we'd used each other for a few months. Then one day she didn't answer my text, so I just assumed she'd moved on.

Now I was thinking she'd found out she was bloody pregnant.

Doing the calculations, that put Millie at around eight or nine months.

Fucking hell.

A knock at the door had me bundling Millie back into her car seat. Her face crumpled as soon as her bum touched the seat. Before she could start wailing again, I lifted her into my arms and cuddled her against my chest. Her wee soft breaths puffed against my neck as she made some gurgling noises and rubbed her face against me. Settling.

Okay, she was tired of the car seat. Understood.

I opened the door as another impatient knock sounded.

Two women stood on the other side and one had a baby in her arms.

"So sorry. Her mum just dumped her on me with no supplies and she won't go back in her car seat and I'm trying to get all the stuff together one-handed," I blurted in an exasperated rush of words.

"Oh dear." The childless woman, who looked to be around my mother's age, stepped forward. "Let me help." Before I could say anything, she'd gathered up the supplies I'd just bought and tucked them all into the car seat. "Can you manage like that? Or do you need some help?"

I gave her a grateful smile as I took the proffered car seat. "No, that's great, thank you."

"Good luck," the younger woman said as I walked away.

First, I had to put the car seat in the car. Millie was sleeping in my arms as I strode back into the supermarket and zeroed in on the baby aisle. There seemed to be a million different kinds of formula and baby food. Harley was fifteen months and ate vegetables and all kinds of things now, but when had that started? I couldn't think. Taking my phone out, I searched online, typing awkwardly with one hand.

According to Google, Millie was still on formula but she'd eat food too.

I should just get her formula and then drop her off at social services.

That was the right thing to do.

Looking down at her face, seeing the sweep of her dark lashes and her tiny wee lips pursing like a goldfish, a pang of panic shocked the fuck out of me.

If this wee girl was mine, I couldn't abandon her.

FOREVER THE HIGHLANDS

Not like I'd been abandoned.

No ... she was staying with me until I had the DNA results.

Decision made, I grabbed some formula and headed to the checkout.

Eighteen
EILIDH

I sat back from the laptop with a crack of my neck.

Staring at the screen, I felt a smile curl my lips. I was proud of the scene I'd just written. Of course, if my show ever got picked up, the script would more than likely go through some changes, but I was happy with how it was coming along. I'd decided to revise what I'd already written and then work on another episode.

My eyes moved from the screen to the shelf above the desk. Previously there had been a vase of silk flowers and a framed print on the shelf. Now it was littered with photographs in simple frames. Me with my family. My eyes lingered on the photo of Lewis, Fyfe, Callie, and me. It was just before Callie and Lewis broke up when we were kids. Fyfe was a gangly teenager but still so freaking cute.

It had been four weeks since our falling-out.

Fyfe had apologized to Lewis two days ago. They'd had a long chat. My brother seemed to think Fyfe did have genuine feelings for me but was too fucked up by his own abandonment issues to explore them. If that was true, it didn't make me feel any better. I wanted someone to love me enough to want to fight to be with me.

Lewis had also told Fyfe he was to stay away from me. While I'd angrily told him that was overstepping, Lewis disagreed.

"You deserve to be able to move on without him messing with your head. And I love him, but I'm not sure I trust him not to mess with your head when he can't even recognize his own bloody feelings."

Since there was truth in that, I let his overstepping go.

Now, however, rumor had it that Fyfe had gone off grid these last two days. Hadn't shown up to meetings. Hadn't shown his face in town. According to Flora, owner of Flora's café, one of his neighbors said there were a strangely large number of deliveries being made to the house, but they hadn't seen him leave.

I was worried. So was my brother. Lewis had called him, but Fyfe said he was fine, just buried with work. I wasn't sure Lewis believed him.

Snapped from my musings by the sound of my phone buzzing, I turned it over and saw Cameron's name on the screen. Smiling, I tapped on the text notification.

Do you like Brie?

I shook my head as I replied.

Not really. I prefer le Roulé.

Tomorrow Cameron was taking me on a picnic. After our dinner at the Gloaming, he discovered what it was like to live in a small town. The next day, one patient after another had commented on the date and that was when he discovered I was a wee bit famous.

152   SAMANTHA YOUNG

"Why didn't you tell me?" he'd asked quietly on the phone that night, sounding uncertain.

"I liked that you didn't know who I was. But I was intending on telling you. I promise."

"I feel a bit of a fool."

"You're not a fool. I was only famous for one show and a couple of movies. If you didn't watch the show or those movies, how were you supposed to know who I was?"

"I feel like we have a lot to talk about on our next date."

"You still want another date?"

"Of course."

On our second date, I'd told Cameron as much as I was comfortable telling him. I didn't mention how difficult things had gotten for me. In fact, I pretty much glossed over the ugliness of the end of my career and merely explained I wasn't happy acting.

The picnic would be our third date.

My phone buzzed again.

> Le Roulé it is. Can't wait to see you.

My smile died a bit.

It wasn't that I wasn't looking forward to the picnic. I liked Cameron. He was sweet and funny and he genuinely seemed to love being a doctor. He was also a very good kisser, which I discovered on date two.

But I couldn't quite say that I couldn't wait to see him. He didn't make my belly flutter or my chest ache like the mere thought of Fyfe did. Yet I'd decided that was a good thing. Being out of control of my emotions had gotten me hurt.

This way I was in control, and I didn't think that was a bad thing at all.

My phone buzzed again, and I picked it up thinking it was Cameron. It wasn't. It was my old landlord back in London.

FOREVER THE HIGHLANDS

"Pete?" I picked up. "Is everything okay?"

"No, luv, it's not. I hate to be the bearer of bad news, but we were doing annual smoke alarm checks on the flat and my bloke found something dodgy."

"Dodgy?"

"There were cameras installed inside the smoke alarms, luv. One in the living space and one in the bedroom."

A wave of nausea rose as I processed why there might be cameras in those smoke alarms. I gulped in a breath, swallowing down the vomit.

"Eilidh, you there?"

"I'm here," I whispered.

"I'm real sorry, luv. We don't keep CCTV footage longer than thirty days and we had the current tenant look and he don't recognize anyone coming into the building as a threat. He's not famous or nothing. Quiet bloke. So we reckon this has to do with you. They had to be installed sometime in the last year. You know we check those things annually," he repeated, sounding just as freaked out as I felt.

"What do you want us to do, luv? I mean I would usually go straight to the police, but with your public profile an' all, I thought you might want to deal with it private like?"

I nodded, even though he couldn't see me. "Pete, can you hold on to them? I ... I need to discuss this with my team and then I'll let you know what we'd like done with the cameras."

"Got them safe and locked away so no one touches them, luv, all right."

"Thank you, Pete."

"I'm real sorry about this, Eilidh."

We hung up and I stared in a daze at the screen.

If someone had been recording me, they most likely had footage of me naked. They might have footage of me in private moments in my bedroom.

Shaking, I felt my panic building. The instinct to keep

this to myself was there. To shield my family from the shit show of public life ... but I'd learned my lesson. Pushing away from my desk, I hurried from the annex and into my parents' house.

Dad was just throwing back the last of his coffee as Mum grabbed her car keys. School was on break for the Easter holidays and Mor had shocked us all by asking to accompany her friend to a caravan park with her friend's parents in the Cairngorms.

"Writing go well?" Mum asked, her dimples flashing. Her smile fell at my expression. "Eilidh, what's wrong?"

Tears burned in my eyes as I looked from my mum to my dad. My gaze locked with Dad's and I wished I were seven years old again and he could make everything better with a hug. Through gritted teeth, I explained what Pete had found in my smoke alarms.

Dad did draw me into his arms, and I let myself cry against his chest as Mum smoothed a hand over my hair.

"Fyfe," Dad announced gruffly. "You need Fyfe to investigate this. It's his job, Eilidh. If there's a way to track this person down via the cameras, Fyfe can do it."

Of course.

Fyfe was the first person I would have thought of under normal circumstances.

As if sensing my hesitancy, Dad withdrew slightly to search my face. "I don't know what happened there, but this is too important. If someone broke into your flat and planted cameras, we need to know who and why."

He was right.

I nodded. "I'll go talk to him."

"Now."

"Me or your dad can come with you," Mum offered.

"You have work."

"Work can wait."

I shook my head, wiping my tears. "No, I can talk to Fyfe alone. I'll go now."

THERE WERE A LOT OF NERVES AND SLIGHT PTSD (considering the results of the last time I drove somewhere to see Fyfe) as I guided my new (well, new to me—the vehicle was five years old) G-Wagon out of the village. A Merc dealership in Inverness happened to have a used G-Wagon with the black and rust leather interior, and it was just bougie but eccentric enough for me to snap it up.

I didn't even know if Fyfe was home. I could call him, but after everything ... aye, I thought it would be better face-to-face.

I couldn't even think about the fact that Mor had stayed with me in that flat and was grateful for the fact that she'd always changed clothes in the privacy of the bathroom during her visit.

Relief and apprehension clenched in my belly as I pulled up to Fyfe's house and noted his SUV out front. I hurried to his door before I could talk myself out of it.

The doorbell was loud on the other side and to my utter shock, I heard a baby's cry follow it. Was Harley here? Had Lewis come to check on Fyfe and brought his daughter along?

I strained to listen and heard Fyfe's muffled curse seconds before the door flew open.

He stood before me, handsome as ever, no glasses so obviously wearing his contacts, hair mussed, a towel over his shoulder, and a bowl of mushy food in one hand. He was dressed casual in jeans and a T-shirt.

The baby continued to cry in the background.

Harassed.

Fyfe looked utterly harassed.

Those beautiful dark eyes of his widened at the sight of me. "Eilidh."

For a second, I forgot everything. Our fight. The creepy camera discovery. "Is Harley here?"

"What? Harley?" He shook his head and muttered another curse. "Come in, come in." Fyfe was hurrying through the hallway away from me before I'd even stepped a foot inside.

Curious as hell, I shut the door behind me and followed him into the open-plan living space only to draw to an abrupt halt.

Sitting in a high chair near the island was a gorgeous baby girl, and she was staring up at Fyfe as he fed her. She wore a soft headband with a big pink bow, so I assumed she was a girl. Her little arms and legs flicked every time he spooned a mouthful of the mush.

"What the ..." I took in the mess.

There were piles of boxes of nappies, baby wipes, and formula all along the base of the island.

A baby's cot was situated behind the sofa. A changing table on the other side of the room near the dining table. There were toys and teddies scattered here and there. And the room smelled of baby powder.

"Fyfe ..." I approached man and child, and he looked at me as he wiped the corner of the baby's mouth.

His eyes gleamed with anguish. "A woman I ... I had a fling with left Millie on my doorstep two days ago. Left a note with Millie telling me she was mine and that she couldn't take care of her anymore."

Oh my fecking gawd.

A slight curl curved his mouth. "Aye, that look on your face is pretty much what I looked like two days ago."

My gaze flew to the wee thing. She was beautiful. "How ... how could she leave her?"

Forever the Highlands

"I don't know," he whispered hoarsely.

Aching for him, I reached out to squeeze his arm. I knew this had to be bringing up his own feelings of abandonment.

Fyfe looked at my hand as if he was shocked I'd touched him.

I withdrew my hand and asked gently, "Are you sure she's yours?"

"No. I did one of those at-home paternity tests yesterday and mailed it out right away. It can take up to two weeks to get the results."

Mind whirring, I glanced around the room again. "You bought all this in two days?"

"I didn't have much choice. Drove to Inverness the day I got Millie, paid extra to have them deliver it next day."

Of course he did. Fyfe thought he wasn't capable of caring about people, but when called upon to do it, he threw all of himself into it. Turning to Millie who was staring at me, I smiled and brushed my fingertips over her soft, rounded cheek. "Aren't you beautiful, wee yin?"

Fyfe sucked in a breath.

"What?"

"That's just ... that's what I've been calling her. Wee yin."

I smiled at Millie. "Wee yin. But you have such a pretty name, Millie Billie. Don't you?" I raised my arms toward her and asked, "May I?"

"Sure."

"How old is she?" I asked as I lifted her from the high chair and into my arms.

"She has to be around nine months, I reckon."

"This ... woman—" I tried not to feel anything at the thought of Fyfe being with someone else and that resulting in him being tied to her forever through their child. "She didn't leave a birth certificate?"

158   SAMANTHA YOUNG

"Nothing but a note that Millie is mine and that she couldn't look after her anymore."

Sympathy scored through me at the anger in his words.

"Oh, Millie." I smoothed a soothing hand over her warm back as she reached for one of my curls. "Everything is going to be all right, my darling. Look how well you're being looked after. Just like the wee princess you are." I grinned at her and her eyes flashed to my smile. "Aren't you the most beautiful baby girl? Oh my goodness, I could eat you up."

She let out a little giggle and my heart swelled. Turning to grin at Fyfe, my lips halted mid curve at the abject longing on his face.

Overanalyzing his expression was asking to have my head messed with again, so I turned away and began walking with Millie through the living space. "Look at this teddy." I picked up the gorgeous white polar bear. "Do you like it? Isn't he pretty?"

Millie grabbed the polar bear in both hands and stuffed his nose into her mouth.

"What shall we call him? Hmm? Mr. Polar?"

She wrinkled her nose.

"No, not very imaginative, is it? What about Snowy?"

She tilted her head as if she was considering it and I laughed. Noting a floor mat on the other side of the sofa, I turned back to Fyfe. "Is she crawling?"

He leaned against the island, arms crossed over his chest, expression neutral again. "Aye. The internet suggested she might, so I ordered a play mat and sure enough, she's been crawling all over the bloody place. I can't take my eyes off her for a second."

Millie dropped the polar bear and reached for my face, making incoherent noises as she touched me inquisitively.

"Have you told anyone?" He certainly hadn't told Lewis!

FOREVER THE HIGHLANDS 159

"No," Fyfe replied. "I wanted to wait to see if she was mine before introducing everyone into her life."

"You need support right now, Fyfe."

"It's fine. I don't deserve ... never mind."

"Call your friends."

"It's fine," he repeated stubbornly. "Why are you here?"

The reason for my visit trembled on the tip of my tongue. However, I stopped myself.

Fyfe had enough on his plate right now.

I could ask Callie's dad, Walker, to look into the camera situation. He was head of security on the estate and he had contacts that might be able to trace the culprit through the cameras.

"It doesn't matter. What can I do to help?"

"Eilidh—"

"Fyfe, what can I do to help?"

He sighed wearily, running a hand through his hair. "Could you just watch her while I have a quick shower?"

"Of course."

As soon as he left the room and I thought he was out of earshot, I turned back to Millie who was surprisingly docile in my arms considering all she'd been through in the last few days. She had to be missing her mummy. The thought made me ache all over again. "Come on, Millie. Let's get Fyfe some help, hmm?"

I settled her down on the mat in front of me with a toy that sang to her every time she pressed a different button, pulled my phone out of my back pocket, and called Lewis.

NINETEEN
FYFE

The last two days with Millie had been a whirlwind of surreal. I'd been so busy keeping the tiny human alive that I hadn't had a moment to overthink.

Now as I showered, safe in the knowledge Eilidh was looking after Millie, it hit me.

This wee girl could be my daughter.

That meant the mother of my child *abandoned* her.

Pamela had fallen pregnant and brought Millie to term, attempted to look after her for around nine months, and in all that time (a year and a half) had not once reached out to tell me I had a daughter.

I'd missed all of it.

The pregnancy, the scans, the time to process my new future as a father. Millie being born. Holding her in my arms the first day she came into this world. Giving her the knowledge that her father was with her from day one. I could never say that now.

Pamela had stolen that from me.

Rage flooded me and I gritted my teeth against it.

I couldn't let that emotion in. It would consume me.

It was so nice to be able to take the time to clean, but I didn't want to leave Eilidh out there alone with Millie for too long. There hadn't been a chance to apologize to her yet, and I couldn't take advantage of her kindness.

As I got out of the shower and changed in my bedroom, I heard voices coming from downstairs. Curious, I hurried toward them, recognizing them as I drew closer. Therefore, I wasn't surprised when I walked into the living room to find Lewis, Callie, and Harley there with Eilidh and Millie.

Harley broke into a smile. Quite a few of her teeth had come in. Millie's wee cheeks were red from teething. She seemed worse at night with it, so I'd ordered a soother online, one that I could cool in the fridge before she chewed on it.

"Bah!" Harley dashed toward me, arms flailing, and I hurried to pick her up. She'd already grown since I'd seen her last.

"Hey, Scooter." I'd called her Scooter as a joke at first to annoy Lewis, but it just kind of stuck. And it suited her now that she was toddling all over the place. I cuddled Harley against me, taking her over to Eilidh who held Millie. "Have you met Millie?"

"Aye."

I froze, my head whipping around to gape at my niece. "Did ... did you just say aye?"

"It's one of her handful of words." Callie stepped up to us, stroking a hand down her daughter's back. "She can say *mum, dad, no,* and *aye.*"

I'd known about mum and dad but not the no and aye. I chuckled, pressing a kiss to her chubby cheek. "A girl who knows what she wants."

"I doubt very much she understood what you asked her." Callie chuckled. "But no and aye being her only words makes for some hilarious conversations."

We shared an easy smile and for a second, I almost forgot how awkward things were between us all.

As if she saw the realization on my face, Callie's smile dimmed. "Why don't I take Harley?" She reached for her daughter. "And you can tell us what's going on?"

Handing Harley over to her mother, I met Eilidh's gaze. Millie was snuggled against Eilidh's neck, her eyelids flickering as if she was fighting sleep. There were new people in her orbit so I understood her curiosity. "You called them?"

"You need your family around you right now, Fyfe."

Longing and gratitude and remorse overwhelmed me. "Eilidh ... I ..."

A hand clamped down on my shoulder. Lewis. His expression was sympathetic. "Let's just focus on Millie for now. How did this happen?"

LEWIS HAD CALLED WORK TO TELL THEM HE WOULD be late into the office today, and I discovered Callie had left her mum handling the bakery when Lewis called her to tell her I needed them. Filled with gratitude, I relayed the last few days to my friends.

"You did all this in two days?" Callie shook her head in amazement as she took in the living space. Harley was toddling around, picking up Millie's toys and playing for a wee bit before getting bored and moving on to the next. "Anyone else would be curled up in a ball. I can't imagine what it would be like if we hadn't had all those months to prepare for Harley coming."

"You would just have gotten on with it." My gaze was on Millie who still slept in Eilidh's arms. "Millie didn't ask for this."

"You could have called social services," Lewis suggested.

FOREVER THE HIGHLANDS 163

"And if she's mine? Handing her over to social services would mean putting her in care and for who knows how long while all the legal stuff gets sorted."

"What if she isn't yours?" Eilidh's question was tentative.

"I have people tracking Pamela down. Once I find her, I'll do my best to find Millie's father if she isn't mine. There must be family out there who are happy to look after her. I don't want her going into the system."

"She's more likely to get adopted at this age." Callie reached out to stroke Millie's hair. "It might be what's best for her if her mother could just leave her out in the cold."

"And all of this is moot if Fyfe is the father," Lewis added.

My stomach twisted with emotion. At this point, I couldn't tell if it was fear or dread, and what of.

Callie turned to me. "How long does the DNA test take?"

"They said up to two weeks."

"Okay." Eilidh pressed a kiss to Millie's head. "Then you'll need help for two weeks. If Millie is yours, then you can think of getting more permanent assistance, but for now, you've got me."

Feeling, too much feeling, crashed over me and I could only stare at the beautiful woman holding my probable daughter in her arms. After everything that had happened between us, Eilidh could put all that behind her to help me?

"Eilidh—"

Lewis cut me off. "I don't think that's a good idea."

"It's not up to you, big brother."

He squeezed the bridge of his nose in frustration. Remembering the promise I made to him, I shook my head. "I don't need your help, Eilidh."

Eilidh huffed. "Don't argue with me or overanalyze it. I'm the only one here who doesn't have a full-time job and a child. I was obsessed with playing mum to Mor when she was a baby and I've had lots of time with Harley these past few weeks, so I feel confident I'm able to look after Millie."

"And you can always call on me or Lewis or Regan, who is an actual qualified childcare professional," Callie pointed out.

"Exactly." Eilidh gave me a nod, a decided smile curling her mouth. "While you work, I'll take care of Millie and I'll even socialize her by taking her to Mum's daycare."

"I ... I can't ask you to do that."

"You didn't. I'm making the decision for you. If you need to work today, you should go to work."

"And tonight we'll come over and cook," Callie offered. "Keep you company."

Gratitude overwhelmed me. "I don't know what to say."

"Aye!" Harley cried, her plump wee legs springing her forward to her dad.

It broke the tension as we all laughed. Lewis lifted his daughter into his arms, grinning. "I think you understand every word we're saying. Do I have a genius on my hands?"

She clapped her hands together. "Aye!"

We all chuckled again and the terror that held me captive these past few days released me, allowing me to breathe again.

TWENTY
FYFE

I was shattered. The last few nights, Millie had kept me awake with her teething. Before the teething ring arrived, I'd let her chew on my fingers because it was the only thing that seemed to stop her crying. While the cold teething ring soothed her, as soon as she woke up, she started bawling again. It broke my fucking heart. Callie told me it should only last a week or two before settling but that she'd have bouts of teething until she was two or three.

It didn't surprise me the way my friends rallied around me.

What did surprise me was Eilidh's support. She seemed to have put what was between us behind her to help out with Millie. Seeing her swoop in to rescue us ... well, it was humbling. I already knew Eilidh Adair was a special person, but she was bloody extraordinary.

I'd had Millie for five days. The DNA results still weren't in, but a contact had tracked Pamela's vehicle. She'd sold it to a garage in Edinburgh. From the car we had her last known address, but that was it. He'd hacked the medical records at the hospital in Inverness to find out Millie's date of birth as well as Pamela's. Millie was born last September, so she was nine months old. Pamela had ghosted me around February of that year after we started hooking up at the end of December.

Pamela's birth date allowed us to get more information about her. My guy was close to finding her.

I didn't know how to feel about any of it.

My life and the life I thought I'd have had been thrown into a complete tailspin. And yet ... I'd bonded myself to this wee human. Or she'd bonded herself to me. All I knew was that only my voice and Eilidh's seemed to settle her, and when she cuddled into me at night, I felt like my heart might explode.

Like ... maybe, finally, I belonged to someone who no one could take away from me.

And that was terrifying because ... what if it turned out she wasn't mine? Or what if she was and she actually *could* be taken from me?

I had a meeting with a potential client via Ardnoch Estate that morning and had just fed Millie when the doorbell rang. I hurried toward it, Millie's belligerent cries and baby words hit my back, words I interpreted as a complaint for leaving her side. I threw open the door to Eilidh. "You know you can just come in without knocking," I told her, fixing my tie as she followed me into the living space.

"Good morning to you too," she teased.

Millie caught sight of Eilidh and broke into the most adorable smile I'd ever seen. She raised her arms toward Eils from her high chair, making happy baby sounds. I lifted her out to hand her over.

"Good morning, Millie Billie!" Eilidh beamed but before she could take her, Millie made a gurgling noise before she puked all over my shirt and neck. She then promptly burst into tears.

"It's all right, wee yin." I kissed her temple before Eilidh took her from me.

"Oh, Millie Billie." Eilidh cuddled her close. "Are you not feeling well?"

"She just ate. I shouldn't have picked her up like that." I scowled at the little dress I'd put her in this morning and the vomit now all over it. "She needs cleaned and changed."

"As do you." Eilidh pressed a palm to Millie's forehead. "She doesn't feel warm, so that's good. Maybe she just had too much to eat. I'll keep an eye on her this morning." She started toward the stairs. "You switch your shirt out. I'll clean Millie up."

"Thanks. It could be her teething. She's not had a lot of sleep."

"Aye, that might be it. Poor wee baby, ay, Millie Billie. Shall we have a long, lovely nap today?"

I tried not to ogle Eilidh's arse as I followed her up but she wore a pair of cut-off denim shorts and a loose, slightly cropped tank top. As she chatted animatedly to Millie, taking the stairs quickly, I could see straight up Eilidh's top. Her back was tan and smooth, her hips sloping gently toward her arse.

Groaning inwardly, I looked at my feet as Eilidh turned toward the bathroom and I walked in the opposite direction toward the primary suite.

I'd just shrugged out of my shirt when Eilidh burst into my room with Millie. "Do you have baby shampoo? It somehow got in—oh!" She stumbled to a halt. Her eyes drifted over my naked torso. "Oh. Sorry." Something like pain tightened her features before she whirled herself and Millie around, giving me their backs. Her words were strained. "I need Millie's shampoo."

Ignoring whatever it was I heard in her voice (or I might just do something we'd both regret), I reached for a clean shirt in my built-in closet. "In the third cupboard above the sink."

"Thanks." She practically ran from the room.

With a sigh, I buttoned up the shirt and pulled on a new

tie. Doing the tie up, I strolled into the bathroom to find Millie naked in a shallow bath. She was slapping her arms in the water, her wee girl giggles filling the air like popping bubbles filled with joy.

Please let her be mine.

I looked at Eilidh to distract myself from the thought. She was bent over the tub, washing Millie gently. The tank top now rode up her slim back. Swallowing hard, I returned my attention to Millie.

"I decided to give her a bath. I hope you don't mind."

"Not at all. I need to go. Are you good?" We already had a bit of a routine down. I still didn't understand why Eilidh was helping us, but if it somehow brought us back together as friends, I wouldn't question it.

"Aye." Eilidh shot me a quick smile. "We'll call if we need you."

Nodding, I stepped into the room to bend down to kiss Millie's head and Eilidh leaned away so I didn't touch her. Frowning, I kissed Millie. "Bye, wee yin. See you soon."

"Bah ga bye!" Millie slapped the water, giggling up at me.

I'd just straightened, but I froze. "Did she ... did she say *bye*?"

Eilidh's laughter warmed me right through. "I think it only sounded like that."

I cupped the back of Millie's damp head. "Did you just say bye? Bye, Millie."

"Goh ka!" She giggled, splashing water at me.

"Bye-bye, Millie."

She made a little hiccupping sound and reached for one of her bath toys.

Eilidh chuckled. "A fluke. But she's around the age babies start saying one or two words."

"Aye? How do you know that?"

"I've been reading that stack of baby books you ordered."

FOREVER THE HIGHLANDS 169

I frowned. "You've been reading the baby books?"

She nodded, kneeling to wash Millie.

Something like pining wrapped itself around me, holding me frozen.

"Aren't you going to be late?" Eilidh asked, tickling Millie with a bath toy.

"Right. Right." I kissed Millie again. "See you both later."

A DIRECTOR AT ARDNOCH ESTATE ALSO HAPPENED to be on the board of an extremely popular British online retailer. They were the target of weekly hacks and the last one managed to get hundreds of thousands of customer details. Thankfully no bank details, but the company was on edge because of the incident. I'd agreed to analyze their current cybersecurity and see how we could tighten it.

It would be a headache on top of looking after Millie right now, but well worth the paycheck.

Walker, Callie's stepfather, accompanied me to the staff car park after the meeting. "Thanks for setting this up."

"No problem. You all right?"

Walker Ironside was a man of few words, but he didn't need them. I could tell by the speculative expression Callie had told him about Millie. Thankfully, I knew Walker kept shit to himself. I didn't want anyone knowing about Millie until I knew for certain if she was mine. If she was, I'd have to set her up with a doctor and a nanny or daycare. As soon as that happened, the cat would be out of the bag. Ardnoch was too small for people not to find out as soon as I stepped into the village with a baby in tow.

"I will be once I know she's mine."

"Aye, I get that." He nodded. "And I know you've got your hands full, so don't worry about this business with Eilidh. I've got someone trying to track who purchased the cameras through the serial numbers."

Confused, I shook my head. "What are you talking about?"

Walker's brows drew together. "Eilidh didn't tell you?"

"Tell me what?"

"Maybe you should ask her."

Walker was trying to trace someone through camera serial numbers. Realization scored through me and with it, a flash of fury. "Did someone plant a camera on Eilidh?"

He nodded grimly. "Her flat in London. Her landlord called because they were doing an annual check on the smoke alarms. They found cameras in them."

Fuck. Was she never to get any peace? "Has anyone contacted Eilidh with footage? Have you found any online?"

"Already got someone checking the dark web. Nothing on there. No one has reached out or blackmailed or threatened her."

"Email me the serial numbers."

"I can deal with it. You've got enough on your plate."

The thought of someone violating Eilidh's privacy made me want to punch a fist through my car window. "Send me those serial numbers, Walker. This is Eilidh."

He clapped me on the back. "I'll email them over now."

As I got in the car, instead of driving toward Ardnoch for coffee like I'd planned, I headed home. The thought of some unknown person owning private, intimate footage of Eilidh was more than I could stand. Hadn't she been through enough? And why hadn't she told me?

I intended to find out.

Storming into the house, I found Eilidh on the couch watching morning television at a low volume. Millie was in her cot. I glanced in it as I passed, relieved to find her sleeping peacefully.

"What are you doing back?" Eilidh whispered.

Instead of answering, I placed the baby monitor by Millie's cot and then gestured toward the stairs. "We need to talk," I whispered back. "I have a monitor in my room."

Eyes wide, she nodded and followed me.

I waited until we reached my bedroom, and I closed the door, my body vibrating with tension.

"What's going on?" Eilidh crossed her arms over her chest.

"Were you ever going to tell me about the cameras someone planted in your flat?"

Her brows drew together. "Walker?"

"Aye, he thought I knew."

"You had enough on your plate." She gestured to the baby monitor.

"Or you didn't tell me because of ... because of e-everything," I sputtered angrily. "But this is bigger than that, Eilidh. This is your safety we're talking about and my area of fucking expertise."

"Don't swear at me." She strode past with a huff and reached for the bedroom door.

I wrapped a hand around her biceps, hauling her closer. "I'm going to find out who did this."

Eilidh licked her lips as she searched my face. "Walker is on it. You just focus on Millie."

My grip on her tightened as she attempted to pull away. "Stop acting like this isn't a big deal. Someone violated your private space."

"I know," she hissed, yanking out of my hold. "I am well aware of that fact."

"Talk to me, Eilidh. I don't want you dealing with this alone."

"I'm not." Her expression closed. "My parents know. Lewis and Callie know. Walker knows. I have support."

"I want to support you too." My tone was almost pleading. After everything she'd done for me ...

Eilidh backed up toward the door. "I don't need that kind of support from you."

Wow.

That fucking hurt more than I could say.

"Eilidh—" But my phone buzzed in my pocket, cutting me off. Cursing under my breath I pulled it out just as Eilidh opened the door to escape. The notification on the screen had me cursing out loud.

Whatever she heard in my voice stopped her in her tracks. "What is it?"

I tapped on the email.

About five gazillion emotions hit me at once as I read it.

"Fyfe ... Fyfe, what is it?" Eilidh's concerned question penetrated those five gazillion emotions.

"She's mine," I wheezed, my knees giving out as I stumbled onto my arse on the bed. "Millie's my daughter." Tears clouded my vision and I covered my face, trying to mask the magnitude of my reaction.

The bed depressed and I felt Eilidh's leg nudge mine, her arm sliding across my back. A sob rattled in my chest as I attempted to hold it inside.

"And ... you don't want her?" Eilidh whispered.

I made an angry noise of denial.

She pressed closer. "You're relieved?"

I nodded.

Eilidh pulled my head to her chest. "I understand," she whispered tearfully. "It's okay, Fyfe. It's okay. She's yours. No one can take her from you. She belongs to you. Always."

Twenty-One
EILIDH

More than once, I'd heard Fyfe say he'd never have kids, and even as I watched him cuddle and play with Harley—calling her that adorable nickname "Scooter"—I believed him. He wasn't interested in being responsible for someone else or committing to a woman or child.

Yet, I'd understood with complete clarity why when, for the first time, I'd witnessed Fyfe cry, all because he was relieved Millie was his biological daughter.

He had no real family.

But now Millie was his.

No one could take that from him.

It was in his control to be a good father to her.

I knew he would be. I knew by the way Fyfe had taken to looking after his adorable baby daughter without complaint from the moment he'd found her on his doorstep. He didn't complain about the lack of sleep or how his formerly pristine home was now a mess of baby things. Not once did he mention how his future had flipped on its head.

Fyfe's true nature had won out with Millie. Deep down,

Fyfe was what I always knew he could be: a nurturer, a protector. He was just terrified to be that man because the one person who was supposed to love him the most had abandoned him.

However, the way he was with Millie ...

Despite our less than pleasant history, I was proud of Fyfe Moray.

"I think you're a moron," my brother had told me bluntly when I called to let him know Fyfe had received the DNA results. When Lewis asked me if Fyfe would hire a nanny now, I'd informed him I was going to continue watching Millie until Fyfe figured out permanent childcare. Calling me a moron was Lewis's response.

"Excuse me?" I'd huffed.

"Look, I love you and I think it's amazing you want to help Fyfe adjust to his new reality as a father, but this is masochistic, Eilidh. Why would you continue to put yourself in his orbit after he rejected you?"

"I'm over it," I'd replied. "I'm dating Cameron."

Lewis sighed. Heavily. "You don't get over the person you love that quickly."

"I'm not you."

"Fine. Then I guess you never really loved Fyfe if it's that easy."

I'd sputtered in outrage.

"Either or, Eils. You're a grown-up. I can't protect you from everything. But please, be smart and don't let yourself get hurt any more than you already have been."

I promised him I wouldn't, but the conversation with Lewis kept coming back to me throughout the next few days. Fyfe had just taken on an important client, he was adamant about finding whoever planted the cameras in my apartment, and he was exhausting all resources to locate Millie's mother so he could come to a legal custody arrangement. I knew he was afraid Pamela would return and try to take his daughter from him.

The thought of Fyfe sharing a child with another woman was still disconcerting, but it wasn't my business anymore.

"You seem preoccupied." Cameron leaned across the table to touch my hand.

I blinked rapidly, guilt flushing through me. Thank goodness I wasn't a blusher. "Oh, sorry. Um, it's just been ... crazy lately."

I was totally zoned out of our date.

Cameron had invited me to his place for dinner. It was our sixth date, and I knew it was time to progress from making out to sex. I wanted to. I was attracted to Cameron. It certainly wasn't fair to him that he worked busy hours at the doctors' surgery but had made time to cook a delicious meal (coq au vin—the name certainly suggested he expected sex) and here I was, thinking about anything but the handsome man before me.

Shit.

Cameron sat back in his chair, a blank look on his face. "You're thinking about Fyfe?"

I'd told Cameron I was babysitting Millie. With childcare taking up so much of my time, I had to. Of course I'd explained who Fyfe was (though I didn't tell Cameron I'd once been in love with my brother's best friend) and I thought he understood. In fact, Cameron seemed to think what I was doing was incredibly sweet.

Or he did think that a few days ago.

"I was thinking about Millie," I corrected him. Dishonestly.

Cameron studied me thoughtfully. "Are you sure there's nothing between you and Fyfe? Romantically, I mean?"

Was I giving off that vibe? How? I couldn't possibly be. I

was over him! "Of course not," I answered truthfully. "I'm just his best friend's wee sister."

He frowned. "That's what you are to him. What is he to you?"

Shrewd. The doctor was way too shrewd. It would be sexy if he wasn't currently interrogating me. "A friend." I crossed my arms, leaning back from the table. "And I don't particularly enjoy being grilled about my relationships with other people."

"I wasn't grilling you. I asked a question."

"Aye, one motivated by jealousy."

Cameron's fist tightened around a fork and he glanced away. "Sorry."

Wariness shot through me. "I don't do jealousy, Cameron. It's kind of a big turnoff for me."

After a few seconds, he released the fork and looked at me calmly. "Understood. It won't happen again. You're just ... so beautiful. I want you to myself."

Internally, I bristled. One: I belonged only to myself. Two: I wanted to be wanted for more than a face and body I hadn't earned. It was a gift of genetics. As someone who was still on a path to liking herself, I needed the person I was dating to want me for *me* and not my looks. I understood physical attraction was a part of human connection, but I needed more than just that.

"Let's forget I asked." He gave me a congenial smile and stood. "More wine?"

"I'm good."

A few minutes later, Cameron led me over to his sofa. He'd rented a spacious bungalow not far from my aunt Arro and uncle Mac's house. It was already furnished when he rented it, and Cameron complained it lacked his personality, but it was stylish and comfortable.

The uneasiness between us settled as we chatted about

FOREVER THE HIGHLANDS

Cameron getting a grip on small-town life.

"And you?" he asked. "How is retirement treating you?"

The truth was my agent, Danny, had been in touch every other day pestering me about my future. He'd warned me my performance in the last season of *Young Adult* had rumors whirring that I would be nominated for a BAFTA again next January. That I owed it to the show to do all the interview requests coming in. He'd been talking to my PR team who he said were inundated with queries. Of course they were. Tell people you no longer wanted something millions of folks would kill to have, and suddenly you were cool as fuck as well as an ungrateful brat and everyone wanted to talk to you about it. It took a minute, but after monologuing exactly how I was feeling, I think I finally got through to Danny.

"He's going to back off?" Cameron asked.

"Yes. I told him I wasn't going to change my mind about quitting acting. That the last few weeks I've been happier than ever. That he should focus his energy on other clients. He said he was sorry to hear it, that he truly believed I was one of his most talented clients, which was lovely, but that he'd back off. And I believe him."

At least that was one thing I didn't have to worry about anymore. Especially with so-called friends from the industry reaching out to ask if I was okay in a tone that most people usually reserved for the terminally ill. Some of them had started sending me articles that trashed me under the pretense of being concerned. I blocked them. Other friends were kinder, if not a little patronizing and disbelieving.

I turned off my Google Alerts and lived in absolute ignorant bliss.

The only downside was Jasper. One of the articles a "friend" sent was an interview he did where he pretty much insinuated that I was a diva who had ruined his chance to remain on a show he loved. Fans adored Jasper. I had no doubt my name was being dragged through the social media mud.

I had to admit, it made me cry.

Not because I was being vilified. I think I'd made peace with my inability to control other people's gossiping ridiculousness.

No, I cried for a friendship lost. I cried because Jasper had betrayed me and because in his twisted, selfish mind, he did it because he thought me putting my mental health before the show was a betrayal of him.

After that, I deleted his contact from my phone.

Finally, my management team, whom I'd kept on to handle tying up my career, had reached out to let me know I'd received some disturbing death threats. I was sad to say it wasn't the first time. When it did happen the first time, I freaked way the fuck out and had security accompany me everywhere. Since then, we just forwarded all that stuff to the police.

But my management company was concerned I was at home without protection. However, I felt the opposite. I felt safer in Ardnoch than anywhere. I told them to forward on the threats to the police as per the usual process. They kept a file of all the creepy emails, DMs, and letters, along with a list of dodgy characters who had revealed themselves and their stalker-like behavior. My security teams used to memorize that list before we went anywhere. I'd asked the team to forward the folder to me because it might prove useful, considering the cameras found in my London flat.

No. I hadn't forgotten about that. I was just trying to compartmentalize that shit.

I stared at Cameron who waited for my answer about how retirement was treating me. "It's good," I replied simply. "Looking after Millie has been a nice change of pace."

"Of course." He nodded. "But you should remember you

came home for yourself. You should concentrate on your writing."

He said it casually, but there was a pointed sharpness to his tone. "I came home for my family. Millie's family. I'll take care of her for as long as she needs."

His smile was soft. "You're a good person."

Hmm.

As if he sensed my uncertainty about his motives, Cameron leaned in to kiss me. He was a good kisser. I'd give him that.

Deepening the kiss, Cameron drew me against him, his hands smoothing around my waist and under my T-shirt.

The image of Fyfe standing half-naked in his bedroom flashed in my mind. I'd stupidly walked into his bedroom without knocking the morning Millie puked up her breakfast. Though I knew Fyfe was built, I'd still been stunned by how beautiful he was. Tight, sculpted muscle wrapped in smooth tan skin. He had a slight dusting of hair on his chest that narrowed downward in a happy trail. I'd seen plenty of men half-naked, men whose sole purpose in life was to look good on camera.

None of them had affected me the way the sight of Fyfe Moray affected me.

Stop thinking about him!

To dismiss Fyfe from my mind, I followed Cameron's lead and pulled his shirt out of his trousers. He groaned into the kiss, pressing me back against the couch as my hands slipped under to smooth over his stomach. There was no happy trail, like Fyfe's.

Stop, stop, stop!

Cameron was attractive.

I was attracted to him.

I moaned deliberately to prove it to myself.

But at the feel of his fingers undoing the top button on my

jeans, I instinctually covered his hand with mine and broke the kiss.

He searched my face. "Are you okay?"

Gently, I pushed his hand from me. "I ... I'm sorry. I ... I'm not ready ..."

"Hey." Cameron cupped my face in his hands. "Eilidh, I'm not in this for a quick roll in the sack. We can take this slow."

Relieved, I nodded. "Thank you. You're a gentleman."

"I want to treat you right. You're so beautiful, Eilidh." He brushed his lips over mine, almost reverently. "I can't wait to make love to you, but I can wait. If that makes sense."

At his smile, I forced a grin.

Make love.

Oh boy.

Not long later, I gave my excuses and left. Cameron kissed me at the door, this time even hungrier than last, his hands squeezing my hips as his erection dug into me. Although I experienced a stirring of arousal, I departed dazed and confused.

Sex had never been a big deal to me. I lost my virginity when I was sixteen and it happened because I wanted it to happen. From that moment on, sex was just for pleasure. It wasn't about intimacy. It was about getting off.

I'd never tied up sex with romance in the past.

Until Fyfe.

And we hadn't even had sex!

So, why oh why did the thought of having sex with a man I wasn't in love with suddenly dampen my libido?

Twenty-Two
FYFE

My house smelled like a home for the first time since I'd bought it.

It smelled of baby—powder, food, and quite often, poop.

This morning it also still held the lingering scent of the sauce Lewis had made to accompany our pasta dinner last night. He and Callie, despite their busy and exhausting lives, took time to make dinner for me and Millie again. It seemed it might turn into a regular thing, and I couldn't say I didn't like the idea. Although Harley was a good nine months older than Millie, they still babbled together. I could already see them growing up as close as sisters.

My friends made the thought of single fatherhood a less terrifying prospect.

Yes, I was relieved as fuck Millie was mine.

However, that didn't mean I'd miraculously shed all my fears. Lewis said if I wasn't scared, then there was a problem. "All new parents have a healthy amount of terror simmering in their system," he promised. "But we're just so fucking exhausted, we get through it."

182 SAMANTHA YOUNG

I'd laughed at that because it was true.

Last night was the first night Millie didn't teethe, but she still woke me up three times.

As I clipped my daughter (still so surreal) into the car seat, I talked away to her about where we were going and what the day held. She interrupted me with a few baby words. Today was the first day Eilidh wasn't here, and I wondered if Millie missed her.

Driving into Ardnoch, I kept talking to Millie because it distracted me from the rage I'd been feeling since yesterday afternoon.

We found Pamela. She was working in Newcastle at a small solicitors' firm. I'd called her office and they patched me through. Our conversation flashed through my mind and my hands tightened on the steering wheel.

"How did you find me?" Her soft voice was harsher than I'd ever heard it. "Leave me alone."

"If you hang up on me, I will bring the wrath of the law down on you and as a solicitor, you know after what you did, I have it in my power to ruin you. So listen up."

I heard her heavy breathing and continued, "The DNA test came back, proving I am Millie's father."

"You thought you weren't?" She had the audacity to sound pissed off.

"A mother who abandons her child outside in the open isn't someone I particularly trust," I snapped. "Now, my solicitor is going to serve you with a document that states you give up all parental rights to Millie. If that's what you want, you sign it. If it's not what you want, we'll need to discuss that further because I need to know you're in the right mental state to look aft—"

"I don't want it."

Stunned silent, it took me a minute to choke out, "It?"

"I don't want it. It was a mistake. You should keep it."

FOREVER THE HIGHLANDS

"It?" I repeated through clenched teeth. "Do you mean her? Our daughter?"

"Don't," Pamela whispered on a sob. "Please ... I can't."

Concern pierced my fury. "Maybe you should talk to someone, Pamela? Before you make any big decisions."

"I don't want it. Send me the document. I'll sign what you want."

"One, call Millie 'it' again and we'll have a problem. Two, Pamela ... you don't sound all right. I think you should talk to someone before you make this decision. Please."

"Not every woman wants to be a mother. I just didn't realize that until ... until *she* came along. I'm not built that way, Fyfe. And I don't ... I don't want to hurt ... *her*." Her sniffling filled the line.

Seething, I replied quietly, "If you sign over your rights now, that's it. If you abandon her now, I won't let you near her in the future if you change your mind. And if you take me to court for custody, I will produce this document and the footage of you abandoning your daughter on my doorstep where she sat in the cold for twenty minutes on her own. That's the man I am. So think carefully that this is what you want ... because if you change your mind later, I will fight with everything I have to keep my daughter from you."

"I won't want her in the future."

Hurt and pain and indignation on Millie's behalf moved through me in a shudder. It took me a second to squeeze the words out around the feelings. "She'll have a beautiful life without you. I'll make sure of it."

"I know you will."

"I need her birth certificate."

"I ... I left it behind."

Shaking my head, I exhaled slowly. "Fine. I'll apply for a new certificate. Please tell me I'm on there as the father?"

"You are. Her ... her legal name on the certificate is Millicent Moray."

She gave her my surname. I assumed then Pamela knew there was no chance anyone else could have been the father.

"I, uh, I named her after my granny. She was the only person who ... well, it seemed right to name her for my granny."

I heard what she didn't say. And if she'd given Millie a name that meant something to her ... "Pamela, we don't have to decide this right now," I repeated. "Why don't you take time to think about it?"

"No! I'm not going to change my mind. I'll sign the document as soon as I receive it."

Fine.

"You'll have it by end of day." I hung up. I'd say the woman I'd just spoken to didn't resemble the woman I'd had an affair with, but the sad truth was, I didn't know anything about Pamela before this. It really had just been sex between us.

Pulling myself out of the memory of yesterday's conversation, I turned off Castle Street, heading toward the doctors' office. "I was thinking we could surprise Auntie Eilidh—"

"Ae!" Millie interrupted me.

"—after we visit the doctor. Maybe stop in to see Auntie Callie at the bakery and get something delicious to thank Auntie Eilidh—"

"Ae!"

I stared at my daughter in the rearview mirror.

"Eilidh," I repeated.

Millie smiled big and beaming, showing off her incoming two front teeth top and bottom. "Ae!"

Was she trying to say Eilidh?

"Eilidh."

"Ae!"

Chuckling to myself, I pulled into the car park at the doctors' office. I couldn't wait to tell Eils about it. This morning my solicitor faxed over the signed document from Pamela. It didn't fill me with the relief I'd hoped for. Instead, though I could tell Pamela was going through something, I still felt furious with her for so easily giving up her child. Moreover, the document held no true meaning under the law in Scotland. A parent couldn't just give up parental rights and responsibilities. It was up to the courts to decide that. So, if one day Pamela did change her mind, I would have to fight to keep Millie.

I tried not to let that thought scare the shit out of me.

After the phone call with Pamela, I'd gone home to find Eilidh with Millie. I'd told Eils everything. She'd wisely advised I take one day at a time. Then she'd said something so profound, it rocked me.

"None of this can be about you or Pamela. This is about Millie. Even if Pamela was to show up tomorrow or next month or in ten years, you can't let the fear of that stop you from loving Millie with everything inside you. You're her father. It's your job to make sure that her life is the best it can be, even knowing one day your heart might break from loving her."

With Eilidh's words of wisdom settled deep inside, that's what I intended to do.

It took me a minute to transfer Millie from her car seat to the baby carrier looped around my shoulders. Once I had her warm weight nestled against me, I locked the car.

"You ready for your first doc appointment, wee yin?" I asked as we strode across the car park.

We'd discovered Millie loved the baby carrier. She stared up at me, wide-eyed, a hilarious smirk curling one side of her mouth.

"I'll take that as a yes." I pressed a kiss to her forehead and

186   SAMANTHA YOUNG

looked up to find the worst person imaginable exiting the doctors' surgery.

Aisla Rankin.

Mrs. Rankin was widowed and a judgmental busybody masquerading as leader of the morality police. When Callie fell pregnant, Aisla Rankin tried to muddy Callie's reputation. The Adairs wouldn't stand for it and Mrs. Rankin found herself persona non grata with the most powerful family in the Scottish Highlands. Stupid auld cow. She deserved it after the rumors she'd spread about Callie.

Unfortunately, she was the worst person I could run into on my first outing with Millie in the village. News of my small companion would be all over Ardnoch by the end of the morning.

Wonderful.

"Fyfe Moray." Mrs. Rankin peered at Millie as she passed us. "What do you have there then?"

"None of *your* business," I replied calmly, snorting when I heard her huff of indignation behind me.

Millie giggled as if she were in on it.

"That's your first encounter with the town gossip, wee yin," I told her softly as I entered the building. "You are to avoid her from now until eternity so she doesn't fill your head with her internalized misogynism and toxic Victorian values."

My daughter blew a bubble at me.

"One day you'll agree." I patted her wee bottom and walked into reception.

There were four people in the room, most familiar faces from the village. I gave them a nod and watched them greet me, their curious gazes on Millie.

"I have an appointment for Millicent Moray," I told the receptionist.

She gaped at me and then Millie. "Oh. Of course, Mr. Moray. Please take a seat."

FOREVER THE HIGHLANDS 187

And so it began.

Even if Aisla didn't do the work, the people at the doctors' office would. Everyone would know by the end of the day that Fyfe Moray was now a single dad.

As soon as I sat down, Millie got antsy.

"It's all right. Won't be long."

Her face crumpled in indignation.

"Fine." I stood and began pacing. Her wee smile returned.

Brilliant. She wasn't even a year old, and she already knew how to get her own way.

Ten minutes later, a man I didn't recognize strode into the reception. He wore a shirt, trousers, and tie and had a lanyard around his neck. He looked around my age, maybe just a tad older. When his gaze landed on me, I could have sworn it hardened. "Fyfe and Millicent Moray?"

"Aye, that's us." I crossed the distance between us. "Doctor ...?"

"Dr. Phillips."

"Are you new in town?"

He gaped at me as if I'd surprised him. "Well ... yes." Shaking his head, he turned around. "This way."

Mildly bemused by the strange welcome, I patted Millie's bottom again and followed him. "Let's follow the doctor, wee yin."

Inside his office, Dr. Phillips was brisk and efficient, checking over Millie.

"Her previous doctor's surgery said they'd email you her medical records," I told him. Pamela had provided all that information to my solicitor.

"Yes, we got them. Nothing untoward there. And Millicent seems in perfect health."

I was a little disconcerted by how unemotional he was with Millie, considering she was cute as fuck and it was physically impossible not to smile at her. Maybe he just wasn't a baby person. I never thought I was until Harley came along. "We call her Millie."

"Eilidh tells me you have full custody of Millie now." Dr. Phillips handed my daughter back to me.

I frowned. "Eilidh?"

The doctor narrowed his eyes. "You do know that we're seeing each other? Me and Eilidh. She's my girlfriend. She didn't tell you?"

What the actual fuck?

Blood rushed in my ears as a sickening roiling sensation moved through me at his revelation.

"You and Eilidh Adair?" I felt the need to confirm.

The bastard smiled smugly. "For weeks now. We're getting quite serious."

A jagged sharpness blazed from my heart.

Jealousy.

It was an ugly fucking emotion.

"Is that right?" I looked away because I was afraid he'd recognize my sudden need to punch his lights out. Instead, I focused on putting Millie back into the baby carrier. "Funny. If you're so serious, why has she never mentioned you?" I felt the words bubbling up before I could stop them as I lifted my chin to meet his gaze in challenge. "She clearly mentioned me and Millie to you."

Dr. Phillips narrowed his eyes. "Well, Eilidh's a kind person who is happy to help out a man she considers a brother."

That's when I knew.

He had no idea Eilidh had admitted to being in love with me.

My gut twisted.

She'd told me she loved me not that long ago and now she was dating this prick? Make that make sense.

FOREVER THE HIGHLANDS 189

"Are we done here?" I stood, and Millie made grumbling noises that suggested if we weren't, she certainly was.

"We're done. You can make an appointment with the receptionist for Millicent's next set of immunizations." He turned away to tap information into Millie's records.

I clenched my teeth, the sudden image of this fucker kissing and touching Eilidh filling my mind and then my chest with a pain I couldn't stand. Possessiveness thrummed through every beat of my heart as I strode to the door and opened it. I blamed it for the devil that rode me as I glanced back at the doctor who watched me with a look in his eyes I did not fucking like. "Just so you know ... Eilidh's never thought of me as a brother. And I *definitely* don't think of her as a sister."

I walked out before he could respond.

Millie chatted to me in her baby voice.

"It's okay, wee yin. Dad's just having a life-changing, ground-shaking epiphany."

"Ae!"

Her hopeful little expression fueled me. "Aye, wee yin. Exactly."

Twenty-Three
EILIDH

It had been a rare day in the Highlands. Summer had come a wee bit early and since Fyfe had Millie all day, I had time to myself to soak up the hot spring sun. I'd taken a lounger and side table out of my parents' storage at the back of the annex and planted it in their back garden. With the sea ahead of me, light glistening on the water, the heat on my skin, I'd lain there and enjoyed the soothing, rhythmic lull of the waves hitting the coastline below. Throughout the afternoon, I vacillated between napping and making notes about my script.

It was the first day in such a long time that I felt truly relaxed.

However, Millie and Fyfe were never far from my thoughts. I was eager to discover how they'd gotten on today. He hadn't said why he was taking the day off work, other than he had some errands to run and he wanted to do them with Millie. Thinking that was so sweet and I was so proud of him I could barely stand it, I didn't question Fyfe any further.

After dragging myself off the lounger just as Mor and Mum arrived home, I tidied everything away and grabbed my

FOREVER THE HIGHLANDS 191

phone from the annex. To my surprise, I had several missed calls from both Fyfe and Cameron.

And a text from each.

Fyfe:

> Sorry to bother you, but we need to talk. Can you come around to the house this afternoon?

Cameron:

> We need to talk. My place? Six thirty?

Bloody hell.

Deciding to text Cameron later, I popped my head into the house to let Mum and Mor know I was heading over to Fyfe's before I jumped into my G-Wagon.

I remembered Fyfe's reaction when he saw the vehicle for the first time.

He'd hooted at the sight of it, chuckling as he rounded the four-by-four.

"What?" I'd mock scowled at him.

"We know you've got money, Eils. You don't need to prove it."

"It's secondhand!"

"Aye, and I know how much a secondhand G-Wagon costs. They don't depreciate like other vehicles."

My cheeks were hot at his teasing. "I'm not showing off. I like it. I like being high off the ground and seeing farther along the road."

"Defender. Wrangler. Those ring a bell? They're high off the ground."

"Everyone around here drives a Defender or a Wrangler. I like to be different. And this is a hybrid, so it's more eco-friendly."

He'd given me a tender smile. "I know, sweetheart. It actually suits you."

"Well, now I don't know how to take that."

He'd considered the vehicle and then me. "It's a Highlander wearing Louis Vuitton."

At that, I'd burst out laughing.

Even now it made me smile.

That smile, however, disappeared rapidly when Fyfe opened the door to me fifteen minutes later. Although his demeanor was calm, there was a hardness in his eyes that made me wary. Following him into the living space, I strolled over to Millie's cot to make sure she was okay. Fyfe had bought another cot and put it in the second bedroom. We were in the process of turning the smaller room into a nursery. All of us were coming together next weekend to decorate it.

Millie was asleep in the living room cot. The urge to reach down to touch her was something I had to physically fight. This wee girl had crawled into my heart so quickly. Every time I thought about Pamela abandoning her, I was heartbroken for Millie. But also worried for Pamela, a stranger I'd never met. I couldn't believe that giving up Millie hadn't greatly affected her. Even if she thought it was for the best. It couldn't be easy.

I didn't say that to Fyfe.

He was too upset for Millie to be sympathetic toward her mother and I understood where he was coming from. Unfortunately, he knew exactly how Millie's mother's abandonment would affect her as she grew old enough to understand.

The difference was, though, unlike Fyfe, Millie would have a father who would never willingly leave her. I knew she was going to be all right. Better than all right.

"What's going on?" I asked quietly, stepping away from her cot.

FOREVER THE HIGHLANDS   193

"Yesterday, you mentioned you asked your team for that file they kept."

"The dodgy creep file," I said with more casualness than I truly felt about the existence of such a thing.

"Aye."

"What of it?"

"I think it's time my people looked through it. We've come to a dead end with the cameras. They were purchased as stock by a guy in London who sells out the back door. Any customers who don't want to leave a trail, they pay in cash and there's no digital footprint. The cameras themselves aren't especially sophisticated. They have to link to an app via the internet, so whoever planted them was piggy-backing off the internet connection in your building. Unfortunately, we couldn't trace them through that because they must have known right away when the cameras were compromised."

"You're kidding me?" I sighed in exasperation. "What now?"

"We comb that file. See if there's any information that could remotely be connected to someone having access to your flat to plant those cameras. We follow every lead."

The thought of Fyfe reading about what some of these sleazy creeps thought of me made my stomach revolt. "*You're* not going to look through it, are you?"

His eyes narrowed. "Only if my team brings something to my attention. I ... I'd lose my mind if I had to read through all that stuff."

I nodded, crossing the room to lean against the other side of the island. I searched his face. "Is that what you needed to talk about so urgently?"

Fyfe rounded the island with a sudden look of determination, and my pulse jumped as he stopped inches from me. I straightened, again wary of his proximity and overall demeanor as I turned toward him. "I took Millie to the doctor today."

"Is she okay?" My gaze flew to her in panic.

"It was a checkup. And an introduction to her new doctor. Though I think I'll be asking to see another doctor next time we visit."

Sudden understanding dawned. "Oh."

The muscle in his strong jaw flexed. "When were you going to tell me you were seeing that guy?"

He spat *that guy* like they were dirty words. Guilt I wasn't sure I should feel flushed through me. "I'm sorry you found out like that. We've only been on a few dates."

He quirked an eyebrow. "Well, your doctor seems to think you two are boyfriend and girlfriend. Very serious."

I ignored his mocking tone because I was concerned by the information he'd just relayed. "Cameron said that?"

"He called you his girlfriend. And said you were getting serious."

"He said that?" Dread filled the pit of my stomach.

"Aye." Fyfe stepped into my personal space. I had to lean back against the island to avoid contact. But he braced his hands on the counter at either side of me, his body flush to mine as I tipped my head back in surprise. The hardness was gone in his dark eyes, replaced with something fiery and hot.

"What are you doing?" I whispered, pressing my palms to his firm chest and then dropping my hands like he was on fire because, whoa, he had *pecs*.

"Tell me how you confess your love for one man one week and start dating another the next?"

He was angry with me?

Was he joking?

"I'll tell you how," I seethed between clenched teeth, my cheeks hot with not-so-old humiliation and hurt. "You get over the first guy when he tells you he can never love you back."

Fyfe licked his lips, his chest heaving a little as if he couldn't quite catch his breath. Then he cupped my face, his palms rough against my skin. I gaped at him as he bent his head to mine, his voice rasping as he said, "We need to talk about that, sweetheart."

No, no, no! "There's nothing to say."

"I fucked up." His words were gruff, thick with emotion. "I was blind. I let myself be blind. But I'm seeing more clearly than ever."

No.

Was he saying what I—

"No!" I yanked his hands off my face. "Don't." Fear of being played, of having a heart that was still bloody broken ripped apart again by this man, had me shoving at his chest.

He was a solid wall of muscle trapping me against the island.

"Eilidh—"

"No!" I yelled in his face and he didn't even flinch. "You don't get to decide you want me because some other guy has me. I'm not a toy."

"Does he have you?" Fyfe glowered.

"None of your business."

"Have you slept with him?"

"How fucking dare you," I hissed. "Get out of my way."

Relief softened his expression. And there was a tiny hint of smugness there too. "You haven't slept with him."

Ugly resentment bubbled over. "Doesn't mean I won't."

His eyes flashed with jealousy. Then his cheek brushed mine and his hands gripped my hips. Fyfe's lips touched my ear. "If you fuck him, I dare you not to close your eyes and imagine it's me inside you."

That dream, that bloody vivid sex dream I had all those

months ago, popped into my head. There had been dreams of Fyfe since, but none had felt as real as that. Arousal flushed through me, my lower belly trembling with it.

Bastard!

With all my strength, I pressed my palms to his chest and shoved him away.

Fyfe didn't even stumble as he took a step back, gaze hungry, like he knew exactly how my body reacted to his words.

"Go fuck yourself," I spat before I marched toward the front door.

"I'd rather fuck you!" he called.

I stumbled and whirled around. "You did not just say that."

His expression was determined as he strode toward me, but I held up my hands, warding him off. Fyfe halted, frustration evident in every bristling line of his body. "Look, I can admit I was jealous when that prick said he was dating you. But I don't want you because someone else has you."

"He doesn't have me," I couldn't help but insert breathlessly.

"I know he doesn't have you. I *know* you, Eilidh." Fyfe's countenance turned pained. "When you told me you loved me, I truly believed that I wasn't worthy of it. That I couldn't protect that love. Or *be* what you deserve. But ... a lot has changed in the last few weeks. Maybe I'm not the man I thought I was. Maybe I can be better. Maybe ... I can try to be worthy of someone as extraordinary as you. All I know is, when you're here with me and Millie, it feels right. The thought of you moving on with someone else scares the shit out of me."

Oh.

I understood now.

Crushing disappointment flooded in and my words were

cooler than I intended as I replied, "A competent nanny will provide that same sense of security." I turned and rushed toward the door.

"Eilidh, please!"

Millie's cries filled the house. I winced, guilt riding me, as I used the distraction to flee the man who had broken my heart more times than I cared to admit.

TWENTY-FOUR
EILIDH

Fueled by my indignation, renewed hurt, and the insidious hope Fyfe had sparked—hope I knew I had to squash—I drove to Cameron's bungalow in a mad dash to clear things up with the doctor.

"How dare you?" I pronounced as soon as he opened his front door.

He scowled. "Excuse me?"

"You told Fyfe that I was your girlfriend and that we're serious? We've been on six dates."

Cameron's frown only deepened. "Maybe we could have this discussion inside."

"No, we can't. I just came here to tell you I need some space."

"Look, Eilidh ..." Cameron stepped outside, reaching for me, but I physically retreated. His expression darkened. "It seems fairly coincidental that your friend acted like a jealous arsehole today when I told him we were dating and now you need some space."

"Don't call Fyfe an arsehole," I defended him, even though he was being an arsehole. Only I was allowed to call Fyfe an

FOREVER THE HIGHLANDS 199

arsehole! "And you're missing the point. Cameron, I've known you a few weeks. We've been on a few dates. Calling me your girlfriend, staking a claim ... no. This is all going too fast for me. Sorry."

Something ugly clouded his expression. "You think you're so special you can have this discussion without caring how I feel about it? I mean, there's a way to tell a man you need space, and this is not it."

I huffed incredulously. "It is if he's lying to people about the status of our relationship. I've had enough people lie about who I am and what I'm doing and who I'm seeing. I don't need that bullshit from you. Forget the space, Cameron. This isn't happening, full stop."

As I turned to leave, I found myself hauled backward and spun, crashing into his chest as pain burned up my arm. He grasped my biceps so tightly and his face was a mask of fury. "Don't walk away from me!"

The shocking transformation from placid doctor to aggressor stunned me for a second.

Only for a second, though. "Get your fucking hand off me before I scream bloody murder."

Cameron released me just as quickly as he'd grabbed me, and I didn't wait around. I ran toward my SUV.

"We'll talk about this later, Eilidh!" he called after me. Calmly. "I'll call you tomorrow."

Holy crap. My entire body shook as I reversed out of his driveway and headed for home.

He had a screw loose.

Bloody hell, I knew how to pick them.

INSTEAD OF RETURNING TO THE ANNEX, I LET MYSELF into my parents' house. Dad's office was at the front and I noted him in there, working on a 3D digital model. He had his concentration face on and I knew if he was working late, it meant he was on deadline. With a sigh, I strolled into the open-plan living space and found it empty.

Muffled music drifted from downstairs and the sound of Lord Huron told me Mor was home. Lewis had given her a bunch of music to listen to, and it turns out she had more in common with his music tastes than mine.

Suspecting where I'd find my mum, I made two cups of chamomile tea to calm my nerves and wandered upstairs. After knocking on my parents' bedroom door, I heard Mum call "Come in."

Inside, I found her in bed on top of the duvet, a paperback in her hand and an empty mug of tea at her side.

She smiled affectionately, her dimples appearing. When I was a kid, I remember asking Santa for dimples like my mum's for Christmas. Obviously, that was disappointing Christmas morning. Until I saw the electric scooter wrapped in a big pink bow.

Handing Mum a fresh cup, I rounded the bed and got in beside her. She dropped her paperback to slide her arm around me, drawing me into her side.

"You okay?"

Instead of answering right away, I asked, "Why are you in here?"

"Mor is in a mood. Your dad is stressed. And I needed some space from them both. Now, what's up with you? You look a bit peaky."

With a heavy exhale, I spent the next twenty minutes telling her everything. About my relationship with Fyfe, confessing my love, his rejection, Cameron, what Fyfe told me this evening, and then Cameron's disturbing behavior.

"Before I say anything else, you need to tell your father about Cameron. And tell Uncle Mac and Walker." Uncle Mac

FOREVER THE HIGHLANDS

gave up his security job, but he used to be head of security at Uncle Lachlan's estate before Walker took over.

"I doubt he's dangerous."

"When people fixate on us, they're dangerous."

I turned to look at Mum's pretty face. Once upon a time, we'd all reaped the consequences of a man fixating on her. I nodded solemnly. "I'll tell Dad. And Uncle Mac and Walker."

"And Fyfe?"

"I don't even know where to start with Fyfe Moray. I mean, I'm right to be pissed off. Right?"

"Men are emotionally constipated sometimes." Mum grimaced. "Your dad made me so mad when we first started seeing each other. And he hurt me. Deeply."

I gaped at her in disbelief. "Dad hurt you?"

She nodded, looking down at her lap. "He loved me so much, but because of our age difference, he thought I couldn't possibly love him back the same way. That I'd grow bored with this 'simple' life in the Highlands and leave for an adventure elsewhere."

"Well, that's the most patronizing thing I've ever heard," I snapped, indignant on her behalf.

Mum chuckled. "I thought so too at the time. But when I realized how much he loved me, I knew it was just his insecurities talking. It was shocking to me that someone as intelligent and charismatic as your father couldn't see his own worth."

Oh my God.

"Are you telling me, I've fallen for a man like my dad?"

At my horrified tone, Mum's whole body shook with laughter.

I playfully smacked her shoulder. "Stop it."

When her laughter died off, she tucked a strand of hair behind my ear and offered quietly, "Think about it, Eilidh. Your birth mum cheated and it completely blindsided him. When someone betrays you in that way, we can't help but wonder why. Is the problem within ourselves? Are we good enough? Are we not lovable enough?"

My heart hurt at the thought of Dad ever believing that of himself, and even worse that my birth mother might have made him feel that way. Had I ever made Fyfe feel that way? No. No, I knew I hadn't. I'd always treated Fyfe like he was someone special to me.

"Fyfe's situation isn't a cheating wife. It was a mother who abandoned him, so I reckon that cut is even deeper."

"You don't think he just wants me because he's afraid to be alone with Millie?"

"No." Mum shook her head. "I think he's just no longer emotionally constipated. I think Millie showed him he's capable of being responsible for another human, capable of committing to someone. And maybe even worthy of love."

"That's what he said." I rested my head on her shoulder, aching so badly. "The thing is, his rejection was a brutal hit because I'm still trying to love myself, to be kinder to myself. Perhaps it was foolish to even try to love someone else while I'm still on that journey."

"Oh, darling, there is no trying or stopping when it comes to love. You just either do or you don't. It's not in our control, and it usually happens at the most inconvenient time."

"What do you think I should do?"

"I think ... you need to put you first. And if you need some time to untangle all your feelings, then you take that time. If Fyfe really does love you, he'll wait for you."

The bedroom door opened and Dad halted at the sight of me cuddled up next to Mum. His expression softened. "Everything okay in here?"

"Just girl talk." Mum kissed my forehead before I straightened.

"I can do girl talk." Dad climbed into the bed on my other

side, making me laugh. He drew me into his side and I cuddled against him, feeling like a wee girl.

It was kind of nice after the day I'd had.

"I'm in love with Fyfe," I blurted out.

Dad gave me a squeeze. "I know, Eilidh-Bug."

"But now he might love me back and I'm scared shitless."

He was silent for a few seconds and then he said, "Ach, then let him work for it. Can't make it too easy for him now, can you?"

Glancing up to find his cheeky grin, I chuckled. "I guess not."

"Oh, and tell him about Cameron," Mum added, tone concerned.

"I'll deal with it," Dad promised in his scary Dad voice once I'd told him about Cameron's reaction.

"How will you deal with it?"

"I'll have a perfectly civil conversation with him. And I might invite all your uncles to said conversation to remind the wee fucker that you have men in your life who can make him disappear, no questions asked, if he doesn't stay away from you."

I met Mum's gaze.

She just shrugged as if to say, "I'm with him."

A knock at the door had us looking up as Mor peeked her head in. "You're all in here?"

Mum patted the bed beside her and Mor bounded onto it like she was five. "Feeling better?" Mum asked, hugging her into her side and smoothing her hair back.

Mor wrapped an arm around Mum's stomach and melted into her with a nod.

"What are we, the Waltons?" Dad teased.

I snorted as my sister wrinkled her nose in confusion. "Who are the Waltons?"

Mum laughed and reached out to smooth a thumb over Dad's cheek. "Dude, you're so old."

Cackling and then apologizing in the face of Dad's mock hurt, I let my worries of the day melt away. I'd be fifty and married with my own kids, and still I knew my family could cure any ailment with just the reminder that they existed and that they loved me.

Twenty-Five
FYFE

Jared and Allegra McCulloch were the farmers who owned the land my home was built on. Since marrying, Allegra had encouraged Jared to be more entrepreneurial. They started with rental properties—glamping pods—and then branched out to the small development of architect-designed homes, including the one I lived in. Then they moved onto a few larger rental properties and now were renting out small cabins as office space. All while still running a working farm.

My home office was a no-go at the moment. It wasn't the sound of Millie that distracted me, it was my need to make sure she was all right any time she made a sound. I required an office away from home, and the McCullochs' small row of office pods were the perfect solution. The house was a mere ten minutes away in case Eilidh needed me.

This morning's handover had been awkward as fuck. Eilidh made it clear she still wasn't ready to talk about last night's discussion, so I gave her that. For now.

I had a shit ton of work on my plate to distract me. Eilidh had provided the dodgy creeps file, as she called it, and I'd forwarded it to a few employees whom I knew were good at research. It was a little outside their purview, but I was paying them overtime to get results quickly. One of the people looking at the files was Evan Willis. He was a security guard at Ardnoch Estate and we got to talking because he had serious computer skills.

First, I'd asked him if he'd like to take on some freelance stuff for my company, and then through that, I'd discovered Evan ran a tae kwon do class in Thurso and was looking for another instructor. He had been taking over my classes for me the past couple of weeks until I could figure out childcare for Millie.

On top of that, I had my regular clients to deal with and the new client who wanted their retailer system gone over with a fine-toothed comb. All the while I was researching nanny services (surprise, surprise, there weren't many options this far north), concluding that Millie would have to go into daycare. I called Regan, but it went to voicemail, so I left a message, asking if she had a space available to take Millie four days a week.

Vision blurred from looking at the screen for hours, I sat back and pushed my glasses up to rub my eyes. I alternated between the glasses and my contacts, especially on days I knew I'd be doing a lot of screen time. It had nothing to do with Eilidh telling me she liked my glasses.

Nothing whatsoever.

Standing to stretch, I picked up my phone and typed out a text to Eilidh, checking in to make sure Millie was good, and then saw Lewis had texted me five minutes ago to say he was on his way.

We were having lunch in my office pod because I needed to talk to him.

My phone buzzed in my hand. It was Eilidh.

FOREVER THE HIGHLANDS

> All good. Taking her for a stroll in the village.
> OK?

I sighed at her abruptness and texted back that it was fine.

Two seconds later, I heard a familiar engine. A large window faced out toward the fields, but the pod didn't have any windows elsewhere. Just a solid door entrance off the small driveway.

I opened the door just as Lewis swung a leg off his Harley-Davidson Fat Boy. He rode it any chance he could, considering he usually had to forsake the bike to drive his daughter in his SUV.

It was so bloody surreal to me that we both had baby daughters now.

That was not something I'd ever seen coming.

In a way, it was kind of all right, though, sharing that experience with my best mate.

Lewis pulled off his helmet and then reached into the saddle compartment and lifted out a cardboard box. "Lunch from Flora's," he announced. "Cakes from Callie."

My stomach grumbled at the thought. I rarely had treats because I believed my body was like a car and it needed the correct fuel to work. Even as exhausted as I was by broken sleep, I still worked out. I had a home gym in my third bedroom, and I'd set Millie up in her bouncy chair as she watched on curiously while I exercised. Sometimes she'd get agitated and bored so I'd have to stop and start, but I was determined not to lose that part of my routine. And treats ... they were something I only indulged in now and then.

"I shouldn't," I replied. "But I'm going to." Callie's desserts were to die for.

Lewis grinned, bounding up the steps and into the office pod. He looked around. The desk sat under the large picture window. There were a few shelves. Tons of plugs for electricals,

208   SAMANTHA YOUNG

USB ports, and a leather sofa on the back wall with a coffee table. "Hey, this is pretty decent."

"Aye, it's good, eh." I reached for the food. "I'm fucking starving."

We settled on the couch with the generous sandwiches and soup. Lewis had even brought coffee from Flora's.

Swallowing a bite of his chicken club, Lewis asked, "What did you want to talk about?"

Even though I knew from our previous conversation that Lewis would be cool, I still felt a surge of nerves. I met his questioning gaze. "I want to be with Eilidh."

Lewis raised an eyebrow and then sank back against the sofa, food forgotten. "Have you told Eilidh this?"

I nodded.

"And?"

"It didn't go down very well."

"Maybe because the timing is suspicious." Lewis took another bite with a casual shrug. Okay, I knew he'd be cool, but he was being very blasé about the whole thing. Too blasé. I waited for him to continue. He wiped his mouth with a napkin. "Millie comes along, your life totally changes, and Eilidh has stepped up to support you the most. Now you want to be with her? I could see how she might not believe you wanted *her* but a live-in nanny."

I scowled. "That's exactly what she fucking said and it pissed me off then too."

Her brother smirked. "Like I said, your timing is shit."

"You don't actually believe that's what I think?"

"No. Look, I've known you forever and you don't latch on to people for the wrong reasons." His expression turned wry. "Plus apparently, I've been in denial about you and Eilidh for a long time. Just ask Callie."

"How so?"

"Callie says she's known how you felt about Eilidh since

our wedding. She suspected before then, but she knew it for certain that night."

"Did she see us kiss?"

He choked on a swig of coffee, his eyes flashing. "You kissed my sister at my wedding?"

Well, fuck.

"It ... it just ... aye." I threw my hands up. "I kissed Eilidh at your wedding. And I kissed her months before that in London. Apparently, you were not alone in your denial!" I stood up, agitated as I began to pace. "Of course, it looks dodgy as fuck now that I can admit I want her. But I've wanted her for a long time ... Definitely since you came home to Ardnoch and she and I started talking again. If I'm honest with myself, maybe even before then. I just didn't think I could have her. That I deserved someone like Eilidh. That I could keep someone like Eilidh interested." There. I admitted it. Beneath the confidence I'd shrugged on like armor as a teen, I still felt like that geeky wee kid whose mother abandoned him.

"I can't believe you kissed my wee sister at my wedding," Lewis grumbled.

"Oh, would you get over it?" I ran a hand through my hair with an exasperated sigh. If I had my way, I'd be doing far worse than kissing her. Filthy, dirty, grown-up things that would make my best friend's head explode.

Lewis aggressively bit off another piece of sandwich, eyeing me as if he wished he were taking a lump out of me.

Sitting back down, I turned to him. "You know you're my family. That's why I want to be straight with you about this. I intend to pursue Eilidh. Romantically."

"And if I say I'm not actually comfortable anymore with the thought of you and Eilidh together?"

A sharp pain pierced between my sternum. "Ah, Lew, I hope that isn't true. I ... you're like a brother to me, but ... I've

210 SAMANTHA YOUNG

been so blind to how much I need Eilidh. The happiest time in my life were the months she and I started talking again. We talked every day. I looked forward to waking up because I knew there would be a text from her and that I'd get to talk to her on the phone or video chat with her in the evening. When that stopped ... I buried how much it hurt not having her in my life. It's not just that I want Eilidh. I *need* her. She's become essential."

"So you're going to go after her with or without my blessing?"

I nodded grimly. "I'm sorry."

Lewis smacked me on my back. Hard. "Don't be. That is the exact right answer."

I gaped at him. He had me in knots for nothing? Thinking I might lose my best mate over this. As a test? "You are an absolute fucker."

He grinned, his eyes flaring comically. "Oh, this is going to be fun."

Twenty-Six
EILIDH

Although all the treats were sold out by the time we got to Callie's Wee Cakery, Callie and Sloane ushered Millie and me into the back of the bakery where they had some malformed desserts that still tasted delicious.

Millie tried to grab Callie's take on a French Fancy out of my hands and grew pretty pissed off when she saw the entire thing disappear into my mouth.

Her wails filled the kitchen and Callie whipped off her apron and lifted Millie out of her stroller. "Oh, it's okay, sweetie. Take a wee walk with Aunt Callie. Hmm. When you're a bit older, you'll get to try a treat, eh? Aw, hush, baby." Callie bounced her gently as she paced up and down the kitchen. Millie's cries gentled. I wasn't surprised. Millie got over her grumbles if someone cuddled her.

"So, has Fyfe worked out permanent childcare?" Callie's mum, Sloane, asked as she wiped down the marble-topped prep counters.

He'd told me he was in the middle of trying to. I hadn't responded with anything but a grunt. After my talk with Mum, I understood him better. I maybe even believed he

212   SAMANTHA YOUNG

thought he truly wanted me, but I couldn't quite trust that. And I wasn't ready to talk to him about it just yet.

"There aren't a lot of people looking to take on full-time nanny positions in a remote Scottish village." I shrugged with more casualness than I felt. "I think Millie will end up at my mum's daycare."

"How does that make you feel?" Callie asked.

Millie was snuggled against her, but her big blue eyes were trained on me.

My heart squeezed. "I will miss the hell out of seeing her every day. But ... I suppose we need to get back to reality."

"So ... things between you and Fyfe?" Callie was wide-eyed with curiosity.

I glanced between her and Sloane, who had stopped cleaning to hear my answer.

"He got jealous over Cameron—who, by the way, giant red flag—and decided he wants me after all."

Sloane frowned. "Go back to the red flag."

I told them about Cameron and how Dad had more than likely already called all my uncles plus Walker to go scare him off.

"You didn't sleep with him, did you?" Callie grimaced.

"No, thank God. There were some orange flags. I thought it was Fyfe who was holding me back from sleeping with Cameron, but maybe it was my instincts."

"Great. So now we have a doctor with possible behavioral issues." Sloane grimaced too, looking so much like her daughter it was uncanny. "Just what Ardnoch needs."

"We'll figure that out later. For now, back to Fyfe." Callie brought Millie over because she was straining for me. I took her warm weight into my arms as she babbled. I nodded at her, smiling brightly so she'd smile back. At her baby giggle, I melted.

"Fyfe?" Callie insisted.

FOREVER THE HIGHLANDS 213

"I need some time." I bounced Millie on my knees and she giggled harder. "Don't I, Millie Billie? Auntie Eilidh needs some time to figure out if your daddy even knows what he really wants. Isn't that right?"

"Ae!" Millie clapped her hands. "Ae!"

I laughed softly but looked up to see Callie giving me a look.

"What?"

She sighed heavily. "Please don't waste time like I did."

"Don't even think about interfering like I did," I said, referring to the fact that I'd deliberately brought Lewis and Callie together at a party in London because I was convinced they were both still in love with each other. I was correct.

Callie shrugged nonchalantly. "Well, it would only be fair. And that worked out great, FYI."

"Callie ..."

"Fine." She threw her palms up. "Waste time dancing around each other instead of banging out your issues."

"Charming." Sloane threw her daughter a wry look.

Callie grinned unrepentantly. "What? Isn't your problem that you're worried Fyfe is only physically attracted to you and clinging to you because you've been such a help with Millie?"

"Stop reading my mind, woman."

"Sleep with him. You'll know after that if it was just an itch you both needed to scratch. Plus, you should have sex before you make any important relationship decisions. What if you're not compatible in the bedroom?"

"There's more to a relationship than sex," I tried to argue.

Callie and Sloane exchanged a look and Sloane offered quietly, "Of course there is. But sex is a big part of intimacy with a partner. If you don't have chemistry, things might get stale fast."

Shit.

I never even considered Fyfe and I might not click in the

214   SAMANTHA YOUNG

bedroom. Maybe because of that infamous sex dream in which he was a phenomenal lover. But that wasn't real. That was all in my head.

Oh my God.

Callie patted my shoulder. "Maybe something to think about."

AS SOON AS I PUSHED MILLIE'S STROLLER OUT OF the bakery, I spotted Cameron exiting Flora's with a to-go cup of coffee in hand. I ducked, veering a sharp left in the opposite direction.

"Eilidh!"

Shit.

Inwardly sighing, I glanced back and saw Cameron looking left and right before jogging across the street. His lanyard bounced against his stomach while his coffee valiantly held on.

That dread I'd felt yesterday during our altercation increased tenfold as he bestowed a white, charming smile on me.

"So glad I caught you before I return to work." He slowed to a stop, searching my face happily like we hadn't seen each other in years. His gaze dropped to Millie in the stroller. "She's so adorable. Out for a walk?"

I gaped at him.

Like ... what the actual fuck?

At my nonresponse, Cameron leaned in and pressed a kiss to my cheek.

I reared backward. "Whoa, okay."

He laughed softly. "Sorry. I, uh ... yeah, yesterday was odd. I thought we could just forget about it and start again. Why don't we go for dinner Saturday night?"

FOREVER THE HIGHLANDS 215

True concern crawled down my spine in an unpleasant shiver. "I think I made it clear yesterday, Cameron, that I'm not interested in pursuing a relationship with you. Any kind of relationship." I pushed the stroller to walk away, and he clamped his fist around the handle to stop me.

The warm, cordial doctor was gone. His expression was hard.

Seriously, he was like a real-life Jekyll & Hyde. I shivered again.

"You might want to rethink giving me another chance," he said quietly, a tinge of menace curdling his tone. "After all, I am Millicent's doctor. One call from me to social services and Fyfe loses his daughter."

He did not just ...

Rage clouded my mind.

He was attempting to blackmail me into dating him?

A cold laugh huffed from between my lips as I stared up at a man I'd thought attractive a mere week ago. Now I thought he was one of the scummiest things I'd ever laid eyes on. And I called him a *thing* because he was not a *man*. "You think you can threaten and blackmail me?"

"No one would dispute the word of a doctor." He shrugged, taking a casual sip of his coffee.

Chuckling at his naivete, I watched his face flush with rage. Oh, he didn't like a woman laughing at him. Safe in the knowledge there was nothing he could do to me in the middle of the street, I scoffed, "You have no idea who you're dealing with."

"A once-famous actor?" He guffawed.

Something snapped in me at that moment.

For years, I'd allowed my power to be taken from me. Allowed others, friends, strangers, to have power over me. Someone had planted a fucking camera in my home and watched me, had *stolen* power from me, and I didn't even know it.

And I was done.

"No. I'm an Adair. You think we're just a family with some money, a few businesses ... You'd be wrong. Our estate isn't some fluffy club for the rich and famous. There are powerful people in that club with connections that would blow your mind. And through them, my family has connections that reach the highest level of government. In multiple countries. One phone call and I could have your medical license stripped from you. Your car license revoked. Evicted. Credit score annihilated. In other words, *Dr. Phillips*, you mess with me, my family, or Fyfe, and I will fucking *ruin* you in every way that matters. You might have gotten away with threatening women in the past, but this time you chose the wrong one. Because I know my own power. And this part's really going to enrage you since you're a little, little man who clearly gets off on making women feel weak ... but I have so much more power than you, that wee threat you just made is a joke my family will be dining on for years to come."

He lunged toward me, teeth bared, like he might hit me.

"Do it," I hissed. "I dare you."

Cameron caught himself, his expression blanking. He glanced around to see if anyone was watching. Then he leaned in and vowed quietly, "This isn't over, you little bitch."

"You're right. It won't be over until you're out of Ardnoch."

"Problem here?"

I looked to my right to find Walker standing outside the bakery. He was parked in the no-parking zone, his piercing eyes fixed on Cameron. When he looked at me, whatever he saw on my face had him striding forward to stand at my back.

"Hi, Walker. Cameron, have you met my sister-in-law's father? Ex-Royal Marine Commando, head of security at the

Forever the Highlands

estate. Walker, I was just telling the new doctor here that maybe it's best he find a job elsewhere. As in not in Ardnoch or anywhere near us."

"Oh aye, your dad called me this morning. So this is the prick?"

"Excuse me?" Cameron straightened his shoulders, appearing affronted. "I don't know what she's told—"

"He just threatened to call social services on Fyfe so they'll take Millie from him unless I agreed to date him," I told Walker with a casualness I didn't feel.

The atmosphere instantly turned ice cold as Walker took a step toward Cameron, towering over him at six and a half feet. "Oh, I think it's definitely time you moved on from Ardnoch, Doctor. Or I might just have to investigate you. I'm sure there are a few skeletons in your closet just rattling to get out and destroy your life as you know it."

"I see threats are a common currency in this village." Cameron glowered.

"Uh, pot meet kettle."

His eyes narrowed on me. "You think I'm afraid of you? After this, you should be afraid of me, Eilidh. I don't take kindly to threats."

Walker stepped right into Cameron's space, not touching him, but his menacing expression was clear. "Neither do I. Don't even think about breathing in her direction because the next time you do ... by the time me, her father, and her uncles are done with you, there won't be a body to find."

This time Cameron was smart enough to show a little fear. Without another word or glance in my direction, he strode off.

Walker and I watched him until he'd turned the corner out of sight. Then Callie's dad looked at me, concern written all over him. "I'm tired of making that threat. Hopefully, that's the last time I have to. But I don't think *that* problem is over.

218 SAMANTHA YOUNG

Until me and your dad finish this, you go nowhere alone. I'll walk you and Millie back to your car."

"Do you think that's necessary?"

"Aye. I've dealt with enough abusive narcissists to recognize one when I see him."

"Bloody hell," I muttered under my breath as I turned the stroller toward the car park. "A few weeks. That's how long I've known the arsehole. How did it escalate to this?"

"With people like him, a fixation can happen almost instantly."

"Wonderful." I had a mystery stalker planting cameras in my old apartment and now a new one who wanted to make my life a misery because I had the audacity to say no to him. "You know, coming home was supposed to be about slowing down."

"This is Ardnoch. We were due a wee bit of danger," Walker replied dryly.

Twenty-Seven
FYFE

It had been a brutal night.

Millie had woken up wailing and when I went to check on her, I discovered she was roasting hot. When I took her temperature, it told me she had a fever. Of course, I went into panic mode and drove to the out-of-hours at the small hospital in Thurso. After waiting for an hour, they checked Millie over and found she had an ear infection. They assured me Millie was fine and that the ear infection would clear up on its own. We were only to see the doctor if she was still in pain after three days. They prescribed pain medicine and saw us on our way.

My daughter slept fitfully, waking up every few hours to cry. It broke my fucking heart. I'd never felt like such a failure in my life, not being able to stop her pain. Finally, I just ended up on the couch, the TV on low, while Millie slept on my chest. I drifted in and out until she woke me again to change her nappy.

At the crack of dawn, I gave her some formula, made myself a coffee, and settled back on the couch. Her fever had come down a little with the meds the docs gave us. Millie rested her chubby wee cheek against my bare chest and fell asleep.

I rubbed my eyes beneath my glasses, staring at the TV screen, feeling like I'd been awake for days instead of hours. Flicking through the apps, I switched over to a well-known streaming platform and the first thing advertised on it was *Young Adult*.

With everything up in the air between us, I hadn't been able to bring myself to watch the last season Eilidh starred in. Curiosity piqued, I switched on the show and turned the volume up just a bit. Eilidh's character Mikayla was the first on-screen.

My pulse picked up speed as I watched her. She was so the opposite of Mikayla that I marveled anyone would mistake her for her character. But she was a bloody great actor, and it made me sad for Eilidh that the joy of acting wasn't enough to outweigh all the other shit that came with the job. Even knowing it wasn't real, I still didn't like it when she shared an on-screen kiss with Jasper Richmond. They had the kind of chemistry that people had gossiped about for years, about if they were a couple in real life.

I saw that Jasper had trash-talked Eilidh lately, though. I wasn't sure if she was aware of it, but I wouldn't bring it up. She was trying to avoid all that rubbish. He was a prick for doing that to her.

"Ae," Millie said.

I looked down to find her eyes on the TV. "Is it Auntie Eilidh?"

She wriggled, and I helped her sit up so she could turn to look at the screen. She let out a sleepy giggle and pointed at the screen. "Ae!"

Holy crap, she *was* trying to say Eilidh's name.

Pride filled me. "That's right, wee yin. That's Auntie Eilidh."

Forever the Highlands 221

Unfortunately, the giggles turned to crying as Millie grew distraught when her Auntie Eilidh didn't come to her out of the TV screen. "Aw, hush, wee yin." I switched off the TV and brought her up to press kisses against her gorgeous chubby cheeks. "That's too confusing for you, eh, my wee darling."

Eventually, my attention soothed her and her crying stopped. She snuggled back on my chest and I felt her breaths slow as she fell asleep. I could feel baby drool on my pec and chuckled to myself.

Life had certainly taken a strange turn.

Looking down at Millie, seeing her long, dark lashes fluttering, her lips moving in a moue, I felt such overwhelming fucking love, it almost cracked me in two.

Aye, life had taken a strange turn. Even stranger ... I'd never been happier.

Twenty-Eight
EILIDH

This was deliberate.

It had to be.

A complete manipulation of my erogenous zones.

I let myself into Fyfe's house this morning, expecting him to be feeding Millie all the while trying to get ready for work, as per usual.

Instead, the house was eerily quiet and I realized why when I rounded Fyfe's large living room sofa to find him on it with Millie, looking like an ad to seduce women into getting pregnant!

Fyfe wore only his pajama trousers and his glasses. His thick hair was tousled and his head lolled back on the sofa as he slept. He didn't snore, though Millie did, gently, her cheek smooshed to his chest. His naked, sculpted man chest.

I was instantly aroused in every way a woman could be aroused. Physically, emotionally, mentally.

How fucking dare he?

Even in my indignation, I had the presence of mind to pull out my phone to take a photo of hot father and sweet child.

"Hullo, new phone wallpaper," I muttered, tapping my screen to do just that. I slipped the phone into my back pocket just as Fyfe blinked sleepily behind his sexy black-framed glasses. I found myself drowning in his warm, dark eyes. "Eils?"

"What happened?" I whispered, my words a wee bit more clipped than usual. He'd totally thrown me with this. It wasn't just that he was hot and I was attracted to him. Fyfe was reminding me that he was a good man. A great father who'd shown in just a few short weeks that he'd fallen in love with his daughter.

I didn't think my heart was ready for that reminder.

He groaned, holding tight to Millie as he sat up. She made grumbly noises but didn't wake. "What time is it?"

"Eight o'clock."

"Oh, bloody hell. I'm late."

"Let me take her."

He nodded and gently eased her off his chest and into my arms. Millie stirred with the transfer but didn't fully awaken. That wasn't like her. Worried, I pressed a kiss to her forehead. She was a little warm.

"She has an ear infection." Fyfe scrubbed his hands over his face, rubbing his eyes beneath his glasses. "Took her to Thurso earlier this morning. They said it'll clear up on its own, but if it doesn't by day three, to bring her back to the docs."

"My poor Millie Billie," I whispered, kissing her again before I gently set her in her cot. She remained deep in sleep. By the looks of things, neither she nor her father had much rest last night.

I turned to Fyfe and whatever I was about to say tumbled right off my tongue.

He stood, stretching, and I attempted not to drool. The tartan pajama trousers he wore had slipped low so I could see the fantastic V-cut of his hips. My gaze devoured every inch of naked skin on display. The taut six-pack, the sculpted chest, the broad shoulders, and just thick enough biceps. He was ludicrously physically perfect.

A throat cleared.

My eyes flew to his.

And then there were his glasses. He'd been wearing them more often lately. Taunting me with that whole hot, genius lost boy vibe I'd fallen for as a teen.

Fyfe wore a far too sexy smirk. "Are you done ogling me?"

I crossed my arms over my chest. "You did this deliberately."

"What?"

I waved at his half-naked gloriousness. "That! The no shirt, glasses on, cute baby sprawled on your man chest."

Fyfe let out a low chuckle. "It wasn't deliberate. But I like how flustered you are right now."

"I'm not flustered."

He cocked his head in contemplation, a certain heat entering his eyes. "Are you turned on?"

Yes! So, so turned on! "Pfft! We're not talking about that stuff in front of Millie."

Fyfe swaggered over to me and I stumbled back against the cot. To my surprise, he cupped my face in his hands and bent his head to mine. I thought he was going to kiss me. But his lips hovered just above mine as he searched my eyes. "Eilidh Adair, if I wasn't so bloody tired right now, I'd throw you over my shoulder and take you upstairs so we could do more than just talk about that stuff."

My lower belly squeezed. Callie's words from yesterday came back to me. "Maybe, when you're not so tired, I'll allow that."

His nostrils flared. "Really?"

I pressed a palm against his naked chest, my fingers flexing against the feel of him. "It would be casual, though."

FOREVER THE HIGHLANDS 225

Fyfe instantly dropped his hand and retreated, his expression shuttered. "Casual?"

"I've been thinking ... before either of us can decide what we want from the other, we should make sure we're sexually compatible."

"We *are* sexually compatible," he bit out angrily.

"You don't know that."

"I fucking do."

"Millie," I hissed, turning to make sure he hadn't woken her up.

"Eilidh ..." Fyfe's jaw clenched as he gritted out, "I am not having casual sex with you."

"Then we're at an impasse because I'm not getting into a relationship with you until we see how physically compatible we are."

He stepped back into my space, bristling in a way that had my blood pumping. His voice was rough like gravel as he declared, "I am going to kiss, lick, suck, and fuck every inch of you, Eilidh, until you come in my mouth, on my face, around my fingers, and all over my cock. And I'm going to have all that from you knowing I have your body as well as your soul. No compromises."

His declaration along with the remembrance of that dream I'd had caused wet heat to pool between my thighs.

Wow.

Okay.

I had never been more aroused in my whole life.

Fyfe ducked his head toward mine. "Can you speak?"

"No!" I shoved his chest, sliding past him. "I'm all ..." I gestured down my body.

He faced me slowly, grinning that cocky grin. "Are you wet, sweetheart?"

"Not in front of the baby."

His eyes dropped to my chest and darkened. "Your nipples are hard. I can't wait to taste them."

Literally, it was like he'd taken my breast in his mouth, his words had such an effect on my body.

I flapped air at my face, trying to cool down, somewhat panicked by the way he'd taken control of this conversation.

He chuckled. A dart down his body told me he was not unaffected by his filthy words or my reaction.

"If you say one more dirty thing to me, Fyfe Moray, I can promise you that the appendage tenting those pajamas right now will get nowhere near me. Ever."

He considered this. "But you'll want me to say dirty things to you in the future, right?"

I made a scoffing sound. "You know ... well ...I mean ..."

"I'll take that as a yes."

"Casual only," I warned him.

"Nope. Not happening."

"You're that convinced we're compatible? All in or nothing?"

"Eilidh, we're standing in my living room, I'm hard, you're wet, and we haven't even touched each other. I'm pretty sure when we have sex, it'll blow our fucking minds."

He was determined to turn me into a horny puddle of goo on his living room floor. I spluttered, unable to form a witty comeback. The bastard. No one had ever flustered me so much they'd stolen my ability to banter!

"Are we in agreement?"

"No," I huffed.

"Eilidh—"

"I'm not ready for the other stuff." My shoulders slumped with despondence. "I'm sorry."

Fyfe barely hid his flinch before he turned from me. He strolled to Millie's cot to look in on her. "I need to get ready for work."

FOREVER THE HIGHLANDS 227

My heart hurting, my mind reeling from the abrupt change in atmosphere between us, I offered quietly, "Why don't you get some sleep?"

"I have a couple of meetings I can't miss."

"Okay." My voice sounded small even to my ears. I was so confused.

Fyfe seemed to sense it. His smile didn't quite reach his eyes, but I knew it was meant to reassure me. "Can you watch her while I get ready?"

"That's ... that's why I'm here." Thoughts of yesterday flitted back. I hadn't mentioned it to Fyfe last night because I didn't want to add to his stress, but I'd realized afterward that he deserved to know. Cameron threatened his relationship with Millie, after all. "Something happened yesterday that we need to discuss. We'll talk after you get dressed."

"Let's talk now."

"I, uh, kind of need you to not be half-naked anymore."

There was that smug smirk again. Fyfe nodded, crossing the room toward the stairwell, which meant passing me. "Your obsession with my body bodes well for me."

"Fuck you," I replied without heat.

"No." He stopped to bend his lips to my ear. "Fuck you, baby. When you agree to be mine, I'm going to fuck you so hard, you'll see heaven."

It took everything within me not to climb him like a goddamn tree.

Fyfe abruptly drew away, walking toward the stairs.

I turned on him. "Well, I'm ... that's ..."

He grinned over his shoulder at me as he climbed. "That's ...?"

"Just you wait." I shook a finger at him. "When you get back down here, I will have a comeback ready and I will skewer you with my wit."

"I'd rather I skewered you with my cock, but okay."

228   SAMANTHA YOUNG

"Uh! That's sounds painful, not sexy." And yet my body thought it sounded hot.

"Oh, it'd be sexy," he called, even as he disappeared out of sight. "Everything I do to you will be sexy, baby, I assure you."

"Stop calling me baby!"

Millie broke into cries.

"Thanks for waking mine!" he yelled back down.

"You started it," I bit out between clenched teeth, hurrying over to the cot. "With your filthy innuendo and dirty talk." Reaching down, I picked Millie up and smelled the poop. "Aw, Millie, it's okay. Auntie Eilidh's here. Let's get your nappy changed. I hope you didn't hear any of that naughty stuff your daddy said or I will skewer him with more than my wit."

TWENTY-NINE
FYFE

"I'm going to kill him." I strode toward my car keys, entire body bristling with unspent fury.

Eilidh had informed me about her altercations with Cameron Phillips.

And now he was a dead man.

"No." Eilidh dove in front of me, arms and legs comically splayed like she was trying to stop a ball from going into a goal.

Millie giggled from her playpen, like she thought we were playing.

First, I'd awoken to find the woman of my dreams standing over me and Millie, only for her to announce she wanted casual sex. Even though I understood she was protecting herself and that I deserved it, the more I thought about it, the angrier I got.

Because that's all sex had ever been to Eilidh as far as I could tell. It's all it had ever been to me.

But buried in my deepest fantasies, I knew one of the reasons I'd vowed not to give into my attraction to Eilidh was because I knew it could *never* be casual between us. It would always mean more.

It pissed me off she ever thought it could be that unremarkable between us.

And now this.

That prick of a doctor using my relationship with my child to blackmail Eilidh into dating him?

Aye, he was so fucking dead, he was a ghost already and didn't know it.

"Out of my way."

"No." Eilidh straightened, a mulish look on her gorgeous face. "I put Cameron in his place. Walker was there, and he rallied my dad and uncles last night, and they all paid the good doctor a visit that almost got them arrested."

"How so?" A flash of spiteful pleasure rushed through me at the thought of the Adair men putting the fear of death in Dr. Dick.

"Cameron made a complaint with the police."

"Fuck."

"It's fine." She waved a hand. "Uncle Lachlan took care of it. Anyway, Uncle Lachlan also informed Dr. Mulligan that the new doctor in his practice is harassing and threatening me, and considering Cameron's contract is for a trial period only, he's fired, and it's all legal. Dr. Mulligan just told him this morning that he wasn't the right fit and they no longer required him. There's nothing Cameron can do about it. Uncle Lachlan texted me while you were in the shower to let me know. Cameron's pretty much dealt with."

Although I was relieved he'd lost his job, I wasn't entirely convinced. "You got him fired and you think he's not going to be pissed off about that?"

"Until he's moved out of the village, I promised my dad and Walker that I wouldn't go anywhere alone."

Annoyance flushed through me. "You came here alone."

"I left the safety of my parents' house and drove to the

Forever the Highlands 231

safety of your house." She shook her head. "I think they just mean while I'm out and about."

"Well, I'm not leaving you here alone."

"Don't you have the best home security system ever?"

I glowered at her dry tone. "Not the point."

"It's very much the point. I'm literally safest in your house. You have panic buttons downstairs *and* upstairs, for goodness' sake."

Rationally, I knew she was correct. I had the kind of security system I didn't actually require, but since it cost me half the price it would cost someone else, I went all out with it. Once that alarm system was on, no one got past it. And whether someone broke in or Eilidh hit a panic button, the security team at Ardnoch (and me) would be alerted immediately to an intruder and my office was ten minutes away. Ardnoch Estate wasn't much farther. "Fine. But, Eilidh, if that bastard comes near you again, I am going to kill him."

"Get in line."

"I mean it."

Her expression gentled. "I know."

Sighing, I grabbed my car keys and strolled over to kiss Millie on the head. She seemed to be doing a lot better this morning, so I hoped her infection was already clearing up. "I'll see you soon, wee yin. Daddy loves you." The words slipped out without thought, and I froze for a second over her pen.

I glanced back at Eilidh and she was smiling, tears bright in her eyes.

There was that overwhelming sensation inside me again, so big, so expanding, it was terrifying.

Millie's babbling brought my head back down. "Daddy loves you, Mills," I repeated intentionally as I stroked my hand over her hair. She beamed up at me, her new teeth making her gummy smile so fucking cute, it killed me.

Swallowing hard, I forced myself away from the pen and strode toward the front door. I stopped at Eilidh's side first.

My heart bloody well ached at the look in Eilidh's eyes. They were filled with hero worship, something she hadn't given me in years. Christ, I'd forgotten how much that look made me feel ten feet tall. And I hadn't realized how much it hurt to have her not look at me like that anymore.

I'd taken so much of Eilidh for granted.

If she'd let me, I'd spend a lifetime making it up to her.

"When I get back, we need to talk about earlier. I won't do casual with you, Eilidh. But I won't let you go without a fight either."

There was a sexual playfulness to this morning's encounter.

It was doused now with abject emotion.

Fear shadowed her features. "I can only offer you casual."

"I can't. I won't."

"That's what I need." She shrugged sadly. "I need time to trust. To take things super slow, no promises, no commitments. Time to know that what's between us is more than you needing a partner, needing a mum for Millie. Because that won't last, Fyfe. Eventually, you'll wake up one day and realize you settled."

I gaped at her, stunned that she could ever think that. "It boggles my mind that you could imagine a man would ever be settling for you. Don't you know how spectacular you are, Eilidh Adair?"

Tears brightened her eyes.

I bent my head to look deep in them. I wanted her to *feel* my sincerity. "I would never start something with you and then abandon you."

"I know. You would never abandon anyone once you committed to them. I don't want someone who'll stay with me out of obligation and a sense of honor. I know that's what

FOREVER THE HIGHLANDS 233

you'd do. I want a man who *wants* to be with me for the rest of his life."

Jesus, she still wasn't getting it. I opened my arms. "Then look no further because here he stands."

She sucked in a breath. "You don't mean that."

"I am not having this conversation with you while I'm rushing out to work. In fact, I'm not having this conversation, period. You will never believe words. You need action. That action starts tonight." I nodded, decided, and strode toward the front door.

"What does that mean?"

I just shot her a cheeky grin over my shoulder and walked out.

"What does that mean, Fyfe Moray!" she yelled as I shut the door behind me.

Thirty
Fyfe

My stomach knotted as I stared at the screen in front of me. Walker leaned back in his desk chair, waiting grimly for my response.

"Do you think he came here to target her?" I straightened.

The information was everything Walker's contacts had dug up on Dr. Cameron Phillips. It seemed he had a history of harassing female colleagues. He'd worked in several general practices around the country in his short career. A little digging uncovered formal complaints in the last two practices (from a female doctor at the previous and a receptionist at the one before that).

It seemed Dr. Dick tended to fixate on a woman. These women had stated in their reports that they had only been dating a few weeks when Dr. Dick became possessive, aggressive, and threatening. When they tried to end things, he turned up at their homes, he called them at all hours of the night, he cornered them at work, and he'd followed them when they were out in public. There were police records for both women, but there was little the police could do unless he physically assaulted them.

FOREVER THE HIGHLANDS 235

The cherry on top was that he'd been engaged to a woman while cheating on her and stalking other women. It appeared the engagement ended when the police got involved.

Dr. Dick hadn't done anything violent yet. He seemed to move on to the next woman before it got that far. However, men like that ... it was usually only a matter of time before they crossed that line.

Eilidh's arse was out there as someone with a public presence. She knew that this kind of behavior from strangers was common toward famous people. But she'd come home to distance herself from her public persona. To start over.

And the first fucking guy she encountered was a stalker.

"You couldn't write this shit." I scrubbed a hand over my face. "We need to get him out of Ardnoch now. Leave no options open to him to be anywhere near Eilidh."

"Blacklist him." Walker nodded. "Lachlan's on it. Gordon owns the house the arsehole is renting." Gordon was an elderly, semiretired businessman who still owned some property in the village. "They've found a loophole in the rental agreement so Gordon's serving an eviction notice today. Unfortunately, it gives the prick a week to find accommodation elsewhere."

"But he won't find it here?"

"Lachlan's put the word out. No one will rent him a property. Arran knows not to let him stay at the Gloaming. From here to Wick, he'll be persona non grata. If he repeats his usual pattern, he'll give up and move on."

The knot in my stomach didn't loosen. It wouldn't until I had confirmation Dr. Dick was far, far away from Eils.

There was a knock on Walker's door and Evan Willis stepped inside. He looked as if he hadn't slept for days—pale, unshaven, dark circles under his eyes.

"Problem?" Walker asked.

"I heard Fyfe was here." Evan nodded at me. "Need a

word."

"You look like shit. Are you okay?"

He scrubbed a hand over his cheeks. "I've been shouldering your classes and this research. Not had much sleep."

Guilt shifted through me. "I'll be back to running my classes as soon as I can get childcare."

"Don't worry about it, mate. You've got bigger worries than that."

Alert, I stiffened. "Whatever you've found, you can say in front of Walker. Eilidh told him about the cameras."

Evan strode into the room. "Well, you owe me big-time for the deep dive I had to take to find this bastard. There are some sick perverts out there."

"I'll pay you a massive bonus if you just get to the point."

He nodded. "In the files, there are emails from the same person. Loads of emails. Coming in to Eilidh's agency addressed to her twice a week at least."

It was sickening to even imagine someone being that obsessed with Eilidh.

"Usual creepy stalkery emails about how they were meant to be. He talked a lot about watching her. Anyone would assume he was talking about her TV show, movies, right?"

"But he wasn't talking about that."

Evan shook his head. "While a lot of the stuff is ... sexual ... sorry—"

I waved off his apology, even though the very thought of someone getting off on watching Eilidh made me want to start snapping necks.

"—they were also more intimate comments. Like how he loved the way emotions played over her face when she was reading a book."

"How would he know that from watching her on television?" Walker asked coldly.

"Exactly. So I scoured through all the emails. Now,

without seeing Eilidh's flat, I don't know for sure if details match, but he talks about watching her lying naked in her bedsheets with the birds printed all over them. How he liked that she kissed her family's photograph before bed every night. There are loads of wee details that her team missed."

My chin jerked back. When I'd been in Eilidh's apartment, I'd seen into her bedroom. She had a bedspread with hummingbirds printed on it. She had a few framed family photographs on a sideboard outside her bedroom too. "It was him. She has bedsheets like that. He planted the cameras. Who is it?"

"Well, Eilidh's security did look into it and tried to trace him through his email, but he'd set up a dummy IP address. I sent it to Lore to see if she could trace him."

Lore was on my payroll and one of the best hackers in the country.

"But while she was working on that, I thought I'd try to find him using his sign-off. Most of these letters and emails Eilidh received have no sign-off. Completely anonymous. But this fucker couldn't help himself. He signed off the email *Domini*. And that word and a sequence of letters and numbers were used in the dummy email address."

"And?"

"Domini means *master* in Latin. And after a search on the dark web, I found the same word and sequence of letters and numbers as a username in several chatrooms. A few were BDSM chatrooms. The other ... well, it's a chatroom where people share their fantasies about what they'd like to do to the people they stalk. We're not just talking rape fantasies, but violence, murder ..."

"What the fuck?" I felt ill.

Evan nodded grimly. "I will never be able to bleach some of that shit out of my head. Ever."

I winced on his behalf.

"And Lore will want a big fat bonus because I had to send her into the chat to trace the fucker from there."

"Who is it?" Walker asked impatiently.

Evan shook his head, expression apologetic. "His name is Peter Pryor."

"That doesn't ring a bell."

"Eilidh's landlord in London. The pervert planted the cameras himself."

My mind raced in horror at the thought of that bastard watching Eilidh. For ages. For maybe as long as she'd lived in the apartment. I wanted him in front of me so I could eviscerate him.

"A quick look into records shows that it wasn't the landlord who ordered the annual smoke alarm check. The smoke alarms were fritzing and the new tenant, for whatever reason, had an outside company come in to check the alarms. *They* found the cameras. Peter was just covering his arse calling Eilidh to let her know."

"And you know this for a fact?"

Evan sighed. "Lore hacked his computer. Lots of disturbing stuff on there. We didn't make a move, but if you're happy to, we'll hand over what we found to the police."

"Do you know ... are the recordings of Eilidh on there?"

My friend's features tightened with anger. "Aye, they're on there. Lore says organized by ... activity."

My hands curled into fists as Walker bit out an angry curse.

Before I could respond or think past the black wrath in my mind, my phone let out a very specific alarm.

No.

A chill slithered down my spine.

"Fuck!" I yanked my phone out of my pocket, the security app open and flashing the alert. Blood rushed in my ears. "Someone just broke into my house."

THIRTY-ONE
EILIDH

To my relief, it seemed Millie was already over her earache. There was some grouchiness when Fyfe left for work, but it didn't last long. I fed her a bit of fruit while I ate my breakfast, and since we were stuck in the house, I let Millie crawl for a while. She liked to be on the go, so I cleared the way for her to explore a little. To my delight, she kept pulling herself up to standing, grabbing onto the couch or my legs. I'd taken her hand and steadied her as she attempted to walk.

Tears burned in my eyes and I wondered if she'd done this for Fyfe yet or if I was witnessing her first attempt at walking.

I couldn't wait to tell him.

It was around lunchtime, Millie was down for a nap, and I was making a snack. The TV was on low in the background with a rom-com playing on a streaming app. So okay, yes, I couldn't get Fyfe's words from this morning out of my mind and I was fluttery with nerves and anticipation for his return, and totally confused about ... everything.

However, other than that, the moment was calm. My life

felt beautifully ordinary and sweet and safe, and it made me happier than any time I'd spent on the set of the show.

I was just thinking how I knew for certain I'd made the right decision walking away from acting when the doorbell rang.

The hair on my neck rose. Attempting to tell myself my reaction was based on Cameron's behavior and nothing else, I tapped on the wall-mounted security panel before the entrance hall. It was connected to the camera outside.

What the ... It was Peter. My landlord.

I hadn't had many dealings with Peter in person. I reckoned he was in his early forties. Kind of nondescript, dressed casually but drove a flashy car. I remembered seeing him pull away from the apartment building in an Aston Martin Vantage. A neighbor had told me Peter owned a ton of real estate and was super well off. He'd always been kind and amiable to me. Though I'd heard he was ruthless when it came to rent. He didn't give people many chances. You didn't pay your rent on time, you were out.

I always paid my rent on time so we never had issues. If there was a maintenance problem with the flat, he'd come to speak to me about it directly if I was home, but that was it.

What the hell was he doing here? And at Fyfe's?

That instinct that had risen the hair on the back of my neck had me pressing the speaker button on the security system instead of opening the door.

"Peter? It's Eilidh. What are you doing here?"

"Eilidh, luv, thank goodness I found you. We got a big problem. Didn't want to take the chance calling you in case my phone was tapped. I know who's been watching you. Can you let me in?"

My heart thumped hard. "How ... how did you know where to find me?"

FOREVER THE HIGHLANDS 241

"I was round your mum's. Explained everything. She told me where to find you."

Mum hadn't called to warn me. And Mum wasn't home today. She was at the daycare.

Finger trembling, I pressed down the speaker button again. "I'm sorry, Peter. I'm going to have to ask you to leave. Why don't I meet you at the Gloaming this evening at five o'clock with Fyfe?"

"We don't have time for that, luv. We're both in real fucking danger here." I could hear the edge in his voice. "Please let me in to explain."

"I'm sorry. I can't."

I released the speaker button and stepped back to stare at the door. There were frosted glass panels on either side, and I saw the shadow of his movement. I couldn't hear anything over the rush of blood in my ears.

I think my body knew before my mind had even caught up.

I'd just turned in search of my phone when a noise blasted through the house. A shattering so loud, it startled Millie out of sleep. Her wails echoed off the walls.

Gasping in fright, I spun toward the front door and saw glass shards from one of the side panels shattered all over the floor. There were pieces at my feet and as my hair fell over my shoulder, I saw tiny shards glisten on the strands.

Pete knocked away bits of glass still stuck to the frame and then squeezed his tall body in through the gap. His once bland, unassuming expression was contorted with furious determination. His dark eyes gleamed with hunger as they dragged down my body and back up again.

"I've missed you, luv."

Millie's cries tugged me toward her, but as I took a step in her direction, Pete warned, "Go near that baby, and I'll kill her."

I froze in horror, gaping at him, trying to make sense of the bizarre turn of events. It was like I'd been drugged and was in the middle of a frightening hallucination. It didn't seem real. "What's going on?"

His expression switched so quickly, it was unnerving. Menace melted to pleading. "I tried to forget you, Eilidh. Once you were gone. I tried so hard that I was stupid enough not to remove the cameras." He took a step toward me as sick realization dawned. "I loved watching you." He spoke calmly, like he wasn't admitting to violating my privacy. "I've loved watching you from the moment you walked into my life. For years, it was enough just to watch."

Oh my god, oh my god, oh my god. Limbs trembling, I took a shaky step back toward the kitchen.

For years, this man whom I'd only known as my landlord, whom I'd never suspected of creeping on me, had violated my privacy every day.

"We have to move quickly." Still, he spoke as if we were talking of everyday things. "I've been watching for days, and I know this house is rigged with a security system that will have alerted the kid's father. We need to leave now."

"If you think I'm going anywhere with you, you sick fucking bastard, you have another thing coming." Because something had flipped in him. Whatever had been holding him back before (probably the access to seeing me whenever he wanted), it no longer existed. And if I let him take me, I wouldn't walk away from the situation.

I knew it deep in my bones.

He seemed shocked by my denial. "You belong to me. Even when you let those other men into your bed like a dirty little slut, you always belonged to me. I'm not waiting anymore."

I glanced at Millie whose cries had decreased to whimpers. She needed me and this bastard was standing in my way. "I will never belong to you. Try to do what you want to me, but do it knowing you will never have me in any way that's real. You spied on me! Violated me!"

"No." He shook his head, a madness glinting in his eyes. "I did it because I loved you. I wanted to protect you. You ... You don't understand." He scowled. "You don't understand because no one has ever loved you properly until now."

Rage simmered with my fear. "That's where you're wrong."

Peter rushed me before I could react. He wasn't overly built, but he was six foot and broad-shouldered. When he threw back his arm and swung it out, his fist clipping my cheek, I had no chance to react or block it.

Pain exploded across my face and knees. Ringing filled my ears, and it took a second for a sense of reality to return. Cheekbone and eye throbbing, I looked up from where I was now sprawled on the floor.

Peter glared down at me. "Now get the fuck up and leave with me." He strode to Millie's cot and I cried out, scrambling to my feet. The room spun a little as Pete stood over Fyfe's daughter. "If you don't agree to leave right now, I'll squeeze the life out of the little girl."

I wasn't afraid for myself. Only the need to protect Millie filled my brain with a buzzing sound. Like something had taken over me, I heard the unfamiliar shriek of fury leave my mouth as I ran at Pete. He wasn't expecting the attack and so when I reached him, arm swung up, he didn't block me as I raked my nails down his face and then dug them into his shoulders. With all my might, I hauled him away from Millie's cot and tried to hit him in the balls with my knee.

But he was too big and strong. We grappled and I managed to wriggle free, turning toward the kitchen for a weapon. He grabbed handfuls of my hair and pain screamed up my scalp, my knees giving way. A hard shove brought me crashing down, my chin jarring off the floor. Pain ricocheted through my head, but I fought through it as Pete's hands tugged and clawed at me. With another roar of outrage, I had just enough strength to turn around.

It was a stupid decision.

The man grew a thousand arms and legs and I found myself pinned beneath his heavy body. He smelled of a spicy aftershave I knew I'd never be able to smell again without feeling sick to my stomach. Flashbacks from childhood blurred before me. Of the man who had hurt Ery and tied me and Lewis up in the annex. Not again. I wouldn't be powerless like that again!

"You shouldn't fight me, luv." Pete slammed my wrists against the floor and tears of pain pooled in the corners of my eyes.

How many times had Lewis and Callie asked me to train with them over the years? To learn how to defend myself. Aunt Robyn had attempted to show me self-defense maneuvers too. I'd never been interested.

This man, this stranger, peering down at me with a mad light in his eyes, was going to win because I wasn't physically strong enough to fight.

No.

No!

He wasn't going to win.

Not powerless.

This bastard had had enough of me.

"No!" I shrieked in his face, making him flinch. Then I bucked and strained and snapped at him with my teeth like an animal. Pete released my wrists to smack me hard across the face again. I'd expected it, I'd wanted it. All so he'd release my hands.

I gritted my teeth against the pain and disorientation, but with my hands freed, I fought my revulsion as I grabbed the appendage between his legs and twisted with all my might.

His bellow of pain shuddered through the house and I clambered out from under him, crawling toward the kitchen.

I was halfway there, his shouts of fury and retribution making me curse my jelly-like limbs. Everything had morphed into agonizing slow motion. The kitchen seemed so far away. Millie's wailing was like a knife twisting in my heart. She must be so afraid.

Keep moving, keep moving.

A hand clamped around my ankle.

No!

Then a masculine bellow of outrage drew my head toward the entrance.

Relief crashed over me at the men hurrying toward us, and I was sobbing before Fyfe had even reached me.

Walker was at his side, his gun clasped with both hands. Fyfe seemed ready to launch himself at me.

But Walker's authoritative voice halted everyone. "Release her or I will shoot you."

I glanced over my shoulder. Pete released my ankle, and I was just about to sag into the floor when he stuck his hand into his inner jacket pocket and pulled out a switchblade. I sucked in a breath, cold shuddering through me as Pete raised his arms, eyes blazing down at me.

A shot rang through the air and Pete jerked. Another shot had the knife slipping from his hand. His mouth gaped open in shock as his entire body fell back onto the hardwood with a dull thud.

"Eilidh!" Fyfe moved toward me.

"Millie!" I cried, gesturing wildly toward her. "Millie first."

Fyfe's face paled. "Did he ...?"

"No. But she's scared."

His hesitance to leave me was obvious.

Walker strode to me, kicking the knife out of Pete's reach. I could hear his gargled breathing, but I didn't want to look at him. Walker stood over him, putting his body between us. "I've got Eilidh. You see to your daughter."

The muscle in Fyfe's jaw clenched, but he hurried over to the cot. I watched him cradle Millie in his arms. Black dots started creeping in on the edge of my vision. "Walk," I mumbled.

"Eilidh, are you okay?"

"Just ... just warning you ... I'm about to pass ..." The darkness drew me in before I could even remember what it was I'd tried to tell him.

Thirty-Two
EILIDH

Everyone was afraid to let me out of their sight.

Feeling guilty for putting them through this, I'd fought my exhaustion as we crowded together in my parents' living room.

But now it was almost midnight. Only my parents, Fyfe, Millie, and Mor lingered. Mor should be in bed, but instead she was cuddled into my side like a little girl. We lay back on the couch, feet up on the chaise, my arm around her as she snuggled against me. I stroked my wee sister's hair in reassurance as our family milled around us.

My aunts and uncles had taken turns popping in to visit after I returned from a quick trip to the emergency room. I'd lost consciousness mostly from shock, though I did have a few bumps and bruises. My chin was swollen and bruised, along with my right eye and cheek. Mum kept bringing over a fresh ice pack to put on my eye until I waved her off, needing a break from the chill of it pressed to my skin.

The adrenaline coursing through my body had dulled the pain. It was only now, hours after the altercation, that the throbbing made itself known. I could feel Fyfe's eyes on me the whole evening, but I couldn't bring myself to look at him. He and Millie were staying at my parents' tonight. I'd given them the annex. Millie was sleeping in a travel cot beside him while my family spoke in hushed tones. Lewis and Callie had reluctantly left a few hours ago to put Harley to bed. My aunts and uncles had slowly departed after that.

Mum and Dad were freaked out and attempting not to show how freaked out they were. I knew one of the reasons they'd secretly hated my career choice was because of the fame. Of the scrutiny it would bring. Of the strange folks who might fixate on me.

Their worst fear had come true.

Mine too.

Peter Pryor had hidden the darkness in him until he no longer could. He was under police supervision while he recovered from his two gunshot wounds (one in each shoulder). The police here coordinated with the Met Police in London. His attack on me was enough to get a hastily processed warrant, and they'd recovered his computer from his home this evening. Fyfe assured my family there was enough evidence on it to put Peter Pryor away for a long time. I despised the fact that there were strangers in the police department combing through recordings of me in my most private moments. And I dreaded the upcoming court case and the media frenzy it would cause.

Yet there was relief in knowing who was behind the violation. Relief in knowing he couldn't hurt me again.

"I think Eilidh needs rest," Fyfe said.

I still couldn't look at him.

"Of course."

"Will you sleep in my bed, Eils?" Mor asked quietly.

I also hated that this darkness I'd attracted had leaked into my family, affecting them too. "Aye," I promised. I pushed to my feet and Morwenna came with me. Kissing my mum and

FOREVER THE HIGHLANDS

dad, I waved in Fyfe's direction without meeting his gaze and called good night to everyone.

Mor's bedroom was a bookworm's dream. Mor and Allegra McCulloch had painted a mural of a misty forest on the wall where Mor's bed was placed. The largest wall in the room was filled with floor-to-ceiling custom shelves, stacked to the brim with books. There was even a ladder on a rail so she could reach the top shelves. Fairy lights were strung around her wrought iron bed frame. The room reminded me of innocence and magic, things I was sorely lacking this evening.

After we'd dressed for bed, we got in and Mor snuggled deep against me. Exhausted, she was out within minutes.

I, however, couldn't sleep.

Not just because today's attack kept playing over and over in my mind, making my heart race and palms slick with sweat, not just because my face was pulsing with pain ... but because I owed Fyfe an apology. I couldn't say it in front of an audience. But I didn't think I could sleep until he knew how sorry I was.

Though my parents were quiet, I heard them come upstairs and close themselves in their bedroom. A while later, being careful not to wake Mor, I climbed out of bed and tiptoed downstairs. Sticking my feet into boots I kept at the side entrance, I let myself out and hurried over to the annex.

I knocked softly. "Fyfe?"

Almost immediately, I heard movement inside and a few seconds later, the door swung open.

Fyfe stepped back to allow me entrance and then closed the door behind me.

The travel cot was set up by the bed and Millie was sound asleep.

Tears brightened my eyes, her wails from earlier filling my mind.

I whirled on Fyfe. He'd put on his glasses and though his hair was mussed and he was half-dressed, he didn't appear as if

250   SAMANTHA YOUNG

I'd woken him up. "I'm so sorry," I whispered on a sob. "I'm so sorry."

His expression tightened before he drew me into his arms.

I buried my face against his naked chest, my tears wetting his skin as I cried quietly.

"Hush. You have nothing to be sorry for," he declared firmly as he stroked a hand down my hair.

I shook my head. "I put Millie in danger."

"No." Fyfe drew me back and gently cradled my bruised face, his head bending to mine. "Baby, no. Please don't take that on."

"Wh-what i-if s-s-something ha-happened t-to her?" I stuttered, struggling to breathe properly through my tears.

Fyfe pressed a firm kiss to my forehead before leading me over to the bed. He took both my hands in his. "Breathe, baby." He pulled in a breath through his nose and slowly exhaled. "Copy me."

My grip on his hands had to be bruising, but Fyfe didn't react, just breathed with me until I'd calmed down.

Eventually, he slid an arm around my shoulders. "Is that why you wouldn't look at me earlier? Because you feel guilty?"

"Yes."

"I ... I was worried you were mad at me. Because I told you that you were safe in my house."

I gaped at him in shock, feeling even worse for my behavior. "No. Fyfe, no. Never."

Familiar guilt reflected in his eyes. "I didn't keep you safe."

"You saved me." Now I cupped his face, his short beard scratching my palms.

"You were doing a pretty damn good job of saving yourself."

My lips trembled. "Is Millie okay?"

"She's completely fine. A resilient wee girl who will never remember this day." Fyfe brushed his fingertips over my

FOREVER THE HIGHLANDS 251

swollen cheek. "If that gun was in my hand and not Walker's, I would have put the bullet through his head."

I shivered at the thought, curling my fingers around his strong wrist. "Then it's a good thing you didn't have the gun. I need you here, Fyfe. Not in prison."

He grew alert. "*Do* you need me?"

Fresh tears burned my eyes. "Far longer than you've ever known."

Fyfe shook his head. "I wish I'd been who I am now back then. Instead of wasting all that time."

I took his hand in mine. "Let's make a pact ... starting now, we learn from the past, but we stop living in it."

His grip on me tightened. "I can do that."

A sweet silence fell between us as we stared at our entwined hands. Then I admitted quietly, "I can't sleep. I keep ... seeing him."

"Stay with me. I'll hold you, watch over you."

Nodding, I kicked off my boots and then slipped into bed. Fyfe removed his glasses, placing them on the bedside cabinet, and slid in beside me. Without hesitation, he pulled me into his arms like I'd always belonged there. I nestled against him, my good cheek pressed to his pecs, the warm weight of his hand comforting on my hip.

"Do you remember when we were kids and we all went camping? You let me stay in your tent, even though I was always making you uncomfortable with my flirting."

Fyfe squeezed me. "I shared my tent with you because you made me laugh and you always made me feel like I was worth something. I shared my tent with you because I wanted you around."

"Really?" I whispered, surprised, emotional too.

"I am done taking you for granted, Eilidh Adair," he whispered in my ear. "I know the woman in my arms is the most extraordinary bloody woman I will ever have the good fortune of knowing. I promise to never let a day pass without making you feel as special as you've made me feel all these years."

When I closed my eyes, tears slipped free. But they were good tears. A release. Relief.

All I could smell and feel was Fyfe.

Like the miracle I'd always thought he was, he held back my intrusive thoughts so blissful sleep could claim me.

THIRTY-THREE
FYFE

Lewis brushed his wet paintbrush over Callie's nose and she squealed before chasing him with hers. Eilidh giggled at their nonsense, shaking her head before turning back to help me with the peel-and-stick mural.

It had been a couple of weeks since Peter Pryor's attack. We'd postponed decorating the nursery because I wanted Eilidh to be a part of it, and I wanted her to feel comfortable in my home again.

Since her attack, a few things had happened.

The media descended on Ardnoch, attempting to hound Eilidh. Like always, Ardnoch rallied around one of their own and made sure the media felt so unwelcome, they fucked off onto the next big story only a few days later.

Walker shooting Peter had the bonus of apparently scaring the shit out of Cameron Phillips. He'd departed Ardnoch before his week was up. Lachlan, never one to let an abuser get away scot-free, was keeping tabs on Dr. Dick. He'd taken a job in Edinburgh. Lachlan had put him on the radar of a journalist down there who was, as we speak, digging up enough dirt to bury the bastard, at least under the scrutiny of public opinion.

As for Peter Pryor, although his attack on Eilidh took place in Scotland, many of the charges he faced had occurred in London, so he was transferred to jail down there where he'll await his hearing in a few weeks. If the case goes to trial, and we'd been advised it most likely would, Eilidh would have to face the bastard again in about four or five months. We'd deal with that then.

Millie was almost eleven months old. Her *Ae*'s were definitely an attempt to say *Eilidh* and best of all, a week ago she'd started calling me *Dada*. I doubt I could ever articulate how it felt to hear my child's first word. Or for that word to be the word that described her attachment to me. The magnitude of it wasn't lost on me. Though I was still scared shitless about somehow finding a way to mess up my kid, I felt a little more confident now that I could be a good father to Millie.

My daughter had settled into daycare with Regan's team, and we'd found a routine together. Lewis's aunt Eredine was happy to watch Millie and Harley twice a week in the evenings so I could return to instructing my tae kwon do classes that Lewis and Callie also attended.

Eilidh had returned to writing, but I knew she stopped by the daycare for hours to see Millie, which was probably why Millie had adjusted to the change so easily. Easing Eilidh into returning to my house was a process. We'd been meeting up at Callie and Lewis's for dinner a few nights a week or catching up for a coffee in the village.

Last week, she agreed to have dinner at my place. Callie and Lewis were there with Harley to offer support. Eilidh had been tense, pale-faced, and I'd regretted suggesting it. However, she told me she didn't want Peter to taint a place she'd grown to love.

I loved that she'd grown to love my home.

FOREVER THE HIGHLANDS

It kept my hope afloat that despite the lack of romantic progress between us, a future together still hovered on the horizon. I was taking it slow because she'd been through so much.

Yet looking at her now, her bruises all healed up, a smile curling her soft mouth, olive skin aglow with health as she helped me decorate my daughter's nursery ... well, it took everything within me to not order Callie and Lewis out of the room.

Eilidh's dark curls were piled on top of her head, a few falling onto her cheeks as she moved. She wore a tank top beneath cotton dungarees. It shouldn't be a sexy outfit, but the tank was short on her and I could see flashes of smooth tan skin. I could slip through the gaps on either side and cup her delicious arse in my hands.

I swallowed hard and returned my focus to the mural.

My need for Eilidh had grown into this hunger I'd never experienced before. I'd had time to think on why, and I assumed it was a mix of impatience to be with her now that I'd finally pulled my head out of my arse. But maybe also to quiet the guilt that had plagued me since Peter attacked her in the house I'd sworn she was safe in. Every time I thought about how close I'd come to losing her, I felt frozen to the bone. I was eager to claim her, not just so we could start our lives together with Millie, but to reassure myself she was alive, that she was mine, and that I'd be there to protect her going forward.

I just wasn't sure if Eilidh was ready.

I'd been waiting for three weeks for her to make a move.

It was only last night and this morning that I'd started to notice her *looking* at me again. For instance, I'd been bending over to take the lids off the paint tin for Lewis and Callie and when I'd straightened, I'd caught Eilidh guiltily turning away from ogling me.

The truth was, I didn't know how much willpower I had left.

"Lewis Adair, you brush any more of that paint on me, and I'll knock you on your arse," Callie warned behind us. "Such a child."

I glanced over my shoulder from smoothing down the mural. Lewis chuckled like a wee boy as he returned to painting.

Eilidh followed my gaze. "If you stop messing about, we might actually finish the nursery so Millie can get into it tomorrow."

"What about the paint fumes?" Callie asked. "Don't you have to let it air out for a few days?"

"Aye," I confirmed.

"Still, we've only got the weekend." Eilidh narrowed her gaze suspiciously on her brother. "Why are you acting like a five-year-old hopped up on Haribo?"

I stepped down from the ladder, watching Lew. He had shown up in an awfully good mood this morning. I'd just assumed it meant he'd gotten some. Lucky bastard.

As Lew stared at his wife with a secret smile, and Callie's cheeks flushed, I saw something else pass between them.

"Wait." Eilidh stepped toward her brother and sister-in-law and they both reluctantly turned to her. "Are you ... oh my god, are you pregnant?"

Callie's lips parted. "How ... how did you know that?"

"Oh my god, you are?"

I met Lewis's gaze, and he grinned smugly like he hadn't just done something many men before him had. "Aye?"

He turned to Callie and she threw her hands up, accidentally brushing the wall with the paintbrush in her hand (luckily, it was the correct wall). "Well, it's out now."

"Ahh!" Eilidh squealed and threw her arms around Callie who laughed, trying to keep the paintbrush away from her while she returned her embrace. "Congratulations!"

I reached out a hand to Lewis; he shook it and we shared a grin. "Pleased as fuck for you, mate."

"Thank you." His voice was gruff with emotion before he accepted Eilidh's hug.

"So happy for you, big brother."

"Thanks, Eils." He grinned at his wife over Eilidh's shoulder. "No getting away from me now."

Callie rolled her eyes. "You make it sound like you're trapping me in this marriage with pregnancy."

"No, he already did that with Harley," Eilidh teased and I laughed.

Lewis shot me a mock hurt look.

Callie chuckled, wrapping her arms around her husband. Lewis snuggled her close, pressing a kiss to the top of her head. I felt a rush of envy. My attention moved to Eilidh, and I reckoned everything I felt was in my eyes because when our gazes locked, her lips parted, her eyes flaring with surprise.

"We aren't telling anyone else just yet because it's such early days," Callie said. "You have to promise not to tell anyone."

Eilidh reluctantly dragged her attention from me to her family. "Not even our parents?"

"Nor mine. Nor anyone's," Callie insisted. "Seriously. I'm only six weeks along. I want to get to at least twelve weeks this time before the entire village finds out."

"I get it. I promise. Just between us. But you two need to do a better job of hiding it. Lewis is acting like a fool."

"Uh!" Lewis's voice went comically high-pitched. "I didn't do anything."

"Other than act like a kid at Christmas, which is the way you acted when Harley was born."

He turned to me for support.

I shrugged. "Sorry, mate. Eils is right."

"Well, excuse me for being excited I'm about to be a father again."

Callie rubbed a soothing hand up his arm. "Just keep the excitement inside for a while."

"You've no chance." Eilidh studied her brother. "Lewis will give you away."

"Your faith is astounding."

Her lips twitched. "It's adorable that you can't hide how happy you are."

"I am not adorable."

Callie scoffed.

Lewis scowled. "What was that?"

She made a "you're so cute" face. "You can be adorable sometimes. In a manly, biker sort of way."

"What is with the roastin'?" Lewis threw his arms up. "A man finds out he's going to be a father again and it calls for a roastin'?"

"Only when that man is absolutely adorable," I teased, leaving the room to the sound of his insults. Shoulders shaking with laughter, I hurried downstairs to grab some bottled water from the fridge and a few snacks before returning to the nursery. I handed water and food to Callie first.

She smiled as she took them. "Thanks. I'm good, by the way. A little morning sickness like with Harley, but otherwise good. Lots of energy." A slight flush on her cheeks was telling.

"Aw, so that's why you're so happy." I handed Lewis his water and snack with a cheeky grin.

"Watch it, Moray."

Chuckling, I turned to Eilidh. She laughed as she took her water and snack but said, "Please don't talk about my brother's sex life in front of me."

"Fine, we'll just talk about mine." Callie grinned wickedly. "This morning, my husband woke me up with his—"

FOREVER THE HIGHLANDS   259

"La la la la la la!" Eilidh yelled, squeezing her eyes closed like a toddler.

We all laughed as we found a seat on the busy floor.

"Okay, let's stop torturing Eilidh because it's slightly torturing me at the same time," Lewis joked. His amusement drifted off as he glanced at me. "Any word from Millie's birth mother?"

An instant chill swept over me. "Not a word so far. Had a look into her family. Dad was out of the picture at an early age, so no reason to believe he'll come looking for a granddaughter. Her mum relocated to Australia and remarried a bloke in Melbourne. There's no one else. No siblings. No close aunts and uncles."

"That's maybe why she thought she couldn't handle raising Millie alone," Callie offered quietly. "I couldn't imagine raising Harley without a support system."

Anger cut through the chill, and I gritted my teeth against it. "Your mum did it for a long time. I know you would do it if you had to."

"Not everyone is made the same way." Lewis sighed heavily. "From what you said about her reaction, it sounds like a messed-up situation for her."

"So?" I scowled at my best friend. "You do not abandon your child. Ever. You compartmentalize whatever the fuck is messing with your head so you can prioritize the innocent child who is relying on you to not only keep her alive, but to make sure she knows she's loved."

Tension crackled between us.

I didn't give a fuck if they thought I wasn't being compassionate toward Pamela. They weren't the ones who somehow had to explain to Millie when she was old enough to understand that her real mother just didn't want her enough to stick around. As a kid who very much understood what that did to a person's sense of self-worth, I *hated* Pamela for putting our child through that.

"Fyfe, I know—"

"Stop, Lewis." Eilidh spoke up. Her tone was like silk over steel. "Fyfe doesn't need to feel anything but what he's feeling."

"I just—"

"No. You're a good person who wants to believe the best in everyone. But sometimes it's more important to just have your friend's back and let him feel what he needs to feel." While I ached for this woman, I watched as she offered her brother a kind smile. "Just ask my therapist."

Callie jumped on the chance to ease the tension. "Are you still seeing her?"

Eilidh nodded. I knew she'd been talking to Diana more recently. "I'd stopped checking in with her for a bit when I came home, but after the incident with Peter, I needed to talk it out."

"Has it helped?"

"Loads."

To my relief, Eilidh had slept in my arms that first night. She'd drifted off easily and hadn't woken up with nightmares. However, there hadn't been a repeat of the sleepover, and many nights since I'd lain awake (instead of grabbing sleep while I could in between Millie's sleep sprints), wondering if Eilidh was sleeping or if she needed me beside her.

We chatted for another ten minutes before getting to work. The afternoon passed quickly, and my mind kept wandering to later that evening. Regan had offered to not only watch Millie with Harley during the day but to keep Millie overnight so I could catch up on sleep. It was overly kind, and I'd tried not to accept the offer, but Regan and Thane had insisted. I trusted them implicitly, so I wasn't worried about Millie being away from me, though I hoped she wouldn't

FOREVER THE HIGHLANDS   261

grow fussy. I'd made Regan assure me she'd call me to come pick Millie up if she couldn't get her to settle.

"It's good for you to be apart," Regan had reassured me. "For Millie too."

Now, with a free evening ahead, it wasn't sleep I was thinking about.

When Eilidh squeezed past while we were trying to hang the last strip of mural, her breasts brushed my chest, and my whole body tightened. The merest touch had me reacting like a fucking teenager.

This need for Eilidh was becoming almost debilitating.

Was she ready for that, though?

Before Peter, she'd been trying to insist on casual.

The night of the attack, she seemed to suggest she was ready to commit to me instead.

But we hadn't discussed our relationship since.

I pushed those thoughts away as we finished up for the evening. Lewis ordered pizza from Thurso and it arrived just as we put the finishing touches on the décor.

"It's going to look amazing," Callie opined as we sat around my dining table to dig into the food. "We'll come back tomorrow to help you put the furniture together."

Gratitude moved me. "I can't thank you enough for your help."

Lewis shrugged. "What is family for?"

My eyes caught Eilidh's and that overwhelming feeling I got when I looked at Millie swelled beyond bearing. They were my family.

Always would be.

But I wanted to one day make it official.

I didn't know if Eilidh read my thoughts, but whatever she saw on my face made her eyes bright and a small, sexy smile curl the corner of her mouth.

THIRTY-FOUR
EILIDH

I ate two slices of pizza before the butterflies forced me to stop.

We chatted a little more about Callie and Lewis's plans to create space for the new baby in the nursery because they wanted Harley and the baby to be together while they were both still young. I could imagine how excited my niece would be once the baby came. Harley would be around two and a half by the time my new niece or nephew arrived, big enough to be aware of the change but not too old it might cause rivalry. Hopefully.

All throughout our chat, I attempted to conceal my anticipation. Lewis and Callie seemed oblivious, but Fyfe had been throwing very hungry looks my way for several days and today the tension crackled between us.

Something shifted for me that night I'd lain in Fyfe's arms after Peter's attack. Trying to force a casual relationship on Fyfe had been born of my fear of rejection again.

But I'd known the moment he'd turned to me, overcome with emotion and guilt, that I meant a great deal to him.

FOREVER THE HIGHLANDS   263

Maybe it wasn't love yet, but I hoped it could turn into love. If I was just brave enough to reach out.

Tonight, I wanted to be brave again. To be the Eilidh who ran toward the things she wanted, instead of hiding from them and the world.

Peter Pryor's sick perversion and obsession had the opposite effect on me from what most people might expect. I didn't want to shy away, to live my life smaller so I wouldn't have to face something as scary as him again.

I wanted to live my life big. But *my* definition of big.

Big to me was being open to the things and people that excited me. To talk to Uncle Brodan and Theo Cavendish about the script that I was more than ready to share.

To spend every second making up for all the years I'd missed out on my beautiful family.

And to throw myself into loving Fyfe because I'd never stopped loving him, and it was foolish to pretend otherwise.

By the time Lewis and Callie were ready to leave, my heart was beating with excitement and my skin was hot. Lewis asked me if I wanted a ride home, but I casually replied, "I'm going to stick around for a wee bit."

Lewis appeared almost pained as he glanced between me and his best friend, but Callie laughed and shoved him out the door.

Silence seemed to scream between me and Fyfe as soon as my brother and sister-in-law departed. Fyfe locked the door and turned to me. He wore his contacts today because he preferred wearing them if he was doing something physical. His Muse T-shirt sculpted to his strong body and his paint-splattered joggers hung low on his waist.

The man was so sexy, I might die from it.

Lewis's SUV purred to life, and we heard it pulling away from the house.

My mouth turned dry, and I didn't know what to do with my hands.

Like always when I couldn't stand the tension, I impatiently blurted, "Well, are you going to just stand there or are you finally going to have your wicked way with me?"

His dark eyes gleamed. "That depends ... do you agree this isn't casual? That if we do this, we're doing it for real?"

"What I feel for you is the most real thing I've ever felt in my life," I whispered bravely. "It isn't casual between us, Fyfe. It's the opposite of casual."

His nostrils flared for just a millisecond and then he bridged the distance between us to haul me into his arms. His lips crashed over mine and I grabbed hold of the front of his T-shirt to pull him down to me as I lifted onto my tiptoes. It was a deep, hungering kiss. Fyfe's hand on my nape, holding me to him. His other pressed low on my back as he dominated our embrace.

His kiss was desperate, and it set every inch of me on fire. It was sexual and consuming. It was years of pent-up longing. It was the kiss we'd shared on my couch months and months ago but set free, not just by sobriety but by acceptance.

This thing between us ... it was meant to be.

Fyfe lifted me under the arms and I instinctually jumped, wrapping my legs around his waist. His strong hands gripped my thighs as we moved backward. Then just as suddenly, my arse was on the dining table, my legs wrapped around Fyfe's hips as his ravenous kisses intensified.

When his mouth eventually left mine, it was to trail along my jaw. The scratch of his beard made me shudder with need as he kissed a path to my ear. "First, you're going to come all over my tongue."

I shivered and Fyfe swallowed my gasp of want to give me another brain-fogging, mind-blowing, scorching kiss. God, no one kissed like him!

FOREVER THE HIGHLANDS 265

He was hard and I undulated against him as he ground his jersey-covered cock against me. My hands explored his taut body over the soft material of his T-shirt, and I desperately wanted to rip everything off him but even more desperately wanted my stupid dungarees off so I could *feel* him.

I panted for breath, my body trembling with need, my knickers damp with arousal.

As if he'd read my mind, Fyfe held my gaze as he unclipped my dungarees.

The least sexy thing I could be wearing right now.

Fyfe didn't seem to think so. He appeared half-starved as he yanked them down and pulled them off, one leg after the other.

I sat atop his dining table in just my tank top and knickers.

Fyfe curled his fingers through my underwear, placing his palm over my pussy, cupping me. I gasped at the tantalizing sensation as he ground his palm against me, fingers flexing on my lower belly as he found me wet.

"Is this for me?" he asked hoarsely. "Just mine, Eilidh?"

The possessive touch was not something I ever thought I'd find sexy because I'd only ever belonged to myself. But I realized it was different when you *wanted* to belong to someone else. When that someone wanted you to belong to them, it was thrilling. I got off on it.

I sat up, blood rushing in my ears as I cupped his crotch. "Is this mine?"

He groaned and nodded, eyelashes fluttering. "Baby, it belongs only to you."

I released him to cover the hand he had pressed between my legs. "Then this is yours."

Fyfe kissed me again like he needed me to breathe. No one had ever kissed me like that. Like I was ... *essential*.

He only broke the kiss to whip my underwear down my legs. His expression had hardened with want and I knew his patience had snapped. My lower belly squeezed with anticipation. I raised my arms to let him haul my tank top off and as he threw it away, I unclipped my bra and shrugged out of it.

"Fuck me," Fyfe muttered as he lifted my breasts into his palms, and a shiver skated down my spine. I moaned as he gently caressed and squeezed my tits. "You're so fucking beautiful. Bone-deep beauty." His lips hovered over mine. "I'm the luckiest fucker in the world."

"Fyfe ... I need you."

He gave me a wicked smile and pulled my arse along the table until I was almost hanging off it and then he pushed my thighs apart. Fyfe lowered to his knees and I groaned. "Yes, yes ..."

Fyfe smoothed his hands along my inner thighs, gazing up at me with that cocky smirk. "Patience, baby."

"Fyfe Moray, you better put your mouth on me right now or I might just come without you."

His rumble of laughter blew across my pussy.

I lifted my hips, my fingers curling into the edge of the table. "Please."

In answer, Fyfe's tongue explored me in a long, slow lick up to my clit. I groaned as sensation spiked down all four limbs. Arousal tightened in exquisite need low in my belly as my heart pounded. My gaze dropped to his, our eyes locking. Excitement shuddered through me at this fantasy brought to life. Fyfe Moray's handsome face buried between my legs.

His fingers dug into my thighs as he licked and sucked at my clit. Just when I would be on the precipice of coming, Fyfe would abandon my clit to push his tongue inside me. He closed his eyes, his grip tightening, and I felt that inner tension grow even tauter at the sight of him tongue-fucking me like he was in ecstasy. Then he returned to that bundle of tormented nerves at my apex, drawing my clit between his tongue and teeth and sucking hard. My body tensed, my thighs closing on him, my chest heaving and shuddering as the sensation spiraled toward explosion.

My cries filled his house as I arched my back, my fingers threading through his silky thick hair to hold on. "Fyfe! Oh god, oh god, oh, ohhh!"

He growled at the tug on his hair as I shattered. I shuddered and shook against his mouth as he lapped up every drop of my orgasm.

When I opened my eyes, Fyfe stood, wiping his mouth with the bottom of his T-shirt. He was visibly very, very hard in his joggers and he looked ready to fuck me until I came a million times over.

I was still trying to catch my breath and hold myself up as he gripped my hips and growled against my lips, "Now we're going to my bedroom so you can ride my face before I ride you hard and good."

Surprise flew through me and I gasped.

Fyfe's eyes narrowed. "What? I thought you liked the dirty talk?"

I swallowed, disbelieving ... but ... "I do. I do ... but ... I had a dream. A sex dream."

His eyebrows rose. "Hopefully about me."

I grimaced. "Of course about you. It was the night after we kissed at my place."

"And?"

"It was so vivid, Fyfe. Like, I could have sworn it was real it was so vivid."

"I would have remembered sex with you, sweetheart," he said gently.

I smiled, reaching to cup his face. "I know. It was just a visceral sex dream ... in which I rode your face and then you fucked me. And I thought it was just my fantasy ... not ... not a premonition."

He grinned, a secretive smile that made my heart skip a

beat. "Baby, do you know how many times I've fantasized about you riding my face?"

"Seriously?"

"But to be fair, I've pretty much fantasized about taking you in every sexual position known to man."

I shivered, sliding my arms around his neck. "Well, that's a lot of positions to get through. We should probably get started."

THIRTY-FIVE
EILIDH

Somehow we made it to his bedroom.

Facing each other. Breathing hard. Me naked. Him still fully clothed.

Fyfe whipped his T-shirt off first. Then his socks. His eyes never left mine as he pushed his joggers and boxers down his legs. He was impressively hard as he kicked himself free of his clothing. He stood before me, at ease with his own nakedness (as he should be), and I devoured him with my gaze. So muscular. So strong. His happy trail led to the cock that strained toward his stomach. Thick and throbbing, precum glistening at the tip. His thighs were crafted with hard work and martial arts, his calf muscles popping as he shifted on his feet.

Beautiful, beautiful man.

But I'd thought so even when he was a skinny nerd.

I'd never loved any man I'd slept with. No one had told me how different it would feel. How heightened.

How much more of a turn-on it was.

The possessiveness I'd experience and how carnal that need was.

Fyfe swallowed hard as his gaze dropped down my naked body. I'd never been body conscious. Thank God because I'd had to show my breasts and naked arse on telly. But I'd also never felt sexier than I did as Fyfe Moray looked his fill. His cock strained harder and he licked his lips. When his dark eyes met mine, there was raw need in them. But I also recognized tenderness.

I approached Fyfe slowly and his eyes fell to my breasts, his hands flexing as my tits bounced with the movement. Feeling smug, I pressed close to him, his erection hot against my skin. I moaned, smoothing my palms over his sculpted pecs. Fyfe thrummed with tension, but he held still for me as I explored.

Lightly trailing my fingertips over his skin, I memorized the contours of his chest, my thumbs stroking over his hard nipples. His abdominal muscles flexed under my touch. I brushed my lips over a nipple and he groaned my name.

I teased his other nipple as my hands coasted up his chest and along his strong shoulders and down his arms. Then I kissed lower, soft, wet kisses down his six-pack.

"Eilidh, fuck, where are you going?"

I followed his happy trail with my mouth and lowered to my knees until I was eye level with his cock.

"Eilidh? Baby, fuck, okay, yes, yes, yes." His groan was long and deep as I took him between my lips. My hands rested on his outer thighs, giving me stability as I eagerly explored him. My tongue learned as much of him as I could, considering I couldn't fit all of him into my mouth. "Eilidh, look at me."

I looked up, breathing through my nose to swallow him deeper. Our eyes locked and he slid his fingers into my hair, his expression taut with pleasure. "You're the sexiest thing I've ever seen," he gasped.

I began to suck, bobbing my head so my mouth slid excruciatingly slowly up and down his length. Sucking hard, like he was a lollipop, I smoothed my hands over his arse as his breathing grew shallow.

Curse words and pleas fell from his lips in mutters and groans, and I could feel the tension in his arse as he tried not to fuck my mouth. I sucked harder.

He let out a shout and came without warning. I released him.

Laughing softly, I reached for his T-shirt to wipe up the mess he'd made of my chin and chest.

"Right. Your turn again." He swept me off the floor like I weighed nothing and settled us on the bed, him flat on his back, me straddling him.

My dream returned to me.

I couldn't believe it was coming to life.

My legs trembled with anticipation. I smiled at his smug smirk as I raised my hips over his face.

Fyfe guided me over him.

I felt his tongue thrust into me, and my back bowed as I gripped the headboard and undulated into his hungry exploration. Just like the dream, his fingers were bruising on my hips as my pants and cries for more filled the bedroom. His tongue was magical, licking and fucking and sucking until I was mindless with need.

I shattered and Fyfe pulled me harder on his mouth, voraciously eating up every second of my orgasm. Before I could catch my breath, Fyfe had me flat on my back, kissing me. His kiss was surprisingly slow, exploring, our tongues tangling. We tasted of each other. Possessiveness roared through me as I crushed my breasts to his hard chest, needing to be closer, needing more, deeper, harder. Fyfe's hands roamed my body as we kissed, squeezing, caressing, and claiming.

Breaking the kiss, his gaze lowered to my breasts.

"Such beautiful tits, Eilidh, sweetheart." His voice was gruff. "That night at your flat, your nipples were hard. I wanted to take them in my mouth and suck until you begged me to fuck you."

"Yes, yes." I wanted that. I wanted that so badly. I arched my back, my nipples pebbling, eager for his mouth. When his thumbs brushed them, I shuddered. *More, more, more.*

"At the wedding, when we kissed ... I was ready to fuck you against the wall," he confessed hoarsely. "Never wanted anyone the way I want you."

My hips squirmed with need at his words, at the way he rolled my nipples between his fingers and thumbs. His gaze was curious, as if he was learning my body, my reactions, my likes and loves. Then he bent his head and covered my right nipple with his mouth and I cried out as sensation scored down my belly and my clit pulsed.

That was new!

"Oh!" My back arched off the bed.

Fyfe made a pleased sound as his other hand dipped between us, his thumb finding my clit.

I jerked at his touch, on sensory overload as he tugged ruthlessly at my nipple, scraping his teeth over it.

The tension coiled tight in my womb and I dug my fingers into his strong shoulders as he moved his mouth to my left breast and treated my other nipple to the same. He raised his head to watch me as he pressed two fingers inside me. We gasped together as he finger-fucked me, his way eased considerably by my arousal.

"Fyfe, Fyfe ... oh god, yes ..."

He bowed his forehead against mine. "Your pussy's so wet. I can't ... I can't believe how wet you are. For me."

"I need you." My fingers bit into his waist. "I need you inside me."

"I need that too," he promised. "But you're going to come again first." He circled my clit with his thumb.

I shattered, crying out his name as I came, shuddering

against him as he licked and kissed my breasts until I was nothing but pleasure-melted goo on the mattress.

Again, he gave me no chance to recover. Fyfe's kisses turned demanding, harder, needful. He reached blindly across me, cursing as he had to break the kiss to open the bedside cabinet. He pulled out a condom, and I was shaking with want as I watched him roll it on. The man had barely secured himself when he was pushing inside me. I wrapped my thighs around him as he braced himself over me and thrust deeper. Needing more, I pushed against his chest. "Sit up."

He sat back, our bodies still locked as I came with him, straddling him, my knees to the mattress, my arms wrapped tight around his neck. Our chests pressed together, I rocked my hips over him.

We moaned against each other's lips before our mouths met fully as I rose again and came down. I clung to his shoulders, flooded with feeling. The overwhelming fullness of him inside me, the hard grip he had on my ass while his other hand squeezed and molded my breast with just the right amount of pressure. I leaned back, breaking the kiss, but only so his cock thrust into me at the most delicious angle. Only so I could watch him. I moved slowly, building toward an exquisite orgasm.

I moved beneath Fyfe's awed gaze, watching the way his nostrils flared as he lingered on my breasts, on the way his eyes dropped to watch me ride him. He gripped me tight, urging me on; his jaw clenched as the heat between us increased. Our gazes locked and everything passed between us.

Connected.

Totally connected.

Not just physically.

My orgasm hit me, and I came around him, my stomach muscles rippling with the release, my inner muscles squeezing him tight.

274 SAMANTHA YOUNG

Fyfe cursed under his breath and pushed me back on the bed mid orgasm. He lifted my hips, gripping them as he knelt between my legs and began to fuck me.

Hard.

Sensation scored through me and I didn't know if it was another orgasm or if he'd just extended the last. Whatever it was, I almost blacked out as incredible pleasure exploded through me.

Thirty-Six
FYFE

Light prodded at my eyelids and I groaned, reluctantly opening them to the request.

I blinked rapidly, my eyes dry and gritty and like there was something foreign in them. Blurred vision cleared somewhat and I realized I'd left my contacts in overnight. Moreover, I'd forgotten to hit the remote on my bedroom blinds, which was why the morning sunlight woke me.

The slight, warm weight of another body had me peering down, and last night came flooding back.

Lying in my arms was the reason I hadn't taken out my contacts and had forgotten to shut the blinds.

Overwhelming realization moved through me as I stared at the beautiful woman half sprawled across me. Eilidh's dark curls tickled my chin as a few errant strands escaped upward. The rest spilled down her slender back. One arm was tucked in at my side, while her other rested over my stomach. Claiming me. Her right leg was tangled with mine. I could feel nearly every inch of her gorgeous body against me. Arousal mixed with the dawning recognition that until this moment, something integral had been missing from my life.

Eilidh. Here. In my arms. Waking up to her after a mind-blowing night of sex and intimacy.

I'd never experienced anything like last night.

And I knew I never would if Eilidh chose not to give that to me again.

The very idea was like ice water in my veins, and my hold on her waist tightened.

Staring down at her face, watching her eyelids tremble in sleep, humbled by the way Eilidh unconsciously wrapped herself around my body, making herself vulnerable to me again ...

I knew.

I was going to marry this woman.

When I put my mind to something, I achieved it.

The sound of my doorbell ruined the tranquil moment, and Eilidh mumbled in her sleep, rubbing her cheek against my chest.

Tenderness washed through me, followed by irritation at whoever was at the door.

Usually my phone would sound an alert if anyone pulled onto the driveway, but last night we'd left our phones downstairs. Not the most responsible thing I could have done as a parent.

Fuck.

I guess I was still learning.

Anxious to ascertain whether Regan had tried to contact me about Millie, I attempted to move out from under Eilidh without waking her. I'd just rested her against my pillow when the doorbell rang again, jerking her out of sleep.

She blinked wearily as I stood to pull on my discarded joggers. There were condom wrappers on the floor of my bedroom and a caveman smugness rushed through me. At least my woman would never complain about my lack of stamina.

FOREVER THE HIGHLANDS 277

"Someone's at the door," I told her, my eyes roaming over her body because I couldn't help myself.

"Oh." She sat up on her elbow and yawned before waving me away as it rang again. "It sounds urgent."

My expression was regretful. I knew she understood because she returned it with a sexy smirk before I hurried downstairs, snatching my phone up first before I checked the security system.

Nothing from Regan, though there was a text from Lewis.

And he and Callie stood outside my front door.

What the ... a quick glance at the time on my phone told me it was nine o'clock.

Shit.

I yanked the front door open, feeling like a wee boy who'd been caught with his hand in the cookie jar.

"Finally." Lewis stepped in, dressed in the same paint-covered clothing from yesterday. Callie followed, a knowing smile trembling on her lips. "Did you sleep in?" Lew asked.

Shutting the door, very much aware I was half-naked and probably reeked of sex and Eilidh, I physically retreated from them, raking a hand through my hair. "Aye, sorry. Just let me shower. Make yourselves at home, have a coffee, there's food in the—"

"Fyfe, is everything okaaaaay—" Eilidh had wandered down the stairs in just my T-shirt and now stood midway, gaping in horror at her brother.

Apparently, we'd both forgotten Lewis and Callie were coming over to help finish the nursery.

A snort covered by a cough came from Callie's direction.

Lewis stared stonily at his sister. Then at me.

I waited, heart pounding.

"Fuck." He grimaced, shielding the sight of her with his palm. "At least do me the courtesy of hiding it for a while."

Callie pressed her cheek against Lewis's back, hugging him

278   SAMANTHA YOUNG

from behind. Laughter trembled on her lips. "It's okay, Adair. Realizing your wee sister is a woman is scary, but we'll get you through it."

"Funny," he huffed but covered her hands with his as he looked at me. "You take care of her or I kill you."

"Fair." I clapped him on the shoulder, relieved he wasn't going to make a big deal out of it. "You guys settle. We'll shower."

"Separately. On entirely different continents." Lewis led Callie into the living space.

"Aye, sure, that's exactly how we'll do it," Eilidh called down to him. "We won't at all be washing each other's bodies while you're downstairs picturing us on separate continents."

Evil. She was truly evil.

My shoulders shook with laughter as I met her on the stairs.

Her eyes danced with amusement.

Fuck, I loved her.

"Payback, Eils. Payback!" Lewis warned from below.

Eilidh giggled and turned upstairs. I followed her, grinning at the flash of the boxers she'd adorned. She'd pulled on a clean pair of my underwear.

I didn't know why that was so sexy, but it was.

Between that and walking back into my bedroom to find it musky with the aroma of our exploits last night, I knew I was about to break the bro code.

Despite what she'd joked, Eilidh sat on the end of the bed. "Do you want to shower first?"

"Sure." I had no intention of showering alone. Instead, I strolled into my bathroom to take my contacts out. The world blurred before me. However, I wasn't so blind I couldn't see enough to shower. I did every day. But Eilidh didn't need to know that. "I'm slightly blind without my contacts. You want to help me out here?"

Forever the Highlands

Eilidh wandered into the bathroom. Her lips trembled with laughter. "You are so full of shit." Without another word, she whipped off my T-shirt and boxers. Grinning like a fool, I got naked too and hauled her into my generously sized shower.

We did wash and shampoo, but it took us longer than usual because our hands kept wandering to places that were very fucking distracting.

Eilidh had to bite her lip to stifle her cries as I made her come. Twice.

THIRTY-SEVEN
EILIDH

The Cavendishes lived in the same development as Fyfe. For a while they used to split their time between here, Gairloch, and London, but when Theo's wife, Sarah, had gotten unexpectedly pregnant (I knew from Callie that the Cavendishes hadn't wanted children, which was difficult to believe considering how much they doted on their daughter Rose), they'd gradually started spending more time in Ardnoch. They wanted Rose to have stability, so they lived in Ardnoch permanently now that she attended primary school.

However, they still traveled during the summer and Theo traveled more often because he was not just a screenwriter but a producer. Now that Rose was a wee bit older, he was starting to work on projects that did require some travel.

His wife, Sarah McCulloch Cavendish, wasn't someone I'd known particularly well as a child, even though she'd lived in Ardnoch her entire life. Her cousin, Jared, had returned to Ardnoch to help their grandfather Collum with the farm, and the three of them kept to themselves. Plus, there was some antagonism between my family and the McCullochs owing to a generations-old land dispute so, growing up, I'd never known if Sarah disliked us. It turned out she couldn't care less about old arguments and was now a good friend to my family.

Sarah had worked as a housekeeper at Ardnoch Estate for years, all the while secretly penning a best-selling crime fiction series. When Collum passed away, she decided to give up the housekeeping job and be open about her success. Her first port of call was asking Theo Cavendish, one of the UK's best screenwriters and producers (and the son of an actual viscount), to consider adapting her series for television. What occurred between them after that only they knew, but the unlikely pair—shy housekeeper and imperious English aristocrat—fell madly in love. They made the television series together and it was a massive hit, won a ton of awards, and had become a cult classic among television shows. I'd even guest-starred on it before its final season.

With the kids now on their summer holidays, it was unusual for the Cavendishes to still be here, but according to Mum, Sarah was on deadline and they weren't planning to travel for another two weeks.

After chatting with my uncle Brodan, he'd suggested Theo was the best person to discuss my script with since he was still in the business. Uncle Brodan, of course, offered to read it, but I knew he was correct. Not just because Theo knew what was relevant and happening in the industry, but because he wasn't someone who had inspired my script like my family had, like Brodan had.

I walked along the farmer's lane that connected the small, sprawled development Jared and Allegra had created, having said goodbye to Fyfe and Millie as he set off to drop her at daycare and then head in for a meeting with a client at Ardnoch. The past few weeks with Fyfe had been nothing short of bliss. After what I'd gone through recently, I hadn't thought I was capable of being this happy. But I finally understood what cloud nine meant.

I was on it. And regularly getting the best orgasms of my life on that thing.

Fyfe, Millie, and I had fallen into a routine so easily, it was like we were built to be a family. I spent most of my nights there, so much so Mum and Dad were angling for a family dinner so they could officially commemorate my relationship with Fyfe. I knew they were pleased for us, but I was a wee bit apprehensive to do any "commemorating." Because as much as I was loving every minute of this life Fyfe and I were creating ... there was just one thing missing.

He hadn't told me he loved me.

I hadn't said it again since that first time I confessed it because ... well ... maybe, a little stubbornly, I wanted him to say it first.

Yet, if he didn't say it soon, I was going to blurt those three words out there and try not to lose my shit if he didn't say them back.

Stubborn male.

I took a deep breath, shoving thoughts of my new relationship with Fyfe from my mind. Now was about *me*. About my possible future career. For a moment, I stood outside the large home that was almost identical to Fyfe's, staring at it. Urging my feet forward.

Theo was expecting me.

I'd called him last night to ask if he had time to talk. He told me he'd be home at 8:30 a.m. after dropping Rose off at the summer school my mum organized on top of her regular daycare. My mother was superwoman. It would be cool to be like Mum. To be able to explore my own passions, all the while helping Fyfe raise Millie.

Mor asked me the other day if that meant I was going to

FOREVER THE HIGHLANDS 283

be Millie's new mum. I hadn't known how to answer. So I'd said maybe. My wee sister had then asked if that scared me.

I answered honestly. "I think it would be arrogant to say no when I'll be responsible for a little human being's happiness. But I'm more excited than scared."

It was true. Millie had weirdly felt like mine from the very beginning. Kind of like how Fyfe had felt like mine since I was eleven years old.

The front door of the Cavendishes' home opened as I stood there lost in my musings.

Theo stepped outside into the bright sunshine. "Are you having our meeting outside on your lonesome or was it your eventual intention to knock on the door?" he drawled in his upper-crust English accent.

I rolled my eyes as I approached the cerebral, sardonic screenwriter. The man had been twice blessed with beauty and intelligence. His golden good-looks and wit were an intimidating combination, but I knew beneath that sarcastic exterior, he was a giant marshmallow who would do anything for those he loved. He was also more obsessed with his wife than any man I knew and that was saying something considering who my family members were. Sarah had softened Theo's edges considerably over the years.

"I was just bracing myself to face your unique brand of wit," I replied as I reached him.

Theo's lips curved upward. He liked when you bit back. "Unique, you say? Always delightful to hear." He gestured me inside the modern house that had almost the exact floor plan as Fyfe's. Fyfe had taken the wall down between the entrance and the rest of the space. Seeing the wall still in place in the Cavendishes' house, I couldn't help but agree with Fyfe's choice to open it all up.

I followed Theo out of the entrance and into the main space. The layout here was almost identical. However, much more lived in. Art on the walls, throws over the furniture, colorful scatter cushions, and rugs breaking up the large expanse of hardwood. A gallery of family photographs ran up the stairwell wall.

It made me realize how much softening we needed to do to Fyfe's home to make it feel ... well ... like a home.

Sarah Cavendish hopped off a stool at the island, a wide smile on her pretty face. For years, Sarah had been so shy and introverted that I'd never paid much attention to her when I saw her out and about.

It was shocking then once Aria and Allegra welcomed her into our circle to discover that Sarah was stunning in a very English rose sort of way. Long, wheat-blond hair, refined features, and the most striking pair of green eyes. Still, I knew for a fact it wasn't just her quiet beauty that lured Theo in. Once you got talking to Sarah, you realized she was one of the most intelligent, nonjudgmental people you were likely to meet.

A strangely perfect match for the prickly aristocrat who doted on her. Theo reminded me of a faithful guard dog, who snuggled and loved all over his owner and growled at anyone else who got too close.

I'm not sure he'd find the description flattering.

"Eilidh, it's so good to see you." Sarah drew me into a hug. When she released me, her gaze was searching. "How are you?"

The memory of Peter Pryor hadn't disappeared just because I was loved up. His court case had been set for November. It would be a long few months knowing what the trial would entail: the media frenzy, the reliving of him violating my privacy, his attack ...

"I'm much better. It's good knowing Peter is behind bars and will probably remain there for a very long time." The Met Police had been in touch regarding the recordings of me they'd discovered on the computer. They needed permission to

Forever the Highlands

submit them as evidence. As much of a violation as that was, I agreed. The recordings would never make it into public consumption. At least they assured me they wouldn't.

"Oh." Sarah shot a quizzical look at her husband as he came to rest his hand on her lower back. "I meant ... I meant about the Jasper Richmond thing."

My stomach knotted. "What Jasper thing?"

At their sudden discomfort, I huffed, "I've been avoiding the internet. I deleted my social media. All so I didn't have to see people gossip about me. But if there's something I need to know, tell me."

Theo nodded grimly and pulled his phone out of his pocket. He tapped on the screen a few times and then handed it over. I hit the video and felt the blood drain from my cheeks as I watched Jasper have a very public meltdown on his social media. In it, he dragged me through the mud. Again! Tears I knew were fake because I'd worked long enough with him to know the difference streamed down his face as he explained how I'd betrayed him in many ways (alluding to the rumors that we'd been in a relationship, which we had not!), and that now his career was stalled because of me. He lied and said I'd gotten him into hard partying and then abandoned him when he needed me. The tears might be fake, but this level of destruction had to be real. No one did this unless their mental health was not at its peak.

"What the fuck is this?"

I was sorry if he was having a hard time, but he didn't seem to care what this would do to *my* mental health. How dare he!

How dare he use me for publicity.

Hands trembling, I handed the phone back and pulled out mine as the Cavendishes watched on in concern. I hit the number for my entertainment lawyer. There was no way I would directly respond to Jasper, but this was slander. He had no proof of the bullshit he spewed because it was all lies.

By the time I hung up with my lawyer, they were already writing up a cease and desist.

"Are you okay?" Sarah asked, handing me a cup of chamomile.

"No. I'm pissed off that I've just used up twenty minutes of your time talking to a lawyer. I'm pissed off that I might have to sue a person I used to think of as a good friend." I sipped at the tea, my hands trembling around the mug. I was so tired of feeling like everywhere I turned I had a battle to face.

I must have said that out loud, because Sarah pressed a comforting hand to my arm and replied, "Sometimes that's just how life feels. It can last a long time or a few months ... but you're not alone, Eilidh. You know that, right?"

Grateful, I nodded. "I know, thank you."

Theo curled an arm over Sarah's shoulders. "Why don't we let Sarah get back to her writing, while you show me this script of yours? Take your mind off things."

I nodded. Because Jasper wasn't going to ruin this for me. And I wouldn't let myself think about how he was slandering my name or what people were saying about me because of it.

None of it mattered.

Not really.

Not in the end.

THIRTY MINUTES LATER, THEO SAT BACK IN HIS chair at their dining table. I'd brought the script on a flash drive and he'd immediately popped it into his laptop. We'd talked a little as he read through the first few episodes, but eventually, he stopped talking and kept reading.

FOREVER THE HIGHLANDS   287

My pulse was so loud in my ears.

He was annoyingly blank-faced.

This man had written some of the best British drama our screens had seen in the last fifteen years. His opinion would buoy me or crush me. I knew it was a lot of power to give him, but I couldn't help it. I'd admired his work for a long time and was honored when he and Sarah had asked me to act in an episode of their show.

Theo looked at me.

"Well?" I huffed impatiently. "Look, if you hate it, just say so. Don't feel like because of Jasper and everything else that you need to pussyfoot around my feelings."

He nodded slowly, contemplating me. "You know I'm not a man inclined toward hyperbole."

I gulped.

"I will say ... I am rather envious that I did not write this."

I sucked in a breath, hope rising.

His expression softened. "You are very talented, Eilidh. And if you need a producer, I would love to work with you on this project."

Tears of happiness brightened my eyes. "Really?"

Theo chuckled. "I never offer to do something I don't want to do. And I rarely offer twice. This is an excellent premise. It has a compelling hook, an interesting cast of characters. I'd be a fool not to jump on it."

Laughing, I wiped away my tears. "I would love to work with you on this. Thank you."

"Good." He slapped his hands on his thighs. "Why don't we have a coffee and talk about that beginning. I have a suggestion."

"Of course. Great. Yes."

Theo shot me a droll look as he stood up. "I suggest you curb your enthusiasm to agree with me. It has a tendency to inflate my ego. Just ask my wife."

288   Samantha Young

So ecstatic I could burst, I bit my lip against more laughter. Despite Jasper, despite everything negative that had come from the industry I'd grown up in ... I was excited to return to it in this capacity. To do something that I'd conjured from my own mind and experiences.

Something I could be truly proud of.

To tell stories... but to do it without leaving behind the people who made *my* story worthwhile.

Thirty-Eight
EILIDH

When Theo Cavendish decided he wanted to do something, he was like a snowball with GPS, rolling downhill but only picking up the people he needed before rolling on to pick up the next person.

Within two weeks, he had his usual team signed off and on board, and we were already pitching the show to several streaming platforms. Between that and dealing with the legal stuff regarding Jasper and Peter Pryor, it had been a full-on couple of weeks.

Fyfe had suggested we take a day off and give Millie her first road trip. As a child, there was nothing I loved more than day trips with my parents. I loved the drive, the scenery, the family time, and we usually stopped off somewhere great to eat. Millie was too young to appreciate that, but I was excited to spend the day with two of my favorite people.

We took Fyfe's Volvo SUV because even though I'd fitted a car seat into my G-Wagon, Millie preferred the one in Fyfe's. I had it on order for my vehicle because she fussed a lot whenever we tried to buckle her into the one I had now. The boot was full of supplies for Millie and a large picnic basket with

290   SAMANTHA YOUNG

sandwiches and snacks from Morag's Deli and a treat or two from Callie's Wee Cakery.

I eagerly strapped myself into the passenger seat and felt like a wee girl again going on a family trip.

Fyfe sensed my excitement as he got comfortable in the driver's seat. He wore his black framed glasses today, along with a Kings of Leon T-shirt and jeans. He looked so sexy I could lick him. All over. "We ready?"

I resisted the urge to jump him and nodded. "Let's hit the road, Jack."

We'd decided to take a road trip through the county and just go with the flow, see where the day took us.

It was the perfect summer's day. A few puffy white clouds in a startlingly blue sky above. Not too hot. Not too cold. I rolled down the window a fraction to let the breeze move through the car, and I talked to Millie, explaining the scenery as we passed. It was mostly so she heard my voice. Her car seat legally had to be rear-facing until she was fifteen months old, so we attached a mirror to the rear seat so we could see her expression.

I chatted to her about the vibrant, varying shades of greens in the grass and the trees, and how they contrasted beautifully against the water on our left. First, we drove past the Dornoch Firth, and then we followed the denim-blue water of the Kyle of Sutherland. Fyfe interjected to share that he and Lewis once jumped into the Kyle butt-naked on a dare from friends when they were sixteen.

I laughed, shaking my head at their nonsense. "Never tell my mother that story." The Kyle of Sutherland was deep, the bottom was treacherous, and the current could be extremely strong. "What else did you two get up to that I don't know about?"

Fyfe chuckled boyishly. "A few things."

"Dada," Millie grumbled from the back seat. "Dada!"

"Just a while longer, wee yin," Fyfe assured her. "Then we'll stop for some food."

Once we'd crossed the River Shin, the roads changed to a single carriageway. It wasn't a particularly busy road during the rest of the year, but there were more tourists around this part of the country in the summer. We got stuck behind a motorhome with a foreign number plate. They were clearly very nervous on the single carriageway, and Millie grew fussier by the second. I attempted to quiet her with more descriptions of our surroundings, but the words alone were not soothing her.

Between Fyfe having to drive at a ridiculously slow pace, the traffic building up behind us, and Millie's ever-increasing volume of protest, I started singing.

I'd only ever sung to Millie when I was on my own. It was the one thing guaranteed to soothe her.

Her favorite was Taylor Swift, which pleased me to no end but did not bode well for my alternative rock–loving boyfriend.

Millie's absolute favorite track was "Bigger Than the Whole Sky." Of course she loved the melody and didn't understand the melancholy lyrics. At least I hoped not.

Just as the motorhome pulled into a stopping place to allow us all to pass, Millie's loud complaints slowly faded to silence. I sang a wee bit longer, just in case, and then let the lyrics trail off.

It was only then I sensed something emanating from Fyfe.

I glanced at him.

Awe saturated his expression, making my next question breathy with wonder. "What is it?"

"How the hell did I not know you can sing like that? You sing like an angel."

Pleasure suffused me. "I guess you never heard me sing in the few musicals I did as a teen. Other than that, I haven't had much cause to sing. But Millie likes it. She's a bit of a Taylor Swift fan, just so you know."

"That was Taylor Swift?"

"Yup."

"It was beautiful," Fyfe opined gruffly. "You're beautiful."

I reached over and pressed a kiss to his cheek, his beard scratching deliciously on my chin before I pulled back. "*You're* beautiful."

He gave a sexy huff of laughter like he wasn't quite sure how to respond.

Not long later, Fyfe indicated left and took a very short track down toward the River Oykel. A footpath through grass-covered dunes led to a small patch of golden sand on the riverbank. It was perfect for a picnic.

Fyfe gathered Millie and the blanket while I grabbed the basket, and we made the very short trek to the riverside. It was a calm, slow flow of sparkling blue water. The hills slowed upward on the other side in patches of forests and spring greens, moss, amber, and copper. It was beautifully secluded, and the landscape created a natural windbreak against the gentle breeze.

Millie giggled as Fyfe held her and I slathered sun protection all over her perfect skin. She wriggled and wrinkled her nose, bearing her four front teeth. "I love you so much I could burst with it." I covered her cheeks in kisses, making her giggle harder. My eyes flew to Fyfe and he gazed at me like ...

Well ... like he loved me.

My heart beat a wee bit faster as I filed his expression away and made sure Millie's cheeks were protected. Fyfe straightened her little hat, keeping her on his lap. I insisted on smoothing sun cream on the back of his neck and arms, and he watched me in that same way as before. With a possessive tenderness that reflected what I felt for him.

Was he ever going to tell me he loved me?

I shoved that worry aside, not wanting it to ruin our day. After we were all sun protected, I set out the picnic on our blanket. Fyfe fed Millie first and then we hungrily started on our food. We gave little bits that Millie could eat to quell her growing agitation at being left out food-wise. She always wanted to eat whatever we were eating.

"This girl is going to love her food, I think," I informed Fyfe.

"Maybe she'll learn to cook and help her auld da out."

"You're a pretty good cook." We'd taken turns with our evening meals and while neither of us were spectacular cooks, we did okay.

"Ae!" Millie reached for the chocolate hazelnut pastry thing Callie had suggested from today's bakery menu. It was bloody heaven in pastry casing. "Ae!"

Happiness overwhelmed me every time Millie used her version of my name. "This one is mine, Mills. You'll get to try this scrumptiousness when you're a wee bit older."

"In moderation," Fyfe added as he stuffed the whole thing in his mouth. He watched me laugh, his eyes twinkling with amusement. When he swallowed, he warned, "If we don't stop eating at Callie's, I'm going to put on weight."

"Put on weight. As long as you're happy, who cares?" I shrugged.

"Seriously?" He raised an eyebrow. "If I didn't work out, you wouldn't care?"

I scowled at him.

Then ... fuck it.

"I loved you when you were a skinny wee Clark Kent and I love you as the built Superman I see before me. I'll love you if you put on weight, lose your hair, go blind and/or deaf, can't walk, can't speak, and need help to dress in the morning. Whatever the future brings, I love *you*, not the fancy wrapping."

"Ae!" Millie clapped with a grin, as if she agreed with me.

Fyfe barely noticed. He was gazing at me as if I'd just hung the moon.

I waited with bated breath.

His lips parted to speak.

Then Millie reached for his glasses, almost breaking the right temple as she curled her tight fist around it and yanked.

"No, wee yin." Fyfe gently removed her grip. He shot me a smirk. "I know you like the glasses, but she can't grab contacts off my face."

Disappointment curled in my stomach, but I forced a smile as I looked down to pull a bottle of water out of the picnic basket. "Then wear your contacts."

A slight tension invaded our picnic. I tried not to let my discontent spoil the day, but I found myself giving all my attention to Millie because I didn't know how to deal with Fyfe's inability to say those three little words.

In a normal relationship, I'd consider it completely understandable to wait several months before saying it.

But we'd known each other since I was ten years old. If he didn't love me now, then he probably never would.

AFTER THE PICNIC, WE GOT BACK INTO THE VOLVO to drive on a little farther. I could feel Fyfe watching me as I tidied everything away and loaded it back into the SUV, but I couldn't look at him.

Today was supposed to be perfect. Maybe that was too much pressure to put on a day, but after the last few weeks, I'd needed perfection.

I'd had to answer a few more questions for the case against Peter Pryor. And when Jasper didn't take down his videos in which he besmirched my name, I began legal action. It was

Forever the Highlands

only then he absolutely shit himself. Danny reckoned Jasper was lulled into thinking I would just take his abuse because he'd gotten away with it for months. Only when he realized I was serious did he backtrack. I agreed not to sue under the proviso he not only take down all content about me but he release a statement retracting his accusations.

He'd done it and hopefully that was the last I'd ever hear of my old friend.

It was heartbreaking to see our friendship turn to such bitterness. It was exhausting too.

I'd just needed one beautiful day with my boyfriend and his daughter, whom I loved.

I couldn't help if wanting more from Fyfe than he could give soured it.

I really ... I thought he might love me.

So why couldn't he say it?

The landscape changed as we traveled farther north. The scenery grew a little marshier, more rusts and browns interrupting the summer greenery. We passed by a couple of lochs and tourists who had stopped to take photographs of the ruins of Ardveck Castle. The white clouds grew closer as we climbed upward. So close you almost felt like you could reach out and touch them. The road was dual carriageway again, but it began to hairpin more dramatically through the rugged, grasscovered rocky hills.

My breath caught as Loch Gleann Dubh (Gaelic for Black Glen Loch) came into sight on our right. At this elevation, there was a slight mist over the water, even during the summer. It was magical. Like it might even be a gateway to Faerie.

"Happy?" Fyfe asked me.

An ache of longing pierced me. "Of course."

A muscle ticked in his jaw, as if he didn't believe me.

We were just approaching the famous Kylesku Bridge, a curved concrete bridge across the waters of Loch a' Chàirn

Bhàin (Gaelic for White Cairn Loch) when Fyfe pulled off into the car park before it. It was busy with tourist traffic.

"What are you doing?"

"Taking Millie for a wee look at the loch before we head home."

Millie was eager to be out of the car seat. Fyfe hooked on her baby carrier, and we settled her into it so she was facing outward against his chest and could see the view. We trekked down as close to the water as we could and watched a boat travel under the bridge.

"Aunt Robyn took a drone shot over the bridge that takes my breath away every time I see it." Robyn was a successful photographer, specializing in photos of the Highlands. She'd taken the Kylesku Bridge photo when she first met my uncle Lachlan. Uncle Lachlan and Robyn loved it so much, they'd blown up the photograph and it now hung in the entryway of their house. "I love that photograph. And I've offered to buy it so many times, but she said she can't part with it for money."

"Aye?" Fyfe smiled in thought. "I don't think I've seen it."

"It captures that feeling you get when you take time to stand on Ardnoch Beach when it's empty. Or stand at the peak of a hill or on the banks of a loch. You know that feeling? Like ... awe, but peace, too, because you realize we're such a small part of something so beautiful. And for a second or two, you forget all the things you worry about on a daily basis. You remember how lucky you are to have this beauty at your fingertips. It isn't scary to realize that it will last long after I'm gone. It's comforting. It puts everything in perspective. Makes the overwhelming stuff feel almost insignificant in the grand scheme of things ... and I just ... I feel at *peace*. Like everything will be okay." I turned to Fyfe. "Does that make sense?"

He nodded, searching my face. "Absolutely."

I shrugged, turning back to the view. "That's what Aunt Robyn's photo captures. Every time I look at it, I feel like I'm on the banks of a loch with no one else around. Utterly at peace because everything will turn out all right in the end."

After a while the tourists who'd accompanied us disappeared and we were on our own. I'd grown up in the Highlands and places like this still took my breath away. We were guardians of such a beautiful planet.

Yet that peace I'd spoken about evaded me. I was hyperaware of the man and child beside me. Fyfe's inability to say he loved me didn't seem like one of those insignificant things I'd spoken of. Realizing I wouldn't find my peace *here*, I wanted to leave.

"I think we should head back." I started climbing up the slight incline toward the car park.

"Eilidh Adair!" Fyfe called.

I spun around to shush him because some people might recognize my name.

He grinned, looking so handsome with his adorable baby daughter strapped to his chest that my lips clamped shut against the admonishment.

"Just thought you should know ... I'm pretty much as in love with you as a person can get."

Joy flushed through me so quickly, I should be terrified by how much this man affected my mood. "Really?"

His expression turned serious. "Now get your arse back here so I can kiss you."

"Bossy," I grumbled but hopped down beside them. "Say it again."

And there it was. That look I'd witnessed earlier. Tenderness and awe and possessiveness. "I love you so fucking much, Eilidh Adair."

I bit my lip to suppress a cheesy grin, and Fyfe reached out to pull me closer. Millie kicked me in the chest as she beamed at my sudden proximity. "You shouldn't swear in front of Mills."

298 Samantha Young

"I'll stop when she's older," he promised. "Now fucking kiss me and tell me you love me."

My laughter was swallowed in his kiss as he maneuvered around Millie to take my mouth. It was short but beautiful and when he released me, I told him what he already knew. "I love you too." My gaze dropped to Millie. "I love you both."

I kissed Millie's cheek and then reached up to kiss Fyfe again.

His voice was gruff as he announced, "Move in with us."

"What?"

"We're already living together. You know we're meant to be a family, so why wait?"

I didn't think it was possible to get any happier than when he'd told me he loved me, but there I was. So giddy, my cheeks hurt from smiling. "Okay."

Fyfe's return smile was so big, it made my heart swell. "Aye?"

"Aye. But I'm buying rugs and throws and cushions and putting up—" He cut me off with another kiss. Millie broke our connection by slapping us as she let out a high-pitched squeal. Laughing, we pulled apart.

"You can do what you want to the house," Fyfe assured me. "It's yours now too."

The bliss was just a wee bit too much and tears blurred my vision.

Fyfe was used to the fact that I'd become a crier. Whether happy, sad, frustrated, or stressed, I was now a big old crier and I couldn't care less. Neither could he. He just pressed a tender kiss to my forehead and laced our fingers together. "Let's go home. Ready to go home, wee yin?" he asked Millie as we climbed up the incline.

"Dada Ae!" she squealed.

And there went my heart, bursting all over the place.

THIRTY-NINE
FYFE

I was only twelve when Lewis first invited me to his parents' house for a family dinner. I'd walked into the beautiful coastal home and looked past the impressive architecture, the privilege, the view ... because I was overwhelmed by the energy in the room. Lewis's aunts and uncles and cousins were like an overfilled fruit bowl. So much color and vibrancy spilling out everywhere.

I'd never known the warmth of camaraderie, teasing banter, the hilarity of multiple conversations going on at once as food was traded up and down two tables. That first dinner was one of the happiest days of my young life, but when I'd returned home to an empty cottage, it had also been the worst.

It was at that moment I'd realized how much was missing from my life, and I'd never resented my mother more.

However, I'd rarely turned down the opportunity to sit in on an Adair family dinner. Eilidh's parents had been attempting to organize a large dinner Millie and I could attend since I'd started seeing their daughter. My girlfriend had been putting it off because she didn't want the scrutiny when we were so new. After I'd finally gotten up the courage to tell her I loved her, I hadn't realized how much insecurity she'd been hoarding. I think I only realized when she immediately started planning all these family events. An official Sunday dinner with the Adairs was the first on the agenda.

Considering how protective the Adair men were, I'd expected threats and warnings. Instead, Eilidh's uncles, much like her father, Thane, gave me big man hugs and relieved grins while thumping me on the back in welcome.

Lewis must have seen my bemusement because he'd leaned in to explain, "They know you. They trust you with her. I do too. And being with you means she's more likely to stick around. You're officially an Adair now. But you always were, mate."

Honestly, I was grateful I didn't start bawling in front of the entire family.

The best part, though, was watching Millie light up under so much attention. I was concerned this many people might be too much for her, but her unintelligible baby words and giggles floated toward me as the Adairs lavished their affection upon her. The only people not in attendance who usually were, were Callie's mum and dad and brother. They were in Italy for ten days' vacation.

The eldest of Lewis and Eilidh's younger cousins were Lachlan and Robyn's daughter, Vivien, and Arrochar and Mac's daughter, Skye. Eilidh had told me the girls were going into their final year of high school after the summer, which seemed mind-boggling because they were toddlers when I'd first met them. Vivien and Skye couldn't be more different, but I'd noticed how close they were at all of these dinners, and I knew from Eils that the cousins were best friends.

All the Adair kids were teens now. Arran and Eredine's twin girls were the youngest along with Robyn and Lachlan's boy, Brechin. They were fourteen, but Keely and Kia (the twins) were turning fifteen this year. Lennox (Nox) Brodan and Monroe's son was sixteen.

Watching them from a father's standpoint felt very different. I could see how quickly the years would pass. I had to make sure I didn't miss a second of Millie's childhood because clearly it would be over before I knew it.

The melancholic thought was stripped away as Kia and Keely asked if they could take Harley and Millie out in their strollers. We agreed, but Eilidh advised they bring Mills back if she was fussing.

As Robyn, Regan, and Thane insisted on cooking, everyone else kept them company, catching up on one another's lives. We didn't discuss anything too serious since most of the teens were still here, even though they didn't appear to be listening to a word we said. They'd congregated over on the couch and now and then looked up from their individual devices to say something to each other.

There was a close call when Lewis nearly slipped up as Regan went to pour Callie a glass of wine. He'd instantly covered the glass and opened his mouth only to slam it shut. I'd smothered a smirk as he shot Callie a wide eyed "fuck" expression.

"I'm driving tomorrow." Callie shrugged nonchalantly. "To Inverness to pick up a piece of equipment for the bakery. I can't drink."

No one was the wiser except the four people in the room who knew Callie was pregnant again.

The twins returned with Millie and Harley and the wee yin seemed perfectly content. Dinner was almost ready, so I set her up in a chair at the end of the table next to Harley's high chair and me and Lewis fed our daughters their dinner before we ate.

We were just chatting among ourselves as Mac and Lachlan rose to help serve the food when Vivien wandered over to the table with Skye at her side. Her attention zeroed in on her parents in the kitchen. Vivien was precocious and extremely confident and always had been. Her boyfriend was a year older, went to college in Inverness, and they'd been dating for nine months. Lachlan hated him. Surprise, surprise. Skye was quieter, a little shyer and more reserved, though much to Mac's chagrin, she also had a boyfriend. A boy in their year at Ardnoch High School who lived in Golspie.

"So ... Skye and I had to do a family tree project for some stupid thing in English class," Vivien announced.

Lachlan looked up from plating food. "And?"

"And ... my brain hurt from trying to work out how we're related. Skye and I are shocked, I tell you. Shocked. Perhaps even traumatized."

Eilidh choked on her swallow of wine and I tried not to laugh.

Robyn narrowed her eyes on her daughter as she rounded the island with a plate of sides in each hand. "Why are you traumatized?"

"Eh, trying to explain to our teacher and the class how we're related, for a start." Vivien threw her hands up. "It is the first time in my life that I have ever acted less than cool."

"You know"—Arran waved a fork at her, already digging into the food before everyone else—"calling yourself cool cancels out the cool."

Brodan chuckled, nodding in agreement.

Vivien ignored both her uncles. "We had to tell our teacher we'd come back and explain it to her once you all explained it to us."

"And you chose now?" Mac's lips curled with suppressed laughter.

"Well, you're all here, Pops."

"You've been calling that man your grandfather since you

FOREVER THE HIGHLANDS 303

could talk and you haven't figured out you and Skye are more than cousins?" Lewis teased.

Everyone burst into laughter.

Vivien sighed heavily with the weariness of being cooler than everyone else in the room. "Aye, but how do you explain that? You try!"

"If Dad is Vivien's grandfather," Skye spoke up, "then how is Mum her aunt Arro?"

"Because I'm both," Arro offered. "And I'm slightly worried that it's taken you almost eighteen years to ask this. No offense, sweeties."

I smothered a snort.

"Like, I've been calling you Aunt Robyn"—Skye directed her attention to Robyn—"but you're actually like my sister?"

"Half sister." Robyn frowned. "We've talked about this. Surely?" She placed more plates in front of folks and stood back, hands on her hips. "We cannot have gone eighteen years without addressing this."

"Well, it is a bit incestuous," Brodan joked.

Monroe shoved him and he gave a bark of laughter.

"It is?" Vivien and Skye asked in unison.

"Ha ha! You're incestuous!" Brechin shouted comically from the living room, not even looking up from his Nintendo.

"If I am, you are too!" Vivien rolled her eyes drolly and gestured over her shoulder. "Worry less about my intelligence and more about the tool behind me."

"I think it's just so intertwined, no one ever talked about it," Eredine said. "The relationship between you all, I mean."

"Explain it from the start," I inserted. "Maybe if we break it down, we can come up with a coherent explanation for your teacher."

"Okay." Vivien pointed to her mother. "Mum married Dad. Dad's sister is Aunt Arro. Mum's dad is Mac, and Mac married Aunt Arro. So ... Mum is Skye's half sister through her dad, but she's also Skye's aunt through Lachlan's sibling relationship to Aunt Arro."

"Correct." Robyn nodded.

"Aunt Arro is technically my aunt but also my grandmother because she's married to my mum's dad."

"Also correct."

Vivien made a face. "And you don't think that's confusing?"

"I have a vague memory of asking that exact question as a child." Eilidh's lips trembled with laughter.

"You forgot the part where Lachlan is Skye's uncle via Arro but also her brother-in-law," Arran added helpfully.

Arro shot her brother a killing look. He grinned unrepentantly.

"So what are me and Skye?" Vivien asked.

"Cousins via your dad and Aunt Arro," Robyn provided. "And technically, Skye is your aunt via me and your pops."

A smug grin curled the corners of Skye's mouth. "Interesting."

Everyone burst into laughter.

Especially when Vivien, who'd always considered herself the more authoritative of the two, contemplated that and said, "I think we should never speak of this weirdness again and go back to being just cousins."

"That might be for the best," Mac agreed with a grin.

"I don't know what you're laughing at. I blame you, Pops."

"What did I do?"

"Married my sister," Lachlan offered helpfully. "Robyn and I married first. You two"—he gestured between Arro and Mac—"are to blame for making it weird by marrying next."

"I was in love with Arro before you even met Robyn. You married my daughter."

They bickered good-naturedly and Brodan turned to his

nieces. "See what you've done? We've gone a decade without this argument recurring."

"Hey, we're the offspring of their weirdness. If anyone has trauma from it, it's us."

"Oh, so much trauma," Lewis teased. "With your privileged lives and loving family. How will you ever cope?"

Vivien very maturely stuck out her tongue at her cousin and settled at the small table with the rest of the teens to eat.

"Have I mentioned lately how much I love your family?" I said to Eilidh as we all dug into eat.

"Your family too." She nudged me before taking a bite of her roast dinner.

Aye, my family too now.

I couldn't wait to make it official. But Eilidh had only just moved in, and her new career was only on its training wheels. Patience. The time would come soon enough.

Forty
FYFE

E ilidh bit her lip, stifling her moans and gasps, as I moved inside her in deep thrusts.

I'd woken up this morning, after just a few hours of sleep, to Eilidh stroking my cock and kissing my chest. It was an hour before my alarm was due to go off, but I didn't care. Millie did not sleep all the way through the night, and Eils and I had to take advantage of any time we could be together.

Watching Eilidh turn her cheek into the pillows, her knuckles in her mouth, teeth biting down, her breasts trembling with every drive into her body, I could feel my balls drawing up tight.

"Come, baby," I growled.

My phone rang on the bedside cabinet.

"Ignore it," I demanded as her eyes flew open.

I braced a hand at her side and slid the other between our legs to rub her clit. A few seconds later, Eilidh stuffed her fist back in her mouth to stifle her cries as she came. Her pussy muscles rippled with the climax, fisting around my dick. Fuck, she felt amazing.

FOREVER THE HIGHLANDS   307

"Eilidh." I groaned, pleasure rolling through my limbs as I emptied into the condom. One day, I was going to come inside this woman with nothing between us, and I couldn't fucking wait.

My phone rang again as we tried to catch our breaths.

Agitation thrummed through me as I reluctantly pulled out of Eilidh and rolled over to pick up the phone. "Whoever this is, it better be important."

"Eh ... Fyfe?"

"Speak."

"It's Adam."

Instantly alert, I pushed to sitting. Adam was an employee, and he was also someone I paid extra to do bonus work for me. Like keeping tabs on people of interest. "What's up?"

"An ambulance was sent to your mum's house last night. Her wife's daughter overdosed. Spoke to someone at the local hospital down there. Girl was DOA. Thought you'd want to know."

Despite everything, compassion for my mother and her wife swarmed through me. "Thanks for letting me know, Adam."

"Sorry it wasn't better news."

"Aye, speak soon." We hung up.

Eilidh rested her chin on my shoulder, her hand smoothing over my chest. "What's wrong?"

I told her the information Adam relayed.

"That's awful." Eilidh kissed my shoulder. "I'm sorry for your mum and her partner."

"Me too."

"Do ... do you want to do anything about it?"

I turned into her, wrapping my arms around her as I rested against the headboard. "Is it terrible if I say no?"

"Of course not."

"I just ... I think all that resentment I felt toward my

mother came hurtling back when Millie entered my life. Knowing that at some point I have to explain to her that Pamela gave her up. And as much as I hate that anyone is going through what my mum and her wife are going through, I don't want my mother around. I don't want to invite that resentment back into my life. Especially now that I have you and Millie to protect too. I can forgive her, but only to free myself. And I don't think I can follow through on that forgiveness if I let her back in. Not that she wants anything to do with me, anyway."

Eilidh's eyes were full of compassion. "I get it. The forgiveness stuff."

"Aye?"

She stroked my cheek tenderly, her fingernails scratching through my beard. "I think forgiveness is earned and when it hasn't been earned, we don't owe that person anything. We only owe ourselves the grace of forgiveness. And I think there are some people who we can only ever forgive if we never have to see them again."

I slid my hand around her nape to pull her in for a kiss. It felt too much, what Eilidh meant to me. Too much for words. I poured all that feeling into our kiss until she was breathless and dazed and everything else but the love between us ceased to exist.

With Theo back from his travels, Eilidh left a few hours later to be in on a meeting Theo had procured with the streaming giant who'd also aired *Young Adult*.

Eilidh was feeling optimistic but trying not to get her hopes up too high. Usually these kinds of things didn't move as quickly as they currently were, and I think she thought it was all a bit too good to be true. I hope Theo proved her wrong.

After dropping Millie at daycare with Regan, I'd returned home, telling Eilidh I could work from home today. The truth was, I was awaiting a delivery.

I sat on the couch with my laptop, feet up on the table, working while I waited. My home was slowly being transformed. Every time I walked in, there was something new. A lamp, a rug, a throw, cushions. Everything Eilidh had promised. There were photographs of us and Millie in frames on a gallery wall in the living room. Framed artwork started appearing too. It was amazing how all those things that made the place more homely also made the place less echoey.

Eilidh had even ordered storage for Millie's toys and she had a dedicated play area beside the living room. The only time I'd gotten a wee bit concerned was when the artwork started going up because I had something in mind for the expanse of wall at the entrance of the house.

Thankfully, Eilidh hadn't gotten to that area yet.

My eyes kept moving to the time on the laptop. Eilidh's meeting would be over soon, and my delivery still hadn't arrived. Just when I was starting to fret, my phone beeped with the alert.

The camera app opened to reveal the Range Rover pulling into my drive. Dumping my laptop, I hurried to the door, throwing it open just as Robyn Adair jumped out of the vehicle. She wore aviator sunglasses, her ponytail blowing in the wind. Smiling broadly, she rounded the SUV to open the boot. "Did I make it in time?"

"Right on time." Anticipation moved through me as I bridged the distance between us. She'd flattened the seats to lay out the large item wrapped in brown paper. "This is it?"

"This is it."

Together we eased it out of the SUV and Robyn followed

me, a professional hanging kit in her hands, as we strolled inside.

"Nice. Perfect place."

"I can't wait to see it."

Carefully, Robyn unwrapped the framed photograph, and I inhaled and exhaled slowly, a little taken aback by my reaction to it.

Eilidh was right.

It was a phenomenal photograph of Kylesku Bridge and the surrounding loch and hills. "Robyn ... you are a very talented photographer."

"Thanks." She patted the frame. "Shall we get it up there?"

Together, we measured the space and attached the hanging kit before carefully placing the photograph onto the wall.

We stepped back, and I stared at it in awe. "I can see why Eilidh loves it so much." I looked at my girlfriend's aunt. I knew she could charge a lot of money for her exclusive photography. "Please let me pay you for it."

"Nope." Robyn shook her head stubbornly. "I always told my niece I could never take money for it. What no one knows about me is I'm kind of a secret romantic. Can't take money, but I'll take being part of a grand gesture I know will make my niece very happy. Not because she's getting a photograph she's admired for years. But because she's getting a man who would have hounded me until the end of time to get it for her. After everything she's been through, Eilidh deserves someone who would do just about anything to make her happy."

Emotion constricted my throat as I looked back at the photograph. I'd approached Robyn almost immediately after our drive out to Kylesku. She'd refused. At first. I'd offered money. Offered tutoring for Vivien and Brechin. And then I'd left her a voicemail explaining why Eilidh loved it so much and how much I loved her and wanted her to have it.

FOREVER THE HIGHLANDS   311

I'd promised to back off if the photograph just held too much sentimental attachment for Robyn to let it go. The next day, Robyn called me, telling me she was happy to gift it.

Now I knew why.

"You are all a very special family," I said gruffly. "I hope you know that."

"I guess ... we've all been through a lot. It makes you appreciate what's truly important. And reminds you every day to take care of it." Robyn squeezed my shoulder. "I need to get back, but it looks good."

"It does. Thank you."

"Oh. The photo looks great. But I was talking about you. Being in love looks good on you." She winked at me and strolled out the door, closing it softly behind her.

I was on absolute tenterhooks waiting for Eilidh to come home.

Wanting a direct line of sight so I could see her reaction without giving anything away, I sat at the island with my laptop. The little beep on my phone had me tensing on the stool. My head turned toward the door as it opened and Eilidh stepped inside, her gaze on me. "I think that went well." She ran a hand over her hair, kicking her shoes off, and her attention snagged on the photograph for a second before she started walking toward me. "I mean it—" Eilidh abruptly halted and spun robotically back toward the photograph. Her jaw literally dropped.

"What the ... how ..." She gestured to it. "That's ... when ... how ..."

Chuckling, I hopped down and strolled across the room. I embraced Eilidh, huddling her against me. "Do you like it there?"

She gaped up at me. "How ... explain?"

I shrugged with more casualness than I felt. "I offered to

pay Robyn for it. She said no. So I explained how much I wanted to give it to you, and she presented it to us as a gift."

"But how?" Eilidh's fingers curled into my shirt. "I've been pleading for years for it."

"Remember Robyn said she wouldn't give it up for money?"

"Aye?"

"Well, she didn't. She gave it up for love."

Tears brightened Eilidh's beautiful eyes. "She gave it up because you love me."

My voice was hoarse as I replied, "So much, Eilidh Adair, I can't even begin to explain how much."

"I can't believe you did this for me."

"Do you love it?"

She nodded, wrapping her arms around me, her cheek pressed to my chest as she looked up at the landscape. "I love it so much. But I love you more. There will never be anyone for me but you."

It had taken me too long to believe that was true, but finally I did. I pressed my cheek to the top of her head, cuddling her tightly. "Aye, nor for me, baby. Nor for me."

Forty-One
EILIDH

My starting-over adventure had been going way too well these last few weeks.

I'd thought the gnawing pit in my stomach had something to do with how quickly my TV show was coming together, a complete industry anomaly.

It turned out, that feeling of dread, of waiting for the other shoe to drop, had nothing to do with how well my career change was going.

It also had nothing to do with me and Fyfe. We'd fallen remarkably easy into a serious relationship and embraced our family unit with Millie.

I was packing for a long weekend business trip with Theo. We were heading to London to meet with the London office of the streaming service who were showing all the signs that they were ready to greenlight this project. Fyfe was at Ardnoch Estate discussing new updates to the security system on the program that housed all their members' personal and financial details.

Contemplating whether three pairs of shoes was overkill,

my phone rang and I strolled toward where I'd placed it on the bed. It was Mum. "Hi," I answered. "Do you think three pairs—"

"Eilidh." Mum gasped out, tears in her voice.

My heart stopped. "What? What is it?"

"Someone took Millie," Mum sobbed. "I'm so sorry."

"Who took Millie?" I demanded, adrenaline rushing through me. An image of a woman I'd never met floated through my mind. Pamela. Millie's mum. "How? When? Who? Have you called the police? Fyfe?"

"Yes. The police are out looking and Fyfe is on his way. I said I'd call you. I wasn't there. My staff were. The kids started screaming at something in the playroom so all my staff went running, leaving the nursery empty for just a few seconds. Millie was napping in one of the cots. When they returned, Millie was gone."

I felt abruptly lightheaded. "Was it Pamela? Did Pamela take her?"

Mum sounded breathless with emotion. "I don't know who did it. I'm driving back from Inverness with your dad. The police are checking the camera feeds. Fyfe is on his way to check them too."

Sickness rolled in my stomach as I hurried downstairs in search of my car keys. "I need to go to him," I told Mum before hanging up. I couldn't fall apart. I had to keep it together. Forcing myself not to think about Millie and how scared she must be, and that someone had stolen her ... I shoved the horror from my mind. Fyfe and Millie needed me to keep my shit together.

Who could have taken Millie?

Was it Pamela? She seemed like the most likely culprit. Right?

Fear curdled my blood.

What if it was Cameron Phillips? What if it was him or another weirdo who had fixated on me and had been watching us?

What if my past had invited another sick bastard into our lives and this was all my fault?

Forty-Two
FYFE

Scrambling for my phone, I pulled up the email Adam had sent me on my mother and her new family. Scrolling through the ID pics, I stared at my mother's wife's photo. "That's her. Right?" I held it out to the police officer who had introduced himself but for the life of me couldn't remember his name.

I'd almost crashed my fucking car driving like a maniac to the daycare center in Caelmore. If I thought too hard on the fact that my daughter was in a stranger's hands, that she'd been kidnapped after only a mere few months in my care, I'd lose my mind.

And I was no good to Millie as a panicked glob of emotion rather than a capable father who could find her.

The officer studied the CCTV footage from the nursery that clearly showed a blond woman skulking into the room and leaving with Millie in her arms. I reached over and paused the footage just as she was departing and looked up at the camera as if she hadn't realized it was there.

The copper studied the image on my phone and nodded grimly. "It looks like a match. Who is it?"

FOREVER THE HIGHLANDS   317

"My mother's wife," I bit out angrily just as the phone buzzed in my hand, startling me. "Unknown caller."

"Put it on speaker," the police officer demanded.

Fingers shaking, I did just that. "Hello."

There was some heavy breathing and a moment of hesitancy before she spoke. "I have your bairn. I'm going to text a bank account number to you. I want fifty grand in that account by the end of the day or you'll never see your daughter again."

"Jay McDonald," I said her name.

There was a wee gasp on the other end of the line.

Rage suffused me.

The police officer mouthed, "Keep her talking."

"We know who you are. You can't get away with this," I gritted out. "If anything happens—"

The copper put a hand on my arm, shaking his head.

Right.

Don't threaten my daughter's kidnapper.

"I couldn't give a shit. Put the money over or you won't see her again. That's a promise." She hung up.

A buzzing filled my brain and I think I might have started trashing Regan's office if my phone hadn't vibrated again with a text. It was the account details.

"Do you have your stepmother's address? We'll send a unit now."

I shook my head, my mind racing. "No. She's not from here. I-I have no idea where she might be hiding." But I knew how to find her. It just wasn't legal. "Excuse me. I need to call my girlfriend and tell her what's happening."

The copper opened his mouth to speak, but I was already hurrying out of the office and past the frightened staff. I couldn't look at them. I knew it wasn't their fault, but I was furious with the world and everyone in it right now.

As soon as I was alone outside, I called Lore and told her

to trace Jay's location from the call. It would mean hacking telecommunications, which was why I hadn't shared my idea with the police. And then I called Eilidh.

She picked up on the first ring. I knew Regan was calling her to inform her of Millie's kidnapping so I just launched in without preamble.

"It's my mum's wife," I announced in frantic outrage. "Eilidh, Mum's wife has Millie. Jay. She called. She wants money in exchange for giving Millie back."

"Has she lost her fucking mind?" Eilidh screeched and there was a sick part of me that took satisfaction in her wrath. I needed her to feel this as deeply as I was and it was a strange comfort that she did. "How does she think she's actually going to get away with this?"

"I don't think she's thinking!" I yelled back but not at Eilidh. "I have Lore tracing the call to find out where the fuck she is."

"She can't be familiar with the area," Eilidh replied.

"I don't know. Maybe she was with my mother when she visited all those months ago. I don't know."

Eilidh was quiet for a few seconds and then, "Do you mean when your mother came to ask you about the cottage?"

"Aye."

"Fyfe, is the cottage empty?"

"Aye, it's not rented out again until Monday."

I heard the squeal of tires in the background. "I'm on my way there."

A different kind of fear scored through me. "You think she's at the cottage?"

"If your mother showed her the house, she might very well be. It's worth checking out."

"Let me talk to the police. Send them in." If Jay could kidnap a baby, who knew what else she was capable of. Buried in the back of my mind was the knowledge that this woman

FOREVER THE HIGHLANDS 319

lost her daughter a few weeks ago. That she was likely suffering some kind of emotional breakdown. "Don't you dare approach that house."

"I'll be safe."

"Eilidh!"

"It's Millie, Fyfe. I'll let you know what I find."

"Eilidh—" She hung up on me.

Abject terror clashed with my fury and I just stopped myself from smashing my phone off the wall. "FUCK!"

Forty-Three
EILIDH

Trying to keep my wits about me, I parked on the street behind Fyfe's old house and switched my phone on silent. All I needed was someone calling me when I was trying to be sneaky. I cut through the gardens at the back, hoping no one would peer out their window and start shouting at me for jumping through their rhododendrons. When I reached Fyfe's old place, I nimbly climbed the white picket fence that bordered the back garden and snuck up to the kitchen window. The only sound in my ears was rushing blood. It deafened me and my knees trembled so badly as I eased slowly upward to peer inside the kitchen window. It was empty.

I was hoping for some kind of confirmation so I could just call Fyfe.

I'd have to go around front and that would alert her if she saw me.

Maybe I could lay a trap out back so if she tried to escape through here, she'd be stopped. But then she might trip with Millie if she had her in her arms.

FOREVER THE HIGHLANDS 321

Shit, shit, shit. My gaze scoured the ground as I attempted to come up with a plan.

That's when I saw the fresh cigarette butt right outside the kitchen door.

So fresh, there was still a wee spark in among the ash.

Arm shaking as badly as my legs, I reached out and gently pushed down on the kitchen door.

My breath caught as it opened.

She was here. I just knew it.

Tiptoeing inside, I craned my neck to hear, willing my heart to slow so I could detect noise over the whooshing of my pulse. That's when Millie's cry rattled through me from somewhere in the cottage. It wasn't a big house. Living room, small kitchen, a hallway off that led to two bedrooms and a bathroom.

Creeping as silently as possible through the kitchen, I poked my head out.

There was no sign of her in the living room.

"Oh, shut up, girl." I heard a husky voice snap at Millie from my right. Toward the bedroom. "Here. Take this. Be quiet."

Millie did not take whatever was offered to her.

My hands curled into fists and I took a step out, holding my breath as my weight bore down on the floorboards. I inhaled a sigh of relief when there was no creak and took another step toward the bedrooms.

A slight squeak had me holding my breath.

Millie's cries must have covered it because there was no reaction from her captor.

A phone rang, startling me, and then I heard a belligerent, "What?"

I took another painfully slow step down the hallway.

"Don't fucking yell at me. I'm doing this for us!"

Another step.

"He owes us this, Innes! We don't have Jen anymore so we need this!" She broke on a sob. "No ... I can't ... I'm sorry ..."

Using her distraction against her, I rushed into the bedroom that was once Fyfe's, spotted his mother's wife at the window, back to me, one hand clenched in her hair, the other around the phone at her ear.

Millie was sprawled on her back on the bed. "Ae!" she sobbed at the sight of me. I grabbed Millie up in my arms just as Jay turned. I was already running out of the door as she yelled for me to stop.

With my baby girl screaming in my arms, I raced down the narrow hallway and into the living room.

A hard yank on my hair hauled me backward. "Stop! No!"

Terrified of getting into a tussle with Millie between us, I held her tight to my chest with one arm and blindly slammed my free elbow backward. It made contact with flesh and a howl of pain hit my ears as I was released.

I didn't stick around.

Sprinting for the door, I threw it open and started screaming bloody murder as soon as my feet hit the path outside. Millie started wailing right along with me. I turned to face the cottage as sirens sounded in the distance, drawing nearer and nearer.

Jay didn't appear, but several neighbors spilled out of their houses to see what the commotion was. One of them was Morag from the deli. My whole body shook with adrenaline and relief as I peppered wet kisses all over Millie's face. Her scared cries were devastating and even though I knew rationally it wouldn't help matters, I couldn't stop my sobs from joining hers. Morag wrapped her arm around me, confused, but supportive as the police car turned onto the street and drove straight for us.

Fyfe launched himself out of it before it drew to a complete stop and my knees almost gave out as he reached us

FOREVER THE HIGHLANDS   323

with tears in his eyes. Without a word, he drew us into his arms, hushing us both, pressing kisses to our cheeks and temples and murmuring over and over again how much he loved us.

At that moment, I didn't care where Jay was. Or what her motivation was.

From the time Mum had called me to the time I'd found Millie, it wasn't even an hour.

And yet it had been the longest period of time I'd ever experienced in my life.

I had nothing but gratitude that Millie was in my arms and that we were all safe.

That we were together.

EPILOGUE
FYFE

In the following nights, Millie slept in the cot I'd arranged at the bottom of our bed. Both Eilidh and I needed her there. Eilidh canceled her business trip, though I told her not to. She said she couldn't leave us. And thankfully the streaming service agreed to rearrange the meeting for next month.

Part of me was pissed off at Eilidh for forging ahead into an unknown situation that could have put both her and Millie at risk. She insisted she wouldn't have done it if she'd thought Millie's kidnapper was truly dangerous. As I pointed out, anyone who kidnapped a child was in a dangerous headspace.

Thankfully, it turned out Jay was the worst kidnapper that had ever existed. The police found her running through the gardens at the back of the village and arrested her. She was charged with kidnapping, child endangerment, and breaking and entering. She'd smashed open the lockbox where the house keys were stored for my holiday home renters.

In the days that followed, I found it hard to shake the jitters or the need to keep both Eilidh and Millie close. I worked from home all week and promised Eilidh I'd return to my regularly scheduled program after the weekend, and that Millie would need to sleep in the cot in her nursery.

The police kept us informed regarding Jay's pending case. She had a hearing in a few weeks, but from what they told us, she was going to cop to the charges and we'd probably not have to face a trial. Which was a relief since we already had one of those on the future docket.

Throughout it all, I never heard one word from Mum, though Eilidh was positive she'd overheard Jay on the phone to her.

It was a shock then when an alert on my phone went off and I saw a familiar Nissan park outside.

When I told Eilidh who was pulling up, her features grew taut with concern, but she told me to stay calm.

That all depended on what my mother had to say.

I opened the front door before she could even knock.

The well-put-together woman who'd stood at my door over a year ago now looked a little older, wearier. A bit bedraggled, even. But sober. Grief darkened her eyes. "Hullo, Fyfe." Her eyes moved to my side, and I glanced down to see Eilidh there. She slipped her arm around me, giving me her silent support. "I recognize you ...?"

"Eilidh Adair," she offered. "Fyfe's girlfriend."

"Right." My mother's gaze returned to mine. "I didn't want to call. What I have to say ... you deserve to hear from me, face-to-face."

A familiar dull ache almost made me slam the door.

However, I knew I'd always wonder. And if she was here to do more damage, at least I had Eilidh at my side.

Sliding my arm around Eilidh's shoulders, I drew her against me and eased her away from the door. "Come in."

Relief flickered over Innes's face as she stepped inside. Millie was in her cot, napping. Next week, we'd get her back to daycare. She needed her routine and Regan needed to know we didn't blame her for what happened. Eilidh's mum kept apologizing every time we saw her, and it was awful to see her so distressed. I think we knew the only way to solve that problem was to show Regan we trusted her. I had no doubt in my mind she would never let anything like this happen again under her watch.

Innes walked hesitantly into the living space, her attention going to Millie. She appeared obviously troubled as she studied me. "I am so sorry."

"You didn't do it."

She bit her trembling lip, glancing between me and Eils. "Could ... could we maybe talk in private?"

"No," I denied. "Whatever you say, I'm going to tell Eilidh, anyway."

I felt Eilidh's fingers curl into the fabric of my T-shirt as she leaned more heavily into me.

Innes nodded, exhaling shakily. "Okay. Well ..." I noted the bleached white of her knuckles as she gripped the strap of her handbag. "First, this is the last you'll see of me. I just wanted to apologize for what happened with Millie. But also what happened last year when I came here. Jay ... Jay talked me into it. She was here with me. That's how she knew about the cottage."

"I gathered," I clipped out.

Eilidh soothed a hand over my stomach and some of my bristling tempered.

"I won't blame Jay for what I did—asking for the cottage. That's on me. I ... Jen, her daughter, she was in with the wrong crowd. Doing drugs. And we thought if we could afford to move out of the area, she'd have a chance at starting over. When she died, Jay ..." Innes's eyes brightened, and she glanced at Millie. "I'll never be able to tell you how sorry I am. I should have tried harder with Jay, to get her some help. I knew she was plummeting off the deep end.

Please know, it was grief. She's never done anything like this before."

I did know that. The police had told me Jay had no criminal record. And I knew that grief was a strange monster. No one knew how it would affect them. I had compassion. To a point. But my daughter was stolen from me and for an hour, we'd all been terrorized by Jay's actions. "It's done."

"I'm not here to ask you to drop charges or anything," Innes reassured me. "She should do the time for what she did to you that morning, and Jay is remorseful. She agrees she should do the time."

"Why *are* you here?" Eilidh asked suspiciously.

"I'm here to be honest with you and to be honest with myself. Seeing Jay fall apart after Jen's death, to see what a mum's love and losing a child could do to a person, well, it clarified things for me ... I ... I wasn't built to be a mum. And I don't want you to think I went off and became a mum to someone else. Because I know that's the picture I painted. But the truth is, Fyfe, I fell in love with Jay and she came with a child. But ... I never wanted children." Her eyes gleamed with apology.

"It's not that I didn't love you, Fyfe. I just don't have it in me to be a mother. And that would be fine. I truly believe some people aren't meant to be parents and shouldn't be and shouldn't be judged for that ... but the reality is, I did have a child. I had a child, and I was terrible to you." A tear slipped down her cheek and she swiped it away. "If I could do it all again, I would never have listened to my mum. I would have given you up for adoption as a baby so you could have had what you deserved. A loving family. If I'd done that, it would have been the best version of my love."

I swallowed hard around the words, feelings, swelling inside.

"I'm sorry," she whispered.

328 SAMANTHA YOUNG

I could only nod.

Eilidh leaned her weight into me, her tone uncharacteristically cool. "Fyfe has a loving family. He's had a loving family since he was twelve years old. And he's had me. Now he has Millie too. For the rest of his life, not a day will pass without him knowing he's loved. So if that's all you came to say, I think it's time to leave."

Innes studied her thoughtfully, then nodded. We followed her to the door. Not another word was exchanged, but I stayed to watch her walk to her car. As she opened the driver's-side door, she looked back at me.

I lifted my hand and gave her a small wave of goodbye.

She pressed her lips together and got in the car as I closed the front door.

"That woman ..." Eilidh trembled with anger beside me.

I pulled her close, pressing a kiss to her hair. "Actually, what she said helped."

Eilidh jerked back. "It did?"

"It did. It made me understand Pamela better. She told me she wasn't built to be a mother and that giving Millie to me was giving her the best chance. Some people shouldn't be parents, Eils. This ... this is the best way Pamela can show her love for our daughter. And maybe I can forgive that after all."

Tilting her head back to stare up at me in awe, Eilidh whispered hoarsely, "You are the best man I know, Fyfe Moray. I'm so grateful I get to do life at your side."

I cupped her face in my hands and brushed a soft kiss across her lips. "Not as grateful as me," I promised her.

Nowhere near as thankful as me.

I was the luckiest man in all the Highlands.

THE END ... ALMOST ...
READ ON FOR A SPECIAL SECOND EPILOGUE

Second Epilogue
A Year Later

WALKER

I missed my wife.

In all the years we'd been together, I'd never missed her quite like this. Moreover, I was worried about her. Sloane had been working overtime at the bakery to cover Callie who was on maternity leave. And when she wasn't working overtime, her brain was worrying about our daughter, fussing over our grandkids Harley and Xander. Our son Harry was fifteen, obsessed with martial arts and football and uninterested in academics. This concerned Sloane who was spreading herself thin trying to make sure everyone had everything they needed from her.

Even with me there to make sure Harry did his homework, was fed, clothed, supported, and attending school and all his extracurriculars, it wasn't enough. I helped out with Callie and the grandkids when I could. But my woman couldn't switch off and it wasn't helping she was practically running that bakery all by herself at the moment. Xander was only a few months old so Callie was at home with him and our granddaughter Harley.

Fuck.

Granddaughter. Grandson.

We weren't old enough for that shit.

Well, I was.

Sloane wasn't.

Parking my SUV in the car park behind the bakery, I carried the flask of decaf coffee I'd made for my wife. The bakery hadn't been open today, but Sloane had gone in this afternoon to prep and she still hadn't come home. She'd texted me earlier to tell me she'd eaten, but I didn't know how much longer she was going to be, and I was sick of waiting at home alone. The bungalow felt so fucking empty.

School started back next week, the summer holidays already almost over, and Harry was making the most of his freedom, staying at his pal's house in Golspie for the night. His friend's parents assured me they were home, there was no partying, and they were holed up inside playing video games.

Far more innocent than the shit I'd gotten up to at fifteen.

I knocked on the back door of the bakery, already anticipating seeing my wife like I hadn't seen her in years.

It felt like it.

Other than when we were in our bed, I hadn't had Sloane to myself in weeks.

"It's me," I called through the door.

A few seconds later, the back entrance swung open. Ever since Callie was attacked at the bakery, I'd made both my wife and daughter promise no loud music when they were on their own and always to ask who was at the door before opening it.

Sloane's gorgeous face split into a happy smile as she stepped back to let me in. "What are you doing here?"

"Thought I'd bring you coffee." My gaze swept the place.

FOREVER THE HIGHLANDS 331

It looked like she was in the middle of cleaning up. There were trays of cakes in airtight containers waiting to be frosted, which I knew she'd do in the morning before opening. Bags of frosting ready to be chilled. Flour and bits of butter still on one of the counters.

Sloane ran a hand through her hair as she watched me set the carafe on her clean counter. Her eyes roamed over me greedily in a way I recognized after many years of marriage. Satisfaction heated my blood.

"I miss you." She gave me a soft smile as she echoed my feelings. "It feels like forever."

We'd been married for almost seventeen years. There had been disagreements and hurt feelings, but I could count those moments on one hand. Despite my resistance in the beginning, my wife had given me a beautiful life. I thought I'd wanted solitude. Instead, she'd given me the chaos of parenthood, as well as the gift of it. She'd filled an emptiness in me. Coming home to her and the kids fixed something broken in me. Sometimes I shuddered to think what my life would look like if Sloane hadn't fought so hard to show me what I needed.

I think that's why I hated sitting in the house alone.

There were very few people I'd admit that to. "Aye, it does feel like forever."

She sighed. "I was just finishing up and then coming home to you."

I shrugged. "I'm here now. Put me to work."

"No. You just sit there and keep me company." Sloane gestured to a couple of footstools over in the corner. "Tell me about your day."

I hungrily watched her as she moved around the bakery cleaning up. "Do you remember Dr. Dick?"

Sloane scowled. "I remember."

Dr. Dick was what Fyfe called Dr. Cameron Phillips. The moniker caught on. After I'd witnessed him trying to intimidate Eilidh into dating him, I'd made it my fucking mission to run the arsehole out of town. Eilidh was Callie's sister-in-law. She was family. I'd known her since she was a kid. No one fucked with my people. Or with women.

Her uncle Lachlan felt the same way. Once we'd discovered Dr. Dick had a habit of harassing and stalking women, Lachlan handed that information over to a journalist down in Edinburgh. Three months ago, the story on Dr. Dick broke. Eilidh, unfortunately, was pulled into another media storm over it. The poor lass. She'd been through a lot lately. But hopefully, this was the end of it and she'd get some peace. "The board revoked his medical license. Decision came in today. Lachlan told me."

Sloane straightened. There was that look in her eye. The one I secretly lived for. The look that said she thought I could do anything. "You and Lachlan did that."

"Mostly Lachlan."

"You both did it." Her smile was soft. "I'm proud of you."

"Proud of you," I murmured truthfully.

Her cheeks flushed and I was already anticipating a night alone in the house with her. "Callie stopped by with Harley and Xander today. I don't think she and Lewis quite realized how hard having two babies was going to be." Worry creased her forehead. "Maybe we could offer to take them for a few days?"

The woman didn't know how to stop. She'd always wanted to protect Callie (and Harry) from absolutely everything. Even new parent exhaustion. "Xander's too young. They wouldn't want to be away from him just now."

"You didn't see her. She's worn thin."

"And she'll get through it," I promised her. "When Xander's a bit older, we'll take them away for a long weekend. All of us. It'll give Callie and Lewis some free time without taking the kids away from them entirely."

Sloane considered the idea. "That could be good."

"They're fine. They're better than fine. This is what they wanted. And they're young enough to have the energy to handle it." When we had Harry, the exhaustion was a shock to my fucking system.

"True."

I cleared my throat, eyes devouring Sloane's every move as she finished cleaning up and began untying her apron. Her hair was scraped tightly back from her face for hygienic reasons, and I itched to tug the hair tie out in favor of my fist. Heat pooled in my gut. "I take it now is a bad time to suggest a holiday just for two? Lachlan offered to take Harry for a week next month. He and Brechin would love it." Brechin, Lachlan and Robyn's son, was in the same year at school and the two lads had become best pals lately. Brechin was also at this lad's sleepover in Golspie because wherever Harry went, Brechin followed.

Sloane turned to me, her pretty blue eyes lit with surprise. Seventeen years. I'd wondered if at some point, I'd lose my need for her. Strangely, my possessiveness for her only increased. "A holiday? Where?"

"Portugal. I might already have booked it." A private villa overlooking the water.

"Seriously?" she asked a bit breathlessly.

"Seriously."

"I'd have to close the bakery. Ask Callie if she minded—"

"Callie already knows. She's happy to close the bakery for a week."

My wife crossed her arms over her chest, a smirk playing on her lips. "You've thought of everything."

"I want my wife to myself."

At the growl in my voice, Sloane's whole body softened in a way I recognized. Fuck, I was a lucky bastard. "I could be alone with you for a week. What do you intend to do with me?"

"I think you know."

"I'd still like to hear about it."

My lips twitched. "Let's just say I made sure the villa has a bed frame I can tie you to."

Her cheeks flushed, eyes gleaming. "Oh, I can definitely close the bakery for that."

"How about I give you a preview this evening?" It had been ages since we could play. Sex had become making love quietly most nights. I still held her down like she liked, sometimes missionary, sometimes on her knees. But always quiet and less energetic than either of us preferred. It was only on nights Harry was out of the house that I could fuck my wife hard and rough just as she liked it.

"Oh, I definitely expect a preview when we get home." She reached up to untie her hair. "But maybe you could give me an appetizer right now."

My already heated blood turned hotter as I raised an eyebrow. "Here?"

As her hair fell around her shoulders, Sloane reached for the zipper on her jeans. "I told you I missed you."

I'd crossed the room and hauled her up onto the counter before she'd barely finished speaking. Her laugh scored through me as my hands coasted possessively over her body. "Fuck, I missed you too."

Sloane's lips brushed mine. "Then stop missing me."

My answer was to kiss her as if she was the fucking oxygen I needed to breathe.

Because that's exactly what Sloane Ironside was.

NORTH

FOREVER THE HIGHLANDS 335

. . .

IT HAD BEEN WEEKS SINCE I'D SEEN MY WIFE AND
son. *Weeks*.

I'd decided to surprise them by returning home a few days
early and was excited to see their faces. I loved my job and I
tried my best to take work that would keep me close. However,
this film opportunity was one I couldn't pass up, even if it
meant filming between LA and Europe for the last four
months. The role was that of a government assassin pulled out
of retirement and was the most physically demanding part I'd
ever played. Before it, I'd been in training for six months to get
my body where it needed to be to do some of the stunts. I'd
promised Aria not all of them, considering I was closer to fifty
than forty now. However, I'd never been in better shape in my
life.

Still, I didn't like my wife worrying about me, so I did
what I could to assuage her concerns by leaving the bigger
stunts to the professionals.

Now that we'd finished filming, I'd have some time at
home until the press tour started for a movie I'd filmed last
year.

School had just started back, so I knew Maddox would be
in class by the time I returned to our home on Ardnoch
Estate. We had a beautiful coastal home, and it meant Aria was
literally a five-minute drive from work. It also had the benefit
of being one of the safest places on the planet for my family to
live, and it gave me comfort knowing they were safe when I
was out of the country filming.

Deciding to stop in at the castle to surprise Aria first, I
asked them not to say anything at the gates as they let my car
through. That meant no one was there to greet me at the main
entrance like usual. The head butler Wakefield had retired last
year, replaced by Stephen, who now went by his surname

336 SAMANTHA YOUNG

Miller. It didn't quite have the same ring to it. I'd suggested to Aria she insist on him taking on a fake surname, but she'd just laughed like she thought I was joking.

I was in fact quite serious.

Miller was a rubbish name for a head butler.

Pushing open one of the double doors at the grand entrance of the castle, I stepped inside to find the great hall empty. My feet echoed off the parquet flooring as I crossed the large expanse and disappeared under one of the arches at the rear. I followed the wide corridor to the left, heading toward my wife's office. Aria was the estate manager now. She'd taken over most of Lachlan Adair's duties, freeing him up for his other business ventures. It kept Aria busier than I'd like when I was home, but it wasn't fair for me to expect her to adjust her schedule just because I was home for a bit.

Weariness crawled through me at the thought. I missed my family. We'd fought so hard to create our family, and I sometimes feared I might look back at my life and regret all the moments I'd missed in favor of my career.

For years, Aria and I had tried to have a child. It didn't happen. Turned out we both had issues in that department, which made us extremely incompatible as procreators. It broke my fucking heart not to be able to give Aria what she wanted. In the darkest moments of our grief, I'd thought I might lose her, even when she assured me I was enough. Eventually, we got to a place where we could talk about adoption. Once we started the process, it took a while, but we eventually got Maddox. He came to us at three years old. His mother overdosed when he was two and he'd been in care ever since. Those first few months were difficult. As to be expected, Mad was a very mixed-up wee boy. It was distressing to see that in a toddler, but it also didn't take long for him to start trusting our permanency. Now he had no memory of that time, and Aria and I were just Mum and Dad.

Forever the Highlands

He was eight years old.

Five years had flown by.

I missed his birthday this year.

I fucking hated that.

Desperate to see my family, I hurried my steps toward Aria. I wondered if I could convince her to take Mad out of school for the day. I threw open the door without knocking and abruptly halted at the sight before me.

Aria sat with her arse against the edge of her desk, her hands braced at either side of her curvy thighs, laughing up at the security guard who stood way too close to her for my comfort.

Perhaps it was just the way I'd been feeling lately, but anger and jealousy flushed through me before I could stop it. "What the fuck?"

Aria's gorgeous eyes flew to me and widened. She straightened up off the desk and her body brushed the arsehole looming over her.

I glowered at the bloke I didn't recognize. "Do you want to step away from my wife." It wasn't a question.

The security guard raised an eyebrow and stepped back from Aria. I could feel her glaring at me, but I didn't take my eyes off the fucker who thought it was appropriate to be in his boss's personal space. He was younger than me. Both of us. At least twenty years younger than me. "I was just relaying some information to Mrs. Hunter," the security guard explained calmly.

"Awful cozy relaying."

He pinched his lips together in displeasure and looked at Aria. "If that's all?"

"Of course, Evan. And apologies for my husband's behavior."

I bristled as he strolled by me, almost daring me to punch him in the face.

338   Samantha Young

As soon as the door closed behind him, I shook my head. "Don't ever fucking apologize for me."

"Don't come barging in here after months of being away and accuse me of ... of ... what exactly?" she hissed, throwing her arms up in disbelief.

"You were flirting with him."

Her outrage should have warned me I was crossing the line. But I was exhausted, lonely, and I missed my fucking family more than anything in the world, and the truth was ... I wasn't even sure they missed me that much when I was gone. Aria never asked me to stay. Whenever I spoke to Maddox on video chat, he filled my ears about days spent with his uncle Jared on the farm or Uncle Walker at the estate or how cool fucking Uncle Lewis's motorbike was and how funny Uncle Theo was.

"I was not flirting with him. He was telling me about an issue with a member and it was kind of funny. That's what you walked in on and the fact that you could even accuse me of flirting with another man pisses me off more than I can say right now because I'm at work and I can't scream at you like I want to," she whisper-shouted, beautiful face flushed with indignation.

"Well, I'm sorry," I whisper-shouted back. "But I missed my fucking wife, and I didn't expect some twenty-year-old to be drooling over her behind my back."

"He's not twenty and he wasn't drooling. Contrary to your belief, North, not every man finds me attractive."

"Then they're fucking blind!"

Her eyes flashed. "Why do I want to rip your clothes off when I'm this mad at you!"

"Because you missed me too!" I crossed the room and pulled her into my arms, crushing whatever angry thing she'd semi-yell at me next. The taste and feel and smell of her filled my senses, and I remembered the months of lonely nights

FOREVER THE HIGHLANDS 339

without her. How I'd imagined her in my arms. And having her now, even like this, made me lose my ever-loving mind with want.

Aria didn't stop me as I tugged and pulled at her mouth, my hands roaming her luscious curves. When she moaned at the feel of my erection, everything blanked but the need to be inside her. It had been so long. Too long.

I spun her around, shoving her things off her desk to clear the way to bend her over it.

"North!" She gasped as I yanked her tight skirt up and over her plump arse. "Oh my god."

"No, gorgeous, it's just me." I tested her, pushing my fingers inside her wet, tight heat. "You did miss me." I scrambled to unzip my jeans and release the raging erection straining to get inside my wife.

"Don't—oh, yes—think this—uhhh—means—ah—I'm not stillmadatyouohhhh!" Her back arched as I thrust my cock into her.

"Oh fuck." I squeezed my eyes closed as I held her hips in place and enjoyed the sensation of her tight heat wrapped around me. Then the memory of her laughing up at the security guard clouded my mind. It wasn't that I believed my wife was flirting with someone else. Or that she'd ever even think of betraying me.

It was that I wasn't the one here on a daily basis making her laugh like that.

Longing scored through me and possessiveness had me clasping her nape in one hand and her hip in my other as I pulled almost all the way out and slammed back into her.

Aria let out a little cry and her fingers bit into the edge of her desk.

"Okay?" I grunted, squeezing her neck.

She nodded. "Fuck me, fuck me, fuck me. I missed you. I'm really mad at you, but I missed you so much."

Euphoria scored through me and I tightened my grip on her as I drove in and out of her body. Her whimpers and low moans, along with the clutch of her wet heat, had my balls drawing up faster than I liked.

"I missed you. I missed this. I miss us." I slammed harder into her. "Do you need me like I need you?"

"Yes, yes, yes," she huffed. "North, please ..."

I slipped a hand between her legs and found her clit.

Just one touch and she went off like a rocket, clamping down around my cock, sucking me deep as her orgasm undulated through her. That's all it took to send me over the edge. I came so fucking hard, I forgot to stifle my shout of release.

My hands caressed Aria's round arse as I slowly pulled out. Watching my cum drip from my wife's body would always and forever be one of my favorite viewing pleasures. I reached across her to the tissues on her desk.

She shivered, her arms shaking, holding her up as I wiped between her legs and then cleaned myself before tucking my cock back in my underwear and jeans.

Aria tossed me a dark, sexy look over her shoulder. "You had to be loud, didn't you. Caveman." She pushed up off the desk, shoving her skirt back down. "If I lose my job for unprofessionalism, I will lose my mind at you."

Feeling too satisfied and smug to engage in another argument, I shrugged. "Worth it."

Hurt flickered over her face. "I can't believe you think I'd flirt with someone else."

Groaning, I tried to reach for her and she rounded the desk, putting it between us. "Gorgeous," I pleaded. "I'm sorry. Look, I know you wouldn't. I'm just tired."

She crossed her arms over her ample chest. "Not good enough."

Frustration gnawed at me. I was home for only a few

weeks. I didn't want to spend that time arguing. "I wasn't thinking clearly."

"Still not good enough."

"Fine." I threw my hands up. "I am sick and tired of missing my family and feeling like they don't give a shit I'm never here. You tell me you miss me, but I don't *feel* it. I miss you, Aria, like I'm walking around without a fucking limb. But you act like everything's fine and dandy, that life goes on just the same whether I'm here or not. And Maddox has plenty of men around him, he barely even notices my absence."

"What do you want me to say?" She shook her head in disbelief. "I knew this was your job when I married you."

"That's it. That's all you have to say." Crushing disappointment had me staggering back.

"No." Tears filled her eyes. "No. But if I said what I truly wanted to say, then you'd make changes and resent me for them. And I don't want you to make changes because of me. I want you to make changes because that's what you want."

"So we're playing games? After almost two decades of marriage, we're playing games?"

"You're the one playing games."

"I miss you. I want to be home more. But not if I'm not needed." There. I'd said it. My worst fears. "Distance doesn't make the heart grow fonder, gorgeous. It makes it insecure and lonely."

"You think I'm not?" She gestured to herself. "When we got married, you chose roles that kept you close to home. Then we got Maddox and we had you all to ourselves for a while. But we weren't enough for you."

"What?" I glowered.

"We weren't." She shrugged. "You needed more. And that's fine. But you were the one who said yes to bigger roles that took you away from us for months out of the year. You did, North. And I agreed to go along with it because I knew what I was signing up for when I married an actor. But you don't get to come marching back after months of being away and accuse us of not missing or needing you. I'm raising our child on my own while holding down a full-time job. So the people around me who love me are stepping in to support us while you're gone. Of course we fucking need you!" she yelled, pain etching her features. Seeing it was like a knife in the heart. "But I will not be the one who asks you to give up something you love. I don't want to have to. As for your son, he talks about you every day. He's just a resilient kid, and he's making the best of not having his dad around."

Longing constricted my chest. "You and Maddox are what I love. The most important thing. This was my mistake. These last few years, they were my mistake. Thinking I could have my cake and eat it too." I shrugged as tears blurred my vision. "I'm not happy without you. I miss you."

Aria licked her lips and asked tentatively, "What does that mean?"

Almost two decades this woman had been mine. I knew her inside and out. So I knew that her tone and that careful expression on her face was her trying not to hope.

Fuck.

She was trying not to hope that I might want to stay home.

That killed me. "Theo wants me to consider a role on his and Eilidh's show. It would mean at least a season of work."

Her lips parted, and I could see the excitement building in her eyes. "They film that forty minutes from here."

I nodded, smiling. "Aye, they do."

The light dimmed in her gaze. "But is that what you really want?"

"Aye." I rounded the desk now, done with it being between us. "It's absolutely what I want." I pulled her into my arms, peppering her cheeks with kisses before cuddling her against me. Her fists tightened in the back of my shirt as she hung on. "I'm sorry for being such a bastard earlier."

"When? When you accused my security guard of flirting with me or when you bent me over the desk and had your wicked away with me?" she teased.

"Should I be sorry for the latter?"

"No," Aria grumbled. "It was hot."

I shook with laughter, pressing a tender kiss to her forehead. "I am sorry. I've just ... all of that shit has been building over months, and it spilled out in the least mature way I could think of."

It was her turn to laugh as she pulled back to grin up at me. "It's okay. But just so you know, we will always need you, North. When you leave, you take a piece of me with you, and that empty place that's left inside aches until you're home again."

"Fuck," I murmured, clasping her beautiful face in my hands. "I love you so much."

"I love you too."

I brushed my lips over hers and we sighed into each other's mouths. After a few moments of just soaking up each other's presence, I said, "Do you think we can take Mad out of school early today?"

"No," she replied instantly and sternly, making me chuckle. "But you can be there to pick him up after school. He'll be so over the moon to see his dad."

"Aye?"

"You're kind of his hero, you know?"

"Really?"

"Yes." She squeezed me. "He thinks you are very cool. And I've been told by those in the know that you should enjoy this time, buddy, because in about five years, he's going to think you and I are the definition of *not* cool."

Chuckling, I nodded. "Got it. Enjoy the cool while we can."

———————

A FEW HOURS LATER, AFTER UNPACKING MY luggage, a quick shower, and food, I drove to Ardnoch Primary. The place was packed with parents picking up their kids, and I ignored the wide-eyed looks of recognition and made my way through the crowd toward familiar faces. My best mate, Theo Cavendish, stood at the school gates with my sister-in-law, Allegra McCulloch. He and Allegra were also related by marriage as Theo was married to Sarah, Allegra's husband's cousin.

Theo's daughter, my pseudo niece, Rose, was six years old, and Theo or Sarah collected her and Mad from primary school every day to help us out. Ally's son, my nephew Collum, had just started school, and Allegra was about four months pregnant with her and Jared's second child.

"Look at these two troublemakers," I announced my presence.

Ally whirled around, eyes wide, and then immediately threw her arms around me. I gave her a tight hug and pulled back to note her slight bump.

"How are you feeling?" I asked. "Doing well? You look happy."

"I am doing well and I'm extremely happy." She nudged me. "So ... are you sticking around for a while?"

My eyes met Theo. "My friend here offered me a part I couldn't refuse."

His lips curled. "I take it that's your way of accepting the role?"

"Aye, if you still want me."

FOREVER THE HIGHLANDS 345

"I'm not sure anyone *wants* you, old boy, but yes, you are rather perfect for the part."

I shook my head at his drollness, my attention moving to the school as the bell rang. My pulse picked up speed. "How is my boy?"

"He's great." Allegra rubbed a soothing hand over my back. "Mad will be so excited to see you."

"Aye. I can't wait to see him."

Conversation passed between my friend and sister-in-law, but I wasn't paying any attention. I strained to see Maddox.

Then there he was.

Strolling out of the building, his backpack too big and bouncing off his back as he skip-walked while chatting with one of his wee pals. The day we picked him up, he'd been shyly hiding behind his social worker. I'd held out my hand to him, at once terrified of being a parent, but also determined to love him as hard as any father had loved a son. Our eyes had met and at that moment, I'd claimed him. My wee boy.

Maddox had looked warily at my hand for a second and then, as if he knew I was his too, he released his hold on his social worker and slowly reached for me. As soon as my fingers curled around his tiny hand, I'd promised to never let go.

All that love swelled up in me, and I pushed past parents so Mad could see me.

His friend saw me first, hitting Mad's shoulder as he pointed at me.

Maddox's head jerked around.

His entire face lit up with surprise and delight. "Dad!" he yelled.

I swear I had to stop myself from bawling like a baby as he ran through the other kids to get to me, beaming from ear to ear.

I didn't care if he was eight and too old for it. I swooped him up into my arms, mine slipping beneath his backpack to hold him close. Maddox wrapped himself around me like a monkey, laughing with joy that I was home.

"When did you get home? Are you staying? Can you cook the chicken wrap thingies I like? When do you leave?" He blurted out all his questions at once as I carried him back toward his aunt and uncle.

"I just got home. Aye, I'm staying. Aye to the wraps and I don't leave for a few weeks. But I won't be long this time. When I come home again, I'll be sticking around. How does that sound?"

He clung to my neck, bobbing his head with excitement. "Good, good. That means we can start a tournament on this new fight game Uncle Fyfe bought me. It'll take us weeks!"

Grinning as I lowered him to the ground, I said truthfully, "Sounds fun, pal."

He grabbed my hand, clutching tightly as he turned to Theo and Ally. "Dad's back!"

"So we see." Ally laughed at his exuberance.

"Sorry, Uncle Theo, but I don't need a lift with you and Rose because Dad's back." He shrugged like he wasn't sorry at all.

"How easily I'm replaced," Theo drawled, eyes dancing with amusement.

"Dad, can we get some sweeties from the shop before we go home?" Maddox asked, already tugging me toward the car.

I nodded, my heart feeling like it might burst as every second word out of his mouth was *Dad*. "Dad, we should get Mum a chocolate bar too," he prattled from the back seat. "She says they stick to her hips—whatever that means—but that you like that they stick to her hips, so we should definitely get Mum chocolate if we're getting chocolate. It's only polite."

My grin almost cracked my cheeks as I laughed, driving slowly out of the car park. "Aye, buddy, we'll get your mum chocolate. What about a chocolate cake to celebrate me being home?"

"Oh, oh, aye, let's go to Aunt Callie's bakery! She does the best chocolate. Dad, Dad"—he was speaking so fast, he had to catch his breath—"did you see Aunt Callie and Uncle Lewis had a baby?"

"I did, Mad. I saw that."

"Did they have chocolate where you were? I bet it wasn't as good as Aunt Callie and Aunt Sloane's chocolate cake? It's good that you're staying for a while." He nodded sagely.

Laughing softly, I agreed wholeheartedly. "Aye, son. It's definitely good that I'm staying home for a long while."

THEO
A few days later

To my utter delight (note the sarcasm), the school called to ask me to come speak to Rose's teacher when I picked her up at day's end. Sarah was worried. I was irritated because there was no way Rose could have done anything untoward while in class. My six-year-old was, to everyone's relief, her *mother's* child.

"I'll see to this." I'd kissed Sarah thoroughly before departing to pick up Rose.

Filming would start on the new season of my current show in just over a month. Eilidh and I were co-showrunners. Co-writers and producers. We filmed it forty minutes south of Ardnoch, just outside Inverness, on an estate similar enough to Ardnoch to make it authentic. It meant I could stay at home, but it also meant I didn't get to spend as much time with Sarah and Rose. So, while I was home, I took Rose to and from school whenever the opportunity presented itself.

Attempting to curb my irritation at being called into school for Rose's sake, I was a mask of cool politeness when I entered the reception area.

The truth of the matter was I had never wanted or planned for children. One of the reasons Sarah was so perfect for me was because she shared the same vision for our future. Just the two of us. Writing, traveling, bantering daily, and gloriously fucking in any room of the house we wanted because there were no small people around to be considerate of.

However, it turned out my super sperm were as attracted to Sarah's eggs as my cock was to her vagina, and no matter she was on the pill, Sarah fell pregnant.

It wasn't in the plan.

Sarah was afraid to tell me, which was rather humbling and distressing.

I loved her.

And she didn't bloody well get pregnant on her own.

Thank you, super sperm and your obsessive fertilization abilities. Just couldn't go for a bloody swim like all the others, could you?

Something changed during Sarah's pregnancy. My possessiveness for her expanded alongside her waistline. That little bump became mine too. Then as soon as the doctor put Rose in my arms, I was unequivocally ruined. I was claimed.

Now two females owned me heart and soul, and there was not a bloody thing I could do about it.

There was not a bloody thing I *wanted* to do about it.

The bell rang for the end of school, and the receptionist gestured for me to go ahead. I was already arguing with Rose's teacher in my head and I had no idea why I'd been called in.

Children filed past me excitedly as I strolled down the

FOREVER THE HIGHLANDS   349

corridor to the primary two classroom where Rose was educated each day. There were silly drawings of iconic Scottish things on the walls outside, and I caught sight of Rose's unicorn (the national "animal"), by far the best among all the drawings. It had her name written under it in very tidy writing too. *My genius child.*

Yes. I thought it. And I'd say it out loud too.

I knocked on the classroom door as I stepped in, my eyes moving from the teacher behind her desk to Rose sitting at a little one in the corner. The classroom was set up for the play-to-learn style the Scots favored. Much of the classroom had different play areas for learning and just a few desks in one corner for more concentrated work.

My daughter's eyes lit up at the sight of me. "Daddy."

Daddy.

It got me every time.

Sarah was forever reminding me that we'd ruin Rose if we let her have her way all the time. I agreed. However, it was tiresome to constantly remind myself every time she said Daddy because the urge to do as she wished was very, very real.

"Hullo, turtle dove." I'd nicknamed her after the pretty little bird because she pecked at her food (we often had to coax her to eat more because she had such a wee appetite) and, like the turtle dove, she was rare. To me, she was a rare, precious little being who had to be protected at all costs.

On that note, I turned my attention to her teacher.

Ms. Carson was young and extremely nervous around me. It didn't stop me from glowering at her.

She stood from her desk and twisted her hands together, giving me a strained smile. "Mr. Cavendish, thank you for coming in."

"What's it all about?"

She winced at my cool tone. "Well, while Rose is usually

350   SAMANTHA YOUNG

very well-behaved, lately we've had some issues with her
making up words."

"Excuse me?"

"Rose is speaking gibberish in class, and when asked to
stop, she insists she's not making up gibberish. I had to send
her to see Mr. Adams this morning because she got very frustrated and angry." The teacher's tone was gentle and placating.
"So I thought we should all have a wee chat and see if we can
sort this out."

"Daddy, I'm not making up words."

"I know, turtle dove."

Ms. Carson's expression tightened. "Mr. Cavendish, I
know it can be difficult to—"

"What words do you think she was making up?" I interrupted impatiently.

"We were talking about doggies and cats," Rose spoke up.
"I said I was a canophile."

I nodded and turned back to the teacher. "And?"

The teacher frowned. "It's a made-up word and it sounds
like ... well, it doesn't sound very nice."

"It is not a made-up word," I gritted out. "It means a
person who loves dogs."

Her eyes widened. "Really?"

"Yes. Google it if you don't believe me."

The woman pulled out her phone and bloody googled
it. "Oh."

"What other words do you believe my daughter is
making up?"

"Mathesis," Rose grumbled, uncharacteristically put out.
"Ms. Carson says it's maths, but I'm not saying *maths*."

"Oh, for goodness' sake," I muttered under my breath.
"Mathesis is not a made-up word. It means learning the
sciences, especially mathematics."

"Oh."

FOREVER THE HIGHLANDS   351

Hearing my wife's voice in my head, pleading with me to be nice to the young teacher, I gritted my teeth around the word *Apologies* and cleared my throat, aiming for politeness, "For any confusion. You see, my wife and I play a word game that we now play with Rose. Who can come up with the most unusual word. We've taught Rose some words that most adults are unaware of, let alone six-year-olds."

"Well, oh. Right." Ms. Carson nodded, visibly embarrassed. "Rose does have a remarkable vocabulary for her age and is very articulate. I'm sorry, Rose."

Rose nodded and sweetly forgave, just like her mother (not like her father). "Apology accepted."

Theo, you know what to say. Sarah Cavendish. My bloody conscience as well as my wife. "If Rose was a tad unruly in her frustration, she would like to apologize also. Wouldn't you, turtle dove?"

She flushed a little, a blusher like her mother. "I'm sorry if I was rude, Ms. Carson."

"Apology accepted, Rose." She turned to me. "Perhaps it would be best if the word games stayed at home and not in the classroom. Some of the words ... they sound like other less innocent words."

My lips twitched, but I fought back my amusement. "Very well. Come on, turtle dove."

ROSE SKIPPED INTO THE HOUSE AHEAD OF ME, already explaining to Sarah exactly what had happened.

"Oh dear. Well, let's just keep our big words at home for now until you get a wee bit older," Sarah suggested to our daughter as I strolled into the kitchen.

"And give into the fascists?" I grumbled under my breath as I pulled a mug out of the cupboard.

"Rose, go change, sweetheart. I'll make you a snack."

Our daughter left the room and I braced.

"You better have been kind to Ms. Carson, Theodore Cavendish."

I was the picture of absolute innocence. "Who me? I'm never anything else."

"Theo."

Switching on the coffee machine, I huffed, "I was very polite, even though they sent our daughter to the principal because they have the vocabulary of Neanderthals."

"Don't be a pretentious prick," Sarah said, but the words were gentle and she soothed a hand over my back as she passed me to reach for the fridge.

I halted her before she could get to it, hauling her into my arms.

"I was very nice, little darling," I murmured against her pretty mouth as I slid my hands down over her pert arse. "Even though I very much desired to be otherwise."

She wound her arms around my neck. "What inspired the angel to kick the devil off your shoulder?"

"You." I kissed her nose. "Don't you know you're my conscience?"

Sarah considered this. "I'm relieved you were kind. Not everyone speaks like a Shakespearean villain, Mr. Cavendish."

"Our daughter will. She'll be the finest Shakespearean villain in all the land."

Her soft body pressed deliciously against the hard lines of mine as she laughed. "What am I going to do with you?"

"Let's start with contrection," I murmured huskily. "This evening. Ten o'clock. Our bed."

Sarah's cheeks flushed with arousal. "I think that can be arranged."

"God, I love you so much it makes me sick." I covered her mouth with mine, kissing the laughter right off her perfect lips.

JARED

WHILE I WAS GRATEFUL THAT USING SOME OF OUR farmland to add developments and rentals had not only saved my grandfather's farm but provided a very good income, sometimes I longed for the days when all I had to deal with were the stresses of the farm. At least then, I was outside, working physically hard and seeing the results of that labor.

Spending the day managing issues with rental properties was not my idea of farm life. By three o'clock that afternoon, everything seemed to be in hand. Allegra was working at her gallery in the village, and it didn't close until six thirty in the summer months. New fencing was required on the border of Caledonia Sky, the field where we'd built the glamping pods. We rotated the farm fields every couple of years and the adjoining field would have livestock in it. The current fence required reinforcing, but we'd need to dig a trench along it. For the past week, I'd been acting like a manager rather than a farmer while Georgie, my farmhand, did most of the grunt work. I needed less paperwork and more dirt, so I changed into my outdoor gear and headed over to the field.

Two hours passed. I'd removed my shirt and sweat dripped down my forehead and torso. I probably had streaks of mud on my face, my hands were caked with it, and my back ached with the constant movement of digging.

It felt fucking great.

Wiping a hand over my forehead, I reached down for the large flask of water I'd brought with me and caught sight of two women sitting outside their glamping pod, blatantly ogling me.

I gave them a nod and turned away.

I could already imagine what Allegra would say. *"Maybe they'll book with us again in the hopes of catching a glimpse of the hot farmer."* My lips tugged up at the corner because that's exactly what my wife would say. No jealousy. No insecurity.

She had no need. I showed her every day how much I loved her. Needed her.

An hour or so later, I pulled my phone out of my back pocket. I had a text from Allegra to say she was home and that our son, Collum (named for my grandfather), was having dinner at Aria and North's this evening. I immediately packed up to return home, my body already vibrating with anticipation. Allegra was four months pregnant and horny as fuck. She'd been the same with Collum. Honestly, if it were up to me, she'd be pregnant all the time.

Allegra home alone, though, meant we could be loud.

I practically raced home. As I burst through the front door of the farmhouse, I called, "Where are you?"

There was no answer.

Striding impatiently through the house, I moved into the kitchen and looked out the back window.

Tenderness clipped my impatience. Letting myself quietly out the back door, I watched as Allegra wandered up and down the chicken run, chatting affectionately with her hens. Her cap-sleeved summer dress fluttered in the slight breeze, the fabric caressing the gently rounded belly where our second child grew.

My wife was and always would be the most beautiful woman I'd ever known. It was the kind of beauty she couldn't see by looking in the mirror, though she'd been very well compensated by the genetic gods. Allegra McCulloch's beauty glowed from the inside out.

I was a blessed man.

FOREVER THE HIGHLANDS   355

She turned, her strands of dark hair falling from the messy bun on top of her head. She smiled slowly. "Hi, husband."

"Hello, wife."

With a skip in her step, Allegra strolled toward me. A heated look entered her eyes. "You're all sweaty."

"Been out in the fields."

"Goody for me." She wound her arms around my neck and drew me down for a hungry, slow kiss. With a hop, she jumped into my arms, legs wrapped around me, and I carried her inside. We didn't have to say a word as I climbed the stairs to our bedroom. I pulled off my T-shirt, throwing it in the corner.

"How was your day?" I asked on a huff as Allegra scraped her teeth over my nipple. Her hands roamed my body, greedy, wanting.

"Fine. Painting sold. All good. Horny."

Chuckling, I helped her unzip my jeans. Then she impatiently wiggled out of her underwear and then tugged me toward the bed.

"Can I get undressed properly first?" I laughed as she yanked my jeans and boxers down just enough to free my cock.

"Nope. Urgent business to attend to." She tugged me down. I braced over her with one hand and guided between her legs as she pulled the skirt of her dress up and out of the way.

Fuck. A guttural groan sounded from my chest as I pushed into her with ease. She was soaked. Allegra moaned, clutching at my arse to pull me deeper.

"I've got you, baby," I promised.

"I'm going to come," she whispered. "This ... this is ridiculous. Too soon, too soon!"

I stifled a laugh at her panicked cries. "Just come. I'll make you come as many times as you want. Just be loud," I demanded. "You know I like you when you're loud, baby."

And we had to be quiet so often now.

In answer, on my next thrust, her pussy clenched around me in tight ripples as she came and my wife cried out my name so loudly, I followed her into climax.

"We're not done," I said once my shuddering had stopped. "Again. This time naked."

"On my knees."

"Always full of good suggestions, baby." I smacked what I could of her rump and pulled out to sit up and noticed the mud on my hands. "Let me wash my hands first."

"Okay." Allegra lay sprawled on the bed, so fucking hot as she slid her hand between her legs. I could feel my balls tightening again. "Come back quickly or I'll come without you."

"You'll wait for your husband," I told her sternly. "Hand off what's mine."

She chuckled throatily but obediently removed her hand. "I love you, you bossy Highlander."

I threw her a cocky grin over my shoulder. "Not as much as this bossy Highlander loves you."

LEWIS

THE CRY OF OUR BABY WAS LIKE AN INSTANT injection of adrenaline. Both Callie and I jolted awake, eyes blinking against the dim light. "I'll get him," we said in unison.

"No, sleep." Callie none-too-gently shoved me down. "You went last time."

"Sure?"

She grunted at me and stumbled upward.

FOREVER THE HIGHLANDS 357

Our son's wailing was joined by our daughter's.

I groaned and threw my legs off the bed first. "I'll get her."

We shuffled out of our bedroom and down the hall. Callie slipped into the nursery to see to our son Xander while I crept into the bedroom opposite to soothe Harley. Because our son and daughter were so close in age, we'd liked the thought of them sharing the nursery. But Harley was just starting to fall into a good routine when Xander's constant waking throughout the night woke her too.

We'd fixed up the other bedroom and for the most part, it worked. But there were still some nights Xander's wailing was so loud, it woke his big sister.

Harley stood in her cot, clutching her favorite teddy her uncle Fyfe had given her, her eyes filled with tears. "Dada!" she cried harder at the sight of me, hiccupping. No matter how exhausted I was, it still hurt like hell to see my baby cry.

"It's all right, *mo leanabh*. Daddy's here." My voice was hoarse with lack of sleep as I lifted Harley out of the cot and into my arms. Noting her dummy had fallen out, I did a quick search and found it on the floor. Harley wriggled and fussed in my arms as I carried her into the bathroom to wash the dummy. Then I offered it to her and she cutely opened her mouth, sucking on it. Sleepily, she rubbed at her eyes and I carried her back into her room.

I could hear Callie soothing Xander, singing softly to him and probably bouncing him because it was the only thing that seemed to help him settle. Easing into Harley's rocking chair, I felt my daughter's warm weight melt into me as she snuggled against my chest, sucking on her pacifier.

I rubbed her back, my eyelids fluttering, fighting, as Harley tried to fall back asleep. "That's right, mo leanabh. Back to sleep. Let Dada sleep." I rubbed my own eyes with my free hand and yawned. "Dada would like to sleep for five years."

In fact, Dada must have fallen asleep because the next

thing I knew, I was being shaken awake by my exhausted-looking wife. Callie eased Harley gently out of my arms and carried her over to the cot. Thankfully, she didn't wake up.

Callie turned to me, a finger to her lips.

I nodded and slowly got up. The two of us crept from the room and down the hallway like we were burgling our own home.

Once we reached it, we hurried back into bed, afraid that at any second, one of them might wake again.

I pulled Callie into my arms and she rested her cheek on my chest. "I'm so tired, every inch of my body hurts. I didn't know this kind of tired existed."

"I'm so tired I feel like there are wee gremlins living in my nerve endings and I just want to scream," Callie whimpered comically. "But I'm too tired to scream." Her laugh ended on a sob that made me chuckle and pull her close for a kiss.

"I know, I know." I did. I totally fucking knew what she meant.

"They're worth it, though. They are worth it, right?"

For some reason, this made us both burst into laughter. And then we had to hush each other so we wouldn't wake the kids.

"We're losing our minds." Callie gasped, trying to stifle the hysteria.

"Just a bit."

"Why is it so hard? I mean, Harley was hard, but it was manageable hard. Two of them ... it's like they've quadrupled on us. Like gremlins when you pour water on them."

I snorted. "What's with the gremlin analogies?"

"Is that an anal ... an anal—"

"Are you saying *anal*?"

Now she snorted. "No anal ... ahnahlgy. Analogy. Couldn't get that out. You're not getting anal, by the way."

Lips trembling with amusement at her tired nonsense, I

FOREVER THE HIGHLANDS 359

replied, "I don't remember asking. Though at least I wouldn't get you pregnant."

"True. We can do anal. When I'm not tired. Which could be awhile. Though I suppose I wouldn't have to do much, so have at it."

"As sexy as that offer was, I'll pass. Mostly because I'm too fucking tired to fuck any part of you." I stared at the ceiling in horror. "What have we become?"

Callie laugh-groaned again and patted my stomach. "Sleep. It'll all seem better in the morning."

I cuddled her closer. "I love you. I love our children, too, by the way."

"Love you and love them and love sleep," Callie mumbled.

My eyes closed and I was out like a light.

AN HOUR LATER, XANDER WOKE US AGAIN.

THE NEXT MORNING I CALLED SLOANE. SHE WAS always offering to help, and I knew Callie didn't want to take her up on it just yet, but we were done. We were both zombies.

I pretended to get ready for work as usual, all the while trying to help Callie change and feed Harley and Xander. About ten minutes before I'd usually leave for work, we heard the vehicle pull up outside.

Callie looked up from putting Harley's shoes on. Xander was in his high chair, slapping his hands against the tray that usually contained his food and thankfully no longer did. "Who could that be?"

"It's your mum."

"My mum? Why?"

"I called her."

My wife's face fell. "Lewis, you didn't."

"Granny!" Harley jumped to her feet from her little stool. "Granny's 'ere!"

"No arguments," I told Callie as I strode downstairs to open the door. Relief thrummed through me at the sight of my sunny mother-in-law on the other side.

"Gran is here to save the day." Sloane swooped in, rushing past me with an energy I envied as she took the stairs two at a time.

"Granny!" I heard Harley scream.

As I came upstairs, Harley was jumping up and down at her granny's feet, showing off her teeth in a delighted grimace.

"Is that a new dance?" Sloane asked, jumping up and down with her.

It made Harley giggle hysterically. "Granny!" She said it as if Sloane were the silly one.

"Mum, you don't need to be here." Callie crossed the room.

"Yes, I do." Sloane ran her eyes over her daughter. "You're exhausted. You both are. I'm going to take the kids today. Walker is off work, so he's going to help. And you two are going to get some sleep."

"Two?" Callie's eyes flew to mine.

"I'm not going in today."

Somehow, that made it easier for her to give in. Together we gathered up all the kids' things and packed them into Sloane's car. Harley was delighted to be spending the day with her gran, enough so not to complain about the car seat. Sloane had two car seats for Harley and Xander already set up in the back.

"Call if you need us. Bring them back if they're fussing."

"I've raised two children, baby girl. I can deal with some fussing." Sloane kissed Callie's forehead. "Now go sleep. I'll bring the kids back around dinnertime."

"Mum—"

Forever the Highlands
361

"Nope. It's done." Sloane threw us a dazzling smile and hopped into her car. She waved as she backed out.

Callie looked ready to burst into tears.

"Hey, hey, come on." I nudged her toward the house. "We are going to sleep, *mo chridhe*, and it will make you feel like a human being again. I promise."

"I feel bad."

"Don't." I took her by the shoulders once we were inside. "Cal, we have to be able to function properly to look after our children, and we're lucky we have support to help us do that." I spun her around before she could protest and guided her toward our bedroom.

Once inside, she eyed the bed longingly.

I almost burst out laughing at how adorable she was. "It's okay? Mum will be okay?"

"She's more than okay. She's ecstatic to spend the day with her grandbabies. And we ... we can sleep. Really sleep, Callie." I gestured to the bed. "Do you remember what it was like to sleep for more than one hour? We could have that today."

Her lips trembled at my melodrama. "We could, couldn't we ..."

"All you have to do is give in."

"Sleep."

"Sleep." I nodded.

Then just like that, we were both stripping off our clothes in a frantic desire for one thing. We whipped back the duvet and dove in. Giggling like excited children, snuggled under the covers, me as the big spoon, Callie as the little spoon.

Despite my exhaustion, my dick reacted to being nestled against my wife's naked ass cheeks.

She felt it. "I love you so much, but I'm soooo tired," she whined.

Chuckling, I buried my face in her neck and then lifted it to reassure her. "Mo chridhe, trust me, my cock and I are on completely different wavelengths right now. Just ignore him. Sleep."

I waited for her response.

A soft snore was it.

Grinning, I hugged her closer and within seconds, I joined her in dreamland.

EILIDH

"MUMMA!" MILLIE CALLED FROM THE LIVING ROOM. "Mumma!"

I glanced up from my laptop to find Millie pointing at the TV. I'd had it on low on one of her cartoon shows while I worked on some rewrites Theo had sent over for our show. Millie, however, must have switched a channel or something because a trailer for *Young Adult* was playing.

Muttering expletives under my breath, I lunged for the remote and changed it back to her cartoon.

"Mumma!" Millie toddled over to me indignantly, reaching for the remote. "No!"

"Mumma's right here." I dropped the remote and lifted Millie into my arms. "You don't need to see Mumma on TV because I'm right here."

"No, no." She stretched toward the remote control, her face crumpling.

The sound of our security system binging had relief flooding through me. "Is that Nana Regan?"

Millie let out a giggle of excitement. "Nana!" I took her hand and we slowly made our way over to the panel on the wall. Sure enough, it was Mum getting out of her car.

She was here to collect Millie because Fyfe and I were celebrating a very belated one-year anniversary this evening.

A lot had happened in the past year.

So much.

Not all of it pleasant.

Of course, I'd had to endure facing Peter Pryor at trial. Had to endure knowing the jury had seen enough of the footage he'd kept of me to know that he'd violated my privacy for years from the age of nineteen. The media were like buzzards all over the trial, trying to pick at my innards. Fyfe and Millie kept me strong. The work Theo and I were doing on the show kept me strong. Knowing I had a beautiful future ahead of me if only I could get through my ugly present kept me going.

Peter Pryor was sentenced to ten years in prison for stalking, assault, and violation of privacy. To me, it wasn't enough.

But it didn't matter.

Pryor died of a stroke three weeks into his sentence.

It was a sad legacy for a man that his death provided nothing but relief for me.

After the trial, I faced another round of scrutiny when I testified against Dr. Cameron Phillips. He wasn't charged, but it was still worth it to go through that because he lost his medical license. Uncle Lachlan told me just yesterday that Dr. Dick, as we called him, had relocated to Australia.

Good fucking riddance.

Though I felt bad for Australia.

They deserved better than Dr. Dick.

There were some lovely moments in the year. Like Millie calling me *Mumma* for the first time instead of *Ae*. And the first time she walked by herself. Now she was toddling around the room, picking up things and usually throwing them. We had to have eyes on the back of our heads.

"Shall we open the door for Nana?" I asked.

Millie clapped her hands and almost stumbled with her exuberance. "Yesh!"

I took her hand again and opened the front door.

Mum's eyes lit up when she saw Millie. "Millie Billie!"

"Nana!" Millie reached out for her with her free hand, all the while straining at my grasp.

My entire family had fallen deeply in love with Millie. To them, she was as good as my biological daughter. Loving Millie made me understand my mum better. There was a small part of me that had always worried since Morwenna came along that Mum might never love me like she loved Mor. But I knew now, loving Millie, that I had nothing to worry about. My heart belonged to Millie just as it would belong to any biological children Fyfe and I might have together.

A half hour later, Mum had departed with Millie and her overnight bag, and I got in the shower. Fyfe and I had a night to ourselves, so I wanted to be plucked and gleaming for what I hoped would be a very energetic evening in bed.

I was straightening my hair when I heard Fyfe downstairs. He didn't call up or come find me, so I finished getting ready and strolled downstairs in the sexy floral summer dress I'd bought just for the occasion. I left my hair down and my feet bare. Rounding the staircase, I turned and abruptly halted. The lights were low and our dining table was aglow with candlelight.

Fyfe had thrown his suit jacket over the back of the couch, removed his socks, shoes, and tie, and rolled up his shirt sleeves while he cooked at the stove. The living space already smelled amazing.

He glanced over at me, his eyes flickering down my body from behind his dark framed glasses. He'd worn them just for me today. "Hi, baby."

I bit my lip against a giddy smile because this man still

Forever the Highlands

made my belly flutter. Probably always would. "What are you making?"

"Spaghetti puttanesca."

"Yum."

"Wine?" He lifted a bottle with his free hand and poured into the empty glass next to his.

"I'm getting the full treatment tonight, huh?" I hopped up onto the stool at the island to watch him. "Anything I can do?"

"Drink your wine, relax." He gave me a sexy grin full of promise.

Oh yes, tonight was going to be good.

I sipped at my wine and told him about how excited Millie was to leave with Nana Regan.

"Until she realizes she's staying the night," Fyfe murmured before taking a drink.

"She'll be fine," I promised. "She'll settle."

"I know."

I loved how he worried about her. I just loved him. "I love you."

He looked at me from beneath his lashes, his lips curling at the corners. "I love you too."

"YOU SURE YOU DON'T WANT ANY MORE?" FYFE asked, standing up to take my plate.

"Nope. I'm good."

"Was it all right?" He scowled at my half-eaten plate.

"It was delicious." I did not lie. "But you promised me tiramisu, so I'm leaving room."

"You'll have plenty of room."

He was so dim sometimes. "Fyfe, I don't want to be

stuffed with food if we're going to be banging each other's brains out in an hour."

Fyfe shot me a smug grin over his shoulder. "I see. Leaving room to be stuffed by my cock."

I walked into that one. "Ha! You're hilarious."

"I am hilarious."

Shaking my head at his nonsense, I couldn't help but admire the sight of him moving around the kitchen. Sometimes it still felt unreal that Fyfe Moray was mine. That he loved me back when the very idea of that had been a deep-seated fantasy I'd carried for years.

He looked over at me, narrowing his eyes.

"Problem?"

"Hmm."

"What?"

"You're watching me. A lot."

"I like watching you."

His brow furrowed in thought.

Weirdo. Laughing under my breath, I stood up. "I'm going to the bathroom. It'll give you a reprieve from my ogling."

"Aye," he agreed a little vehemently. "You do that. You should do that."

"*Okaaaay*. I will." Thinking on it, Fyfe had been acting odd all evening. Fidgety. Like he was waiting for something to happen.

I'd just assumed he was eager for us to eat so we could get to the sex part of our belated anniversary activities.

When I returned from the bathroom, Fyfe didn't look at me as he moved around the kitchen. "Desserts just coming."

I nodded and sat back down at the table. I was mid sip of refreshed wine when Fyfe announced from the kitchen, "You know, I always pictured doing this somewhere exotic. With a scenic backdrop and some kind of romantic relevance."

"Doing what?"

He grabbed a plate off the island, what I assumed was dessert, and moved slowly toward me as he continued, as if I hadn't asked a question. "But then I thought I wanted to do this where you and I truly began. In this place ...," he said, setting the plate in front of me, "where you told me you loved me and where I realized I'd loved you for far longer than I'd ever admitted to myself."

My heart hammered as I stared at what was on the plate.

Not dessert.

An open black velvet ring box with a solitaire diamond engagement ring nestled within it.

"Here is where I somehow fell more in love with you than I thought possible as I watched you fall in love with Millie. Here is where I knew that I would spend the rest of my life with you."

I wrenched my gaze from the ring, eyes blurry with tears as I gaped up at my boyfriend. "Fyfe?"

His smile was slow and seductive as he reached over and plucked the ring from the box. Then he lowered to his knee in front of me and raised my left hand in his. "Eilidh Francine Adair, will you do me the greatest honor of my life by becoming my wife?"

I didn't need to think about it.

"Yes." I nodded, tears spilling quick and fast down my cheeks. "Yes."

Fyfe slipped the ring onto my finger and I barely had time to look at it before he scooped me into his arms, kissing me hard and hungrily, swinging me around as if I weighed nothing. We knocked off his glasses we kissed so hard.

He eventually lowered me but only to clasp my face in his hands and kiss me more reverently, gently, like I was the most precious thing in the world. "I love you so much," he whispered gruffly against my lips. "I can't wait until I can call you Mrs. Moray."

I clung to him, my fingers curling in his shirt to pull him closer, deeper. "I love you."

Fyfe released me to press his forehead to mine. "I've had that ring burning a hole in my pocket for six months."

I reared back. "What? No way!"

He nodded. "I wanted it to be perfect, so I kept planning all these proposals and none of them felt right. Then I realized that it didn't need to be some grand thing ... and that I just wanted you to be mine."

"This was perfect," I promised him. "Fyfe, this is our home. It's where our family lives. It's perfect." I wriggled my fingers, watching the diamond sparkle beautifully in the light. The ring was classic, elegant, no fuss or frills, and so me. "The ring is perfect too."

"I'm glad you like it."

"I love it." I beamed at him. "Millie will love it too. Her mumma and dada are getting married. She can be our flower girl."

Cuddling me close, Fyfe brushed the hair off my face and asked, "Small or big wedding?"

"Small. By the loch on my uncle's estate. He'll close it off for a private event."

"Sounds great. Can he do that next month?"

"What? Why?"

"Because I don't want to wait to call you my wife."

"Then don't." I tugged on his shirt with a sexy smirk before taking him by the hand to lead him upstairs. "Marriage is just a piece of paper, after all."

"I like the way you think, Eilidh Moray."

A delicious shiver skated down my spine. "Then come, husband. Make love to your wife." My sudden squeals of laughter could be heard through the house as Fyfe lunged, chasing me upstairs to our bedroom.

Hours later, replete and so blissed out with happiness I couldn't speak, I lay in my husband-to-be's arms and considered how different life was now. How just a few short years ago, I'd felt so lost, wandering the world without an anchor.

Because it was here. With Fyfe. In the Highlands.

Waiting for me to find him. To find myself.

To find our forever together.

Printed in the USA
CPSIA information can be obtained
at www.ICGtesting.com
LVHW031103081124
796007LV00013B/18